# THE MYSTERY OF THE HAWKE SAPPHIRES

*Charles Dickens Investigations*
*Book Seven*

## J C Briggs

SAPERE
BOOKS

# THE MYSTERY OF THE HAWKE SAPPHIRES

Published by Sapere Books.

20 Windermere Drive, Leeds, England, LS17 7UZ,
United Kingdom

saperebooks.com

ISBN: 978-1-80055-169-5

# CHARACTERS IN THE SERIES

Charles Dickens
Catherine, his wife
Superintendent Sam Jones of Bow Street
Elizabeth Jones, his wife
Eleanor and Tom Brim, their adopted children
Sergeant Alf Rogers of Bow Street
Mollie, his wife, (formerly Spoon) who runs the stationery shop for Eleanor and Tom Brim, whose father is dead
Scrap, shop assistant, messenger boy, and amateur detective
Constables Stemp and Feak of Bow Street
Fikey Chubb, known fence and criminal

## IN THIS NOVEL:

### At Kirkdale Hall in the North of England:
Sir Robert Trent
Lady Alice, his wife
Doctor Frederick Sutton
Margery Robb, the nurse
Moses Rigg, driver
Reverend Stephen Hardy
Jane, his sister

### At Hawke Court, not far from London:
Sir Gerald Hawke
Sapphire Hawke, his ward
Esther Stoneridge, his housekeeper
George, her son

Reverend Meredith Case, Sir Gerald's heir
Reverend Octavius Swann, the vicar at Hawke Village
Abe Black, landlord of The Hawke Arms
Maggie, his wife

**In London:**
Sarah Hamilton
Addy Finch
James Semple, book gilder and brother of Constable John Semple
Mr Dalrymple of Clement's Inn, Sir Gerald's lawyer
Alexander, his son
Joah Danks, his clerk
Edward Temple, Mr Dalrymple's tenant
Mr Francis Gresham of Lincoln's Inn, cousin of the murdered Felix Gresham
Mr Codlin, his clerk
Mr Ernest Gresham, deceased, father of the murdered Felix Gresham
Bella Screech, daughter of Ebenezer Screech who owns a junk shop near the bookshop
Johnny, her son, aged seven years
Ruby Kiss, a prostitute
The Captain, her lover
Phoebe Green, a dancer
Old Sal, a woman whose job it is to follow the prostitutes who work for Ma Bailey, the brothel keeper
Percy Oakes, the landlord of The Blade and Bone pub
Susan, his daughter
Eddie Grant, the potboy, brother of Ruby Kiss
Mrs Bradbury of Tavistock Square, a school friend of Sapphire Hawke

Mr Mansion, her footman

Miss Gauntlett of Park Lane, once the town house of the Hawke family

Mrs Pottage, her housekeeper

Josephine Parker, formerly a lady's maid to the Hawke family, whereabouts unknown

Finny Morton, owner of the shooting gallery and army comrade of Mrs Stoneridge's son, George

# PROLOGUE

## *Kirkdale Hall, 1817*

'A son?' Sir Robert Trent's eyes were alight with hope.

Doctor Frederick Sutton looked at the man in the bed, a man who was near death; a man who wanted a son; a man who would never have another child; a man whose hopes had been blasted time and again; a good man who had loved his wife and had hidden his anguish at the birth of too many dead children. And Doctor Sutton knew how much this man had longed for news of the birth of a son. As had his wife.

Sutton had not been able to say no. He had hated the idea, but it would be over soon, and Lady Alice had entreated him.

'Let him go to his grave in peace, Doctor Sutton, I beg you. What harm can it do? Only Margery will know, and she won't tell.'

'But after?' Sutton had worried. 'What if — well, how will it be if the babe is a girl — it must be known eventually…'

It was rare, but in his long career as a doctor, Sutton had seen it before — a baby born where the sex was not determinable. When he had started out in an industrial town, he had delivered the bastard child of a servant girl, a child born with such deformed parts that he had not known what to say. Of course, he knew the term 'hermaphrodite', but that would not have helped the illiterate girl who had lain exhausted on the bed, and who had not even wanted to look at the child, never mind hold it. Boy or girl, she didn't care. She had turned her face to the wall; he had been left to give the child up to the parish. 'Girl,' he had said to the overseer, thinking that a girl might have an easier time; to say 'boy' might have led to a life of hard labour for which the child might have been unfitted.

Sutton had often wondered what had become of that poor infant, and with this child it was also hard to tell. The baby was healthy, as evidenced by its lusty cry. *The life force*, thought Sutton, as its little hand had gripped his finger and its lips sought the breast.

Lady Alice Trent had looked at him. He had seen the unshed tears. 'I want to give him this one last thing. I owe it to him after all my — failures. He has never reproached me. He has been the best of husbands.'

Lady Alice was all that Sutton thought a woman should be. She was beautiful in a quiet way with fine features, a pale complexion and brown, shining hair that curled above a broad white brow which gave her face distinction. She had, so it was said, aristocratic connections in the south of England. She had married the Squire of Kirkdale for love and he had married her for the same cause. The Squire was a man proud of his role as landowner and magistrate and he was a not ungenerous landlord. His was not a great estate, but he would be content to leave it unencumbered to his first son. He was conscious that the land upon which he walked and worked had been owned for generations by men of his own blood and bone, and glad that it would continue to be so. A second son would be a churchman. Daughters? Well, they would marry into county families. Sir Robert had had no ambitions beyond the mountains and valleys of the Lake Country. Howbeit — sons first.

But there had been none in the ten years of their marriage, and now he was dying. And Lady Alice held her handkerchief to her soft hazel eyes.

'Yes — a fine boy,' Sutton said.

The fine boy was brought to his father, tightly swaddled. Sutton saw the man's joy and was glad. It was right that a good man should die content. But when he saw the colour return to the faded cheeks and felt the stronger grip of the hand that shook his, the sickness of doubt rose in his throat. He was very afraid that Sir Robert Trent might live.

# 1: A DEATH

## *Hawke Court, 1851*

The stench of corruption. It came to clergyman, Meredith Case under the lavender scent which was meant to disguise the sickly smell of decay. Here you could see Death at his work, eating away flesh as if the worms were already at Sir Gerald Hawke, lying in the bed. The deaths Meredith had seen were never like this.

The room was oppressively hot from the fire that burned in the great black oak fireplace. Meredith Case noticed the black wooden candlesticks on a chest — carved skulls with hideous teeth grinned at him. He could see how the red silk on the walls was coming away in strips; under his feet there was a carpet the colour of dried blood, and the thick bed curtains looked black and rotten.

There was nothing left of Sir Gerald. A handful of bones on the counterpane. Another skull on the pillow. Some blackened thing that had been the long Hawke nose. Only the eyes were alive, deep, dark eyes in which something glittered, some last spark of life. At each laboured breath, the stench came to him and Meredith felt a sickness move in his veins. The prayer he had thought to offer died on his lips. God was not here. He glanced at the doctor's impassive face, and at the grey-robed nurse whose hands were calmly folded. Her eyes were lowered. The very air about him seemed tainted, but they did not seem to notice.

At the foot of the bed, Meredith could not move. It would not be long, the saturnine-faced doctor had said. Perhaps Mr

Case would care to say his farewell? His tone was sardonic. It was the last thing Meredith Case wanted. He had never met Sir Gerald Hawke, though it seemed he was the heir to the little was left of his fortune, and to this house. It was a house that had been a beauty in its youth. Now, like some raddled, ancient dowager, it was crumbling. The lawyer, Mr Simeon Dalrymple, had shaken his dome of a head, sighed, and advised him to leave it to rot. There was not enough money to restore it. There was enough to bury the old man in the black vault that held the dead bones of the Hawkes — the title would die with the man. Only the son could inherit that, and he was dead.

Meredith understood that Sir Gerald Hawke had been a cousin several times removed. His mother had been proud of her Hawke connections. He had not paid much attention, though he had seen his name in the papers. Sir Gerald had been notorious for gambling, for his whores, for a duel fought in France, for the deaths of his wives and his son — his second wife dead at the foot of a staircase.

Meredith had made his own way. His father, a manufacturer in a small way, had left him an income, and the capital, though not large, had sustained him at Oxford and given him enough to take his orders. He was vicar now of a small country parish, and content enough to preach to his small congregation, marry them, christen their babies, give solace at their sickbeds, bless their calm passing, and bury them in their simple graves. Earth to earth. Thy will be done. But this was the devil's work.

The handful of bones moved. The rotting smell caught Meredith's throat so that he almost gagged. The burning eyes looked at him. The claw beckoned. Meredith moved nearer, his own hands clenched by his sides, the nails digging into his palms. He forced himself to look at those eyes in which some terrible knowledge glittered. Meredith did not want to know.

The doctor went away. The nurse glided after him. Meredith heard the door shut.

Alone with this, Meredith licked his dry lips and tasted death. His heart raced. It was a terrible face. The nose was eaten away. The burning eyes stared at him and the blackened mouth opened. The breath released was foetid, so vile that he thought it infected him. He felt the sweat on his back as if he were suddenly taken by a fever.

'Come near.' The voice was a whisper, yet there was menace in it. It had the power to compel. Meredith thought that it was a voice that had always compelled. The voice of a man whose last words would exact some dreadful command, that would place some burden on the living man that he would not be able to lift until the last wish was executed. Meredith did not want this, had not asked for it. His faith was not equal to it.

He stepped nearer and felt the dry bones of the hand on his in the grip of a vice. The eyes moved in the yellow bones of the sockets. The mouth twisted as if the skull grinned.

'Well, well, Meredith Case, man of God.' The breath again as if hell itself had opened. 'The heir, though not of my body, alas. I have a wish, a dying man's wish.'

Meredith found his voice. 'Sir?'

'A dying man's wish may not be thwarted. You will swear, man of God?'

'I — don't —'

'Swear.'

Meredith Case opened his mouth, but no words came. He could not breathe.

Another gasping breath. 'Find Sapphire Hawke.'

The eyes closed. The iron grip slackened. Meredith Case drew his hand away. A last gust of contagion and Sir Gerald Hawke was dead.

# 2: OBITUARY

## *THE MORNING POST*

*We regret to announce the death of Sir Gerald Hawke, Bt., who expired on Saturday forenoon after a protracted illness. Sir Gerald was the elder son of Sir Alexander Hawke by the Honourable Susan Mary Flower, third daughter of Maurice Flower, the Right Honourable the Viscount Charswell. He was born 9th July, 1775. The late Sir Gerald was twice married: first, 8th October, 1800 to Millicent, only daughter of the late general Sir Augustus Barnard and Lady Amelia Barnard; secondly to Miss Colman, daughter of Mr Jeffery Colman of Dublin. By his first wife, Sir Gerald had one son, Augustus Gerald, who died of a wasting sickness in 1820. The second Lady Hawke died suddenly and tragically from a fall. There was no issue of this marriage.*

*Sir Gerald has lived a retired life for the last several years at his country seat, Hawke Court, his health having declined. Disease of the heart is given as the cause of death.*

*Hideous old man*, thought Dickens, putting down the newspaper. He had met Sir Gerald Hawke once at Lady Blessington's, at Gore House. Years ago — Hawke had looked an old man then. The deceased second Lady Hawke had been a cousin or some distant relation of Lady Blessington, which was why Hawke was there. Gossip had it that Hawke had wanted an heir and had married an Irish lawyer's young daughter. "Wasting sickness", forsooth — his only son had died syphilitic and mad. Not at all surprising, given the father's reputation. He had heard that the second Lady Hawke had died of a fall down the stairs. No issue. An accident — Hawke had probably pushed her.

Dickens had been introduced at the reception. He had felt a kind of revulsion for the man, as if some taint of corruption had emanated from the powdered creature. He had looked half-dead then — something of the cadaver about him — but Hawke had looked down his long nose at Dickens, presented to him as the author of *Pickwick Papers* and *Oliver Twist* — not a reader, Sir Gerald Hawke, unless it was *The Sporting Times* — a gambler, too, his fortune tossed away like a pack of cards spilt on the gaming table.

Dickens had bowed, but without looking again at the obsidian eye, magnified by the quizzing glass so that it looked like a stone; he had turned away to find more congenial company in his friend, Walter Landor, and the poet Samuel Rogers, their laughter as fresh as the rain, dispersing the atmosphere of decay that had surrounded that man.

He had not seen Hawke again. And Lady Blessington was dead, too — she had died in Paris of a burst heart. Her heart had been three times the size of a normal heart — a generous woman and a witty one.

Heart disease had killed Sir Gerald Hawke. Now that he could not believe — the man had not had one. There had been a scandal, he recalled, years back. A young man had been shot at Hawke Court — the verdict had been suicide. Gambling debts, unsurprisingly.

Well, the old horror was dead; his purposeless life had done no good for anyone. His house was ruined and there was no son to inherit. Served him right. He might have been better remembered had he given some of his gold to poor Hannah Haycock, whose death had also been reported in the paper — a young woman who had died of cold in an alley: *her death accelerated by the extreme emaciation of her body through want of the common necessities of life,* so the inquest had found. And buried in a pauper's grave, for no one came to claim her. It was enough to break a man's heart.

Dickens turned to other news. Ah, the inquest on Felix Gresham. He had been shocked to the core to read of the murder when he had come back from Paris. Poor young man — Dickens had not known him, but he had met old Ernest Gresham who had been a solicitor in the Court of Chancery. It was back in 1844 when Dickens had sued the publisher, Parley, for bringing out a pirated version of *A Christmas Carol.* Dickens had won the case, but Parley had declared himself bankrupt and the whole thing had cost Dickens seven hundred pounds in legal fees. He remembered how angry he had been at the entire business. Ernest Gresham, a dry as dust stick of a man, who had won his own case and netted damages for his client, had merely opined, in passing Dickens and his own counsel, Mr Talfourd, that the law had its ways, mysterious though they might be. Then he had bowed — Dickens had expected him to creak — and gone back to his own office. Thomas Talfourd had remarked that there was no man shrewder in his knowledge of the law — and probably no man richer.

But, to lose his only son — what a tragedy. He remembered meeting Mrs Gresham at Talfourd's house. She had been pretty and charming — another wife much younger than her husband. Her boy, Felix, was destined for the law, she had told him, but she was not sure. Felix, she had said, was of a more literary bent. He wrote poems — perhaps Mr Dickens might be kind enough to advise the boy. Of course, he had said he would, but he'd heard nothing more. He thought now that probably Mr Ernest Gresham had prevailed.

The young man had been murdered on the steps of a bookshop — a bookshop Dickens knew. The verdict was:

*wilful murder against some person or persons unknown.* He read on:

*As there had not been sufficient evidence to implicate any person in the crime, the coroner, Mr Dyer, had directed that the jury would be justified in leaving the affair for further investigation in the hands of the police. Superintendent Samuel Jones and Sergeant Rogers of E Division at Bow Street had given their evidence. The deceased young man had been found stabbed to death in the doorway of a bookshop in St. Anne's Court at one o'clock in the morning. The owner of the shop, Miss Sarah Hamilton, had been woken up by the knocking of Police Constable Feak of E Division. Although the deceased was known to her as a customer at the shop, she had no idea why he should be at her door at such a late hour. Other members of the household were roused and could give no pertinent evidence. A female assistant to Miss Hamilton had heard a cab in the night, but she could not say at what time. The police are continuing their enquiries into the life and background of the unfortunate young man.*

*Mr Turtle, Assistant Surgeon at King's College Hospital in Portugal Street, confirmed that the young man had been killed by a single stab wound to the neck and had been dead at least an hour before a passer-by had found him and called the police…*

*The voice of the turtle is heard in the land*, thought Dickens. What a mystery, though. B. and T. Chantrey, booksellers and bookbinders, the shop now run by Miss Sarah Hamilton and her assistant Miss Addy Finch. At Christmas they made and sold keepsake books, pretty albums, pocketbooks, and journals, all bound in velvet, silk or satin, or leather for the more masculine journals. He had bought a charming scrapbook for his daughter Katey's birthday back in October.

The bookshop, known as Chantrey's, was in St. Anne's Court off Church Lane just before St. Anne's Church — a sequestered spot of quiet eighteenth-century houses and a few shops, but there were always customers at the bookshop. Bartholomew and Thyrza Chantrey, brother and sister, had been the proprietors. Dickens had browsed there sometimes in earlier days, but he hadn't been in for years until he had called in on a whim a couple of years ago to find the shop had changed hands. He had been on his way to the stationery shop in Crown Street, owned by Mr Robert Brim until he died of consumption. The stationery shop was run by the wife of Sergeant Rogers — Mollie, who had been Mollie Spoon. Mr Brim's children, Eleanor and Tom, had been adopted by Superintendent Jones and his wife. The shop would be the children's one day. Mollie Rogers must know Miss Hamilton and Miss Finch — the two shops were near enough.

*Further investigation* — Dickens wondered how Sam was getting along. Sam would have asked Mollie about the two ladies, no doubt. He looked at the broken spine of a book on his desk: *The Deluge*, a poem of 1821 — not a volume he valued much. He couldn't remember where he'd picked it up — perhaps at Chantrey's. It had a pretty binding. Worth repairing? His own bookbinder was Thomas Eeles in Cursitor Street, but a man could make a change — surely.

He took up the book and leafed through the pages, stopping suddenly at the lines: *Where are you? Dy'd in the blood of recent murder...* Well, if he needed a sign, this was it. Where are you, indeed?

And a deluge, too. He listened to the rain beating at the window.

# 3: THE WILL

'Sir Gerald said nothing of Sapphire Hawke at the — er — last?' asked Mr Dalrymple, the lawyer, next morning after the will had been read, as was proper, though only Meredith Case and the housekeeper had been there to hear.

Meredith wanted to say no, but he had already given himself away. He knew it by the heat that had rushed to his face when Mr Dalrymple had said the name when he had read out the will. He felt the flush now. Curse his tell-tale face. Sir Gerald Hawke had probably never blushed in his life.

'He told me to find her.'

'And you agreed? A promise to a dying man?'

'No, there was not time.'

'So what do you intend?'

'Nothing. It is no concern of mine.'

'The jewels are hers — the will stated so. The Hawke sapphires have been left to Sir Gerald's ward, Sapphire Hawke, and should she not be found, they must come to you.'

'I tell you I don't want them. I don't want anything from this house. It's…' Meredith knew he sounded foolish — like a sulky child, and, worse, he didn't know what he wanted. 'Surely it is your duty to find her as the family's lawyer.'

'He did not ask me.'

'In any case, how should I, a country parson, set about finding a woman who has been missing for twenty years?'

'There are papers at my office — there might be something. The last I heard of her, she was at a convent in Bruges.'

'I don't want to know. I have duties elsewhere.'

Mr Dalrymple bowed. 'Very well; however, if you should

change your mind, come to see me in London. I shall have a look through the family papers.'

Mr Dalrymple departed with the sapphires. Meredith, decisive suddenly, went to ask Mrs Stoneridge, the housekeeper, to bring down his valise and to order the trap to take him to the to the railway station at Slough.

He returned to the library, which smelt of mildew and decay like everywhere else in this cursed house. The glass-fronted bookcases were discoloured with mould, the books within just shadows, the work of dead hands. Meredith fancied himself a scholar, but he had no desire to look at any of them. They could burn them for all he cared. There was little else in the room other than the table at which Mr Dalrymple had spread his papers and the two chairs where they had sat, the two remaining actors in the sordid drama of Sir Gerald Hawke's life.

He looked at the various Hawke portraits, their surfaces blackened, the likenesses almost obliterated. A pair of black eyes glittered at him. He knew whose they were. *Damn it, leave me be*, he thought, but he was drawn to the picture, the glittering eyes willing him to look closer. He brushed away the dust and revealed Sir Gerald's face with its long nose and hard jaw. More brushing showed the baronet leading a powerful horse with wild eyes, one hand gripping the reins, forcing the beast into submission. Sweat gleamed on its flanks. The other hand stretched out. Surely, there was another figure.

Meredith brushed again, and then spat on his handkerchief and rubbed gently at the shadowy form. Something dirty white appeared. He dipped his handkerchief in a glass of water on the table. He was careful. The figure of a girl emerged. He could see now that Sir Gerald's other hand seemed to grip the girl's thin shoulder. He ran the damp handkerchief over the face. A young girl, perhaps about twelve. She appeared to be tall and thin. It was not a pretty face, being rather long for that, very pale with dark brows drawn into perfect arcs. It was impossible to tell the colour of the eyes, but the expression was unsmiling as she looked out at him. Not a happy child, he was sure of that. There was a taut stillness about her, as if she were poised for flight. Now, it seemed as if Sir Gerald's eyes were on the girl. It was not a tender look — not the look of a father to a daughter. There was cruelty in those glittering eyes.

Mrs Stoneridge came in. Meredith pointed to the picture. 'Is this Sapphire Hawke?'

'I wouldn't know, sir. She was here before my time.'

'What do you know of her?'

'Nothing, sir. She wasn't talked of.'

Mrs Stoneridge looked at him without expression. Her lips were compressed into a thin line and her eyes were hard. He felt a shiver of distaste and smelt corruption again.

Meredith surprised himself. He would not have thought this before about a woman. Now, looking at those cold yellowish eyes, he thought her sly and insolent. She did know something. He wanted to shout at her that he was master here, but he thought about this wreck of a house and knew he would look a fool.

He said mildly, 'Never mind, Mrs Stoneridge, it is not important.'

'The trap is here.'

'I shall bid you good day, then. I shall not be back. Mr Dalrymple will inform you of all the arrangements.'

She did not respond, just looked at him coldly.

Meredith left her. Something hardened in him. She thought him of no consequence — not a Hawke, of course. That would be it. She resented him as the heir. The trap was waiting. He asked the man to take him to the village. He had an idea. He would talk to the clergyman who had conducted the funeral — he was elderly, he must know something of the past times at Hawke Court.

He looked back at the dark clouds that furled above the house — the black banners of the Hawkes. The trap turned a corner. Hawke Court vanished. Meredith stared ahead.

It seemed he was looking for Sapphire Hawke. A rattle of mocking rooks shot up from the tall elms to bid him farewell.

# 4: DISINHERITED

The Reverend Octavius Swann greeted the heir of Hawke Court kindly, though he looked interrogatively at Meredith's collar and black stock, wondering perhaps at the absence of the broad white neckband that a clergyman usually wore.

They went into a book-lined study very like Meredith's own. Reverend Swann saw him look at the papers piled on the desk. 'I am presently at work on a paper. My interest lies in etymology — the word "prise" is of particular significance in the development of the local dialect. It means "hold" — "lost my prise", the locals say. From the French, you see, and pleonastic phrases abound as in "along with" for "with". Very interesting — very. Ah, yes, and "blackwork" for the undertaker's business. Most fascinating, if a rather melancholy thought.' He tidied his papers carefully and wiped his pen.

Meredith could have laughed. What did this mild scholarly man know of the evil he had felt in that hot red room with its leering candlesticks? He sniffed. It was here — that faint smell of corruption, as if it were emanating from him. He felt unclean. *I should go*, he thought. *I've made a mistake.*

Reverend Swann motioned him to a chair. It would be ridiculous to turn on his heel. He would ask about Sapphire Hawke and then make up his mind.

'You were present at the death of Sir Gerald — a peaceful end, I hope,' the Reverend ventured.

'You knew him?'

'Not really. He did not — er — attend the — er — church. I called, of course, but the housekeeper…'

'Told you that you were not needed —' Reverend Swann

nodded — 'Then you will be able to guess what kind of death it was. Blackwork, indeed.' Meredith wondered at the harshness in his own voice. Another time he would have spared the old man's feelings and merely said that he hoped the deceased was at peace.

'I am sorry for it. I shall pray for him,' the old man said gently.

Meredith looked at the faded kindly eyes that invited his confidence. 'I regret that I could not pray for him. There was something, Mr Swann, something in that death bedroom which I had never come across before, some sense of evil done that frightened me.'

Reverend Swann looked at him gravely. 'I understand you, Mr Case. That was a house in which dreadful things happened. Sir Gerald's only son died raving. His second wife was unable to give him an heir. A most unhappy young woman whose death … well, let us say it was untimely. There were no more marriages. Sir Gerald's reputation was so tarnished by the rumours surrounding his second wife's death that it was impossible to think of any family that would wish a daughter to marry him. And no more heirs, of course.'

'Except me,' said Meredith, 'not that I want any of it. It seems a cursed place to me. However, Sir Gerald left me a dying wish. His last words were "Find Sapphire Hawke." I do not even know who she is. I had not intended to carry out his injunction — I don't know yet if I will. I asked Mrs Stoneridge. She bluntly told me that she knew nothing. I don't know why, but I didn't believe her and that made me curious, I suppose. Do you know anything of Sapphire Hawke?'

'Take some of my fine old sherry, Mr Case, and I will tell you what I know — no one has mentioned that name for twenty years, it must be.'

He went to pour the sherry. Meredith thought about the girl in the portrait. The face of an unhappy child, he thought again. And Sir Gerald's hand on her shoulder as if he detained her — or owned her.

Reverend Swann sat down, and they sipped their sherry. It was fine; it tasted of sherry rather than corruption, and Meredith felt warmer for it. He felt better than he had felt since the moment he had stepped over the threshold of Hawke Court.

'Sapphire Hawke was Sir Gerald's ward, an orphan whose family was connected to the Hawkes. I don't quite know how. There was surprise that Sir Gerald should take in a child. The second Lady Hawke was long dead, as was young Augustus, the heir. The child came to live at Hawke Court in 1828, I think. I seem to think that she had lived in London at first, but I cannot be sure of that.'

'How old was she?'

'Twelve or thirteen, I think. I am not sure when she was orphaned. She was a quiet child — understandable, of course. She came to church occasionally with the then-housekeeper, Mrs Drummond, and there were governesses. None stayed long. It must have been a lonely childhood. Sir Gerald came from time to time with his guests. They were not church-goers, so we saw little of them, but, of course, we heard of the parties and the gambling and the love affairs — quite scandalous the rumours were.'

*Poor child*, Meredith thought. To be an orphan in that dreadful house, it was unthinkable.

Reverend Swann continued, 'When the child was about fifteen or sixteen, she was sent abroad, to a convent — in Bruges, I think. The house was more or less shut up then — there had been another death. A guest of Sir Gerald's, a young man called Arthur Sinclair, was shot. After the inquest, which returned a verdict of accident, Sir Gerald went to London. I never knew what happened to Miss Sapphire Hawke. I presumed that she stayed abroad.'

'Is there anyone else in the village who might know anything? What about the housekeeper, Mrs Drummond?'

'She is dead, I'm afraid. Mrs Stoneridge could tell you, but you say she refused?'

'She claimed not to have been there when Sapphire Hawke lived there.'

'She was — she was a kitchen maid and I married her to Joshua Stoneridge, one of the gardeners. She was a pretty girl, I recall, and intelligent. I remember thinking that they would do well. They left Hawke Court, I remember, to set up a market garden business. Joshua Stoneridge had inherited money. Mrs Drummond died about ten years ago. Housekeepers came and went — too lonely, I should think, and the old house falling into disrepair, and very few servants who came and went very quickly.'

'Are there any other servants who might remember Sapphire Hawke?'

'It was a long time ago, Mr Case. The old servants were turned off after the house was shut up; only Mrs Drummond remained, and a few new servants, and they never stayed long. Then Mrs Stoneridge came back as housekeeper. Perhaps you could go back to her.'

Meredith shook his head. He thought of that closed-up face and those hostile eyes. She wouldn't tell him. He felt relief. He had made an attempt — he had failed, and he owed that wicked old man nothing more. He rose to go.

'If I think of any names from that old time, I will write to you if you give me your address,' offered Reverend Swann.

'I am not sure where I will be — I might go to Wales. Write care of Mr Dalrymple, the lawyer at Clement's Inn. I will communicate my whereabouts to him. Thank you, anyway, for your kindness. I rather think I have done all I can.'

'If I can do anything else for you, I will. You have been troubled by what you have seen. Bless you, my child. My prayers will go with you.'

After the door of the rectory closed behind him, a sense of utter loneliness swept over Meredith Case. The late morning was chill; the dripping churchyard looked bleak under a sky of uniform grey, and looking at the Hawke vault, he tasted corruption again. The dry, warm taste of the Reverend Swann's sherry dissolved into the sickly taste of death. Was he always to be thus haunted? It was as if the ghost of Sir Gerald Hawke took up all the room in his life.

He would go to London; he would see Mr Dalrymple and leave in his hands all the matters to do with Hawke Court; he would be firm and tell him only to write to him when all was settled; he would tell him that he could not search for Sapphire Hawke, and then he would go home and tend to his parish. He would emulate the Reverend Swann and take up some scholarly work in his spare time. He would look after the poor and the needy and be the good clergyman he had hoped to be at the beginning of his service. "Choose whom you will serve," so the Bible taught. Well, it was time for him to choose between God and the devil he had glimpsed in that hot room where a wicked man had died.

It was quiet in the Hawke Arms. George ordered a pot of ale and exchanged pleasantries with the landlord, Abe Black, a red-faced, garrulous sort, always willing to talk if it kept a customer free with his purse. *Like his father*, thought George, remembering old Henry Black. Abe Black wouldn't know him. He'd not remember a gardener's boy from all those years ago. George stood at the bar at an angle from which he could keep an eye on the rectory.

'Passin' through, sir?' enquired Abe.

'On my way to Windsor. Snug place you have, Mr —'

'Abe Black, sir. Aye, 'twas my father's before me — a comfortable spot, and we get a passin' trade from time to time. Travellers like yourself.'

'The Hawke Arms? Family name, is it?'

'Aye, sir, Hawke family's bin here for generations, though no more. Sir Gerald was the last. Died only two days ago.'

'You'll have had good trade for the funeral, I daresay.'

'No, sir. Sir Gerald was a sick man. Only the lawyer, the doctor an' the heir attended. We all watched, o' course — glad to see the back o' the old lord.'

'Only three, eh? Not much good to you, I suppose.'

'Well, local folk came the night before to talk of it an' there was good business after. Just the one stranger — a young man on 'is way to somewhere. Can't remember where.'

'A young man, you say? Well, a friend of mine was coming down to Windsor before me. He might have stopped. What was the man's name?'

'Dale — Frederick Dale? Know 'im, do thee?'

'No, Mr Black, not my friend. He must have gone on, as I must, too. Thank you for the ale. I shall return, perhaps, on my way back.' George had seen the front door of the rectory open and Meredith Case talking to the parson.

He bade Abe Black farewell and went to the stable for his horse, all the while keeping his eye on the scene at the rectory. The ostler gave up the horse and George lingered in the doorway, adjusting his stirrup and girth. He watched Meredith

Case come down the path by the churchyard and pause to look at the Hawke vault. He saw the unhappiness and uncertainty on his face. Now what was that about? Had the old vicar told him something about Sapphire Hawke? He felt guilty, maybe, about his inheritance? George Stoneridge was a gambler; he would bet Lady Millicent's diamond that Meredith Case would look for Sapphire Hawke. And George would be right behind him.

# 5: PRAYERS

Mrs Stoneridge heard the front door close. From the window, she saw Meredith Case climb in, and the trap went slowly away.

She turned away. 'You heard. He'll not be back. Just a milksop parson, and there's nothing he wants from here. He's not interested in Sapphire Hawke.'

The man who had emerged from behind a Chinese screen frowned. 'I saw him rubbing at the picture — he was curious enough to do that.'

'It don't matter — she was about thirteen when that was painted. He wouldn't know her from a dirty old picture. Twenty-odd years will have changed her. In any case, she's long gone — went to that convent in Bruges and never came back — dead, most likely.'

'Let's hope so. Still, I'll ride after him — I want to make sure that he's gone, and I'm still wondering about that stranger I saw watching the house from the woods. I saw him in the crowd at the funeral.'

'I wish you hadn't gone anywhere near that funeral. I told you —'

'I kept well out of the way and I came back through the woods. Then I saw him from the window. I want to know who the hell he is. We don't want any other of Sir Gerald's bastards sniffing about.'

'George, watch your mouth.'

'It's true. There might be others still alive.'

'I doubt that. I'd have heard.'

'That girl — the one —'

'Vanished years ago — dead by now. A drunk, like her

mother. Meant for the streets, that one. Anyway, the stranger could just have been a traveller. Mebbe curious about the house. Hawke's death has been in all the papers. Some folk are just nosey.'

'I'll go to the Hawke Arms. Ask a few questions — see if I can find out. He might have stayed there.'

'I don't want you seen.'

'No one will recognise me — I've changed too, remember. It's years since I was here.'

'True, but you have his nose and eyes. I don't like it, George — suppose the landlord —'

'Why should he? Hawke was an old man. No one's set eyes on him for years, and if they had, they'd not have seen a nose — the old —'

'Be careful — don't stay drinkin'. Ask your questions and get out.'

'I have been careful for the last two weeks —'

'I don't know why you wanted to come and hang about here. I told you I didn't like it, that it was too risky.'

'I came because I wanted to be here when that old devil died — and I've been left nothing. Not even a mention.'

'God knows I tried, George, but I had to be careful. You know what he was like — and half mad at the end. I kept hinting —'

'Fat lot of good that did. Anyway, I've had enough of this dreary mausoleum. After I've made a few enquiries, it's back to London. I need to keep a watch on Dalrymple's chambers. See who comes and goes — and if the parson claims those jewels. What's to stop me making a claim to him? It'll be his Christian duty to compensate me. And I've got some unfinished business with a lady.'

'You an' your women, George Stoneridge, you want to be

careful. Concentrate on those jewels, never mind women. Keep your head down.'

George wasn't listening. He was thinking about his London business and the possible danger from a girl with a sweet mouth but a loose one, a girl who was beginning to want too much from him. She wouldn't be wearing the Hawke Sapphires; nor would he if he didn't do something.

'George, you hear me — there's too much at stake for you to wreck it all. I'm tellin' you, leave the women alone — time for all that when —'

'Our fortune's made. I know that. I'll watch my step. In the meantime, got anything for me? I'll need money in London.'

Mrs Stoneridge flashed him a look. 'Not more debts?'

'I told you, I've dealt with all that — the debts are paid, dead and gone, but I'm not flush and I'll have expenses. Can't live like a pauper.'

'I wasn't asking you to. I've got these.' Mrs Stoneridge reached into her pocket. 'Two rings — the signet ring was in the folds of the bed linen after he died. And this one —' she held up a diamond solitaire — 'was Lady Millicent's. Worth a pretty sum.'

Her companion took it. 'She'll not miss it, will she? It'll fetch plenty. I know just the man who'll give me cash on it — no questions asked. And this —' he took the signet ring — 'I'll keep.'

'For God's sake, George, don't be wearing it now if you're going to the Hawke's Arms.'

'I'm not such a fool as that. What else have you? I tell you I need some ready money.'

'I've given you plenty of trinkets. What about the sovereigns I gave you? You've spent nothing here.' Esther Stoneridge saw that he would not be satisfied until he had something else.

'There's this —' she offered a gold watch chain — 'worth a bit — it's heavy enough.'

George weighed it, found it not wanting, and slipped it in his pocket. 'I'd best get off if I'm to catch up with the trap.'

'Write and let me know what you're up to.'

She watched through the window as George Stoneridge rode off on the big chestnut — he made a fine figure, she thought, but he could be reckless — like his father.

In her own room, she took out a jewellery box. There were still a few valuables. George couldn't have everything. She didn't quite trust him — he was too much of a spender. She needed insurance in case things went wrong. There had been plenty of pickings over the last five years. Sir Gerald hadn't noticed — too drunk and latterly too sick, and she ruled here anyway, only taking on servants for rough work and never the same ones. She had been glad to see the back of Mr Case and that lawyer.

Pity about the sapphires — locked away all those years. She had known about them, wondered why Sir Gerald hadn't sold them. Now she knew — old Dalrymple had said. She'd heard the will read. She was to stay until further notice, and she'd been left a hundred pounds. She had lowered her eyes modestly — grateful for her master's beneficence. Little did they know that she had far more in her pocket at that very moment. But not enough — after what had been done to her. Married off to suit the convenience of Sir Gerald Hawke, and she who had given birth to the only lusty son Hawke had ever fathered. And everything left to that parson.

# 6: A PUBLIC DUTY

'Naturally, private feelings must yield to a stern sense of public duty, and when one knows —'

'Ah, a concerned citizen, of course,' Superintendent Sam Jones observed drily to Dickens, who had come to express his interest in the murder of Felix Gresham.

'And you have come to present vital evidence which, unaccountably, I have overlooked. In short, as your Mr Micawber would say, you are cognisant of the villain who perpetrated the horrid deed. Pray, divulge the identity of the person or persons unknown — and be quick about it. I haven't got all day. An arrest imminent and all that.' Jones picked up his pen.

'Samivel, don't be in such a perspiration — jeer, sneer and taunt me, but, as Iago said, I know what I know —' Dickens tapped his nose.

'Which is?'

'Which is, my ancient, that I met Felix Gresham's father, and his mother for that matter, and I know Miss Hamilton and Miss Finch — well, not "know", exactly, but I am acquainted — in the book buying way. Now, was there ever a thing more fated than that I should come to you with this information?'

'Much obliged, I'm sure — and you wish to —'

'Assist the authorities with their enquiries, as the newspapers say — have you seen Mrs Gresham?'

'Not yet.'

'I could, of course, come with you.'

'You could, and we will pay a visit, but just now tell me about the booksellers.'

'You don't suspect them? I read about the cab heard in the night.'

'No — not necessarily suspect, but there was something they were uneasy about. I had an impression that they were holding something back.'

'Secrets?'

'There are always secrets — in every case you and I have worked on, the things that folk want to forget always come to the surface whether or not they are guilty of the actual crime. That's murder for you.'

'So it is — secrets guarded for twenty years or more, sometimes. Scars of old wounds opened again to bleed afresh. Horrible —' Dickens thought for a moment — 'One on whom a secret sorrow preys.'

'Who?'

'Miss Hamilton — there is a remoteness about her. She resists knowing — a self-contained creature in whose heart there are secret chambers. Dangerous secrets, perhaps.'

'Secrets are very often dangerous —'

'And don't always go to the grave — people have a nasty habit of digging them up.'

'Like the police, for instance.'

'Biographers, I was thinking of.'

'Well, no one will be writing mine.'

'I don't know — I could. How about "A Faithful Account of the Fortunes, Misfortunes —'

'You can stop at misfortunes if you will —'

Dickens ignored him. '"Uprisings, Downfallings — in short — The Complete Career of Samuel Jones, the Younger?" Your father was a Samuel, was he not?'

'He was — not an imaginative man. My mother wanted Adolphus — she had ambitions —'

Dickens snorted. 'Dolly Jones, eh? What a swell.'

'If you've just come to distract me —' but Jones was smiling — 'let's stick to the present narrative. You knew Bartholomew and Thryza Chantrey who owned the bookshop?'

'Not well — years ago, I used to haunt those places around Wardour Street where all the curiosity shops are. There's one round the corner from St. Anne's Court in Crooked Alley — one Ebenezer Screech —' Dickens saw Jones's grimace — 'Know 'im, do thee?'

'Smelt 'im — Rogers and I questioned him about the night of the murder.'

'Saw nothink, 'eard nothink, in me innercent bed, yer 'onour. Not that I think he sleeps in a bed — under a toadstool, I'll wager. Something of the gnome about him. I don't think he has what we would call bedrooms. I call in from time to time — just to gaze upon him and all his works — time and decay and all that. The place is like a warehouse and full of junk, though I did buy a rosewood table once — not bad under the grime of decades, or centuries.'

'We couldn't shift him — he wouldn't have heard the cab, and though he's probably a crook, I've no reason to link him with Felix Gresham.'

'I went into the bookshop sometimes in the old days. A kindly sort of couple, unworldly, I thought, as if they'd stepped off the page of an old book — a fairy story. Like two paper cut-outs.'

'Mr Brim knew the Chantreys — and Mollie Rogers knows the two ladies slightly as customers. Not much is known, but Mollie seems to think that Miss Hamilton is some kind of relation of theirs. She came to live with them years back — an orphan. She took over the shop when they died. It was in the cholera epidemic in '46.'

'What about the other young woman?'

'Miss Addy Finch. I asked Constable Semple — his brother is a book-edge gilder in Star Court off Dean Street who does gilding for them, but Semple could tell me nothing except that the two women are friends — cousins, he thought.'

'Another orphan? It is like a fairy story.'

Jones grinned. 'Just up your street. I don't want to press Semple. He is very anxious that his brother is not caught up in all this, but, as I said, they are holding something back and there were other things that I preferred not to dwell on at the inquest.'

Dickens's eyes gleamed. He could feel the weight of the book in his coat pocket. It might be useful yet. 'Such as?'

'There was a young woman, a Phoebe Green, a lodger. She heard the cab; she was definite about that, but she couldn't say the time.'

'Could it have been another vehicle — private carriage?'

'That's what I wondered. Phoebe Green assumed it was a cab. Something was there, I don't doubt. We found no weapon, so it wasn't suicide. Rogers had a good look at the body on the steps. There should have been much more blood on those steps — there was some, but not enough to show that he had been killed there. Rogers thinks that Felix Gresham may have been killed elsewhere. The assistant surgeon, Mr Turtle, has asked Doctor Woodhall at King's College Hospital to take a closer look — I'm waiting on his report. I trust him — he was very helpful over the captain's murder.'

Dickens knew Allen Woodhall — he had had dealings with him about the Sanitary Commission looking into the state of London's old graveyards. There was a particularly noxious one by the hospital, and Allen Woodhall had been very useful to him and Sam over the case of Captain Louis Valentine, who had been murdered a while back on his ship *The Redemption*.

'You think the body might have been left deliberately in St. Anne's Court?'

'Felix Gresham was stabbed by a very sharp blade, according Mr Turtle's evidence, a single-edged blade which severed the carotid artery. He probably died immediately, and there would have been copious bleeding where he was killed. And, even if he had died after some time, the wound would have continued to bleed and there would have been an effusion of blood on those steps. So he must have been dead some time.'

'Bookbinders use very sharp paring knives for the leather.'

'So they do. But we didn't find a blood-stained knife, alas.'

'No knife missing from their workshop?'

'They said not, but unless we find the weapon, I can't accuse them of anything. There was no sign of any disturbance in the bookbinding room or in the shop — no tell-tale splashes of blood on the floor. We did look. But they knew Felix Gresham. They might well know who he knew.'

'You've asked, of course.'

'I have — they were not forthcoming, but I've spoken to Gresham's lawyer, a Mr Edward Temple, of Clement's Inn. He couldn't tell me much, either. Gresham had made a will — not that he had anything much to leave, so Temple said. His income came from his mother. He wouldn't inherit his father's legacy until he was twenty-five. According to Temple, the money would revert to his mother should he die before her. No one killed him for his inheritance. Temple did tell me that Gresham was something of a swell — liked his pleasures — clubs, gambling — that sort of thing. He mentioned a few places of entertainment: the Coal Hole in the Strand, the Cyder Cellars in Maiden Lane, Evans's in Covent Garden, the Garrick's Head down the road — you know the sort of thing

— drinking, singing, gambling.'

'Hardly Miss Hamilton's type.'

'No, indeed — which is why I wonder if whoever killed him is connected to his life about town. A wealthy widowed mother, an only son not short of money to lend to his cronies, perhaps.'

'You think someone owed him and couldn't or wouldn't pay?'

'That's the line I'm taking, and I've sent Rogers to his lodgings to find out what he can about his friends.'

'What about the cab?'

'There are six thousand cabs plying their trade, so I'm told. And any number of private carriages, so I can only look at the places I've mentioned so far. I've sent Inspector Grove and Constables Feak, Stemp and Dacres to them. They might turn up a cabman who remembers taking two men to St. Anne's Court on the night of the murder.'

'One of whom was so drunk he couldn't walk. One man drags the other out, pays the cabbie, who drives off, then walks his chalks, leaving the cadaver neatly arranged on the steps — cold-blooded, ain't it?'

'Disappears down Crooked Alley, turns in to Dean Street, into another cab, and he's away.'

'And if the poor fellow was left deliberately on Miss Hamilton's doorstep, then did that someone seek to blame her or Miss Finch?'

'I asked myself about that — of course, it is possible, but it might be simply that he was looking for a quiet spot and that was it — the cabman had to think that the sick young man was being taken home.'

'To a shop?'

'Why not? In any case, there's a house next door. It might

not have mattered exactly where the body was left.'

'True, my sage. But I suppose someone at the house or shop could have done it. Easy enough to leave him on the steps, slip back into the shop, and be woken from your innocent sleep sometime later.'

'And cleaned up the blood? I doubt that, but I need to keep my eye upon them — the murderer might well be a customer, someone who knew the shop. They might know something.'

'Ah, well, have a look at this —' Dickens took out the book with the broken spine — 'I happened to pick this up as I was coming out this morning — it needs repairing.'

'Happened, eh?'

'"The readiness is all", as Hamlet said. I could engage Miss Addy Finch in conversation, I daresay. She's more approachable than the other.'

'Go on, then. I can't stop you doing a bit of shopping. It might help. I should like to eliminate them if only for James Semple's sake — he likes them and he won't want to lose the work.'

'It shall be done.'

'A public duty, of course.'

'"Blessed is he that sitteth not in the seat of the scornful", Mr Jones. A touch on the crusty side, this morning, I'd say. Howsumever, I thinks yer mind needs divertin'. Now if you was ter take up skittles —'

'Get out of it.' Jones threw a scrunched-up piece of paper.

Dickens grinned and went out smartly, tipping his hat to Sergeant Rogers as he passed him in the corridor.

Rogers smiled to himself. He had a very good idea of what Mr Dickens had been discussing with Superintendent Jones: the murder of Felix Gresham.

# 7: REFLECTIONS ON MURDER

Addy Finch woke with a start, her feet slipping off the fender. The fire was nearly out, and the lamp had almost burned down. She stood to stretch and to look at the mantel clock. Ten minutes before one o'clock. At one o'clock in the morning three days ago Felix Gresham had been found murdered at their front door — *by person or persons unknown*. So the papers had reported.

And neither she nor Sarah had known who had done it — they had said so at the inquest and to the Superintendent from Bow Street. Addy had liked him, but he gave nothing away and the investigation would continue. If they did remember something pertinent to Mr Gresham's life, they should come to Bow Street. But they were disturbed. They had too much to hide to be comfortable under the gaze of the policeman. His grey eyes were sharp, as if he saw into things but he wasn't going to tell you what he saw.

Why, they had wondered, had Felix Gresham been murdered on their doorstep? Had he been coming to them and been attacked as he went up their steps? But why would Felix come to the shop in the middle of the night? In trouble, perhaps? Drunk, probably. Locked out of his lodgings. Lost all his money. Gambling again, no doubt.

Addy was aware, as she was thinking, that she was holding her breath and that she was listening, straining to hear. What had woken her? Was someone there? She watched the clock — Bartholomew's old clock, once so comforting, but now too loud in the silence as the hands drew nearer to the hour. The sound seemed to fill the room. She wanted to hurl it against the wall. Anything to stop it. Someone could be coming up the stairs.

Bartholomew's clock struck one and she heard the clock of St. Anne's Church sound the hour, and beyond that the echoes of other clocks, and still she stood waiting. Silence settled again in the room and the old clock went on ticking innocently. Addy felt the sharpness of her nails digging into her palms and uncurled her hands. She went to the window to peer through the hole in the shutters that they used to spy on late visitors — visitors who were not expected. There was no one outside the shop, but there was someone walking away on the other side of the street. A man, she thought, seeing him turn round to look back, his face a pale shape under the lamp over the door opposite. She shrank back as if he might see her, though she knew he could not. But she had an idea who he was.

She opened the parlour door and stared down the empty staircase. She lit a candle and went down to check. The shop door was bolted. The door of the bookbinding room which led to the yard was locked, too. No one could have got in.

She breathed in the familiar smell of leather and glue and her heartbeat slowed. Nothing must spoil this. This place where she and Sarah had found their peace, where the slow, careful work of their hands, folding the paper with the bone folders, stitching, tightening the cords, smoothing the leather or velvet or cool silk ready for pasting to the boards, all brought them a quiet satisfaction. They kept shop and worked on the books, and their tranquil, even days, regular as breathing, had closed like a series of doors sealing up the past. And all had been well until their door had opened onto the murdered body of Felix Gresham.

The candlelight lit up the gilt edges and letters on the leather-bound books waiting for repair, and it picked out the tools —

the mallets, the paste brushes, the awls, the hand pallets for decoration, the embossing tools, the fillets for inscribing the fine lines on the leather covers and the sharp knives for cutting the leather and cloth. Addy looked and thought about a missing knife.

The police had looked at the tools, especially at the knives. The Superintendent had questioned them, and James Semple, the book edge gilder, who lived in Star Court just a few minutes away off Dean Street. Addy had known that a knife was missing — because it had been Thyrza Chantrey's knife, an old one which Addy used and kept sharp in memory of that patient, gentle woman who had taught everything she knew to a girl who knew nothing and wept very often because it was so hard. Addy had not lost it, but she had said nothing when the policeman had asked if anything was missing, not daring to look at Sarah — Sarah had known, too. Someone had taken that knife. Someone who had been in the workshop in the days or weeks before Felix had died? Someone they knew?

Blood. She thought about Sarah, who was her sister in all the ways that counted, even in blood, probably. Sarah who would surely come this morning. Lord, it was morning already. What a long night it had seemed.

And she thought about a girl called Ruby Kiss and wondered why she had not come to see them about Felix Gresham.

# 8: EARS TO HEAR

Miss Addy Finch had an appealing face, Dickens thought, like a little cat's, and dark eyes, which usually glinted with humour, but she seemed out of sorts this afternoon and she looked tired, as if she hadn't slept. The murder, perhaps. She was certainly not inclined to conversation. He could hardly mention it without seeming merely inquisitive, and he didn't know her well enough to ask if she had recovered from the ordeal of a murdered man found on their steps. He had told her that he thought he had bought his book from Mr Chantrey's shop and asked if it could be repaired.

Behind Miss Finch, there was a door into the binding workshop in which there was a window, behind which he thought he saw a movement — a gloved hand lifted up and brought down again with something black — a hat, possibly. It was gone in a second, but he had an impression of a man's sleeve.

Addy looked up from her examination of the book. 'It is Mr Chantrey's work. I can tell — the gold leaf is his work, and he liked this olive-coloured morocco to work on. These stamps on the corners — the acorns and leaves — are his design, I'm sure, and the black leather insert with the title on the spine. The lettering, too. It's very simple and small — a bit old-fashioned now.'

'You can repair it?'

'Yes, of course. We don't do a lot of this kind of work. The albums and journals sell better with the coloured silks and velvets, but Bartholomew and Thyrza taught Sar— Miss Hamilton the leather-binding work. Yes, I'm sure she can do it,

Mr Dickens.'

'I'm obliged — I don't know how it was damaged. One of my boys, I suppose — my boy Wally is a clumsy fellow at times —' *Shouldn't be slandering poor Walter*, he thought, but anything to keep the conversation going — 'and I should like to keep it, though it's not much of a poem. A bit long and dreary, but it's nice to have something of Bartholomew's.'

Addy took up the book. 'Yes, indeed. I can send a message when it's done. We have your card.'

Dickens was about to take the hint when the door opened, and a young man came in. Addy frowned. She was not pleased to see whoever it was.

'I'll just browse for a while, Miss Finch — it is my eldest daughter's birthday soon. My other daughter loved her scrapbook. Perhaps I'll find a pretty journal for Miss Mamie.'

Dickens moved over to the shelves where the journals and albums were displayed. It was Mamie's birthday soon — well, in a few weeks, next month on March 7th, and he would buy her something. He turned over the albums, admiring the lovely silk covers, and all the while listening to the muted words of the two at the counter.

'She's not here, Ned,' Addy was saying impatiently. 'I've told you, I don't know when she'll be back.'

'Where's she gone?'

'Business — and it's not yours, and we haven't seen Ruby so there's no use you asking. What's your interest, anyway?'

'Only that Ruby was close to Felix — I wondered if —'

'It's nothing to do with Ruby. She's not been around for ages — all that with Felix was finished. She's moved on, I daresay. Now, leave it, Ned. No use hanging about here. It was you last night?'

'I only wanted to ask about Ruby.'

'At one o'clock in the morning?'

'I didn't think —'

'Sarah will get in touch with you — if she wants to.'

Dickens didn't hear the young man's reply, but he did hear the door open and close. He picked up an album with a sky-blue silk cover embroidered with flowers and took it to the counter. He saw how Miss Finch's face was pink with anger, but he made no comment, merely saying that he would take the blue one for his daughter.

Addy took scissors and string to wrap up the parcel. Neat, deft fingers, she had, thought Dickens as he watched her. An idea came to him.

'Er — bookbinding — you know my magazine *Household Words*?'

'Yes, of course. We take it and enjoy it very much.'

'You know that there are always pieces on interesting processes. I should very much like to do a piece on bookbinding — such a skill and two lady bookbinders, what could be more interesting? Two ladies earning their independent living.'

'Not us?' Addy sounded alarmed.

'Why not?' Dickens gestured to the album and to the shelves. 'You make beautiful things.'

'No, no, Mr Dickens, I beg you. We don't want any more publicity after — after —'

'Oh, I do beg your pardon — you mean after the young man, Mr — er?'

'Felix, Mr Gresham, yes — you've no idea, Mr Dickens, how we've been pestered by people staring, standing out there, looking for the blood — folk on their way to church an' on their way back. Praying, indeed, an' then staring an' grinning at where a murder — ghouls, they are.'

'Your customer —' Dickens indicated the door — 'a journalist, perhaps?'

'No, no — just a nuisance — he knew Felix. He just wants — never mind him. We just don't want more people. They're not coming to buy — just to idle about an' gape, an' there's neighbours. Bella Screech asking questions.'

'Bella who?' Not a wife, surely. He thought of gnomish Screech and gaped himself.

'Screech — daughter of Ebenezer at the curiosity shop off Crooked Alley. Barmaid at The Mischief when she's not poking her nose in here. No, Mr Dickens, you mustn't think of it.'

'I wouldn't name you, of course. I could make up two ladies — sisters — in a small country town, Chertsey, perhaps.'

Addy Finch looked even more alarmed. 'Not Chertsey, no.'

'Why ever not?'

'We — have customers there.'

'Rochester, then, where I lived as a boy.'

'I shall have to ask Sarah — she might not —'

'I only want to see how it is done. When my book is repaired, send a message to my office in Wellington Street, and when I come to collect it, perhaps Miss Hamilton will show me the process. I wouldn't think of publishing for a few months yet. The murder business will be forgotten. The ghouls will have moved on.'

Addy answered his smile, though she felt little to smile about. She felt she had been caught out, that she had shown too much alarm, and to mention Chertsey, that was stupid. She handed him the wrapped book. 'I'll ask her, Mr Dickens, and I'll let you know when — if she has time.'

She watched him go out and sat down behind the counter. She felt besieged: first Ned Temple asking about Ruby an' now

Mr Dickens poking his nose in, his kind eyes making her talk too much — and protest too much, but it was true — folk had been gaping. That was a reason in itself not to want publicity.

And Mr Dickens would be a good customer. He was often at the stationery shop in Crown Street. Mollie Rogers knew — Addy gripped the counter suddenly — Mollie Rogers's husband was a policeman. Constable Rogers who had come with the Superintendent. Mollie talked a lot about Mr Dickens and how he had come to her wedding.

She looked at the pretty book with its broken spine. Coincidence? She went to the door and put up the closed sign. Then she went through into the binding workshop.

# 9: THE OLD CURIOSITY SHOP

Dickens stood in the street. Interesting that Miss Finch did not seem to like him — the friend of Felix Gresham. "Felix", Miss Finch had called him — more than once. Surely not just a customer? And who was Ruby, who had not been seen for weeks and whom Ned was anxious to see? Ned?

He walked towards Crooked Alley, intending to go by Dean Street into Oxford Street and then home. He thought about Miss Finch's alarm at the thought of a piece in *Household Words*. Secrets, Sam had said. They had something to hide, but whether it was to do with the murder of Felix Gresham, it was impossible to say. Whose was that arm he had glimpsed? A man's, surely. James Semple, the book-edge gilder, maybe? He couldn't see the two women as a pair of murderesses, but one never knew. He thought of the murderers he and Sam had encountered — two of them women, driven by passionate hatred for their victims, hatred borne of a desire for revenge, and the secret, whispered words like ghostly nooses had emerged from the shadowy past to encircle one slender neck and to hang her.

And Bella Screech, eh? Now that was a staggerer. The old gnome had a daughter. Still, he had often observed that men who were very hideous and disagreeable were frequently successful in matrimonial adventures — one of the mysteries of human existence. But Miss Screech he would very much like to see. Perhaps she did know something about the murder. Perhaps she had known Felix Gresham. She'd asked questions about him. She could have met him at The Mischief — properly known as The Load of Mischief on Oxford Street. It wasn't far from Crooked Alley.

Dickens turned in to the alley and then left into the tunnel of a passage where Screech's shop was. A gloomy place even when daylight was not fading. There was no pavement, and on the step and on the stones of the passage a jumble of Screech's goods almost blocked the way. Any passer-by — and who might pass, Dickens couldn't think — had to walk into the filthy sewer that went down the middle of the alley where all the water and litter collected. A man fleeing from a murder scene must have tripped over the collection of junk. Screech would have heard that, though he'd surely take in his valuables at night.

Anyway, he was certain it was a dead end. He had never ventured beyond the shop door, but it was worth a look. He picked his way past an iron fender and a birdcage. You'd think Screech had left it there on purpose to arrest the flight of would-be thieves, though who could possibly want to steal a rusty old parrot's cage? There was a market for everything, he supposed, stepping over a bundle of old clothes and coming face to face with a cavalier pasted on a rickety screen whose lace was distinctly sooty and whose plumes drooped forlornly in the shadows. A peculiar-looking bamboo chair, of eastern origin, it seemed, had toppled over, its legs in the air like a great fallen bird, blocking his way. Perhaps Screech sat enthroned on summer evenings smoking his hookah, surveying his tattered empire.

The dead wall loomed like a great tombstone, but as he came closer, he saw that there was a tiny passage to the right, only wide enough for a grown person to edge sideways. A murderer couldn't dash down there — but he wouldn't need to. Felix Gresham had been found at one o'clock. He could have been dumped earlier. No one about in quiet St. Anne's Court — slip away through Crooked Alley, pass the shop and squeeze into Dark Entry — Dickens noted the name — and away.

Just as he was about to turn away, he heard running footsteps and a small boy shot out of the passage, rushed past him and down towards Screech's shop, where he paused to kick at the goods on the pavement, scattering a set of fire irons with peculiar ferocity. He let out a great yell of execration, kicked the parrot's cage, and ran on before Dickens had time to move.

He went back down Crooked Alley. He could try the shop. The daughter might be there — if not, he could try The Mischief. For now, he might just browse and engage Screech in conversation. Folk always wanted to talk about murder — they couldn't help themselves.

He picked up the fallen parrot's cage and peered in at the window, hoping he might catch a glimpse of the phenomenon — for such she must be — Miss Bella Screech, but something which seemed to be affixed to the inside of the murky windowpane caused him to step back smartly and entangle his foot in the fire irons which rattled indignantly. He righted himself and looked again. Something flat and white pressed against the window like a slug. It moved up and down, leaving a slimy trail. The thing unpeeled itself and he saw that it was attached to a face — the unprepossessing visage of Ebenezer Screech, whose eyes were gazing malevolently back at him over his nose, which he wiped with a grimy hand. Then he vanished. Dickens heard the door and there he was, leering at Dickens like a face on an old water-spout. He looked at the scattered fire irons.

'Mr Dickin — yer 'onour —' Screech always called him that. Dickens never bothered to correct him. The mistake had been made before by a Mrs Beadnall, mother of Maria, whom he had so passionately loved as a young man. His name had not mattered to Mrs Beadnall — that young man with so few prospects was not going to marry her treasure. Maria's father had been a City banker. *The whirligig of time brings in his revenges*, he thought. Mrs Beadnall forever linked to Ebenezer Screech in his back alley.

'Mr Screech, my compliments.'

'Them fire irons is agoin' cheap — damaged goods, see —' Screech chuckled at his own joke — 'but I'll not charge ye fer the damage.'

'I didn't —' Dickens thought of the angry boy — 'obliged to you, but I'm not in the market for fire irons.'

'Step in, then — I've some good silver. A bargin, Mr Dickin.'

Screech stepped back into his shop and Dickens followed. Screech continued to walk backwards in an odd crab-wise movement, all the while leering ingratiatingly at Dickens. *Keeping his eye on me — in case I pocket a silver spoon.* Screech was unerring in his progress through the shop, sliding past tottering piles of objects which any man, even going forward, would have dislodged as Dickens did, reaching out a startled hand to right a pair of stag's horns which stabbed him in the cheek. The place was alive with articles in dark conspiracy against intruders. He dodged the embrace of part of a ship's figurehead — some battered, peeling goddess. A fire dog, in the shape of Mr Punch and a replica of Screech in chin and nose, barked his shin. A fishing net attempted to suffocate him. He fought it off. A line of ragged bunting attempted strangulation. Extricating himself, he put his foot in a chamber pot which he dashed against a hideous iron fire screen. It broke into pieces.

Screech gave a cry of anguish. 'Mr Dickin, I'd ask ye to be careful with my property. That chamber pot —' he turned his lamp on the broken pieces — 'belonged to the Duchess of Bolton.'

Dickens looked at the shards of pottery. He saw a faded gilded crest and some very unpleasant-looking stains. The Duchess was a woman like any other. He caught up with Screech at his counter where he wiped his runny nose again with his grubby hand. Screech's chin jutted at him like a shovel about to scrape up the ashes of the miserable fire behind him.

'Now yer will 'ave ter pay fer that — I'll overlook the fire irons, but that was a val'able piece — 'istory in it.'

There certainly was. Dickens said mildly, 'By all means. Two bob do you?'

'Yer will 'ave yer little joke, Mr Dickin — quite a card, ain't yer?'

'What about the silver, Mr Screech? Perhaps I can make it up to you for my clumsiness.'

Screech darted behind his counter from which he brought out a velvet box, much scuffed and worn and tied with a bit of old string, which he cut with a sharp knife. He opened it to reveal a set of very nice silver spoons — there were only five and they were a bit tarnished, but worth considering. He picked one up to look for the hallmark. He could hear Screech licking his lips.

'A very great pity about Mr Gresham,' Dickens observed, keeping his eyes on the spoons. He'd have to buy them, he supposed. Well, he hadn't been born with one in his infant mouth. Tin spoons had been his legacy — and they'd been pawned. A man, not unlike Screech in avariciousness, had given him tuppence.

'Knew 'im, did yer?'

In the interests of truth, Dickens replied, 'Slightly —' and in the interests of verisimilitude, he went on — 'I knew his late father, and, of course, his poor mother who is, naturally, grief-stricken.' That last part was true, surely. Dickens did not know her really, but he knew that her sorrow must be profound — an only child. 'My boy, Felix', she had said, fondly. She had fancied him a poet. Surely even Screech must respond to the portrait of the sorrowing mother — a parent himself, incredible though it might seem.

'Widder, then,' Screech said, screwing up his eyes and cocking his head, as if she were standing before him and he was calculating how much she was worth.

That was some progress. Improvising, Dickens went on, 'Yes, these many years. I fear that she has not seen enough of her son recently.' Dickens looked up quickly and met Screech's eyes. 'Did you know him?' He saw that Screech did, and that Screech knew that he saw.

'Came in 'ere a few times.'

'Ah, a good customer?'

'Sellin', cos 'e knowed that Screech'd give a good price.'

'Naturally.'

Screech's eyes gleamed suddenly like little jet beads. 'Yer'd be int'rested in a little memento — fer the widder?'

'Of course, I am sure it would be a great comfort to her if she could have something of his returned.'

Screech scrabbled about in a tray of rusty keys, the largest of which might have opened the great door of Newgate Gaol, and selected one with which he opened a cupboard behind. He rummaged in the voluminous pockets of his coat and brought out a smaller key and opened a metal box. He brought a small canvas bag to the counter and placed before Dickens a diamond pin — the kind with which you would fasten a cravat.

Dickens examined it. It looked valuable. 'Mr Gresham sold you this?'

'Needed the readies — said I'd 'ang on to it o' course, in case 'e wanted it back, but now 'e's gorn, well, a dead man's goods, I dunno, Mr Dickin, I got feelin's —'

Dickens thought of all the dead men's things acquired by Screech at bargain prices, no doubt. 'I suppose you'd take less than —'

'Less!' Screech was aghast.

Dickens's ears tingled. 'I'm thinking of the poor, bereaved mother, Mr Screech.'

'A diamon's a diamon', Mr Dickin, yer 'onour, an' it's worth wot it's worth.'

'Which is?'

Screech named his price. 'Five guineas, yer 'onour — an' I'm makin' precious little on that. A man's gotter live, Mr Dickin.'

'Too much, I'm afraid, Mr Screech, for Mrs Gresham, but I will speak to her about it.'

Screech's face fell, but rallying, he turned once more to the spoons. 'Best quality, yer can see that fer yerself.'

Dickens eyed the tarnish. If he were to get anything more from Screech, he'd have to pay without too much quibbling. The spoons were better than most of the other stock — a rusty parrot's cage, for example, or a duchess's chamber pot. 'How much?'

'Thirty bob — an' that's a bargain. Silver spoons, Mr Dickin. They'll polish up beautiful.'

'Too dear, Mr Screech — say five and I'll take them now. It's not a full set.'

'Yer'd not rob a poor old man, Mr Dickin — fifteen an' that is a bargain.'

'Ten.'

'Twelve an' that's yer lot.' Screech's chin jutted again.

Best not push him too far. 'Very well.' Dickens fished in his pocket for the shillings and, beginning to count them out very slowly, he asked, 'Did Mr Gresham ever come here with a friend?'

Screech eyed him suspiciously. 'Deal o' questions, Mr Dickin.'

'For the sake of the widow, Mr Screech. I could perhaps introduce Mrs Gresham to one of her son's friends — she knows little of his London life, I'm afraid. It might be a comfort to her in the circumstances —' Dickens saw Screech's eyes clear, and couldn't help adding a flourish — 'Murder, Mr Screech — how can a mother bear that?'

Screech certainly could bear it. He looked at the coins on the counter. Dickens saw how he gnawed his lip. There were only eight coins so far. There was a silence and Screech looked up, his eyes thoughtful. 'There was that lawyer, Temple — aye, Ned Temple —' he looked at Dickens's hand — 'saw Mr Gresham give 'im the money from the pin. Owed 'im, p'raps. Graspin' lot, lawyers, like maggots in nuts.' His grimy claw swept up the coins as Dickens put the rest down. Screech put them into the tin box which he locked before Mr Dickin could change his mind.

'No one else you can tell me about?'

'Can't say as I recall —' Screech turned away to his cupboard suddenly, then, turning back, he said — 'couple o' young swells like Mr Gresham. Don't remember no one else.'

'Well, I'll find Mr Temple in one of the Inns of Court and ask him to see Mrs Gresham. I'm much obliged to you, Mr Screech.'

Dickens picked up the box of spoons, sidled past a drooping, yellowing bridal gown, kicked aside the remnants of the duchess's chamber pot, wafted away the bunting, avoided being beheaded by a rusty pike, and found the door.

He took a last look at Dark Entry, resisted temptation, and made his way back to Bow Street, musing on Ned Temple, who hadn't been able to tell Superintendent Jones very much about his client, but had been given the proceeds of a diamond pin.

# 10: TESTIMONY

'Anything interesting from Montague Street?' Jones asked of his sergeant, Alf Rogers.

'I spoke to the landlady, Mrs Flax. Nothing there, o' course. All his possessions had been cleared out — by his lawyer.'

'Mr Edward Temple.'

'The same — landlady knew him, so she had no reason to prevent him. Mr Temple said he would return Mr Gresham's clothes and possessions to his mother at Richmond an' off he went.'

'And his private papers and letters, I presume.'

'Everythin'.'

'I shall have to see Mr Temple again. There might be something in his papers or letters to tell us about his private life.'

'Mrs Flax — the landlady — was fond o' the young man — supposed to be studying for the bar, but she didn't see much evidence of studyin' anythin' 'cept the horses, but he paid his rent on time an' was pretty generous to his friends, gaddin' about, goin' to his club, restaurants, the theatre, music halls —'

'So Mr Temple told me.'

'She mentioned the Casino de Venise in particular — he and Mr Temple used to —'

Dickens came in. 'That's a name I've just heard.'

'I'm interested,' said Jones, 'but first, I'd like to hear what Alf has to tell me about Mr Temple, who I've been led to believe was only Felix Gresham's lawyer not his particular friend.'

Rogers continued his tale. 'Landlady, Mrs Flax, mentioned the Casino de Venise as a favourite haunt, and that Mr

Gresham was very thick with Mr Temple — they went about together a lot.'

'Now, Mr Temple mentioned all kinds of places, but not, I note, the Casino de Venise. So, what can you tell us, Charles, about the very interesting Mr Temple?'

Dickens told of his visit to Screech's shop, his mention of Ned Temple, and of the detail about the money and the diamond pin.

'Screech involved in Gresham's death, do you think?'

'He'd squeeze the last drop of profit from a shrivelled lemon, but I doubt he'd kill a man. No need. He wouldn't hate a man or envy him, but he'd screw him until he starved.'

'That'd be murder,' Rogers said indignantly.

'So it would, Alf, but we can't arrest a man for that. However, we'll keep him in mind — unlicensed pawnbroking is a nice little implement should we wish to squeeze him for any more information. Now this Mr Temple, lending or borrowing, I wonder?'

'Why'd Gresham be sellin' a diamond pin? Mrs Flax said he had plenty, though if he was gamblin' at the Casino, he might have been short o' cash.'

'Mr Temple, a borrower, perhaps. Mrs Flax said that Mr Temple had cleared out all Felix Gresham's possessions — the rooms were empty. No papers, no letters, nothing.'

'No little bills promising to pay up,' said Dickens.

'There won't be any now signed by Mr Temple, I'll be bound,' Jones said. 'Anything else?'

'Indeed, there is. I did go to the bookshop and a young man called Ned came in — a tall, fair-haired young man with a moustache and brown eyes.'

'Sounds very like Edward Temple.'

'Miss Finch was not pleased to see him. He was asking for

Sarah Hamilton and he mentioned someone called Ruby who had some connection with Felix Gresham. Miss Finch told him that whatever it had been, it was all over, and that Ruby had moved on, and that Mr Temple was not to keep hanging about. Mr Temple had called the night before at one o'clock in the morning — he must be very anxious to find this Ruby.'

'They said all this before you?'

'Not exactly — Miss Finch had received my commission for the book I wanted repairing and Mr Temple came in as I was about to go. I was curious so I went to look at some keepsake albums and I couldn't help overhearing — quite accidental, I assure you.'

'Of course — just an ordinary customer whose ears happened to be twitching.'

'He that hath ears to hear, Mr Jones, must employ them in the interests of his dearest friends.'

'Much obliged, Mr Dickens.'

Dickens grinned. 'Then I had a rather brilliant notion — when Mr Temple had departed, I asked if I might watch the bookbinding process for a piece for *Household Words*. Miss Finch was very reluctant. They didn't want the publicity — given that too many people were coming round to gaze at the place where a murder had happened. Even when I promised not to use their shop, only the idea of two lady bookbinders, she was not convinced. I thought of your idea about secrets — something's bothering them.'

'Something they know about Felix Gresham and don't want to tell me.'

'Now that could well be, because Miss Finch referred to Mr Gresham as Felix — twice.'

'More than a customer, then. Why keep that quiet?'

'Some sort o' romance? Mrs Flax said that Mr Gresham was engaged to a lady, but he might have been —' Rogers offered.

'Applying himself to the cultivation of wild oats — it wouldn't surprise me, though I don't know about Miss Finch. This missing Ruby might be more likely.'

'Then, Sergeant, I suggest you take yourself to the Casino de Venise to see if you can find out anything about her since that was their favourite haunt. Meanwhile, I'll need another talk with Mr Temple.'

'I'll walk with you as far as Clement's Inn. I'm away to Lincoln's Inn Fields to see my friend, Mr Forster.'

# 11: PRESUMPTION OF DEATH

Simeon Dalrymple sneezed — very loudly. He felt dreadful. The funeral had been a cold and damp affair, ruinous to the chest. He shivered at the memory of that chilly dinner in that dreary dining room at Hawke Court. What a mean sort of woman Mrs Stoneridge was. Sour as that dreadful port. The library had been worse, colder than a tomb. Now he had a heavy cold which he felt deep in his bones, and he was disturbed. The sight of Sir Gerald Hawke in his deathbed had not surprised him — the man had been a thoroughly bad lot, but he had been shocked by the ruined face. That's what the pox did, and it served the man right, but it had sickened him; he had seen the same feeling in the face of Meredith Case.

He had been glad to get back to London, to his wholesome wife and daughter, and his cheerful son. He had hoped that the Hawke family affairs could be finished with once the heir had signed the necessary papers. But the matter of Sapphire Hawke and the sapphires was very unsatisfactory. He had remembered something — not that he had found anything new in the papers. He recalled that Sir Gerald Hawke's cousin, Miss Henrietta Hawke, had visited some relatives up in the north somewhere. Sapphire Hawke, he knew, had lived at Hawke's London house, but she must have come from somewhere — the north, perhaps? He'd have to think — see if he could remember any more detail.

Not that it mattered. He did not think Sapphire Hawke would be found after all these years. His theory was that she had stayed in the convent whither she had been sent after the scandal of the shooting. He had thought that Sir Gerald had

63

become bored by his role as guardian and had packed her off to Bruges.

But why he should leave her the sapphires and why he should want her found was a mystery. It wasn't his business. He didn't blame Meredith Case for not wanting to search, but legally he felt uncomfortable about it. If the Reverend Case would not act, then somehow he felt it to be his duty; however much he might disapprove of his client, as he had of Sir Gerald Hawke, a family solicitor had an obligation. Whatever would ensue if such a man shirked his duty out of niceness about the reputation of his client? The duty of a family solicitor was a clear-cut thing, especially where property was concerned — property was nothing to do with feeling. Property belonged legally to a man — or a woman in this case — or it did not. And the sapphires, according to Sir Gerald's properly attested will, belonged to Miss Sapphire Hawke — who might be dead. Simeon Dalrymple wanted the matter tidied up — nothing was more satisfactory than a case closed, the papers rolled up, the wax seal stamped, and the whole lot placed in its proper box. And, he admitted to himself, there was the matter of his legal fees — Sir Gerald Hawke had never paid his bills. Those sapphires ought to be sold — by Miss Sapphire Hawke or Mr Case.

There was one obvious thing to do — if Mr Case would not act, then he, the legal representative of the Hawke family, must set in motion the business of having Sapphire Hawke declared legally dead. Simeon Dalrymple had given this matter thought when he had drawn up Sir Gerald's last will. The old man had demanded the codicil with regard to the sapphires. Simeon Dalrymple had complied; he knew better than to ask any questions. Sir Gerald Hawke was not a man to have his wishes questioned. Mr Dalrymple had felt the lash of his tongue more than once.

Simeon Dalrymple knew the law which stated that that the absentee's death was a presumption of law, rather than a fact inferred from absence. He took down the volume where he had marked the place. It was his job to be exact. The statutes of 1837 regarding wills and property of the deceased were what he was after.

The 1837 statute made it perfectly clear: the Chief Justice of the Exchequer Chamber had stated that "Where a person goes abroad, and is not heard of for seven years, the law presumes in fact that such person is dead." Meredith Case could apply to the court for the presumption of death.

Simeon felt better. Statutes and cases were always a comfort. He turned to the case of Watson v England, heard in 1844. The judge there had added that if the absentee were living, it could be assumed that he or she would have communicated with some friend or relative. All well and good — there was no evidence of any communication between Sir Gerald and his ward. However — here Mr Dalrymple frowned — there was a rub. In the case of France v Andrews, heard very recently, the judge had opined that the plaintiff must show that enquiries had been made as to the whereabouts of the absentee.

But this could be done by sending to Bruges; surely the convent could be found, and he could establish if Sapphire Hawke were there — a nun, perhaps — or if she were dead. There could be no other explanation of her absence, "beyond the seas or elsewhere", as the statute had it. And when he had his answer, the jewels could be given to her if she lived. If she were dead, then Meredith Case could instruct him to sell them. He might be made to see that their sale could benefit his church in some way.

That was the case he would put to the Reverend Mr Case

when he arrived. Fifteen minutes late. Unreliable. One wanted steadiness from a clergyman. Mr Dalrymple put down his gold watch on his desk and rang the bell for his clerk, Joah Danks. He felt better; hot tea and more coals for the fire would be most welcome now.

An hour later, Joah Danks's unblinking eyes watched Meredith Case walk down the stairs. *Somethin' wrong with him*, he thought — looked like he'd seen a ghost. His mind turned over the fragments he had heard. Joah Danks eavesdropped very often. He liked to know what was going on. He knew a deal about Dalrymple's son, Alexander, that his pa might not like; he knew a deal about that lawyer downstairs, Ned Temple, that Temple wouldn't like known. Thought themselves too good for Joah Danks. Looked right through him. He'd asked Temple about where a man could meet a girl like the one he'd seen him with. Temple had looked sick as an old maid. Said it wasn't Danks's business and just walked off. He might regret that someday.

Old Dalrymple had looked a bit sick, too, when he'd come back from the Hawke funeral, and now Mr Alexander was goin' to Bruges to find someone, or was it to the north? Westmorland? Had that been the name he'd heard? He couldn't hear whether it was a person or a place. And there was somethin' about real sapphires — jewels in old Dalrymple's safe. Joah Danks licked his dry lips. He knew a man who would pay good money for what Joah Danks knew.

# 12: INHERITANCE

Jones looked over the few papers that Felix Gresham had left behind him. He took his time, aware of a certain tension about Mr Ned Temple, whose hands played with a quill pen, and under whose eyes there were dark circles. There were a few letters from a lady residing at Richmond — a young lady, by the sound of it, who expressed her pleasure in Felix's company at various picnics and suppers, and whose mama would be very glad to receive Mr Gresham on any Sunday he cared to call. There was the will that Temple had mentioned — in the event of the young man's death, the fortune he would have inherited remained in his mother's possession; there were some few bequests of negligible significance and one legacy in particular upon which Jones did not comment, merely observing that it seemed all very straightforward. He put down the papers on the desk and saw how Mr Temple seemed to relax.

'Yes, it is,' Ned Temple replied, 'Felix would not inherit until he was twenty-five years.'

'So you told me —' *He is eager to stress that*, Jones thought, *eager to insist that he has no motive. Well, we shall see* — 'Rather older than is usual, perhaps.'

'Felix's father was a lawyer, a very wealthy one, and a cautious man — far-sighted, too. He was elderly when Felix was born. He wanted to be sure that his considerable fortune would be in safe hands. I think he would have stipulated forty years as a suitable age if Mrs Gresham had not persuaded him that such an inheritance would be sure to —'

'Yes?'

'I was going to say that she thought that Felix would be sufficiently mature at twenty-five. She wanted him to marry and settle down.'

'With the young lady?' Jones pointed to the letters.

'Yes, there was an understanding, but Felix was — not ready, I think.'

'Mr Gresham, the elder, had some doubts about his son?'

'Mr Ernest Gresham was a man who cared about money. He was paid very well to look after his wealthy clients' interests, and — well — he kept a tight rein on Felix.'

'When did Mr Ernest Gresham die?'

'Five years ago — Mrs Gresham was left in control of Felix's money, but she was always generous to him.'

'And to you, I see. Mrs Gresham would have sanctioned Felix's legacy to you.'

Ned Temple blinked. 'She did — not that I ever expected to receive it. Felix was only just twenty-four, Mr Jones. I hope you are not suggesting —'

Jones noted the flush at his jaw. 'I am only pursuing enquiries, Mr Temple; I must establish the facts about Felix Gresham's life. He was murdered and I wish to know if anyone had a motive — money is a very powerful motive, in my experience.'

'I beg your pardon, Mr Jones; of course, I see that you must investigate thoroughly. Felix's death has been most distressing. I cannot think who — only that it was a random act. It is quite beyond my understanding.'

'How came you to be Felix's lawyer?'

'I was articled in Mr Ernest Gresham's chambers. I knew Felix from when he was a boy of fifteen or so. Mrs Gresham was indebted to me, or so she thought, and when I set up on my own, she — er — wanted me to act for him.'

'And the nature of this debt she thought she owed?'

'I was able to extricate Felix from a difficulty when he was a youth of seventeen.'

'He was in some trouble?' Jones pressed. He wanted to know all about Mr Gresham and his relationship with Ned Temple.

'An entanglement with a young lady who was not suitable — a young lady to whom Felix fancied he was betrothed. I —'

'Paid her off?' *Let's not mince words*, thought Jones — *let's have it all out in the open.*

'I acted for Mr Ernest Gresham — he trusted me to deal with the matter, and I did. The girl was quite satisfied with the sum of money she was given.'

'I see. So you became a kind of protector — an older brother, perhaps?'

'Mrs Gresham saw me in that light.'

'And how did you see it?'

'In the same way, really. Felix could be — well, I told you before, he enjoyed his freedom, his night life in the clubs, the music halls and so on.'

Time to pounce. 'And the Casino de Venise?' He looked directly at Temple.

Ned Temple held his gaze, but Jones was aware of the clenching of his fingers on the quill pen.

'Yes, it was one of his favourite haunts.'

'And you went with him there?'

'Sometimes — to keep an eye on him — for his mother's sake. He liked gambling rather too much —'

'Lost money, did he?'

'Sometimes he'd overspend his allowance, and I had to apply to his mother. I promised her I would advise Felix, but he could be — Superintendent Jones, I do not wish to speak ill of Felix — your questions are —'

'Necessary, I'm afraid. Did Mr Gresham owe money to anyone?'

'I see what you are getting at — motive, of course — but I know only of trifling sums which were paid back to friends. Of course, Felix might have been in difficulties about which he had not wanted to confide — not wanting me to approach his mother. There might be someone, I suppose.'

'Did anyone owe Mr Gresham money — a substantial amount of money?'

Ned Temple looked at the quill pen. 'I have no idea — I doubt it — I cannot think of anyone.'

'I shall certainly pursue that line of enquiry. Now, you say that Mr Gresham was not eager to marry the young woman. Perhaps there was another lady — someone he met at, say, the Casino de Venise?' Jones was cautious — he couldn't afford to mention Ruby Kiss. Temple might ask how he knew of her. He had no intention of introducing the bookshop into the case. Temple might remember seeing Charles Dickens there. And, for all he knew, he might well be putting Miss Addy Finch in some danger from the man who had been outside the shop at one o'clock in the morning.

'Not that I know of. He'd treat a girl, of course, take her to supper — you know the sort of thing.'

'Any girl in particular?'

The red appeared at Ned Temple's jaw again. 'I've no idea, Superintendent — I did not keep Felix on leading reins.' However, he reined in his temper. 'I'm a busy, professional man. Felix was —'

Jones rose to go. 'I am obliged to you, Mr Temple. You have been most helpful.'

Ned Temple stood up and went to open the door. He took the policeman's proffered hand with some reluctance. Jones felt the dampness in Temple's hand.

Ned Temple went back into his room to open a window. He loosened his cravat and breathed in the damp air. He thought about the Casino de Venise and he thought about a particular girl. Could the Superintendent know about Ruby Kiss?

He thought about Ruby in this very room, putting a quill pen among the feathers in her hair, telling him that no sensible girl came back to one of the lawyers' Inns — it was well-known that a girl could come to grief there, but you're all right, Neddy-boy, ain't yer? She was lovely, good-natured and generous with her body, peeling off his coat and trousers, laughing all the while and drinking. He'd liked her, but it wouldn't have done too often. Suppose someone important had seen the rising lawyer taking a tart into his chambers. Joah Danks had seen him — not that that mattered, but he might have told Simeon Dalrymple. Danks had a sly look about him. Without much regret he'd passed her on to Felix Gresham. Ruby hadn't minded. Felix Gresham had more money than he had, and Ruby did like a good time.

Ruby and Felix — Ruby who knew all about Ned Temple's debts, and Felix — Felix who had also known all about Ned Temple's debts. Felix who had been able to afford to laugh off his own debts and make a jest of others' debts. Felix who had received a thousand a year from his mother. Felix who had no idea that a man might find ruin staring him in the face — ruin with the face of a man in full-bottomed wig and scarlet robes. Felix who was dead. He felt the sweat start under his armpits and the sting of tears.

He continued to stare out into the dark. He could hear the rush of traffic on The Strand. She was out there somewhere, Ruby Kiss, and he had to find her before Superintendent Jones did. She mustn't tell what she knew about that night — or any night.

And that damned screw, Ebenezer Screech — Ned Temple trembled when he thought of the bills bearing his own name that Screech had in that tin box of his. Oh, God, to have borrowed from such a man. What a fool he had been. Screech had his watch, too, and the gold toothpick his godfather had given him.

# 13: SOMETHING OF THE GRAVE

Dickens walked back from John Forster's through Lincoln's Inn Fields where in the cold dark of the evening under a sky lit by a bright gibbous moon, three-quarters full, and under the pinpoints of stars, he came across a solitary figure, standing like a statue in the silver light. It was the figure of a man whose top hat had fallen off and whose thrown-back face gazed up as though he were an astrologer reading his own fortune there in the heavens.

*There's a story*, Dickens thought as he passed him. A broken heart, a death, a parting, debt, drink — any one of the thousand natural shocks the flesh is heir to, but something profoundly miserable had brought that glint of wet on his cheeks. He looked back, and the face looked at him.

Dickens, surprised into immobility, saw a face he knew. 'Mr Case — what on earth? What brings you here? I thought you were snugly tucked away in your little parish — so Mr White tells me.'

Meredith Case came to at the mention of the Reverend James White, their mutual friend, whose curate he had been, and looked at Charles Dickens. 'Everything is changed — as if a darkness has come upon me. I am changed — death is everywhere — corruption is everywhere —' his words came tumbling out — 'in that street yonder, I saw such sights — a girl, no more than a child, accosted me, asked for money, said she would — a man with no legs clawed at me from a doorway. I felt no pity — only revulsion. I fled — a man of God and I fled —'

He pulled at his cravat as if he were choking, his face as pale as parchment, and the perspiration standing out on his brow. *Good Lord*, thought Dickens, *here's a man in crisis.* He reached into his pocket for his flask.

'Come, sit down here on this bench and take some of this. It will steady you.'

'I cannot eat or drink — the taste —' but he allowed Dickens to lead him to the seat.

'Try it, I beg you.'

Meredith Case took the flask and sniffed it, looked at Dickens, took a gulp and then another. Dickens watched and saw some colour come back into his face.

'I looked into the heavens at those stars and the bright moon and felt only a terrible cold. I am so changed, Mr Dickens.'

'Tell me; it will be better if you can explain what has happened to you.'

Meredith Case looked at the face of the man at his side — a face which spoke of life and action — a strong man, determined and courageous, a man who stood up for the poor and the weak. He thought of the children about whose terrors he wrote, for whom the world was cruel. *A child*, he thought, looking at Dickens's eyes, warm and full of sympathy, *I am like a child in a dark wood.*

'You'll think me mad …' he faltered.

'But north-north-west — as we all are in this whirling world. You can tell a hawk from a handsaw, I don't doubt.'

'Oh, God, a hawk — that name — I don't know that I can tell you. Everything is so…'

'Mr Case, you seem most distressed. Let me take you to some shelter — let us sit by a fire. Let me get you something to eat?'

'I — I don't know that I can eat. It's the taste —'

'Taste?'

'Everything tastes of him, of that place…'

'What place?'

'Hawke Court.'

*Here's a mystery* — Sir Gerald Hawke, indeed. Dickens asked no more questions but took Meredith Case's arm and led him out of the fields to Gate Street and The Ship Tavern, where the landlord would find them a quiet nook by the fire. It was like leading a blind man. Mr Case seemed to have no idea where he was.

Dickens settled him in one of the booths by the fire and brought back a bottle, a jug of hot water and two glasses.

'Now, what can I do? What have you to do with Hawke? I saw the death notice.'

'My mother had a connection with the family — not close, of course, but she valued it, and I am his heir.'

'Good Lord, come into a fortune?'

'No, he left nothing but a mouldering house and some jewels — I was present at his death, Mr Dickens. You have no idea; it was the most dreadful thing I have ever seen — as though corruption itself lay in that bed, and when he spoke, his breath gusted at me as if it came from hell itself — a wicked man, sir. I do not know what he has done, but there was evil in that place. I could taste it — I have tasted it ever since.'

Dickens poured the brandy and hot water. 'Drink this. It will warm you.' *And me*, he thought, remembering the whiff of corruption he had tasted when he had met Sir Gerald Hawke. But the man was dead.

Meredith Case drank again, and Dickens said, 'Hawke is dead. You need not return there. Surely the family lawyer can deal with the property and servants.'

'Sir Gerald — he asked me — no, commanded me — to do a thing which I cannot do. He asked me to swear, but he died before I could make any promise, yet — may I tell you, Mr Dickens? You understand the human heart, its doubts, its fears, its horrors.'

'Of course, I will do what I can to advise you.'

Meredith Case told him, albeit haltingly, about the death of Hawke, the command to find Sapphire Hawke, Mrs Stoneridge's denial that she had known Sapphire Hawke, and about Octavius Swann with whom he had felt calmed until he'd laid eyes on the Hawke tomb again.

'I am so changed, Mr Dickens. I sense corruption everywhere — Mrs Stoneridge — I felt I hated her. Even Mr Dalrymple, the lawyer — I have just come from him at Clement's Inn — even he seemed tainted, even his clerk — just a harmless young man, but I shrank from him, I smelt corruption about him. It is as if I am infected — my blood runs thick with some disease.'

'Yet the Reverend Swann affected you — you felt his goodness.'

'I did, and I felt pity for the child, Sapphire Hawke — an orphan brought up in that house, a poor girl, all alone. What precepts could he have taught her? According to the Reverend Swann, governesses came and went. Hawke came with his set of rakes and gamblers. Such scandals — his wife dead at the foot of the stairs, a young man shot to death, women of the town living with him. A child, sir, brought up in that house.'

'What happened to her?'

'Mr Dalrymple told me that she was sent to a convent in Bruges after the death of the young man, Arthur Sinclair — that was over twenty years ago, and she was never heard of again — but he — Hawke — commanded me to find her. I do not know why —'

'What was her story before she became Hawke's ward?'

'Mr Swann thought she came from London, but he could tell me nothing of her antecedents, or why Sir Gerald became her guardian.'

'Then I do not see what you can do. You made no promise to Hawke and nothing has been heard of the girl for twenty years. You should go back to your parish, Mr Case. This has all been too much for you. Let Mr Dalrymple deal with it.'

'There are two things more — one is that Sir Gerald left the Hawke jewels to Sapphire Hawke — they are sapphires. Mr Dalrymple insists that if she cannot be found, they must come to me. The will is proved — at a cost of so many hundreds — in the Chancery Court —'

*It would be*, thought Dickens — even an uncontested will had to be proved so that the chancery lawyers could get their fees.

'To be paid for by whatever is left, and Mr Dalrymple is to be paid. That is why he wants me to take the sapphires, but I don't want anything from that wicked man.'

'And the second thing?'

Meredith Case looked more troubled than ever. Dickens saw how his pleasant round face looked like a boy's — a bewildered boy who had found out for the first time that the world holds unimaginable darkness and that he is trapped in it. There was an innocence about him. James White had always thought so, but had said that he would do well enough as a country parson. Dickens saw tears in the clouded blue eyes.

'A portrait — I think I saw a picture of Sapphire Hawke, though Mrs Stoneridge denied it. In the picture, Sir Gerald was holding the reins of a wild-looking horse. Long, cruel hands, Mr Dickens — one hand tight on the reins, and the other, heavy on the shoulder of a young girl with a solemn, unhappy face — too old a sorrow for such a child, and his face, his eyes —'

Dickens thought of Hawke's stony eye all those years ago. And that poor Lady Hawke, who had fallen to her death. Here was, perhaps, another victim, a pale child, emerging from a portrait like a ghost returned after twenty years or more. And a broken man before him. He caught another whiff of corruption and suppressed a shudder. What had Hawke done?

'Hawke's look in the portrait — there was nothing tender in it. Not a father's look, and his heavy hand on her shoulder as if she were to be tamed like the horse. I felt pity then, and I went to see the Reverend Swann and came to London to see Mr Dalrymple who tells me that his son is to go to Bruges — if Miss Hawke is not there, the law may declare her dead.'

'And that troubles you?'

'Death, Mr Dickens, is something monumental, awful, yet the law can pronounce it into the air. Sapphire Hawke might not be dead. It would be as if she were consigned to some dreadful limbo, out of the known world, because the law cared more about a handful of jewels than that poor girl.'

'But Mr Dalrymple's son may find that she is alive and in her convent, and then the matter of the jewels will rest with her.'

'That is true, but if she is not there — suppose she is somewhere else and nothing more is done for her. I cannot forget her — what must she have suffered after the deaths of her parents, never mind at the hands of that vile man?'

'We may imagine all kinds of things, Mr Case, but it is my belief that we are here to do as well as imagine — our business is to use life well, to act where there is wrong done whatever the cost to ourselves. You can do something, or you can suffer in your conscience.'

Meredith Case looked at him. 'I have been weak, Mr Dickens, I am weak — and cowardly, running away from evil when it is my duty to stand up to it — you would have done something, I know it. I have read what you have written about children and their terrors — such cruelty is done to children. I ought to find out what became of Sapphire Hawke.'

'Have you any other information about her?'

'There was a Miss Henrietta Hawke — I met her once, an unpleasant, grasping woman — she went to a place in Westmorland to visit relations. Mr Dalrymple wondered if Sapphire Hawke had come from there. He is trying to remember the name of the house.'

'Then you must go there, Mr Case, if you can, and find out about the family there.'

'But Mr Dalrymple is not sure … I…'

'But you will have acted. You will have tried. And when you have, you will find that the memories of Hawke and his death will fade because, even in a small way, and it may not be so small, you have stood against his wickedness. Of this, I am certain. And if those sapphires are to be yours, think what good you might do — some good may come out of Hawke's wickedness, after all.'

Meredith Case took some more of the brandy. 'I will — you have done me good, Mr Dickens.'

'Go back to Mr Dalrymple, tell him of your plans, confound him — and when you come back, I shall be waiting to know all you have discovered. Now, I will walk with you to Clement's Inn.'

At the archway which led into the courtyard of the Inn, Dickens shook Case's hand. 'Courage, persevere. If you remain in Westmorland for any length of time, write to me, send me instruction. I can see Mr Dalrymple for you, find out about Bruges, and write to you.'

As he spoke, a man appeared beside them as if he had risen

from the stones, a slight, creeping fellow, all in black. *Like a beetle*, thought Dickens, looking at the black-gloved hands which seemed to be groping the air like antennae, as if he lived his life underground.

A yellowy, waxy face looked up and smiled at Meredith Case — a smile with a sneer in it. 'Good evening, sir. Mr Dalrymple is still at his labour, if you wish to see him again — the law is a hard task mistress, but my master loves her. Loves her precedents, her statutes, her wills — and her legacies.' He looked at Meredith Case as if he knew a joke about him.

He looked at Dickens, his black hands seeming to reach for him. Dickens felt a shudder, but resisted the temptation to step back. Something of the grave about him. Something damp and decaying. He understood what Meredith Case had felt.

'Mr Dickens, this is Mr Joah Danks, Mr Dalrymple's clerk.'

Dickens had no choice but to take the gloved hand, hard and bony as a beetle's carapace. 'Mr Danks, a pleasure.'

'Mr Dickens, an honour, I'm sure. Mr Case is fortunate in his friends. I'll bid you goodnight and make my weary way. Until next time, Mr Case.'

Meredith Case watched him go and Dickens saw the troubled look on his face.

'Courage, Mr Case; think of the fresh air of the Lake Country.'

'I will — I promise you. I will go as soon as Mr Dalrymple can tell me the name of the house.'

Dickens went on his way. Ahead of him, he saw Joah Danks creeping on his way, keeping close to the walls as if he were listening to their secrets.

# 14: FIND THE LADY

Ned Temple slept badly. He'd been to the Casino de Venise — very late, but there had been no sign of Ruby. He hadn't dared ask. That policeman would be bound to ask questions there. Someone would say he'd asked about her. But he'd have to try again — he couldn't think where else. She could be anywhere, but the Casino was her favourite. He'd have a few drinks, watch the show, keep his eyes open for Ruby. No one would notice. There'd be a crowd in tonight for the musical contortionist. They loved him, and his antics always provoked screams of laughter. Ned Temple didn't feel like laughing.

He jingled the few coins in his pocket — he was broke. It would take time for Felix's legacy to come through — if it ever did. In the meantime, he needed money from somewhere. Dalrymple's son, Alexander, might be good for another few guineas. Ned had borrowed before and had not paid back, but Alexander knew of the legacy now. He was a good sort — he'd not turn a fellow down. There were precious few good sorts when a fellow was down on his luck. There was nothing else for him to do. No work coming in. He made his precarious living as a legal pleader, employed by various solicitors, including Simeon Dalrymple, from whom he rented these two rooms which he called his chambers. He slept in this room on a couch. He hadn't mentioned to Dalrymple that he'd given up his lodgings. Prospective clients — when there were any — used the other room — his office. It looked well enough. The furniture belonged to Dalrymple.

He'd taken up as a legal pleader because it was a practical way of gaining a reputation among the lawyers and of making some money — half a guinea was the going rate for reading and preparing a defence plea for a busy solicitor. Sometimes he devilled for a barrister — reading and summarising briefs. Some pleaders made a fortune — preparing cases, taking pupils, even, but somehow, neither money nor pupils had come. Humiliating — for a man of decent family who ought to be at the bar — deserved to be at the bar — but it was a damned expensive game — you needed family connections and he had none, only a dead clergyman for a father and a mother living on a pittance in the country.

He had had hopes of old Mr Gresham, but they had come to nothing, like all his hopes. Old Gresham hadn't liked him. He had made that clear — and after all he'd done for Felix. He tapped his mother for a few pounds when he went down to see her, but he felt guilty about it. His sister had married a farmer and they'd gone out to Australia. Australia — he shuddered at the thought. The word brought no fond memories of his sister — only of transportation, arriving in that far-off place in leg irons — or worse. Or worse. He looked at his shaking hands.

He got up from the couch — he felt like an old man — and went to his washstand to shave. He looked in his mirror. Unlucky, he thought. People didn't seem to trust him, didn't like him — apart from Felix, and that because he let him do as he liked, and the women he picked up at the Casino de Venise — a man had a right to some pleasure before he settled down.

He'd tried to cultivate a wide acquaintance in order to get commissions, but 'hugging' as it was called — seeking favours — was frowned upon. Someone had joked that the only way forward was to marry a solicitor's daughter, be she ever so ugly. He'd met Dalrymple's daughter at his house in Caroline Street. Maud Dalrymple was very pretty, but she had looked at him indifferently and yawned. She had preferred the attentions of Henry Meteyard, a barrister with a rising reputation in Lincoln's Inn, rumoured to make a thousand a year. Son of a butcher down in Limehouse and his own father a gentleman. Dalrymple hadn't invited him again — he wondered if that reptile, Joah Danks, had said something about Ruby. Danks had seen her that night — drunk. He'd helped her up when she had fallen. He'd even had the cheek to ask Ned where he could find a girl like that. Ned had sent him off with a flea in his ear.

He spat out the water when he cleaned his teeth. He felt the dreadful bile of bitterness rise in his throat. He looked again at his own face — he looked ill, haunted — well, he damn well was. Oh, God, to be such a fool — to gamble with a man like that — and to lose everything — to think that he would ever have had any luck. His hand shook and he staggered to the table, where he poured a glass of brandy and drank it straight off, tempted to drink it all and have done with it. *I should blow my brains out — cut my throat — who'd give a damn?* But he put down the glass and took up his coat from where he had flung it the night before.

Nothing for it but to go upstairs and see Alexander Dalrymple, and then he'd go out, go down to the casino and look about. Anything was better than brooding here. He went out into the hall just as someone came clattering down the stairs. He looked up to see Alexander Dalrymple descending, carrying a travelling bag.

Ned Temple forced a cheerful tone. 'Good morning. Off somewhere?'

'Bruges,' answered Alexander brightly, 'to find a lady.'

'Sounds tempting.' It was, thought Ned, wishing at that moment that he could be away to the continent, Bruges, Paris, anywhere — even Australia. Alexander Dalrymple was all right. Old Dalrymple was rich as Croesus, they said. How often he had wished for a wealthy father. He wouldn't have touched the law, and he wouldn't be in this mess.

'I doubt it. She'll be thirty-five if she's a day, and she might be in a convent. It's some business of my father's and a parson. Money in it, I daresay, and property. It'll be a change from all this —' he gestured vaguely upstairs — 'the law can be a damned dull business sometimes. Anyway, I must be away for the steam ferry.'

He went out, leaving Ned in the hall, still almost penniless.

# 15: A NIGHT ON THE TILES

'Two thousand pounds —' Dickens whistled — 'nice little windfall for Mr Temple from his grateful client.'

'Hm, a little bit more than that — Gresham's mother approved the legacy. Apparently, Mr Temple extricated young Felix from the clutches of an undesirable female. Something of an elder brother to the lad, keeping an eye on him for Mrs Gresham — at the Casino de Venise, for example.'

'That was his story?'

'Oh, yes, never expected to come into the money, of course, but he looked a bit shaky when I asked if Felix Gresham was involved with any particular lady at the casino. That I knew about the Casino de Venise gave him a turn, I could tell.'

'You didn't mention Ruby Kiss?'

'No, I didn't want to involve your booksellers — not yet, at any rate. Didn't want to put them in any danger, nor do I want any collusion. They knew Felix Gresham, they know Ned Temple — they must all know Ruby Kiss, so what's the big secret, I wonder?'

'Did Rogers find out anything at the casino?'

'No one's seen Ruby Kiss for a while — not since before the murder.'

'Significant?'

'Could be. One of the bar girls remembered seeing her with a toff some weeks back — she couldn't remember when, of course, and she didn't remember seeing her on the night of the murder, but the place is always packed, so why would she?'

'Anything useful on the toff?'

'Tall, dark — nothing that would distinguish him from a

thousand others. Just one thing, though, the bar girl thought he was in the army. Didn't know why — just thought she'd heard it said.'

'He could be away with his regiment now.'

'Exactly, and Ruby Kiss could have moved onto someone else. These girls come and go. However, the bar girl did know that Ruby had been fond of Felix Gresham, as she delicately put it. Gresham was often there with Temple and Ruby and various other swells and girls, but she didn't see either Gresham or Temple on the night of the murder.'

'They could have been somewhere else.'

'Any one of a hundred places. In any case, they could have been there — it's always crowded.'

'Is it worth going back to the Casino?'

'I thought of sending Rogers again — he thought he saw Phoebe Green, the one who gave evidence at the inquest, but in the crush he missed her.'

'Night on the tiles?'

'What?'

'You and me — a bachelor night out in the interests of crime.'

'Rogers is quite capable of —'

'Ah, but he's been seen, and heard, no doubt. Policeman making enquiries — there'll be a rush for the exit, but two swells —'

'No — I'm too old for that kind of thing. Take — oh, I don't know — take Constable Feak. He'll scrub up nicely.'

Dickens laughed. 'His mother won't like it.' Constable Feak was a plain and homely young man whose mother Mrs Feak was a nurse, and her word was Feak's law. And a wise woman she was.

'Neither will my wife.'

'But you will be with me.'

'That's what worries me — we'll be mobbed.'

'But I won't be Charles Dickens, I'll be someone else.'

'I shudder to think who — well, something may come of it, I suppose —'

'And I hope it mayn't be human gore.'

'Go home.'

'Nine o'clock, then?'

Jones didn't answer, but Dickens saw a twinkle in his eye. He'd come.


Dickens strode away from Bow Street, planning his disguise. A swell in a silk hat and lilac gloves. An opera cloak, perhaps? Sam would wear his old coat, no doubt — he was always himself. True as steel, and so was Sergeant Rogers. How insubstantial Dickens felt himself at times, and how he liked to be someone else — all the lives he could live, liberating all the reaches of his many selves. Acting, just as writing, was an escape from himself, he knew that, from the secret agony he often felt, as if — surrounded by others, his wife, his sister-in-law, even his children — he were on a desert island or in some frozen waste of the Arctic like poor Franklin, still missing.

He thought of Paris, where he'd been a few weeks ago — like a dream now on a dreary afternoon in that sooty spectre, London. Dark already and beginning to be foggy. Ah, well, the Casino de Venise might shed some of its bright lights on the murder of Felix Gresham. He walked along Oxford Street. The Man with a Load of Mischief wasn't far — perhaps Bella Screech would be there. She might know something of Felix — her father knew him. Felix had been a regular customer at the Curiosity Shop. And, he admitted, he was curious. Like her father, probably, a grasping sort of girl — well, if she looked anything like Ebenezer, she'd not have many suitors, though, he often thought, a woman with expectations might marry whom she pleased whatever she was in the looks department — or murder whom she pleased.

With that sobering thought, he went through the door of The Mischief — into a smoky, yellowy, taper-waxy, tobacco-fumed, firelit, crowded room where he could stand for a moment in the press of men and look about him. As he looked towards the bar, he saw a very attractive young woman come in through an inner door, pinning up her dark hair. The landlord nodded at her and she took her place at the bar to serve a customer. Dickens went to the bar to order a pale ale. The landlord served him, so he went to take a seat by the fire. He would wait to see if the probably dwarfish Miss Screech came to carry out her duties, whatever they might be. He'd know her, he was sure.

Someone came in, a slinking figure in black with his hands groping before him — Joah Danks. Dickens turned away before he could be seen. Joah Danks went up to the bar, where he exchanged some words with the pretty barmaid. Joah Danks turned to look about him and Dickens kept his head down. A man came in — broad-shouldered and upright with short dark hair and a fine moustache. The young woman gave him a smile as he approached, and Dickens saw him talking to Joah Danks. The two men walked away to one of the booths and the woman came from behind the bar, carrying a tray, the brandy bottle, hot water and glasses. Then all three were lost to sight.

Dickens could hardly go ask about Bella Screech now — he had no wish to be seen by Joah Danks. He made his way to the door, which at that moment flung open to reveal the angry little boy, still running, it seemed, who careered into him again.

'Ma,' the boy cried.

'Sorry, sir,' the woman said, coming over, 'he never looks where he's going.'

'No harm done,' Dickens said, smiling at her. He made a business about fishing his stick from behind the table and dropping a glove. Who was this boy? A nice-looking little fellow, dark-haired and tall like his mother. Not the street urchin he had presumed when he had seen him kicking about Screech's stock. About seven, he thought, judging the child by his own son, Frank, who had turned seven in January.

'Where've you been?' she asked. 'You were to get a potato from the man — five minutes, I said. You ain't been near the shop?'

'No, Ma.'

'Leave him be, the old miser.' She sounded angry, but she took the boy gently by the shoulder and walked him away. 'Now, get upstairs and eat your potato before it goes cold. I'll be up in a bit —'

'Bella!' shouted the landlord.

The young woman looked up and Dickens saw how her eyes flashed. He looked after her as she took her boy away. Well, well, beautiful Bella — and she was beautiful at close quarters — daughter of Ebenezer Screech, and the boy his grandson. Not a happy family, it seemed.

He saw then that there was another exit just beyond the booth where Danks and his companion had gone to sit. He went that way, glancing in the bar mirrors as he passed the booth. His swift look showed him Danks's face looking up. He turned away and hurried out, hoping he hadn't been seen.

He found himself in a backyard. Fortunately, there was a door across the way through which he went into an alley which led into Dean Street. He thought about Joah Danks as he walked back into Oxford Street — something avid in that expression, and something malevolent, but whether it was directed at him or Danks's companion, he could not tell. But a man with a load of mischief, indeed.

Wearing his best silk top hat and a rather fetching cloak as well as the lilac gloves, a patch over one eye and the false moustache he kept for just such occasions, Dickens knocked at Jones's door at nine o'clock. Thankfully, the fog had changed its mind and had wafted away, perhaps to the farther reaches of the Thames to coil itself among the masts of the great ships going out into Sea Reach. The rain, however, did not put a damper on his spirits.

He knocked and heard Poll the dog's answering bark. *Let slip the dogs of war — the game's afoot.* The door opened and there stood Elizabeth, Sam's wife.

She laughed as she saw the eye patch. 'La, sir, you're wounded, I see.'

'A duel, a matter of honour, ma'am. You should have seen the other fellow — cut to ribbons.'

'He lives, I hope, Mr…?'

'Fledgeby, ma'am; Fascination, my friends call me. He lives, the blackguard. Is Sir Barnet dressed — his wig, you know?'

'He says it scratches his pate.'

'Dolly, my boy,' Dickens greeted Jones, who appeared at the door — in his familiar greatcoat.

'Fledgeling, did you say?'

'Deuced droll, Mr Jones — deuced dull coat, sir.'

'Deuced cold — I'll leave the peacocking to you.'

Dickens tipped his hat to Elizabeth and they went to find a cab to take them to the Casino de Venise.

# 16: AT THE CASINO DE VENISE

Ruby Kiss fingered the knife in her pocket. It was well to be wary. Ruby had a practical attitude to her profession. 'Yer think it's worse than a stingy missus in Camden, 'apin 'er betters an' payin' five pound a year fer a scullery maid ter rule as a slave. Yer think I'd be better off emptyin' the bank clerk's chamber pot, an' miss, beggin' yer pardon, you ain't 'ad ter do it. An' I ain't goin' 'ome — not that I 'ave one — cos if you knew me ma — a devil, she is. 'An' 'as 'ard as a butter pat an' a face as sour as an old dish clout.' Thus she had spoken to Sarah Hamilton, who had given her refuge. Ruby Kiss knew what she was about, she said.

But the Felix Gresham business had upset her. She'd liked him. She knew he was a fool, but he was handsome, good-natured and generous, lendin' money 'ere an' there, an' signin' 'is name ter bits o' paper. Borrowin' from money lenders, pawnin' 'is bits an' pieces, but that was the way o' things. She'd 'ad them that wouldn't pay. The knife showed 'em.

But tonight, champagne, and plenty of it. She'd wanted lights, company, music, good food and all paid for by someone else. Ruby loved the Casino de Venise. It was a glittering, raucous pleasure palace with immense mirrors reflecting the laughing, talking customers. There were deep-piled red velvet sofas and handsome carpets. Best of all, Ruby loved the dancing and the music. She usually laughed until she cried at the Tennessee Minstrels playing their bone castanets, banjos and flutinas. Mr De Benner was a marvel — a musical contortionist playing his violin with the bow in his mouth, playing it behind his back, under his arm, between his legs —

catcalls greeted that. He'd be on later.

But tonight, nothing felt right. The music was too raucous, and the champagne tasted bitter. She couldn't relax. Why should she feel sorry? You 'ad ter look after number one in this world.

She finished her drink. Her companion offered the bottle. If she drank enough, she'd feel better. The Ethiopian Serenaders came on and she clapped and whistled with the rest. That was when she saw the lawyer, Ned Temple. Drownin' 'is sorrows, she supposed, about Felix. Bugger. Felix again. Another drink.

She didn't think Ned Temple had seen her. Best to avoid him. He knew too much about her and Felix, and she knew a bit too much about him. She licked her carmined lips, patted her red curls, and smiled at her companion. 'Early night, capt'in? Back to your rooms, then? I don't wanter go 'ome.'

He smiled back. 'I have something for you, little Ruby, but you will have to pay for it.' He picked up her hand, put it to his beautiful lips and bit her middle finger — not hard. Then he laughed. His eyes gleamed in the light. *Tha's better*, she thought.

'I've had to move on — let's say that where I am is for gentlemen only.'

'Army pals, is it?'

'Temporary H.Q. — somewhere finer, one day, Ruby, one day.'

'Supper at the Garrick's 'Ead, darlin' — we can get a room there. 'S'nice there, my Capt'in.'

'No, Ruby, not tonight. It'll have to be the delights of your little bed tonight — I'm sure you can fit me in — somewhere.' He put her finger in his mouth again.

Ruby laughed — a loud rippling, gurgling sound of glee. *Unmistakeable*, Ned Temple thought, looking up from his drink. *Found her.* He watched her go towards the door, Ruby staggering and her companion holding her up.

Superintendent Jones kept his coat on — not that anyone was looking. All eyes were on the musical contortionist who was doing some unspeakable things with his violin. *You couldn't call it music*, he thought. He kept his eyes down, looking into his glass of beer. He had drawn the line at champagne on the grounds that he already had indigestion and that he was too hot.

'You might go in for the contortionist line, Mr Jones, shake you up a bit — good for the digestion. Or yer might jest take —'

'Not skittles again.'

'I was merely going to suggest — humbly, bashfully — that you might take off your coat.'

'Just go and find the girl, will you, before she vanishes.'

'I'm agoin' — but order some champagne for her. It'll loosen her tongue.'

Jones had recognised Phoebe Green in the chorus. Dickens was to go to the dressing room in his guise of swell about town, inveigle her to the table with the promise of champagne, and then Jones would ask his questions.

The contortionist unravelled himself, took his bow, and went away to great cheers and whistles. Dickens came back with Phoebe Green, who looked somewhat crushed about the feathers and smudged about the rouge than she had on stage where distance had lent, if not enchantment, some glamour, but she was smiling at her swell whose eye patch gave him the look of a pirate from a pantomime. *He's enjoying himself at least*, Jones thought.

'Oo's this? Brought yer pa ter —' her good humour vanished when Jones looked up and she turned to Dickens — "ere, wot's your game? Yer said a glass o' champagne, not the bleedin' rozzers.'

'You shall have that, too, to go with your talk with Mr Jones.' Dickens sat her down firmly and so fast that she had no time to resist. Dickens gave her a glass. She drank it all at once.

'I told yer, I don't know nothin' more about Felix Gresham — yer can't say I does.' She shook her feathers like a petulant little hen. 'I told yer the truth, I did.'

Dickens gave her more champagne. Jones waited until she had drunk some more. *Patience*, he thought. 'I know that, Miss Green. I want to know about a girl called Ruby Kiss.'

'Ruby ain't done nothin' — Ruby liked Felix. She was good ter 'im. He was good ter Ruby, as well.'

'I know that, too, but I would like to speak to her about him — that's all. Now, drink up and tell me what she looks like and where I can find her.'

'Good-lookin', Ruby. Men like 'er red 'air, I think, all them curls. Only a little thing, too. Some men like that in a girl — like 'em small. Saw 'er before the show — she ain't bin around fer a while, but she was 'ere with 'er fancy man —' Phoebe looked round — 'musta gone.'

'Where does she live?'

'I dunno now — she was a dress lodger at Ma Bailey's in Lewkner's Lane — yer know 'ow it works.'

Jones knew what it meant. Ruby would have worked for a brothel keeper who lent her the clothes for her nightly pick-ups, and to whom she paid over most of her takings. 'I know Mrs Bailey. When was this?'

'Few weeks ago — when I saw Ruby with the gent. Asked 'er if she was livin' with 'im, but she wouldn't say. Just said that Ma Bailey could go whistle fer 'er dresses when the time came, but she'd give old Sal somethin' —'

'Sal?'

'Watcher — yer knows — follers the girl ter keep an eye on 'er. She might know where Ruby's lodgin's is. If yer goes to Lewkner's Lane in the mornin' yer might find Sal. Fond o' Ruby, she is. Fond o' gin, too.'

'What can you tell me about Ruby's new gent? His name?'

'Called 'im capt'in — that's all. Big man — well set-up, yer know. Money, I'd say —' Phoebe Green looked wistful — 'all the luck Ruby 'as, but yer can't 'elp likin' 'er. Allus generous. I 'opes the capt'in treats 'er right.'

'Any reason why he shouldn't?' asked Dickens.

'Dunno — it's jest that some yer meets they can be — well, I've 'ad some beatin's an' from them as oughter know better. Yer'd think their mothers'd tell em 'ow ter treat a girl. An' they think 'emselves better than us cos they's born ter riches. Should think 'e's a temper, the capt'in. 'As a look about 'im. 'An'some, though.'

'And tonight is the first time you've seen Ruby for a few weeks?'

'Yes — dunno where's she's bin — livin' with the toff, I serpose.'

'You don't know if she was here the night Felix was killed?'

'Yer think 'e was 'ere?'

'I don't know. It's just that the place was mentioned by Felix's lawyer as a place he liked to come to.'

'Ned Temple, yer mean?'

'You know him?'

'Came 'ere with Felix mostly. Saw 'im ternight, drinkin on 'is own. Looked as if 'e'd lost a shillin' an' found a penny. Gone now. Don't know where 'e went.'

'Did he know Ruby?'

'Yes, we woz all tergether some nights — me an' some of the

95

other girls, Ruby, Ned, Felix. Plenty of money, Felix 'ad — spender.'

'What about Mr Temple?'

'Dunno — never thought about it. Felix paid gen'rally.'

'And you weren't here on the night Felix was killed?'

'No, I was at Miss 'Amilton's then. Told yer before.'

'How did you come to be at the bookshop?' Dickens asked.

Phoebe Green hesitated. 'She — Miss 'Amilton — was tryin' ter 'elp me get a place. She'd 'elped Ruby when — well, it don't matter why — but she an' Addy, they was good ter Ruby, and when I — was beat up — Miss 'Amilton let me stay an' she thought I could try the millinery, but it want fer me so I came back 'ere — yer niver knows, I might be lucky.'

'I hope so, Miss Green, but you should take care.'

'Easy fer you ter say — yer a toff, yerself. You knew Felix, did yer?'

'Yes — that's why I'm helping the police.'

'Takin' a girl in like that —'

Dickens poured her more champagne and took a glass for himself. 'I beg your pardon, Miss Phoebe, but it was necessary if Mr Jones is to find Felix's killer. You liked him, I know, and he didn't deserve a knife in his back.'

She succumbed to his charm and to the pity in his eyes, and, hardened as she was, remembered Felix's laughing face. She clinked her glass with his. 'Well, if yer puts it like that — I gotter go. Stayin' fer the Ethiopian Serenaders? 'Ave another drink later?'

'Er, no, we'll have to go now.'

She gave Jones a look of scorn. She wasn't going to forgive the policeman. 'Oh, gotter take yer pa 'ome, ave yer?' And away she flounced.

Dickens made to help Jones to his feet. 'Come along, my

ancient, let's find a cab.'

'Before we go, ask at the bar about this captain. I'll wait outside.'

Dickens pushed his way to the bar. The crush was ten deep, but he managed to squeeze himself through to order a brandy and soda water and to begin his enquiries.

'My cousin Feenix of the thirty-fifth —' Dickens hoped the captain wasn't of the thirty-fifth — if it existed — 'lookin' for an old comrade. Any military men about?'

'Dozens,' the barman replied. 'Could win Waterloo again some nights in 'ere. Any name?'

'Captain —'

'They're all captains, sir. Why, some are even generals — wot's 'e like, this captain o' yer cousin's?'

'Deuced handsome — dark hair — tall — well set-up — friendly — young lady — red head — name of Ruby.'

'Oh, it's little Ruby yer after, is it?' The barman winked at him. 'Don't be shy. Ruby's spoken for by the captain — so 'e says 'e is — but there's plenty more'll give yer a good time. Kitty, there — she's a pretty girl — willin' as well if yer've got the money. Got 'er eye on you already.'

Dickens turned to see Kitty in red satin and a good many bows, plying her feather fan. 'Er, not tonight. I really do want to find the captain.'

'Owes yer, does 'e, Mr...?'

'Fledgeby — 'fraid he does — money to my cousin — Feenix — mentioned him — man of honour, sir.'

'So yer did. Well, the captain ain't about — went off with Miss Ruby.'

'Do you know where?'

'Can't say, sir. Word o' warnin' — I'd leave 'im alone if I was you.'

Before Dickens could ask any more, the barman went away. Something poked him in the back. He turned to find Kitty eyeing him up with a distinctly predatory look. She gave him a smile — not many teeth. It was time to go.

Dickens thought about money as he made his way home from Jones's house in Norfolk Street, cutting through Carburton Street. He and Sam had discussed what they had found out from Phoebe Green. 'Lewkner's Lane, tomorrow morning,' Sam had said, 'let's find this Sal and see if we can trace Ruby Kiss before Ned Temple finds her. He's obviously looking.'

'I wonder about this captain — the barman warned me off him. I hope Miss Ruby can take care of herself.'

'I hope so — it makes me sick. "Like 'em small," Phoebe said.'

'Little more than children, some of them — and some still children.'

Now he was thinking about a young man wanting to make his way in the law and facing ruin, perhaps, if he were in very deep — the creditors on the stairs, lurking in the stairwells, in the hall, on the steps outside with their ironical cries of, "Pay us, will yer? Don't be mean." Ned Temple was a lawyer. He would know all the downward steps that led to disgrace: the arrival of the sheriff's officers, the sponging house — that halfway station where the debtor waited for someone to come with the money — then the debtors' court — the King's Bench. Dickens knew all about it, too. His father, John Dickens, unable to pay his debts, borrowing from here and there: his mother, his brother, his brother-in-law, all of whom lost patience.

Then the Marshalsea, the debtors' prison, where a man might die forgotten, or come out again, still forgotten, ruined, a solitary lounger at street corners in a threadbare shiny suit out at the elbows with a yellowing handkerchief at his throat to conceal the absence of a shirt. He had seen such men, slinking away down alleys with the furtive, half-ashamed look of stray dogs. Ned Temple would have seen them.

John Dickens had come out of the Marshalsea because his mother, old Mrs Dickens, had died and left him a legacy of four hundred and fifty pounds. Legacy — Ned Temple stood to inherit two thousand pounds if his young friend, Felix Gresham, were to die. But Felix Gresham had been a young man. How long would Ned Temple have had to wait?

Dickens thought of the young man he had seen at the bookshop. He recalled a thin face — a weak face. Something petulant about the mouth. Angry when Miss Finch was short with him. Envious, perhaps, of his careless, cheerful, spendthrift friend, who had no way to make in the dusty regions of the Inns of Court. And desperate, perhaps, the strangling net of debts winding its way about him so that there was no way out but utter disgrace, or — murder?

John Dickens was not, nor ever could be, a murderer — his father, careless, genial, always the optimist, who floated cork-like on the surface, and sinking to the bottom, was always apt to bob up again. But he wasn't a wicked man, nor a greedy one, nor an envious one. Had Ned Temple been bitterly envious of Felix Gresham?

# 17: MOTHER'S RUIN

In the cold grey of early morning under an ashen sky, they made their way to Lewkner's Lane. The streets had that half-awake, weary look of the sleeper who has had a restless night. There were still a few ragged bundles of sleepers in doorways. A swell wearing a crooked top hat and a black eye smoked a cigar in another doorway. In the street, a man with a basket on his back was picking up rubbish — looking for something to sell. There was a spiky-haired child in the basket, hanging on to the man's hair as he bent down. He passed her a muddy heel of bread. Breakfast, no doubt. At a gin shop, a sleepy-eyed man was taking down his shutters. They dodged by a trap opening in the pavement, from which a dirty-faced sewer man emerged like a devil in a pantomime. A coal wagon rattled by, with a yawning lad hanging on the tail.

In the more respectable streets, maids were polishing brass door knockers and cleaning steps. A little scullery maid's face stared at them through some area railings, her red swollen hands gripping the bars. The smell of frying bacon and the smoke of sea coal drifted through the open kitchen door, and a voice cried, 'Betsy Clark, get in 'ere, now.' Betsy Clark blinked and vanished. Dickens glanced up. The rich curtains at the upstairs windows were still closed.

Jones knew Ma Bailey's house, which was still slumbering — a late night, it would have had. The shutters were still closed, though the front door was ajar — there'd be a skivvy at her work, no doubt. Some of the girls were boarders — as if it were a girls' school, Jones had said. School for scandal, Dickens had quipped. Some, like Ruby, lived elsewhere.

However, Ma Bailey would not have been pleased if Ruby had vanished with her clothes and her takings. It was a risk for Ruby, but, if Phoebe Green were right, Ruby had been tempted by the attentions of her toff.

The front door to Ma Bailey's was open. Inside, they found an old woman seated on a chair in the hall. Blood was pouring down her face and she was moaning.

'Can I help?' asked Dickens, stepping forward.

'Fell over me own feet. Gawd, I'm bleedin' ter death.'

He could smell the gin. No wonder she'd fallen. 'Head wounds always bleed a lot. Is there a doctor nearby, Mrs…?'

'Just Sal, dearie, old Sal. Ma won't pay fer no doctor — just 'elp me downstairs.' She closed her eyes and moaned again.

Jones stepped over to Dickens. 'Take her downstairs — if she needs a doctor, come back and tell me. Ma Bailey can pay. But if she doesn't need one, find out what you can. No need to mention the police. I'll wait down the area steps.'

Sham respectability was for the ground floor — potted palms and a Chinese screen and velvet curtains. Here was the truth of Ma Bailey's boarding establishment. Dickens helped old Sal to a small room off the basement kitchen. Here was the smell of gin and poverty and neglected old age. There was a truckle bed with a ragged blanket and musty-smelling sheets, a rickety table, one upright chair, and a shabby armchair by a little grate where a few coals smouldered. Dickens settled the woman in the armchair, went to the kitchen to dampen his handkerchief, and returned to wipe away the blood. The wound wasn't much, just a scrape — he'd seen worse on his sons' knees — but the grit and dirt needed cleaning off.

'I have brandy here.'

'Give us the bottle. No need fer a glass.'

He couldn't help laughing. 'I was going to clean the wound with it.'

The old woman made a raspy choking noise which sounded more like bronchitis than laughter, but her eyes gleamed with humour. 'I'll need the drink first.'

Dickens gave her his flask from which she took a large swig before handing it back. He wetted his handkerchief and applied the brandy to the wound, holding the handkerchief in place. The old woman winced and gestured for the flask again.

'Nice, gentle touch, you 'ave, sir. Kids, 'ave yer?'

'A few — nine, in fact, one just a baby girl.'

Sal's eyes flew open. 'Blimey, yer 'ave bin busy —' she looked at him — 'fer a young 'un — cost a lot, all them mouths ter feed. Still, if yer've got it … I 'ad a little girl … tried ter keep 'er, but it want no good. Died — fer the best. Can't remember 'er face now or what I called 'er…' She took another drink.

Dickens took the flask before she became insensible. 'I was looking for someone here when I found you — a girl called Ruby Kiss.'

'Does yer wife know?' She chuckled again, coughed, and held out her hand for the flask. He gave it to her and waited until the coughing subsided. She took another drink.

'No, no, not that — I want to find her because she knew a friend of mine, and he's missing.'

Old Sal made to take another swig. ''Ere, it's empty — there's gin in the cupboard. Go an' get it, dearie — no need fer a glass, neither.'

Against his better judgement, Dickens went to get the bottle. She wouldn't tell him anything more without a drink. Thankfully, there wasn't much left.

He gave her the bottle and asked if she knew where Ruby Kiss was.

'She don't work fer Ma Bailey no more.'

'Do you know where she's gone?'

''Er new gent woz takin' 'er away from all this. Tol' me weeks ago she wouldn't come back when 'er time came. But Ma Bailey sent me ter the Casino de Venise an' there she woz — Ruby, I means. Saw 'er come out wiv 'im. Tol' Ma Bailey I couldn't find 'er. She want pleased — dint get no pay that night, but Ruby'd give me somethin' an' I got a bottle. 'Tis a comfort when you ain't got nothin' else, dearie.' She took another swig and her eyes closed.

Dickens had to be quick. 'Where was she living?'

The bleary eyes opened. He saw a flicker of something, but she closed them again. ''T'ain't much of a life fer an ol' woman like me. Ma Bailey'll give me the push one o' these days. I ain't much use as a watcher — can't keep up with the girls. Can yer spare a few bob, dearie?'

Dickens looked down at her. Old Sal was nothing but a collection of bones, fragile as twigs, and the hacking cough suggested that there was not much left of a wretched life, but she'd weighed him up and his nine children and scented money. He couldn't blame her. Perhaps the money would help her remember. 'I can, Sal, if you'll just tell me if you know where she might be.'

'Good girl, Ruby — she give me money that night an' I thought she'd make 'er fortune. Gent, see, 'e woz — looked like money. Seen 'im wiv Ruby a few times, then she woz fed up cos 'e'd buggered off. But then, I sees 'er wiv 'im so it's awright — yer needn't worry abaht Ruby. She can take care of 'erself.'

'Please, Sal, think. I need to find her. Where was she living after she left here?'

Sal shook her befuddled head. 'Las' night — yers. I woz followin' Lucy, one o' the girls. Lost 'er, but Ruby woz there outside the Casino — remember now.'

'The Casino de Venise.'

'Wiv 'er gent —'

*Hopeless*, thought Dickens. They knew where she'd been last night. He tried again. 'Where —'

But Sal wasn't listening. 'Not sermuchas a gent as Ruby thort. I wenter speak ter Ruby. Ruby knew me an' giv me two bob … but 'e pushed me outa the way. Caught me on the face wiv 'is ring or somethin'… Temper, I thort. Called me an old 'ag… Shoulda seen me in t'old days — got plenty o' men, I did, an' money — where's it gone, I'd like ter know…' Old Sal closed her eyes again. 'Gi' me the bottle, dearie…'

He gave up. He put the bottle in one of her hands and half a crown on the table next to her. She'd spend it on drink, no doubt, and Ma Bailey would kick her out. She'd end up in the workhouse, or dead in the street.

He found Jones and told him that it was no use. Ruby Kiss was with her toff, it seemed. Old Sal had seen her at the Casino de Venise, but she hadn't been able to say where Ruby lived.

'I thought she was going to tell me at one point, but she was too fuddled with drink. Not too fuddled that she didn't tap me for money. She rambled on about Ruby's gentleman friend who'd pushed her out of the way when she tried to approach Ruby last night. You can see why — he probably thought she was begging, but he caught her on the face. From what Phoebe and Sal say, he doesn't sound like the gentle type. That barman, too, told me to leave him alone.'

'I know — these girls get taken in by the money and end up beaten half to death by some rake who thinks he owns the world.'

'Perhaps she'll turn up at the bookshop — like Phoebe. It's interesting that Miss Hamilton and Miss Addy give them succour. I wonder what was in their past.'

They walked on. Jones was thinking about the booksellers. 'Odd types they mix with — Ruby Kiss, Phoebe Green, Ned Temple and Felix Gresham — what's the connection, I wonder? Are they protecting someone?'

'What if they know something, but don't want to say because of their own pasts? Miss Addy Finch was very alarmed when I mentioned the piece for *Household Words*.'

'Then you'll have to go back there — for your poetry book. See what you can find out.'

'Do you know, Sam, I think that they are too used to concealment to give anything away.'

'Not even to you? You seem to find out all the secrets of those girls from the home easily enough.'

'The girls at Urania Cottage want my help, need my help. I'm not so sure about Miss Hamilton or Miss Finch.'

'They'll keep for the time being — I doubt they'll disappear, but we'll act quickly if we find anything which links them to the murder. What did you give Old Sal in the way of help? I know you.'

'Half a crown — poor old thing. She'd had a child once — a little girl, and she couldn't even remember her name.'

'Dear God — what a world we live in. My Edith's face is engraved on my heart. She's been dead these ten years. I can bring that sweet face to mind as we stand here. Phoebe Green reminds us that men like little girls, and there's a mother who's forgotten her own child's name.'

'I know, Sam, it's enough to break the heart and hope of any man, but Old Sal is so sodden with drink. It's all she has. I could have taken the bottle from her, but I hadn't the heart. It's too late — too late.'

They walked away from Lewkner's Lane. Dickens was right. Old Sal would never recall her child, or anything else. She spent her half-crown on gin and dropped dead in the street. Ma Bailey didn't claim her, and the parish gave her a pauper's grave.

# 18: IN CHANCERY

'What now?' asked Dickens.

'Lincoln's Inn.'

'And our purpose in storming that stronghold of melancholy — that hopeless haunt of the hapless and the helpless?'

Jones grinned. 'To see a lawyer.'

'Ah, well, you'll need twenty lawyers if you are engaged in a suit there, and two guineas a day for each of them to tell you to wait upon events — events that never come. Or, if they do, it's at the end of a hundred years. *Men have died — and worms have eaten them.*'

'We have an appointment with just the one lawyer — and he'll not charge the police. He knows it's a murder case.'

'Who?'

'Ernest Gresham was a solicitor in Chancery.'

'I know. Are you sure he's dead?'

'Why?'

'I don't believe they do die — in suspension, he'll be, waiting like something in the deep, to rise to the surface and pounce, shark-like, to gobble up his next victim. The business of Chancery is, I read, presently moribund. The Lord High Chancellor is in chancery himself — confined to bed — nothin' to be done — for any plaintiff or defendant, or widow, or wife, or damsel, or daughter, or orphan in rags — but to wait upon his Lordship's pulse which is so slow as to render him as near death as any living organism could be — a sponge, perhaps —'

Dickens's peroration on the state of Chancery was interrupted by the need to dodge the surging traffic in Great

Queen Street which led them into the quiet of Lincoln's Inn Fields where Dickens had met Meredith Case. Away in Westmorland now — that is, if he had gone. Not simply vanished like Sapphire Hawke. He hoped that Mr Dalrymple had remembered rightly, and that poor Meredith Case had not been sent on a wild goose chase.

Jones interrupted his thoughts. 'There's a Mr Francis Gresham —' Dickens stopped and looked at him — 'I was about to tell you then you took flight into chancery and its evils.'

'Beg pardon, Mr Jones, it's a habit I have — distractin', the law, or it is to me just at present. There's an idea brewing in my brain about a suit in Chancery — like the Jennens case. That man William Jennens left two million pounds. The case went on in Chancery for a hundred years because he hadn't signed his will, and not a penny left at the end of it. That's the law for you — an ass.'

'Ass or not, I want Mr Francis Gresham to tell me about Felix and Ned Temple — here we are. His office is in Stone Buildings.'

'The way to dusty death,' observed Dickens as they approached the usual dark and mysterious staircase, a feature of all the gloomy law chambers he had ever been to, which pointed them up to Mr Gresham's chambers — *no light ever shone on the tenfold darknesses of the law*, he thought, negotiating an inconveniently placed black chest — for coals — or corpses, more like — the last resting place of some victim of the Jennens case, no doubt. The stairs creaked, but the banister rail seemed solid enough, and up they went to knock at the oaken door.

Francis Gresham's little venerable clerk — Mr Codlin — let them in. A fishy sort of face — a face with watery grey eyes that looked at them suspiciously. There was a lot of flat pale cheek, and not much nose, or mouth, come to think of it, thought Dickens. A bit of a beard — very like a codfish. Did he imagine that very ancient fish-like smell? Jones introduced himself.

'Superintendent Jones,' Mr Codlin repeated, opening and closing his mouth in a distinctly codfish-like manner.

*Is it only when I'm with Charles Dickens that I meet such odd people?* Jones asked himself, but he exercised patience. 'Yes — to see Mr Gresham.'

'Appointment?'

'Yes.'

Codfish turned to Dickens. 'Appointment?'

'Mr Charles Dickens to see Mr Gresham.'

The mouth dropped open, closed again, and opened to say, 'Mr Charles Dickens of —'

'Devonshire Terrace to see Mr Francis Gresham, with Mr Superintendent Samuel Jones of Bow Street to see Mr Francis Gresham of this office. Mr Francis Gresham to see us.'

'By appointment,' Jones added with a touch of cruelty. *The law is an ass, sometimes*, he thought.

Codfish looked from one to the other. *Comedians?* Uncertainty creased his pale brow, but he collected his dusty dignity about him. 'I shall enquire if Mr Gresham is available.'

'Much obliged,' said Jones, and gave him a metaphorical shove, 'it is about Mr Felix Gresham — victim of murder.'

Mr Codlin scuttled, crab-like now, away into another room. 'Fish out of water,' whispered Dickens.

'Sprat to catch a mackerel.'

Mr Francis Gresham bore no resemblance to any fish of any species, large or small — or any mammal for that matter. Jones was much relieved to see an ordinarily constituted human being of moderate height, moderate looks, moderate age — about thirty-five — and perfectly good-humoured courtesy, and frank as his name suggested when he introduced himself. He accepted the presence of Charles Dickens with simple pleasure. He did not ask why Dickens was there.

'It is very good to meet you, Mr Dickens — I have so envied Henry Meteyard who speaks of you so often. I followed that case of the murdered captain of *The Redemption*, too, and my aunt, Mrs Gresham, spoke of meeting you some years ago.'

'Mrs Gresham?' asked Jones. 'Is it possible to see her?'

'I think not, Superintendent Jones. She is sick with grief, attended by a nurse and her housekeeper. I have hardly dared speak of Felix to her. I'm sure that I can tell you what you wish to know. Mrs Gresham knew little of Felix's life in London — thank goodness.'

'Yes, I have gathered from Mr Temple that Felix led a rather rackety life.'

Frank Gresham's genial face darkened. 'I am sure he did, and Ned Temple encouraged him in his scrapes, though he was supposed to keep an eye on him. Mrs Gresham was too soft — and too trusting of that young man.'

'Temple told me that he'd incurred Mrs Gresham's gratitude by rescuing Felix from some embarrassment.'

'Yes, he got involved with some unsuitable girl — wanted to marry her. In any case, he was only seventeen so it wouldn't have done at all. My uncle paid her off through Temple, who treated with the father of the girl. Temple had his fee, too.'

'Ned Temple's legacy.'

'He was paid for his trouble at the time — a hundred pounds, I think. As to the legacy, my aunt — oh, I see — you're asking about Temple because —'

'Someone murdered your cousin, Mr Gresham. Mr Temple

inherits a large sum of money, so I need to know about him. He told me that he began his career with Mr Ernest Gresham — why didn't he stay with Gresham's?'

'My uncle was a thorough lawyer — no one doubted his law. The truth was to be found there in the clause, the case, the precedent, and, despite what you might sometimes write, Mr Dickens —' he smiled at Dickens — 'and your lawyers are very funny — my uncle was high-principled and honest in his narrow, strict way. He did not care for Ned Temple — he did not trust him. He could see through people — he thought Ned Temple a poor student and clerk — too fond of pleasure. In any case, he hoped that Felix would come into chambers and I, of course, would be the senior partner. My father was Ernest Gresham's elder brother. He died when I was a boy, but it was always Gresham and Gresham. There was a Wigs once, but he —'

'Took to his box.' Dickens pointed to the wig box on Gresham's desk.

'Didn't last, I was going to say,' Francis Gresham smiled. 'My father didn't care for the name — thought it would attract the wrong sort of comment. The law is no place for comedy, he always said, though Wigs is with Witty now — Gray's Inn.'

Jones interrupted Dickens's snort of laughter. 'Why did Mr Gresham trust him so far as to have him act in the case of the unsuitable girl?'

'That was my aunt's doing. She thought Ned Temple, as a young man, might be more persuasive. She liked him — of course, she felt sorry for him. He has only his mother, who is quite poor, I believe. His father was a country parson on eighty pounds a year and he left nothing. Only a legacy from an uncle allowed him to begin his law studies, and he had a cheerful way about him with Felix. My uncle was a stern father, I'm afraid.'

'Do you think Ned Temple led him astray with this young woman?' asked Dickens. 'Did Ned Temple, perhaps, know her?'

'I wondered that, but the matter caused so much upset between Felix and his father that I forbore to mention it. Ned Temple moved on and Felix began with a barrister — not that I thought it would do any good. After my uncle died, Felix kept on for his mother's sake, but I knew his heart wasn't in it.'

'So how was it that Ned Temple became Felix's lawyer?' Jones asked.

Francis Gresham looked astonished. 'He wasn't.'

'He told me he was — that's why I went to him first. I thought you were at the inquest as a family member. I beg your pardon, Mr Gresham — I should have come to you had I not been misled.'

'I expected you, of course. When I saw you with him, I assumed you were asking about Felix's friends. What did he tell you?'

'He told me about the places Felix frequented — the clubs, the casinos, but I discovered that he'd been to Felix's lodgings to clear out his possessions and his papers — he showed me the will and some letters.'

'Felix must have given him a copy of the will — to show him the legacy, I'd guess, but Ned Temple was not, in any official way, Felix's lawyer. I am. Were there any other papers?'

'Nothing useful, but he was not at ease — hiding something, I thought. I wondered about debts — if Ned Temple destroyed evidence of money owing to Felix by him?'

'It wouldn't surprise me — Felix was careless about money. He spent his allowance and went to his mother for more. She gave it, of course, and I couldn't do a thing about it. How could I tell her of the life he was leading? I thought that in time

—' his open face clouded — 'poor lad, poor aunt…'

Dickens said, 'I went to an old pawnbroker and found out that Felix had pawned a gold pin and given the money to Ned Temple.'

'I remember that pin — his mother gave it to him. There was a diamond ring —'

'Stolen at the time of the murder, possibly.'

'Superintendent Jones, do you think it possible that Ned Temple killed Felix?'

'I don't know, of course, but the circumstantial evidence may point that way. I shall be seeing him again. I wonder, Mr Gresham, if you might look at any papers at Mrs Gresham's house. It would be very helpful if I could find evidence of any money owed by Ned Temple.'

'I doubt there's anything, Superintendent, but I will look. Felix was careless — there might be letters, I suppose.'

Jones rose to go. 'We'll bid you good day, Mr Gresham. I am much obliged for your assistance.'

'I am obliged to you, Superintendent Jones, and to you, Mr Dickens. I hope you will be able to find out who did this. Felix was a foolish young man in many ways, but he was likeable and good-natured. He did not deserve this — and nor did my aunt.'

'We will do our best, Mr Gresham.'

They shook hands. Dickens had a sudden thought. 'The young woman — she wasn't a Ruby Kiss?'

'No, I'd have remembered that name. Who is she?'

'Someone Felix knew,' Jones explained.

'By the name — a prostitute?'

'I'm afraid so.'

'What about the name Phoebe Green?'

Frank Gresham looked at Dickens. 'No, it means nothing. I

don't know that I ever knew her name, and there's no record, of course. Mr Gresham was a very cautious man — cash only. No trace of any payment.'

'Would Mrs Gresham know?'

'Possibly, but I shouldn't like to rake the thing up — in the circumstances.'

'I understand,' said Jones, 'we shall have to ask Mr Temple.'

'Mr Codlin might remember. He was very close to Mr Gresham, who had absolute trust in him.' He grinned. 'Of course, I'm not half the lawyer my uncle was. Codlin knows everything, I should think, from the last fifty years, longer probably.' Frank Gresham stood up. 'I'll ask him to come in.'

Mr Codlin came in and looked from Jones to Dickens as a man might look for whom the earth had suddenly shifted. His mouth opened and closed. He looked at Frank Gresham.

'Mr Codlin, Superintendent Jones is making enquiries about the death of Mr Felix. The matter of the — er — young lady — you remember when Mr Temple acted for Mr Gresham?'

Mr Codlin made one of his codfish attempts to speak, caught his breath and answered, 'I do, sir. Mr Temple was entrusted with five hundred pounds — too much, I opined to Mr Gresham. That young man was not to be trusted with so large a sum. Very fond of his pleasures, I recall. The law is a serious matter. Mr Gresham was of my opinion, but Mrs Gresham, I believe, exerted an — influence.'

'Do you recall the young lady's name?'

'I should hardly call her —' Codlin caught sight of Jones's face — 'the name was mentioned by Mr Felix. Mr Temple hushed him — no names, he said, but I seem to remember —'

Dickens felt that he would like to stun him before throwing him back into the Thames, but he was not entirely surprised to hear the old man's conclusion.

'It was Isabella — Bella, Mr Felix called her.'

Dickens thought about the angry boy.

Dickens and Jones sat down on the bench in Lincoln's Inn Fields where Dickens had sat with Meredith Case.

'Bella?' Jones raised an eloquent eyebrow. 'I saw a light in your eyes. Don't tell me you know who she is.'

Dickens explained about Bella Screech and her boy. 'It could be, Sam — Felix and Ned Temple, both known by Screech and Miss Finch, told me that Bella Screech had asked a deal of questions when Felix Gresham was murdered. Suppose she had Felix's child?'

'How old do you reckon the child is?'

'About seven, I should think.'

'Felix Gresham was twenty-four.'

'And he was seventeen when he formed this unsuitable liaison. It could be, Sam, and she's about twenty-four or so — and very beautiful, incredible though it seems with Screech as a father.'

Jones thought for a moment. 'Ernest Gresham might have known that the girl was pregnant. Hence the five hundred pounds — it's a large sum.'

'If she got it all — old codfish, there, said Ned Temple wasn't to be trusted. He had a hundred pounds for his role as go-between. It wouldn't seem much in the light of five hundred. Tempting to a poor man with his way to make — and he'd think he could get away with it.'

'But it was a risk — even if Screech got half of it, Temple and Gresham still visited Screech.'

'Ned Temple's the sort who would think he could get one over the likes of Screech, though I'll bet Screech has had it back tenfold in interest on loans — it wouldn't surprise me to find that Ned Temple owed Screech.'

Jones nodded. 'I wouldn't be surprised at that. Now, I wonder if Felix Gresham was still paying something to Screech. That'd let out Screech. Killing the goose and all that —'

'Spot of blackmail — or just that the boy ought to be supported. Appeal to the young man's honour. Ned Temple in cahoots with Screech, maybe — getting a cut. And Bella Screech wouldn't want Felix dead if he were still paying.'

'So, perhaps, he had stopped paying — there's a motive for someone. All the more reason for me to question Mr Temple. He knows something, even if he's not the killer. I'll go to Bow Street and get Rogers. You'd better not come — he'll remember you from the bookshop, and that's a complication.'

'Pity, I should like to see his face when you tell him what you know. I'll walk with you and go back to Wellington Street.'

Sergeant Rogers was just coming out of Bow Street Police Station when they arrived. He was in a hurry.

'What's up?'

'Ebenezer Screech — found dead. Constable Feak sent a message. Murdered, he says.'

# 19: THE HEIRESS

*Death on his pale horse had galloped by*, thought Dickens as they turned in to Crooked Alley and he saw Screech's goods scattered across the passage. The cavalier had met his end, too, bowled over and lying in the gutter. Not that Death could have galloped out by Dark Entry. A murderer could have slipped through there, though.

Ebenezer Screech lay on his side. Mr Punch with all the stuffing knocked out of him, almost in the embrace of Judy, or rather the wood-wormed Britannia who had fallen with him. A good deal of his other decaying stock had collapsed about him, ready for the dust heap. Dickens noted that the cupboard door was hanging open. The box of keys was overturned, and the keys spilled everywhere on the counter.

'Bashed on the head, I should think,' Feak told them, 'with this —' he pointed to the poker at a little distance from the corpse — 'blood on it. His daughter's in the back room. Her boy found him, she says, went for her at The Mischief — she works there.'

'Has the boy said anything?'

'No, sir, too shocked, I think.'

Jones looked at the body and saw that Screech had been felled by a blow from the fire iron. The left-hand side of his face bore the marks of a sudden blow to his temple — a right-handed blow. Blood stained the ragged bunting onto which he had fallen.

'Feak, go to King's Hospital and see if you can bring Doctor Woodhall. Tell him what's happened, and ask if he can arrange for the body to be taken to his mortuary.'

Dickens pointed to the cupboard. 'He kept that locked — he brought out Felix Gresham's gold pin from a locked metal box inside. The key to the cupboard was in that tray with all the others — you'd not know which one it was unless —'

'You'd watched him carefully. Someone who knew — who came here regularly, perhaps.'

'I saw it once, but I wouldn't be able to tell which it was — there are dozens. The key to the box was in one of his pockets.'

Jones looked into the cupboard. 'There's no metal box now. Rogers, have a look for a key in his pocket.'

'A robbery?'

Rogers stood up. 'There are some small keys under the body and a few scattered about. None in his pockets.'

'Someone in a hurry — knew he kept keys on him, but didn't know which one. It would be quicker to take the box and run.' Jones looked back at Screech and the poker. The killer had cast it away and fled. 'A row of some sort — someone wanting money — someone who needed it badly. Screech refuses. The killer picks up the poker, threatens Screech, who still refuses, and in a sudden rage lashes out.'

'I can imagine that,' Dickens said. 'Screech had no heart — no tale of poverty would move him. No more pity than that fire iron. He'd be implacable. Liked his power, I daresay, and he'd expect his importuner to slink away. Someone at the end of his tether.'

'Not intending to kill, perhaps — but desperate enough. Let's go and see the daughter —'

Dickens lowered his voice. 'The boy — who we think might be —'

'Yes, he complicates things. Let's stick to this death for the time being. See if we can find out if the boy saw anyone.'

'His mother told him to keep away — the old miser, she called him.'

'No love lost, then.'

'Didn't seem like it.' Dickens thought about Bella Screech, taller than her father, and stronger, and she had a temper. He remembered her flashing eyes in The Mischief. Screech would drive a saint to murder.

Rogers was left to look about the shop while Jones and Dickens went into the back. Two other constables had been detailed to search the alley and Dark Entry.

The back room was just as crowded as the shop. It was very cold and smelt of old clothes and sweat and stale food. An oil lamp smoked on a table near the cold grate. Bella sat on a moth-eaten sofa, the boy next to her, his head burrowed into her shoulder and her arm about him.

'Superintendent Jones from Bow Street, Miss Screech.'

She looked up and saw Dickens. 'You were at The Mischief.'

'I was.'

'Police, are you?'

Jones didn't let him answer. 'Miss Screech, what can you tell us?'

'Johnny came and told me that the old man at the shop was hurt. I came and found him. Went to find a policeman. That's all.' She spoke without any emotion at all. The boy didn't move.

'Is there anyone to look after your boy? At The Mischief, perhaps? I need to ask questions about your father. You might not want him to hear it all.'

'There's no one. In any case, he won't leave me.' She held her son tighter.

'The unlocked cupboard and the keys thrown about — anything missing?'

'Didn't look — that cupboard's always locked.'

'What did he keep in there?'

'A metal box — valuables in it — gold, silver, jewellery that he bought.'

'It's not there now.'

'Robbed, then — plenty of folk who know about it.'

She wasn't hostile, exactly, thought Dickens, more indifferent. Perhaps she had done it and thought she couldn't be found out — taken the box as evidence of a robbery. It could be anywhere in this chaotic place. It would take forever to search. She could have hidden it already. Or, the boy? Was she so calm to protect him? She was holding him very close. Screech had been a horror — no doubt of that. Had the boy lashed out with something that had come to hand? Screech had been a very small man.

Jones was unreadable, too, just asking his questions, making no inferences. 'Did your father have creditors?'

Bella Screech nodded. 'We weren't close. He — well, my boy hasn't a father. Not married, see. My father didn't like it. He didn't tell me about his — business dealings.'

'He threw you out?' Dickens asked, knowing very well that even a father as crooked as Screech could find a straight path to the high moral ground over a daughter's virtue.

'Not exactly — we just didn't get on.'

'You don't know the names of any of his creditors?' asked Jones, thinking of Ned Temple and Felix Gresham.

'There was a book — kept his accounts in it. He was a secretive devil. It'll be upstairs — under the bed. Lot of boxes there — where he kept his money.'

Interesting that she didn't mention the two names, but that would keep. Jones merely asked, 'Plenty of it?'

'I suppose so. He never gave me any of it — or my boy.'

'Did he make a will?'

'Him? Leave anythin' to anyone? It'd have broken his heart — he'd have made plans with the devil to take it with him.'

'Have I your permission to search the premises?'

'Yes, I don't care what you do.'

Rogers came in to say that Doctor Woodhall had come from the hospital. Dickens stayed where he was.

'You didn't say who you are,' Bella said to him.

She didn't miss much. *Tell her*, Dickens thought. He might get her to talk. 'My name is Charles Dickens.'

'You mean —'

'Yes.'

'What've you to do with all this?'

'I was with the Superintendent when we heard. I came because I'd been in the shop only a day or two ago.'

'Not pawnin' your watch, I daresay,' she said drily.

This was his chance. 'No, I was asking about Felix Gresham — the young man who was murdered by the bookshop.'

Bella didn't speak, but she looked at her boy and shifted him so that he was more comfortable. He was asleep and didn't stir. Dickens just waited.

'You knew him?'

'Not well. I knew his mother some years ago when Felix was about seventeen.'

She looked at him then — that same fierce look she had given the landlord of The Mischief. 'You know, don't you — she tell you, the mother?'

He evaded the question. 'She didn't know about Johnny.'

'How'd you know, then?'

'I guessed.'

'Clever, ain't you? But I know that.' Her eyes flashed at him. 'I can read, you know. So can my boy.' She laid him gently down and put her shawl over him. He looked just a baby with his thumb in his mouth — like little Frank when he was sleeping.

'Shall I light the fire?' There was some wood and a few pieces of coal in a bucket on the hearth.

'Yes, it's freezin' in here. There's brandy. I'll get some. You'll have to drink it from a cup. He don't — didn't do glasses. Hardly did cups — too mean.'

Dickens got the fire going and lit a couple of candles. It was getting darker in the room. They sat with their cups of brandy. Dickens tasted his and felt the warmth slip down his throat, but he waited for Bella to speak again, feeling that she would not be pushed. She'd do things her way. She sipped her drink. The firelight flickered. He sensed a change in her, saw how her shoulders relaxed, but still he waited and watched. *Patience*, he thought.

She turned to him at last, and seeing a pair of mesmerising eyes, spoke in a faraway tone. '*The secret agony of my soul* — I've read it. About that poor boy in the bottle factory — David Copperfield. Like me in this shop. Like him, I wanted something better. Screech — Pa — was a terror — give you a slap as soon as look at you, and worse. Until I was taller — and stronger. I had my dreams, Mr Dickens…'

'We all have dreams —' he said quietly.

'Yours came true, I think.'

'Not all of them… I think what a dream we live in — the saddest dream that was ever dreamed…'

Bella looked at him, her expression half puzzled, half surprised. She nodded and looked into the fire.

He heard footsteps on the stairs — Sam going up to search, but Bella Screech did not look up. He watched her as she gazed into the growing flames. She was beautiful with creamy skin and full red lips. Her hair in the candlelight shone a rich brown. At sixteen or seventeen, how lovely a girl she must have been — and Felix Gresham just a boy. Dreams, eh? He thought of his passionate devotion to Maria Beadnall — his first love — and how his heart had broken when she'd rejected him. Bella turned her head, but she looked as if she were not seeing him. Her dark eyes had a wistful, longing look now that her fierceness had subsided. He couldn't think of her murdering Felix Gresham, or her father. But who could know to what a man or woman might be driven? And yet there was her tenderness for her child.

'Tell me about Felix.'

'He was just a boy — a lonely boy. His grandmother lived on Frith Street near St. Anne's Church. Felix's mother looked after her. His father was a miserable type — strict with Felix. Never good enough, I suppose. Felix roamed about during his school holidays — he liked the old couple in the bookshop. We met in the churchyard. I was just sittin' by my ma's grave. Didn't remember her much — just that she was a little woman with fair hair, but I used to dream that she p'raps wasn't dead at all an' she'd come for me in a carriage... Anyway, Felix an' me, both lonely. We roamed about together, then he went back to school. Thought I wouldn't see him again, but he turned up next holidays an' the next — wrote to me — love letters. I believed him. Didn't think about his pa, o' course — we'd get married an' they'd see — oh, what's the use of goin' over it? That was years ago. We were two fools, that's all.'

'Mr Jones and I found out that Mr Ernest Gresham —'

'Paid us off — so, he did — two hundred and fifty pounds — they were frightened they'd be sued for breach of promise. Not that I saw much of it. I was eighteen, but I never said about the baby. Midwife came. Pa didn't know. He never looked at me anyway —' she grinned at him suddenly — 'but he got a shock all right when he saw the baby. Not that he cared. Anyway, soon as I could I helped myself to what money I could — he didn't come after me. I knew he wouldn't. Thought he'd got off cheaply, I suppose. I took lodgings with a widow I knew. She didn't mind. She looked after Johnny when I went to work an' I did housework for her — rent was cheap. When she died, I went to work at The Mischief. I have rooms there. It's a home — of sorts. The landlord's all right. He lives in the house next door.'

'Ned Temple paid the money to your father.'

'How'd you know all this? You ain't that clever.'

'Mr Jones has been investigating Felix's death — he has questioned Ned Temple and the lawyer, Mr Francis Gresham.'

'Never liked him, Temple — saw him about here sometimes — had money dealin's with my pa, no doubt.'

'Did you ever see Felix?'

'I did — saw him once goin' down Dark Entry. Wondered what he was about. I followed. He met Ned Temple and they both went into the shop.'

'Did you speak to him?'

'I did — when they came out. Course, he knew me. He was embarrassed — tried to laugh it all off, but he wouldn't look me in the eye. Temple stood there sniggerin'. Maybe Felix was ashamed — the money. Remembered the promises he'd made. Oh, I don't know. I didn't know him at all. He expected I was married now with a brood of kids clingin' to my skirts — brood — you can tell what he thought of me.'

'Did you tell him?'

Bella looked at her child again and adjusted the shawl — not that it was necessary. 'I wanted to — I wanted to see his face, but no, I didn't tell him. I didn't feel anything about him. That boy — the boy he was had gone. Such a toff, he looked … made me feel a fool — nothing more than some serving wench —' her eyes flashed again suddenly — '"investigatin", you said — is that what you're about for him upstairs? Want to know if I killed Felix? Is that your game?'

The spell was broken — he should have been more careful. 'No, I just —'

She stood up. 'Copper's nark, are you, Mr Story-teller? Tell that copper, he knows where to find me.' She shook the child gently. 'Come on, Johnny — time to go home.'

# 20: CRACKING THE CODE

Dickens went upstairs. The banister rail was festooned with old clothes — a soldier's red jacket slipped off at his feet. Of the thirty-fifth, perhaps. He picked it up and put it back. It smelt as if it had been last worn at Waterloo. Coats, dresses, pairs of boots, single ones and single shoes crowded the staircase. He picked his way to the top. A rusty black bonnet perched like a ragged crow on the newel post. Something pale and suspicious dangled from a hook — the dim light suggested a ghostly figure waiting for him. But it was a dress that had once been white in the Regency style, decorated with dirty lace and tarnished silver thread — the Duchess of Bolton's, perhaps, he thought, remembering the chamber pot — if she had ever existed. Duchess of the cotton mills.

On the landing he heard voices and made his way to the first of two open doors. In the first room, the mattress and bedding had been taken from the bed, drawers were open, and Rogers knelt with his head in a trunk. Dickens heard the chink of coins.

'Double ducats,' he said.

'Lot o' money, here — sovereigns mostly — he was a miser. Ebenezer Scrooge, eh?' Rogers grinned at Dickens and began to take out a quantity of bags.

Jones was standing in the little light from the window, turning the pages of a book. 'Miss Screech?' he asked.

'Gone, I'm afraid.'

'I thought you were getting along famously. I heard your confidential tones in there.'

'We were, but she became suspicious when I asked about

Felix Gresham — thought I was a copper's nark.'

Jones grinned. 'Well, you are. What did you find out?'

'Temple paid Screech two hundred and fifty pounds, not five hundred. I don't know if Screech knew — he might have found out and confronted Temple.'

'Gresham let it slip, maybe — about the five hundred pounds, I mean.'

'That would put Mr Temple in a very awkward spot,' Rogers put in, 'if he'd stolen money from a lawyer. He'd have a motive for both murders — an' him a lawyer — facin' ruin, I'd say.'

'You'd say right, Rogers, but it's odd that the killings are different — murderers tend to use the same method. This one bespeaks sudden rage. Still, that doesn't rule him out if he owed Screech money he couldn't pay. Screech blackmailing him, perhaps. Did Bella Screech know about the five hundred pounds?'

'I don't think so — she just said two hundred and fifty, and she didn't see much of it. The old skinflint kept it. She kept her pregnancy secret and left home as soon as she could after the boy was born — he is Felix's son, by the way.'

'Did Gresham know?'

'She says not. She met him a while back. Temple was with Gresham. I didn't have the chance to ask when. Gresham took it lightly — thought she'd be married with a brood of kids.'

'Brood — he used that word?'

'He did — she used it with a certain amount of bitterness, I thought. She said he looked such a toff.'

'Humiliated, and resented him?'

'She thought he was ashamed, too — about the money, but she said she felt a fool. He treated her like a serving girl. That's when she flared up. Told me you'd know where to find her.'

'The boy? Could he have?'

'He was asleep. He looked such a baby, but — when I saw him first, he kicked out at Screech's goods outside the shop and yelled out. He was very angry — but I'd not like to think —'

'That a kiddie'd do that,' said Rogers. 'Nor would I, Mr Dickens, but, you know, it happens — could have been temper. An' there was that lad, William Allnutt —'

'I know — he murdered his grandfather, but that wasn't temper, it was poison — twelve years old.'

'We'll have to keep it in mind,' Jones said. 'I'll get Constable Feak to watch The Mischief. Anything else about Temple?'

'Bella said he was always hanging about — money dealings with Screech, she assumed.'

'But she said that she kept away and told the boy not to come near the shop. Bit contradictory.'

'I suppose it is.'

'She might be directing our thoughts to Temple. She'd seen him with Felix Gresham. Now, have a look at this — lists of names, last names and numbers — money owed, I imagine.'

Constable Feak came in to say that the room next door was full of junk and that they hadn't found anything valuable yet. Jones told him to carry on — every drawer and cupboard had to be searched.

Dickens turned the pages. There were a lot of names, some repeated — double, triple debts? He focused on one section. He couldn't see Temple or Gresham. There was nothing familiar:

*Gray, M 3*
*Noel, S 24*
*King, N 40*
*Church, S 28*

*Dean, J 45*
*Park, A 50*
*Clement, T 8*


He turned another page and scanned the list, then turned back to the page he'd looked at first. 'Where did you say Felix Gresham lived?'

'Montague Street, number 15.'

'Look at this.'

Jones read aloud, 'Montague, G 15.'

'It's a code — of sorts. They're all street names.'

'So they are — all hereabouts — Dean Street, Noel Street, King Street — are the numbers the house numbers?'

'I'll bet — the numbers are very small for owings. Wrote down these for quick reference. The list of monies owed might be somewhere else — or in Screech's head.'

'There is no Gray Street round here — oh, wait a minute — Clement, T. I've got it — Edward Temple of Clement's Inn where I saw him. Gray could be Gray's Inn. Number eight, Clement's Inn, Ned Temple's rooms — cunning devil. There'll be names somewhere.'

'Number eight Clement's Inn — the chambers of Mr Simeon Dalrymple.'

'Know him?'

'Of him — I'll tell you another time. It's a very pretty little mystery. But this list, is it enough?'

'I want to double check. Church Street's the nearest. Rogers, get along to number 28, find out who knows Screech and tell them he's dead. Someone might be willing to admit being in his debt, someone whose initial is 'S' — don't mention murder. Then go to Dean Street — just to be sure that's what all this means. Then we'll approach Temple.'

Rogers went away. Jones fished under the bed and pulled out a battered tin box. 'Is this the one you saw in the cupboard?'

'No, wrong colour — the other was black.'

Jones tried the keys Rogers had picked up and found one that opened it. He took out various little bags made of sacking. Several contained more gold sovereigns. From the other, he took a diamond ring. 'Felix Gresham's, I wonder?'

'Stolen on the night of the murder, pawned by the murderer?'

'A murderer who needed money fast.'

'Temple?' asked Dickens.

'Well, no doubt we shall see — I'll show it to him. That might give him a shock. Let's see what else there is.'

There were a bracelet set with rubies and a sapphire ring. 'Stolen, I should think — not the sort of thing you'd find round Dean Street.'

'Montague Street?'

'More likely.'

Jones emptied more of the bags. There were several silver boxes, a silver-backed mirror with the monogram JAC, a gold snuffbox with a different monogram, AAH, another snuffbox, plain this time, but surely gold, another gold bracelet, a gold cravat pin, a cameo ring, a gold locket without its chain — with the same monogram as the mirror — some silver napkin rings, a silver cup with what looked like a coat of arms which had almost been polished away, but with the initials SMF engraved on it, a gold pencil case with same initials, a little gold pencil, marked with the initials MMB, two gold thimbles, and two diamond-studded shoe buckles — the sort a courtier might wear.

'Quite a haul,' Jones observed, 'from someone with access to a wealthy household, a servant, maybe, but not necessarily to do with the murder. If someone wanted this lot back, they'd have come upstairs to find it —'

'Unless our someone was disturbed.'

'The boy, you mean — you didn't ask?'

'I didn't dare — as it was, I overstepped the mark, I think. She talked about herself and Felix — two lonely children who met by chance and fell in love and thought they could marry — two dreamers. For a few minutes, she confided and then — sorry, Sam.'

'Never mind — Temple is our priority at the moment, and this ring. I'll put Inspector Grove onto these valuables. He can investigate any robberies reported and the other debtors who live close by.'

Rogers came back to report that he'd spoken to two of Screech's customers; one was a Stephen Munton of Church Street who had been delighted to hear of his death and had readily admitted to owing money.

'And the other?'

Rogers looked uncomfortable. 'Dean Street, sir, it was James Semple.'

'Awkward. What do you think?'

'He admitted to owing Screech and said that Screech was a bloodsucker. He hadn't told his brother — too embarrassed, but I don't think —'

'That he killed Screech?'

'Doubt it, sir — he's not the violent type.'

'All right, but if any evidence comes up, we can't ignore it for Constable Semple's sake.'

'I know, sir.'

Jones gave Rogers his instructions to tell Feak and the other constable that the valuables and money and any papers were to be packed up and taken to Bow Street and the shop locked up.

'I want to know how much Ned Temple owed — useful evidence. And, Rogers, you'll have to inform Miss Screech.'

'Turn-up for her, sir, a fortune — an heiress, she'll be, even if some of the stuff has to be returned to the rightful owners,' Rogers said. 'Makes you wonder.'

Dickens wondered, too. "No love lost," Jones had said, but he hoped that Bella Screech had not killed her father — nor that little boy with his thumb in his mouth.

'I'll bear that in mind,' Jones said to Rogers. 'Now, I'm going to Clement's Inn to find Ned Temple and he can tell me all about his dealings with Mr Screech.'

# 21: NEWS FROM THE NORTH

The child was sleeping. Little Dora, Dickens's little pet, his baby girl, who had been so poorly with convulsions only a couple of weeks ago. The Reverend James White, Meredith Case's friend, had been dining with them on the night the baby had been so ill. Dickens and Catherine had asked him to baptise her — so dreadful had it been. It had been a comfort. She was rather better now, quite tranquil in her sleep — no sign of innocence more touching than the smile of a sleeping infant.

Dickens closed the nursery door very quietly and tip-toed away, the pain about his heart less sharp. He went down to his study and sat at his desk. He had been reading about sleep and dreams, talking about them to his friend, Doctor Stone, who was writing a piece for *Household Words*. He read Stone's words: *The lover dreams of his mistress. The miser dreams of his gold.* Shylock had dreamt of moneybags the night before his daughter had eloped. Had Screech dreamt of his gold the night before his death when all his riches would be lost to him? Bella Screech had said that Screech would be in league with the devil to take it with him — he'd have found out now that it was all gone. His ducats and his daughter.

Bella Screech had had dreams — dreams that had been crushed. There was a loneliness about her. She had suffered. *The secret agony of the soul* — she had remembered that from *David Copperfield*. Women, Dickens often thought, could bear adversity better than men. Bella had borne hers and had brought up the child. He could read, she had said. Taught by Bella, he reckoned. Felix Gresham had suffered as a boy, but he had made his rebellion by leading a dissipated life, careless and unthinking. But then, he'd had no child to rear.

Dickens thought about the sleeping boy. He had lain quite still on that shabby sofa — the sleep of innocence, he was sure, so different from the sleep of guilt. But he might have seen something. Perhaps Bella would forgive him, and he could ask — perhaps not.

Ah, well, there were letters to deal with now. Now, here was one in an unfamiliar hand. He opened it and looked at the sender's address: The Rectory, Kirkdale, Westmorland. Ah, Mr Case, he presumed. Mr Dalrymple had remembered.

*My Dear Mr Dickens,*

*You will see from the address that I have found sanctuary — the Reverend Stephen Hardy and his kind sister have taken me in. I shall not be returning to London for some while for I have suffered a serious sprain to my ankle, the circumstances of which accident I shall relate before I end my letter.*

*I stayed a night in Kendal and took the branch line to Windermere, where I found a man called Moses Rigg who was at the station waiting for a parcel of books for Mr Hardy. He was pointed out to me as a man from Kirkdale. Mr Dalrymple recalled the name of the house where Miss Henrietta Hawke visited.*

*Mr Rigg was not a communicative man, but directed me to Kirkdale Hall, though he warned me that I would find nothing there. I hardly understood him until I saw that the house is a ruin, destroyed by fire in 1828. The Squire, Sir Robert Trent, perished. His only son survived and was looked after by a Doctor Sutton, now, alas, dead, and later, he was adopted by relatives.*

*None of the natives here are very forthcoming. The Squire was highly thought of and they do not trust strangers enough to talk of the family or the fire. Stephen Hardy and his sister have been here for about five years.*

*Naturally, they know nothing of a Sapphire Hawke, nor can any local people shed light upon the matter. I asked about the visit of Miss Henrietta Hawke, but there was no memory of her coming to the hall.*

*I have visited a Miss Margery Robb who was nurse to the son, Sydney Trent, but she could tell me nothing, only that when the boy was well enough after the ordeal of the fire, a lawyer came from London to take him to his new home with connections of the family. Miss Robb seemed to have little interest in the child's fate, merely saying that she had done her duty and that rich folks did as they pleased in her experience which was rather at odds with the opinion generally given of Sir Robert Trent. I supposed that she was one of those rather sour individuals who are never pleased, though I did wonder what kind of a nurse she made. She was rather a stern, unbending woman, I thought. She remembered the fire, of course. The boy had been with her and they escaped from the nursery floor while the fire took hold below where the Squire slept. She also said that they were taken in by Doctor Sutton who looked after the boy. Doctor Sutton died some years ago. Miss Robb knew nothing of Sapphire Hawke nor of Miss Henrietta Hawke, though she believed that there might have been a distant connection between the Trent family and the Hawke family. More than that she could not say.*

*Lady Alice Trent, the boy's mother, died in childbed five years after her first son's birth. The newborn would have been a second son, but did not survive.*

*It does seem a tragic family. I found the ruins most sombre and melancholy, but Mr Hardy's church is a very peaceful and simple white-washed place. Mr Hardy is a good and simple man — a fine scholar, I think, and his sister who is only about twenty-five is a most charming young lady. I do feel as if I have found friends.*

*Miss Hardy showed me the memorials in this quiet church. The Squire's and his lady's are very affecting and testament to his great love for her. I could not help feeling the sadness of their only son's fate. I saw the memorial to her brother's predecessor, the Reverend Alexander Hamilton* and his wife, Adeline. Mr Hamilton, too, was a good servant to his parish for many, many years. An example for me, I felt.

I injured my ankle when I went back to the ruins for a last look. I had hoped to return to London that very day, but my kind hosts insist that I must stay with them until I am recovered, and as I can do no more for Sapphire Hawke, I shall stay. You were right about the fresh air. I feel much better and the Reverend Hardy is helping me to recover my spiritual health.

I wonder, Mr Dickens, if you would oblige me by communicating my news to Mr Dalrymple. I should also like to hear if there is any news from Bruges. It is quite clear that Sapphire Hawke did not come here. Mr Dalrymple may wish to pursue his enquiries at Hawke Village. As far as the sapphires are concerned, I am content to leave the matter for the time being.

You gave me good advice, sir, and I am humbly grateful to you. I remain,

Faithfully yours,
Meredith Case

Dickens felt pleased for Meredith Case, but what an extraordinary business — no trace of Sapphire Hawke. Did she exist, or was she a false creation — like Macbeth's dagger — from Meredith Case's overheated brain? But, no, she was palpable enough to Mr Dalrymple, and to Sir Gerald Hawke who had left her his sapphires. A pretty little mystery, indeed. Tomorrow afternoon he would go to see Mr Dalrymple of Clement's Inn. He wondered if Ned Temple would be there — you couldn't call that a pretty mystery. Not pretty at all, he thought, remembering Ebenezer Screech's battered face.

# 22: UNDER LOCK AND KEY

*If I had an enemy whom I hated — which Heaven forbid! — and if I knew something that sat heavy on his conscience...*

Dickens was in his office at Wellington Street beginning a new article for *Household Words*; its title was *Bill-Sticking*. There were bill-posters everywhere these days, a sort of pasted rash of them, advertising every possible thing: wigs, waxworks, perfumes, potions for the anointing of bald heads, hair, hands; potations, pills — pyramids, even. He'd seen a great van advertising the *Pyramid Panorama*, rolling down the street and blocking the traffic. There'd been a pagoda once. The idea for the piece had come to him when he'd seen a poster advertising the Bramah Lock Company — their locks were supposedly unpickable. They'd offered a reward to any man who could pick their so-called challenge lock displayed at their premises in Piccadilly. He'd like to have tried that. *A living key, to keep the list'ners from the ministry*, so an old rhyme went about Bramah's locks.

Locks had brought to mind that great gaol key of Screech's — what door did that open? He wondered if there were a cellar at the shop where yet more of Screech's secrets could be found. He'd mention it to Sam.

Murder was on his mind, and keys — secret keys provided the starting point for his article. A man who had stolen a key, haunted by bill-posters put up by his enemy with the headline: *SECRET KEYS*. The haunted man would see his conscience glaring down on him from every window and lamp post, gazing at him from every omnibus. He would see the fatal words lurking under every archway. Ned Temple would see the ghastly word *MURDER* as he walked to his chambers. *MURDER* in bloody letters emblazoned on posters — murder coming towards him in the shape of a man sandwiched between two boards.

Dickens was tempted to dash out then to Clement's Inn to see if Ned Temple were there, but he disciplined his thoughts and wrote on. Strike while the iron is hot — he might lose the thread of it.

He went on and did not look up until his secretary, Harry Wills, came to tell him that he was leaving for an appointment. It was almost lunchtime. He would go to Clement's Inn to see Mr Dalrymple, calling in on Sam on the way. Perhaps Ned Temple was already in one of those gloomy cells. No key to let him out.

At Bow Street, Jones was putting on his coat. He, too, was on his way to Clement's Inn.

'Mr Temple was not at his chambers yesterday evening. He's not been there all night. I've Stemp keeping a very close eye on number eight.'

'Temple won't get past him,' Dickens observed. Constable Stemp was a burly individual and quite intimidating. He'd been very useful in their past cases. Inexhaustible, too. He could go without sleep for days, it seemed.

'He's sent word. Temple has not been there this morning. I'm on my way to ask Mr Dalrymple if he knows where Temple lives.'

'I'm on my way there, too, on an errand for a Reverend Case — he is Sir Gerald Hawke's heir. The mystery I spoke of. It seems that there is a missing heiress — a Miss Sapphire Hawke.'

'What's she in line for?'

'Some very valuable sapphires.'

Jones whistled. 'Tell me on the way.'

The noise of traffic and voices and countless marching feet faded as they went through the archway into the ancient Inn of St Clement's, the garden of which in its quietness and with its few trees gave the impression of a churchyard — much neglected. All the dead lawyers were quiet at last, their mouths stopped by death's black sealing wax. Only a tall man in a grey hat and long grey coat glided soundlessly through an archway into the shadows beyond. The ghost of Master Justice Shallow, once of Clement's Inn? *Death is certain to all*, Shallow had said. Or perhaps it was the ghost of Silence, that other justice of the peace. Shakespeare, perhaps, walked these paths, his head busy with Sir John Falstaff's japes. Shakespeare was good at names — all that company of Master Shallow's: Shadow, Wart, Feeble and —

'Mouldy,' Dickens said.

'I suppose it is,' Jones said, looking ahead towards the building in which Mr Dalrymple ought to be found.

'I was thinking of Shakespeare: *Let's kill all the lawyers.*'

'Save me this one. I've business to do.'

Joah Danks let them in. *A face made for hanging*, thought Dickens, as Danks said how honoured he was to see Mr Dickens again. Was Mr Case coming, too?

Dickens exerted himself to courtesy, though his instinct recoiled. Something in Danks's tone grated, and he saw that flash of avid curiosity in his dark eyes. He did not mention Westmorland or Meredith Case's injury. Danks said he would tell Mr Dalrymple that Superintendent Jones and Mr Dickens wished to see him. Mr Dalrymple appeared at his door to greet them. *Another thorough lawyer*, thought Dickens, noting his high-domed head and gold eyeglasses, and the heavy gold chain across his waistcoat, from which dangled various portentous seals and keys. A half-moon of watch dial showed above a pocket — a large gold watch, no doubt. Its face would say: time is money.

Jones broached the subject of Ned Temple's whereabouts first, but Mr Dalrymple had no idea where he could be. It would be possible for Superintendent Jones to look at his rooms, but if he might enquire why?

'Mr Temple was the friend of Felix Gresham — you know, the young man that was murdered.'

'I do — a most dreadful occurrence.'

'Mr Temple has some letters and papers of Mr Gresham's, which I should like to look at. It is a matter of urgency.'

'Mr Temple is my tenant. I am certain that it is in order for me to authorise this. Mr Danks will let you in.'

'Do you know where Mr Temple lives?'

'I am sure it will be written down somewhere. I will ask Mr Danks.'

Joah Danks came in with a book. 'The address written here is 15, Montague Street —' *Felix Gresham's address*, Jones thought, but he didn't comment — 'Some weeks ago, I had occasion to ask — for my records, Mr Dalrymple. I like things to be up to date. Mr Temple informed me that he had moved. However, I think he might have been lodging downstairs —'

'How so?' asked Mr Dalrymple sharply.

'I saw him go into his rooms the other night — when you were here, Mr Dickens, but when he came out in the morning he was dressed in different clothes.'

'Perhaps he stayed the night, though I can hardly imagine why. Montague Street is hardly far.'

'I'm sorry, sir, for not mentioning it sooner, but I rather think he made a habit of sleeping in his rooms. I saw him a month or so back come out one night — I was working late on the Abercrombie papers.'

'Ah, yes, and you saw him?'

Joah Danks gave a little cough and put his hand to his mouth. 'Yes, sir, I didn't want to say — er — it was rather awkward — Mr Temple was with a young lady who was —'

Danks looked down as if embarrassed, but when he looked up at Mr Dalrymple again, Dickens, who was watching him carefully, thought that there was a good deal of feigned humility about Danks. He caught a brief gleam of malice in those black eyes. Joah Danks did not like Ned Temple. He had waited for this moment — how fortuitous that a policeman was present, too.

'Go on, Mr Danks, if you please.'

'Inebriated, sir. I was going out myself. Naturally, I held the door for the young lady and Mr Temple and —' *a pattern of humility*, thought Dickens — 'the young lady slipped, and I caught her.'

'You had a good look at her,' said Jones.

'She had red hair and wore feathers in it, and a rather garish red dress, I'm afraid, which was somewhat — er — rumpled...' Danks looked as pained as a temperance curate offered a beaker of gin.

Mr Dalrymple made a tutting sound — the idea of such a person on his premises. Jones was just forthright. 'She wasn't a lady.'

'I shouldn't say so, sir.'

'Name?'

'He called her Ruby.'

'Thank you, Mr Danks; now if you would let me into Mr

Temple's rooms, I'd be obliged. Then you can return to your duties.'

'You wish to speak to me, Mr Dickens?' asked Mr Dalrymple, seeing that Dickens did not go out with the policeman.

'I do. It is about the Reverend Mr Case. He is a friend of mine.'

'Oh, you know his circumstances.'

'I do — if I might sit down.'

'Of course, forgive me, I am rather shocked by what I have heard —' he tutted again — 'Mr Temple, dear me, dear me.' Whether he was more shocked by murder or a dolly-mop in his chambers, Dickens wasn't sure.

Dickens took out Meredith Case's letter. 'Mr Case has written to me from Westmorland and asked me to tell you his news. He has found no trace of Miss Sapphire Hawke — no one remembers her, or, indeed, Miss Henrietta Hawke. Kirkdale Hall was burnt down in 1828. Sir Robert Trent perished in the fire; his only son survived and was looked after by a Doctor Sutton — he is dead now — until he was adopted by Trent relatives, though Mr Case did not discover where they might be.'

Mr Dalrymple looked pained now. 'Ah, well, it was mere speculation on my part. The whole matter of Sir Gerald's ward was never fully communicated to me. He was a secretive man, and an irascible one — he liked his own way. One didn't like to…'

Dickens could well believe it. 'Mr Case is staying at the rectory in Kirkdale. He has a badly sprained ankle and will not return to London for a while yet. He asked me to send him any news from Bruges.'

'Miss Sapphire Hawke was certainly a pupil-boarder there

according to the records my son was shown. It was thought she might be destined for the cloister, but Sir Gerald sent for her. The former Mother Superior was close to her, but she is no longer there — dead, I suppose.'

'Have you any further ideas?'

'There was one piece of information which my son sent. Miss Hawke left the convent in April, 1832. She travelled back to England by steamboat in the company of a Miss Marianne Hopkins and her servant. Miss Hopkins was the daughter of a wealthy East India merchant, Mr Herbert Hopkins, who lived at Tavistock Square. He is still there. My clerk, Mr Danks, found that out. I wonder —'

'Mr Danks is not party to these matters?'

'Certainly not, Mr Dickens — that would hardly be appropriate.' Mr Dalrymple was snappish. 'The Hawke family matters are the concern of the senior members of this office. My clerk knows only that I wished to find information about Mr Hopkins on a legal matter. These things are sometimes necessary. Information is useful.'

Dickens adopted a suitably apologetic expression, but he thought of Joah Danks with his ear to the walls in the street. 'I do beg your pardon, Mr Dalrymple. Please, do go on.'

Mollified, Mr Dalrymple continued, 'I have pursued my own inquiries. Miss Hopkins is now a widow, Mrs Bradbury. She lives with her father in Tavistock Square, number twenty-six. I was going to apprise Mr Case of these facts to see if he would want to pursue the matter.'

'Perhaps I could see her on his behalf?'

Mr Dalrymple thought. 'I see no objection. I am sure that Mr Hopkins would be pleased to see you, Mr Dickens, if you are sure.'

'My very old friend, the Reverend Mr James White, has taken

a great interest in Mr Case, who is a protege of his, you might say. I am in Mr White's debt — a deeply personal matter — and I should like to assist Mr Case on his behalf as well as Mr Case's.'

'Indeed, indeed. I do wish to see the matter settled — it is very unsatisfactory as it stands.'

'Perhaps Mrs Bradbury will be able to tell me something of Miss Hawke's character — what kind of girl she was.'

Mr Dalrymple frowned. He did not see that the girl's character was relevant — the sapphires were the important matter. 'You may find out what happened when the steamboat came into St Katherine's wharf. Find out if Mrs Bradbury knows where Miss Hawke went.'

'I wonder why, Mr Dalrymple. We know that Sapphire Hawke disappeared, but why did she? And did she disappear with someone?'

Mr Dalrymple thought of his daughter, Maud, so doting on her loving father. Mr Dalrymple, though a stern servant of his exacting mistress, the law, and sometimes an overly expectant father to his only son, had a very soft heart where his pretty Maud was concerned. She was eighteen now. He thought of a young man called Simon Clavering and how pretty Maud's eyes strayed to him across the dinner table and how she blushed when he brought her a bouquet. Mr Dalrymple was not entirely fond of the young men who lounged about his drawing room with Alexander. He wasn't sure about Henry Meteyard either — his father a butcher in Limehouse. Maud seemed to like him, too. He thought of more blushes. Maud would not, surely.

'A young man — an elopement, you think? Dear me, I suppose it has happened before. Perhaps she did not care for the life of a nun. Perhaps that is why Sir Gerald washed his hands of her.'

'But the sapphires?'

'Sir Gerald Hawke was unpredictable — perhaps he wished to make amends.'

Dickens could not imagine Sir Gerald Hawke making amends for anything. He'd probably left the jewels to Sapphire to complicate matters, to make life difficult for Meredith Case, an unlikely and unwelcome heir, and difficult for Mr Dalrymple. Hawke would have known his man — Simeon Dalrymple, exact and punctilious. How the old man would have relished the thought of his discomfort. Hawke would have relished the last laugh, too.

Mr Dalrymple was looking at him. 'Quite,' said Dickens, 'I suppose he might.'

'The reason is not pertinent, Mr Dickens. The will assigns the sapphires to Miss Hawke. Property, Mr Dickens, property must go to the rightful heir. A matter of law — the law cannot be trifled with. The papers must be signed and sealed.'

'A valuable property.'

'It is, it is. I will show you the jewels — you will see what is at stake.'

Mr Dalrymple took one of the keys from his watch chain and opened a drawer in his desk from which he took a metal box. Dickens was reminded of Screech and his keys as Dalrymple opened the box with a second key from his chain and removed yet another key which he used to open the safe which was concealed behind a portrait of some long-ago Dalrymple, identifiable by the same domed head and large ears. From the safe he took a wooden box and unlocked it with another small key from the chain. Inside the wooden box was a velvet one. In that were the sapphires, blue stones separated with diamonds. There were earrings to match. They shimmered in the gaslight, ice blue and dazzling white, almost unreal. Worth a great deal of money, he supposed.

'They are very beautiful. A fortune for Miss Hawke.'

'If she is still alive.'

Dickens bade farewell to Mr Dalrymple, who saw him to the door which, Dickens noted, was not fully closed. Joah Danks was perched on his high stool, busy with his pen. Yet there was a slight disturbance in the air, as if someone had moved. Danks had been listening, he was sure.

He went down to Ned Temple's rooms. Jones and Rogers had searched his desk and the inner room.

'Mr Danks was right. He was living here — and he gave Felix Gresham's address,' Jones said by way of greeting.

'Couldn't afford lodgings, I'll bet.'

'Habitual liar, Mr Temple, and that makes me suspicious.'

'Found anything interesting?'

'A lethal-looking paper knife on his desk.' Jones showed the knife, which was fashioned as a dagger.

'No gouts of blood?'

'Perfectly clean, but I'll take it to Doctor Woodhall at the hospital. I'd like him to examine it with regard to the wound in Felix's throat. He can compare the edges of the wound with the blade of this — you never know.'

'He wouldn't leave the murder weapon here, surely.'

'You'd think not, but he could have wiped it clean. There was a case in which the pathologist removed the handle of a seemingly clean knife and found dried blood between the handle and the rivet that held it. Doctor Woodhall could remove this brass handle and its collar.'

'Anything else?'

'Only a fire grate full of ashes. He'd been burning his papers. But there are records of the people he worked for as a pleader or preparing briefs — one of them Mr Henry Meteyard.'

'I wonder what Henry thinks of him.' Dickens and Jones knew Henry Meteyard, a barrister whose father was a butcher in Limehouse. Dickens had known the family when he'd visited his godfather in Limehouse as a boy. Henry Meteyard had helped them in the matter of the murder of the captain of *The Redemption*. Dickens trusted his judgement.

'Not a great deal, I shouldn't think — I shall certainly go to see him. His opinion will be worth something, and he might be able to tell us about any other acquaintance — anywhere Temple might have gone.'

'His clothes are still here,' Rogers said. 'P'raps he is comin' back.'

'Perhaps he's out searching for a red-headed woman called Ruby — she seems to be an old acquaintance. Also, I've found a letter from his mother, who lives at somewhere called Bennett's End, near Wycombe. He could have gone there. I'll send a man by train — plain clothes. No, not you —' Jones laughed; Dickens suddenly seemed to be two feet smaller with a hunched back — 'someone would notice a dwarf.'

'Oh, I don't know — pedlar and his boy — Scrap and I do a very nice line in father and son vagabonds.'

'Someone threw an ale pot at you last time, as I remember.'

'Mistaken identity, yer 'onour. I shall not forget that bruise in a hurry. Alas, Mr Jones, I cannot don my motley for you at present. I am bound for Tavistock Square.'

'Ah, Mr Dalrymple shed some light on your missing heiress?'

'Let us say the dull gleam of a tallow candle.'

# 23: MRS BRADBURY REMEMBERS

No tallow candle lit the home of Mr Herbert Hopkins, the wealthy East India Company merchant. Lights gleamed from the polished windows. Number twenty-six was on the west side of Tavistock Square, a fine, white-stuccoed house with a pillared portico and a smartly painted double front door with a gleaming brass knocker in the shape of a turbaned head with which Dickens knocked. *Open sesame*, he thought — perhaps some *Arabian Nights* magician would sprinkle him with golden water, and he would find the truth.

No magician opened the door, but there was a stately liveried footman as tall and solemn as one of the marble pillars. Dickens handed in his card and asked if Mr Hopkins was at home.

The footman read the card. His powdered head shot up and two eyes gazed at him in wonder. It was as if one of the columns had come to life, its marble iciness turned to human flesh.

'Mr Dickens, sir, it is an honour this — my word —' But no word came. The footman continued to gaze.

'Mr Hopkins?' Dickens gave him a broad smile.

'Oh, sir — of course — Mr Hopkins is not at home, I'm afraid, but I feel sure that Mrs Bradbury — Mr Hopkins's daughter, that is, would — that is — you must come in, sir.'

Dickens stepped into the hall with its black and white floor. A great staircase curled up to the next floor. A chandelier on a long, thick golden chain lit up the white-panelled walls and the pictures on them. The footman took his hat, examined it as if he hardly believed in its reality, took his stick, examined that, placed both reverently on a chair, gazed back at the visitor, said again, 'My word!' and held out his hands. Dickens understood that he was meant to offer his gloves — he would be naked at this rate.

'Mrs Bradbury?'

'Yes, of course, Mr Dickens. My word!'

Dickens grinned at him. 'A pleasure to meet you, Mr…?'

'Mansion, sir — ironic, that — never thought I'd work in one.'

'You do it proud, Mr Mansion.' Dickens held out his hand.

'Never thought I'd shake hands with Charles Dickens.'

'Never thought I'd shake hands with a mansion.'

Mr Mansion grinned back. 'I'll take up your card to Mrs Bradbury. Stand by the fire, Mr Dickens, while you wait — warm yourself, sir.' He picked up his salver, was transformed in that instant to a stately pillar, and made his solemn way up the staircase.

Dickens warmed himself by the fire and stared at the silver candlesticks and the replica of a scimitar mounted in gold with a jewelled handle. *The Arabian Nights again*, he thought. A bit of magic would be handy.


Mrs Bradbury was dressed in lavender with black trimmings and wore a lace widow's cap. She was a plump, rather matronly woman with a good-humoured face and a wide smile. She rose immediately to greet Dickens as he came in. He caught the footman's eye as he turned to leave the room. Mansion gave him a conspiratorial wink.

'Mr Dickens, you are most welcome. I am very sorry that my father is not here to see you — I don't think he was expecting you. I know he would have told me — my late husband was a connection of your Mr Bradbury. I thought, perhaps —'

'No, no, Mrs Bradbury, I had no idea of your connection with my publisher, though I am very glad to know it.'

'He is very kind to send me your *Household Words*. I am rather enjoying your *Child's History of England*. I'm afraid my education was somewhat deficient in history, but you are putting me right, and my daughters, too. But, Mr Dickens, do forgive me, I am not allowing you to tell me how I can be of service to you. Will you sit down?'

Dickens sat opposite his hostess who had given him his opening. 'It is about education, in a way — about your schooldays, and a fellow pupil at the convent in Bruges — Miss Sapphire Hawke.'

'This is most extraordinary. I read about Sir Gerald Hawke's death. I thought about Sapphire Hawke then. I had not thought about her for years — and now you are asking about her.'

Dickens explained about Meredith Case and the sapphires and his visit to Mr Dalrymple. 'He told me that Miss Hawke came to London by boat with you. Do you remember?'

'Oh, I do, Mr Dickens, because it was rather peculiar. Sapphire Hawke disappeared after the ship docked at Saint Katherine's wharf. I was seasick and felt very ill, so it didn't register very much at the time. I just wanted to get home. My maid was much put out. Sapphire said she would try to find our coachman, but she did not come back, and my maid had to go to find it. Mind you, Sapphire Hawke was an odd girl. We were never really friends. I wrote to her at Hawke Court — just to ask, you understand, if she had got home safely. I didn't reproach her or anything, but she never wrote back. I was disappointed, but I forgot it all eventually. Our paths never crossed. I suppose I thought she must have stayed in the country. It was only when I read of Sir Gerald's death that I thought of her again.'

'You have no idea where she went?'

'Well, I don't, I'm afraid. I was so poorly, you see. I suppose I assumed she would go to the Hawke town house — it was on Park Lane, I think. I supposed — if I thought at all — that someone had met her, and she had forgotten about our coach. She had said she was to go to Hawke Court, so it would have made sense to go from the town house. When I didn't hear from her, I did wonder if she had gone back to the convent. We all thought she would become a nun. She was very close to the Mother Superior and she wasn't like the rest of the girls. We were very silly, I suppose, only thinking about getting out of school, the clothes we would have, and the husbands, of course.'

'No, she didn't go back. Mr Dalrymple's son found that out and the Mother Superior is no longer there.'

'Oh, dear — she was very strict, as I remember. Do you mean to say that Sapphire Hawke did not go back to Hawke Court?'

'I do. No one has seen or heard of her since you saw her at Saint Katherine's Wharf.'

'Good gracious — I can hardly believe it. How is it possible that a girl could just disappear? She can't have been kidnapped — or worse — it would have been all over the papers. But why wasn't it, anyway? Surely Sir Gerald Hawke must have looked for her.'

'Apparently not. It seems that everyone thought she had stayed at the convent.'

'But why didn't he? She was his ward. It's mad. But then he was mad, they say. He had a dreadful reputation. Do you think she ran away?'

Dickens thought of Sir Gerald Hawke, eaten up by

corruption, the tales of his mistresses and debauchery. That might well be the reason that Sapphire Hawke had vanished.

'I don't know, Mrs Bradbury, but it is possible. But where would she go? You don't think that Miss Hawke might have arranged to go away with someone?'

'A man? An elopement?' Mrs Bradbury shook her head. 'No, Mr Dickens, it is out of the question. Many of us giggled and speculated about our future, but Sapphire Hawke never did. I really cannot think of anything to help you. A young woman — from a convent — alone in London. It is a terrifying thought.'

'Yes, it is — I hardly dare speak to you of what might have happened.'

'Mother Mary Theresa at the convent thought I was a fool, but I have grown up, Mr Dickens. I have four children, two girls whose lives I cherish, as I was cherished, but I read the papers. I know what some women's lives are. I know about your home for fallen women. Perhaps Sapphire is dead. I wonder — there are many unknown women who are found dead and never claimed, never identified. Think of Waterloo Bridge. There was a case the other day. A poor, desperate girl threw herself into the river.'

'It may be so, Mrs Bradbury. I had not thought of any of these things, and I must investigate. There will be records of such deaths, and we know the date of Sapphire's return to London. In the meantime, is there anything else at all you can remember?'

'Sapphire was clever and bookish. She never talked — oh, wait, I'd forgotten this. She was kind to me when I felt sick, and she did sit with me in the cabin. I remember now. She was very good, holding the bowl and bathing my temples — not a bit squeamish. I doubt I'd have done the same for her. And when I felt a little better, she did talk to me, or rather she did distract me by getting me to talk. I don't suppose she was much interested in my ramblings about young men.'

'She didn't talk about herself?'

'I'm sure I would have asked her about her future plans, but I don't remember that she told me anything about herself or her future plans. I didn't really pay much attention —' she gave Dickens a rueful smile — 'I daresay I was too wrapped up in my own concerns.'

'She didn't mention any friends, any place she might have gone?'

Marianne Bradbury thought. 'I honestly cannot remember, Mr Dickens.' She seemed to be thinking again, looking back to the time when school was over, and she would begin a new, exciting life which would bring her the joy of marriage and children. It was obvious that she had been a happy woman, reflected Dickens, thinking about Sapphire Hawke. What future had she found on the streets of London into which she had disappeared?

'I can only think of the Hawke town house.'

'Mr Dalrymple has not mentioned it, as far as I know, to Mr Case.'

'Perhaps it was sold. Sir Gerald had debts, so it is said. You should ask Mr Dalrymple — he might know what happened to the servants. There might be someone who remembers if Sapphire returned there.'

'I will. I am much obliged to you for your help, Mrs Bradbury.'

'I am sorry I could do no more. It is a very sad story, Mr Dickens. I cannot help wondering if she is dead.'

Dickens walked away, having been shown out by his new friend, Mr Mansion, who had brushed his hat for him, and probably polished his stick. It looked very shiny. He went down into Bedford Place, thinking about Sapphire Hawke, that unhappy, solemn girl in the portrait Meredith Case had seen, who had become a serious, bookish and reserved young woman.

He thought about Sir Gerald Hawke and the young Irish bride who had died of a fall. Sold by an ambitious father in Dublin? Trapped in a marriage to a hideously debauched rake, had she, in a desperate attempt to escape him, flung herself down those stairs? Sapphire Hawke, sent to a convent, finding sanctuary there, had she, too, risked her life rather than go back to Hawke Court?

Sir Gerald Hawke's reputation was enough to explain why. She had been fifteen or so when she'd left for her convent. Hawke had lived in London after the death of the young man, Arthur Sinclair. Had Hawke intended some dissolute crony there as a husband for her?

But where had she gone — an unprotected young woman from a convent in Bruges? Not an elopement — that was clear. Perhaps there had been someone she'd trusted at the town house? Park Lane, Mrs Bradbury had thought. It would be easy enough to find Sir Gerald Hawke's town house, and even if it had been sold, easy enough to find out who lived there now. There might be some servant from Hawke's days who might remember Sapphire Hawke. He could invent some tale — distant cousin, the Reverend Mr Case, now the heir, looking for Miss Hawke — that was true, at any rate. He wouldn't mention the sapphires.

Dickens quickened his pace, hurrying through Russell Square and down into Montague Street, where he slowed down to look at number fifteen. Sergeant Rogers came out. He had been asking Mrs Flax, the landlady, if she knew where Ned Temple had lodged. Mr Jones wondered if he might have returned to his old lodgings or someone might know him there.

'Did she know?' Dickens asked.

'No — and he hadn't lodged at her house at any time.'

'He could be anywhere, Rogers, in any hotel — on a steamer to the continent.'

'That's the trouble, Mr Dickens. Mr Jones has gone to see Mr Meteyard at Lincoln's Inn — see if he knows anything. Should be back by now. You comin' to Bow Street?'

'Yes, I'll come before I go back to the office.'

# 24: TO A HAYSEED

Henry Meteyard had not been able to tell Jones anything more about Ned Temple except that he had not liked him very much, but had employed him occasionally in the past on briefs. Temple was able enough, but Henry had disliked Temple's obvious resentment of the success of others. Henry had met him socially once at Mr Dalrymple's house. Temple had not been a success. Miss Maud Dalrymple had been unimpressed, making her preference for Henry Meteyard quite clear. Not that Henry was interested in Miss Dalrymple, but he had been irritated by Temple's somewhat disparaging reference to Henry's butcher connections in Limehouse. He hadn't employed Temple again.

'Not much help,' Jones observed to Dickens and Rogers.

'No, but it does add to the impression we get of Temple — resentful, envious, bitter, even. Had he the same feelings for Felix Gresham — friends on the surface, but debts mounting and nowhere to turn?'

'Very likely — there is something else. I went to see Doctor Woodhall about Screech's death. He only confirmed what we saw — killed by the blow which cracked his temple bone. There was hair on that poker as well as blood. An effusion of blood in the substance of the brain killed him. He had a particularly thin skull.'

'Manslaughter, then?'

'I should think so. There's more — with regard to Felix Gresham. Doctor Woodhall examined the paper knife — yes, it could have been the same knife, but there was no blood to be found. And he examined the stab wound again — under the microscope this time — and he saw something else: a few very small, sticky pieces which he found to be hayseeds.'

'Killed in the cab?'

'I doubt it — the cabbie would have reported bloodstains. Stables, more likely. Now, we've questioned all the cab drivers around the Casino de Venise — not that we've any proof that either Gresham or Temple were there that night. We've tried the Cyder House, the Coal Hole, the Garrick's Head — all the places Temple mentioned. No one remembers. Why would they, with the number of drunk folk they carry about? I hate to think about the number of stables we'd have to search.'

'What were Gresham and Temple doing in a stable? Neither of them had a horse, as far as we know,' said Rogers.

'Quarrelling — row about money — they dodge into a stable by an inn, say, to continue their row. Temple stabs Gresham, who is drunk — not taking it seriously. Not listening to Temple's woes —'

Jones interrupted, 'Like Screech — not different murders, just different weapons. The same anger prompted both.'

'The cup is bitter to the brim for Temple. He feels a bitter sense of dependence — even of degradation. Think what he said to Henry, Henry Meteyard who has risen high, and his father a butcher. Look at my friend, John Forster, son of a butcher and now editor of *The Examiner* and Thomas Carlyle, a Scottish farmer's boy turned into a famous author — things have been said. Envy's a deadly poison.'

'It all makes sense — but, if it was Temple possessed by a sudden rage, what was he doing with a knife?'

'He might have had two or three knives — the one on his desk, another paper knife, a pen knife for sharpening quills — he could have had one in his pocket by chance. Absent-mindedly put it in his pocket — I find the strangest things in my pockets sometimes.'

'Now you say that, I suppose it could be.'

'What about his mother?' asked Rogers.

'I sent Inspector Grove and Constable Dacres. An hour on the train to Wycombe — a couple of miles to this Bennett's End. Dacres will stay —' Jones looked at his pocket watch — 'Inspector Grove won't be back for a couple of hours at least.'

'Anything else on Screech?'

'No — no robberies nearby — no reports on any of the objects we found.'

'They're all small, Sam, portable — I wonder if they were missed. You know these fine houses, full of little gee-gaws left about. Someone could pick them up one at a time — even from different houses.'

'Very true. Now, Alf, tell Mr Dickens about the bookshop.'

'I called in to ask if they had seen anyone about — you know — about the time Screech was killed. Saw Miss Hamilton — she said she was workin' at her bookbinding. Miss Finch had been at the counter, but she was out. The shop was closed. I told her we were looking for Mr Temple's friend, Miss Ruby Kiss —'

'What did she say to that?'

'Said she did know Ruby — it was when Ruby was in need of help, but she hadn't seen her for weeks. She knew about Lewkner's Lane. She was quite matter o' fact about it — for a lady, I mean. Said she hadn't seen Ned Temple, but she knew he was a friend of Ruby and Felix Gresham.'

'Did you believe her?'

Rogers scratched his thick hair. 'D'you know, Mr Dickens, I did. She looked me straight in the eye. Somethin' about her — I dunno what. Honest, somehow. Serious about things.'

'Well, I trust you, Alf,' Jones said.

'I doubt they'd be protecting Ned Temple from what I heard between him and Miss Finch.'

'They might protect Ruby Kiss from Ned Temple, however. Ruby knew Felix Gresham. Felix Gresham is murdered.'

Dickens looked at Jones. 'What might Ruby Kiss know about Ned Temple?'

# 25: THE CUPS THAT CHEER

Dickens stood at Stanhope Gate, just on Park Lane by Hyde Park. He was looking across to the Crystal Palace, almost ready for the Great Exhibition. The Fairy Palace, people called it, and on this grey morning with drizzle falling like a ghostly curtain before his eyes, it looked as insubstantial as a dream, seeming to shimmer and hover just above the green ground. He wouldn't have been surprised if it had floated away into the misty sky — a cloud-capped palace dissolved into thin air. Yet, all the world's treasures would be displayed there when it opened in May — from railway engines to the Koh-i-Noor diamond, owned by the Queen. One hundred and eighty-six carats, so they said. Not that he particularly wanted to see it, he thought, feeling the rain drip down the back of his neck. Sapphires were his business today. Though he had scant hope that there would be anything. Hawke had sold his house sixteen years ago — there wouldn't be any of his servants in Park Lane now. Hawke had lived in apartments in The Albany until he'd returned to Hawke Court.

Dickens turned to look at Sir Gerald Hawke's former town house opposite Stanhope Gate. He had found it in *The Royal Blue Book*, a compendium of all the noteworthy residents of the town. Dickens was in it — at number one Devonshire Terrace. Not for much longer. The lease was nearly up, and he had to find another house. *Not Park Lane*, he thought. He was choosy about his neighbours. Too many dukes and duchesses hereabouts.

The house was in the possession of a Miss Jane Gauntlett — another heiress. But, obviously, she had come into her inheritance — she must be a single lady of some means to live at number twelve. Her near neighbour was the Duchess of Gloucester and opposite, the Marquess of Stafford, whose carriage was just rolling out of his gates, judging by the coat of arms on its black door. He wouldn't be walking, of course, fat as the old Prince Regent. Dickens, slim as a lath, had walked from Devonshire Terrace, only a mile of his often seventeen miles a day.

His knock was answered by a small, round woman with a rather blue nose to whom he gave his card. She let him in. He was to wait. Her mistress was busy in her library. Mornings were her time for correspondence and writing her papers. She had important work to do for the Temperance Society. Dickens kept a straight face. Somehow, he was not surprised. The woman went to knock on a door leading off the glacial hall. No wonder her nose was blue. He half-expected an icicle to form on his own nose. The place was freezing.

Mrs Blue-nose came out and motioned him to enter. He saw a tall, spare woman of about forty years, dressed in black relieved only by a white starched collar. A rather hideous white cap covered her iron-grey hair. She looked like a female Oliver Cromwell. Old Ironsides. A breastplate and gauntlets would have suited her. She had a long, sallow face and chilly grey eyes which looked at him suspiciously. An iceberg would have been more welcoming. Clearly meeting Charles Dickens had no charms for her. She was not, presumably, a novel reader. He saw a Temperance Movement pamphlet in her hand. There was no fire in the grate and the library was as cold as the hall — colder probably, with Miss Gauntlett in it. There were a large desk and a variety of upright chairs with black leather seats. Miss Gauntlett lived, he gathered, on the total abstinence principle — the abstinence from comfort as well as strong drink.

Her chilly demeanour did not improve when he mentioned Sir Gerald Hawke. She looked at Dickens as if he probably took a daily pint of gin for breakfast and dined every night on turtle and sherry soup. However, he persevered and told his story of the most respectable reverend gentleman who was the unwilling heir to his distant cousin, Sir Gerald, and who was most anxious to seek out any other relations. Legacies, he said vaguely, throwing in Mr Dalrymple of Clement's Inn and the Court of Chancery for good measure — his own credentials were obviously not very impressive.

Miss Gauntlett thawed slightly, enough to ask him his own interest. He took the opportunity to emphasise his friendship with Mr Case and their mutual friendship with the Reverend Mr James White. She inclined her head at White's name. He wrote for various periodicals — she probably wouldn't know that White was also a novelist and poet. Dickens moved swiftly on to explain that the Reverend Mr Case was indisposed so he, Mr Dickens, was acting for his clerical friends.

'I never met Sir Gerald Hawke, I am glad to say. A most dreadful reputation. My father purchased this house. It was sadly neglected. Much restoration work was required.'

*Got it cheap*, thought Dickens. 'It is not about Sir Gerald Hawke that I wish to enquire. I wanted to ask if there were any servants retained from the days of his possession.'

'There may have been. Of course, it is a long time ago and my mother would have dealt with the matter of servants — through her housekeeper, of course.' Miss Gauntlett's narrow nostrils dilated. Mama deal with servants — hardly.

*I know that, you piece of frozen misery*, Dickens wanted to say, but he only asked if her own housekeeper might know of any of the Hawke servants. Miss Gauntlett graciously agreed to ring for her housekeeper. Mr Dickens could ask. He must excuse her. He might wait in the hall. Mrs Pottage would answer the bell. She turned back to her desk. *Oh*, he thought. The conversation — if you could call it that — was over. Her sentences snapped off like shards of icicle.

Mrs Pottage, whose nose seemed to have warmed up, met him in the hall where he explained his purpose.

'You don't mind the kitchen?'

No, he did not — there ought to be a fire, surely. He followed her down a set of stairs to the basement kitchen. She saw him glance at the fire.

'Get yourself warm, Mr Dickens.' She was smiling. 'A nice hot cup of tea — nothing stronger, I'm afraid.'

'The cups that cheer but not inebriate.'

'So Miss Gauntlett says — often.'

'William Cowper said it first.' He saw her blank look. 'Poet.'

'Don't know him, but I know who you are, sir. I do a bit of reading —' she smiled — 'down here when I've finished the latest tract against the evils of drink.'

'I've brandy in my flask — medicinal purposes, of course. I think I feel a chill coming on.'

Mrs Pottage laughed. 'Don't you dare, sir. She'd smell it from the library. Lord, sir, we'd be out on the street in two seconds. Now, sit you down.'

He sat by the fire while Mrs Pottage poured the tea from a homely brown pot and buttered him a scone.

'She's not a bad old stick — not so old, really — I keep to the rules upstairs, but down here, well, she's not a great interest in kitchen matters. She'd have cold food only if I didn't serve up some warming dishes. She'll take a thin soup and a little white chicken meat. Scones, I keep for the kitchen, and visitors, of course. Miss Gauntlett's not one for sweet things.

Lonely soul, really. Looked after her father then — well, too late. Took up her cause.'

A shrewd body, Mrs Pottage, and as warm as her name. 'I'm here about Sir Gerald Hawke.'

'Dead, I believe. Saw it in the newspaper. I never met him. It was before my time. Bad lot, they say.'

'He was not a good man. His property goes to a clergyman.' Dickens told his story again and asked if she had any knowledge of any of Hawke's servants.

'There was a parlour maid. I started in the kitchen — and that was sixteen years ago. Her name was Josephine — I remember because I was only a bit of a cook in training and she seemed so high, having worked for Sir Gerald. We all thought it grand to work for a title — she'd been maid to Lady Julia Hawke, though she'd died. Josephine used to tell how she'd found Lady Julia's body all crushed at the bottom of the stairs at Hawke Court. Don't know if it was true, but it made an impression on me. Mr and Mrs Gauntlett seemed very ordinary. Mrs Gauntlett was a very plain lady — so was her own maid, for that matter.'

'What happened to Josephine?'

'I think she went home to Hawkstone village to get married — that was the talk. A surprise, it was. She was thirty if she was a day, but a fine-looking woman, nevertheless.'

'What was her other name?'

'Let me think — the family used our second names. There was Harris, and Polly Thompson, and Mrs Batty, the cook, and Josephine, Josephine — P — Parker — that was it. Parker.' Mrs Pottage looked at him in triumph.

'You have a good memory, Mrs Pottage, and this scone is excellent — Miss Gauntlett is missing a treat.'

Dickens finished his tea, brushed the crumbs from his coat

and Mrs Pottage showed him to the front door. The library door was still closed. *Busy fulminating against the bottle*, he thought.

Outside, on Park Lane, Dickens found a cab to take him to Wellington Street — his mornings were for work — and for a better cause than temperance. He was almost tempted to throw down his own gauntlet, rush to his office, and pen an indignant piece on the real causes of intemperance: the filth and degradation of too many hopeless lives. Like Old Sal — no comfort but the bottle. However, while he had been talking to Mrs Pottage about Josephine Parker, he had had an idea. He would have to go down to Hawke Court, and a rather ingenious scheme was forming in his head. He knocked on the roof of the cab. The cabman's face appeared like a red moon at the trapdoor in the roof — certainly not a temperance man.

'Changed my mind,' Dickens told him. 'Clement's Lane, if you please.'

# 26: THE CHILL OF AN ICY FINGER

Dickens waited to cross the road to enter the archway of Clement's Inn, but he darted back, seeing Joah Danks slinking out, and slipped into a shop doorway from where he watched that creeping young man sidle along Clement's Lane towards Lincoln's Inn.

When Danks had vanished, Dickens made his way into Mr Dalrymple's building where he met Alexander Dalrymple, who had just come down the stairs. Alexander Dalrymple, a bright-faced young blade with eyes like his father's, only brighter, greeted Dickens with hearty good cheer.

'Good morning, Mr Dickens, come to see father?'

'I have.'

'He's there. No Danks, though — bit of a blight on the place sometimes, I think. Still, you'll find the pa at his tomes — not that he needs to read it all up. Has it all at his fingertips. A formidable memory, he has — unlike mine. Dashed serious business, the law — not to be laughed at.'

'No, indeed.'

'Can't help it, though. Lord, Mr Dickens, Dodson and Fogg — Fogg and his vegetable diet — very droll, sir. Fog is just what I'm in when I'm readin' all the cases.'

Dickens wished he'd keep his voice down. Mr Dalrymple would hardly like to be reminded of Mr Dickens's lawyers. That would not advance the scheme he was going to suggest. 'I'm glad you enjoyed them. Not all lawyers do.' He glanced up the staircase.

'No, indeed, but don't worry. He reads your books — on the quiet. I've heard him chuckling in his study at home. He's not as austere as you think him, and you don't like to let him down.' Alexander Dalrymple glanced at Ned Temple's closed door and did lower his voice to ask if anything had been heard.

'Nothing, I'm afraid. You have no ideas, I suppose?'

'Superintendent Jones fixed me with his gimlet eye. I felt —'

'Peppered, salted, and grilled on a gridiron.' Sam Jones could be very formidable when he chose.

Alexander laughed. 'That's about it, Mr Dickens.'

'Guilty conscience?'

'No, no, only — well, the governor don't care much for loose living, so I couldn't say much while he was listening.'

'You'd better tell me.'

Alexander blushed. 'It's not much — just — I lent Ned money. He didn't pay me back, of course, but then a fellow knows that, I suppose. I thought he was going to ask me again on the day I met him in the hall, but I was on my way to Bruges. There was a fellow just coming in. Thought he might have a client, but perhaps not — pity for Ned.'

'Did you go out and about with him?'

'A few times, but they were out of my league, Ned Temple and Felix Gresham. You know how a fellow gets too much claret and champagne in him. I woke up a few times with a very sore head, and my pockets were empty — too many cards. They were very fond of cards, those two.'

'You didn't speak of Temple's debts to your father?'

'Not a thing a fellow does, Mr Dickens — you know that. Honour and so forth.'

'You withdrew the hem of your garment, so to speak.'

Alexander grinned. 'The governor has a way with him. Nothing said — just a look — pained, you know, and irritable in the office next day.'

'Did you know Ruby Kiss?'

'I met her — a good sort. She and Felix Gresham were — close. She sort of mothered him. It wouldn't do, of course.'

'You know the Superintendent is looking for her — she's missing. According to Mr Danks, she came here. She was with Ned Temple.'

'So my father said — I was very glad I wasn't in the room at the time.'

'You've no idea where she might be?'

'I told Superintendent Jones about the places I'd been with them — the Casino and so on — he gave me a look, too. Stern, you know. I tried to remember, but with the pa listening, I'm afraid I was rather muddled.'

'Casino de Venise and so on — anywhere else you recall?'

'There was a place I went to. Other than the clubs, I mean. We — that is — Ned, Felix and I — went to a place called Lantern Yard, somewhere off Whetstone Place. I'm not quite sure where. Horrible labyrinth of alleys — stinking, and black as your hat. Gresham liked that sort of thing — adventurous type, he was, enjoyed a whiff of danger … Giff's Court, I think the name was — the place where Ruby lived. There was Ruby and another girl — I don't know who, but I didn't actually go into the court. Peeled off before we went in. Spare part, I suppose.'

'I'll tell Mr Jones. It might be useful. Now, I need to speak to your father, so I'll bid you farewell.'

Dickens made to go up the stairs, but stopped suddenly. Lantern Yard. He felt a tingle at the back of his neck as if an icy finger had touched him there. A sudden rush of fear. Sam ought to know about this. The Hawke sapphires could wait. They'd lain untouched at Hawke Court for years and Mr Dalrymple had them safely under lock and key.

He turned and went across the quiet garden. The man in the long grey coat and grey hat stood contemplating the statue of the black boy in his circle of rusty iron railings. He merely nodded as Dickens sped by. Master Justice Silence, then. *I'm right, though*, Dickens said to himself, *it is urgent*. At the archway, he turned to look back. The stranger had gone. The light had thickened in the garden. *Ghosts*, he thought. *A girl called Patience Brooke. Ruby Kiss.*

# 27: MONEY TALKS

At an anonymous chop house somewhere near Lincoln's Inn, George Stoneridge was waiting for Joah Danks. Joah Danks was a catch — a lovely tickled trout. George Stoneridge had fished in a lot of ponds — and stews — in his time.

George had first followed Joah Danks to The Load of Mischief, engaged him in conversation, bought him a few drinks, and mentioned his need for a clever lawyer. Over a confidential pie and more drinks, Joah Danks had thawed nicely. George was a good listener, and the money did the talking. Mr Joah Danks, it seemed, had no particular loyalty to Mr Dalrymple, and a particular antipathy to Mr Alexander Dalrymple who had gone to Bruges. George had agreed that it was hard for a man to make his way without family connections. Joah Danks should certainly look about him. It had been easy enough. George had only asked for information — so far. He did not want to frighten off his spy, and Danks was quite prepared to eavesdrop and report back for his fee.

Joah Danks came in. George ordered the chops — his treat, of course, and whatever Mr Danks would care to drink. Champagne if he wanted. Right, brandy and warm, it would be — straightaway. George went to the bar while Joah Danks settled himself in, brought back the drinks and waited while Joah took a swig.

'What news?'

'The parson's up in Westmorland, Mr Stoneridge. Seems this Miss Hawke might have come from there, but Case didn't find her. A friend of his, Mr Dickens, brought a letter.'

*So*, thought George, *not in Bruges and not in Westmorland. Dead then, surely.* 'Any other useful snippets?'

'Someone called Hopkins. Old Dalrymple asked me to find out about him — East India man lives in Tavistock Square. I thought Dalrymple had somethin' on him, but white as the driven, it seems. Then I hear the name when he's talkin' to Mr Dickens, and there was mention of a woman. Bradbury's the name — Mr Dickens was to go and see her. Seems to be actin' for Case. I wondered if she could be the lady — married by now.'

'Could be. Try to find out.'

'I will — and now, Mr Stoneridge, there's sapphires — seen 'em. Belong to the girl. Old Dalrymple took 'em from the safe, showed 'em to Mr Dickens —' Joah's pale face sweated in the gaslight and the black eyes gleamed yellow for a moment — 'You didn't say about them. Worth a deal, I should think, if the girl's dead.'

Danks was brighter than he looked, George thought. He had told him that he had been cheated out of money from the Hawke estate. He had been saving the sapphires until he knew that Sapphire Hawke was dead. Still, no matter.

'Sharp, ain't you, Mr Danks, but I like that. Think about it. Why should I show all my cards? Had to be sure I could trust you.'

'Deal o' money, Mr Stoneridge.'

George laughed. 'It will be if we —' he chose the "we" carefully — 'get our hands on them, but patience, sir, patience. I see it this way: let's say that Miss Hawke is dead; you say that the parson don't want the jewels; the jewels go missing. Who cares?'

'Old Dalrymple will, an' what about me as chief suspect? Dangerous, that.'

'But you won't be around to answer him because, Joah, my

lad, you'll be a wealthy man. Ever been to Paris?'

Joah's eyes widened. 'Paris — in France?'

'Where else? Lie low there, Danks, taste the delights of the mamselles, and come back when it's all forgotten.'

Joah wasn't entirely a fool. 'An' where'll you be, George?'

George didn't blink, even at the use of his forename by this little rat-faced creature. 'Meet you in Paris?'

'All right, but I'll need something on account. I'm takin' all the risks just now.'

*Little you know*, thought George. 'Naturally. I won't keep you short, and I said I'd trust you. Works both ways, you know, and as I say, let's not rush at the gems. Play the long game, Joah, and we'll do all right. Find the lady, eh?'

He took three cards from his pocket. 'Go on, have a go.' Joah couldn't find the lady, but George did. He put the cards away. 'I'll show you the trick of it — when we know each other better — just you remember: them as don't play, don't win.'

Joah's eyes were dazzled. George's hand went to his pocket again, jingled the coins there, and thought of the young man he'd seen at Hawke Court, the young man who had stayed at the Hawke Arms. 'No one called Dale mentioned — Frederick Dale?'

'Didn't hear. Who's he?'

'Just someone I heard about — not important now.'

'There's another thing — Mr Dickens was at Dalrymple's with a policeman — from Bow Street.'

'Dalrymple fiddling the books?'

'They were lookin' for a lawyer named Temple — Ned Temple. Seems he's gone missin'.'

'What do they want him for?' George betrayed nothing — kept his poker face, though he knew the name well enough.

Joah Danks licked his lips. 'Murder.'

'You don't say.'

'Well, not exactly, but remember that murder case, man called Felix Gresham murdered near a bookshop?'

'I read about it. I was away in the country at the time.'

'Temple was a friend of this Gresham's an' the policeman wanted to search his rooms — rents 'em from Dalrymple — makes you think.'

'What were they looking for?'

'Papers — bills, I'll bet. Temple's in debt — given up his lodgings an' sleepin' in his rooms. Told the policeman that.'

'Not a friend of yours, Mr Temple?'

'Temple thinks himself quite above me, but I'd got some juicy information — made Dalrymple sit up. I can tell you.'

'Always useful to have a bit of information on a man, Joah, my boy. Tell me more.' So, it was, he thought. He filled Joah's glass and took a good swig from his own.

'Saw 'em,' Danks repeated. 'Temple and his dolly-mop.'

'Not a crime, is it? Bet you've been seen with a fancy girl a time or two.'

'Course I have, but I knew Dalrymple wouldn't like it. Anyhow, that's not the point — I knew her name an' so did that policeman. She meant somethin', I could tell.'

'Very observant, Joah, no flies on you — so what's the name?'

'Ruby Kiss — drunk, she was. Asked Temple if he could get me a girl like that. Turned shirty — well, he's in it now. Police'll be lookin' for that girl — bet she can tell a tale or two about Ned Temple.'

'You did your duty, Joah. I mean, suppose Ned Temple was involved in the death of — what was his name?'

'Felix Gresham.'

'Ought not to get away with it, and Joah, my lad, think of how it'll look for you. Honest Joah Danks, ready to do what's right. You might remember a few more snippets about Ned Temple's doings — if you think hard enough.'

Joah Danks's eyes gleamed again. He understood very well how it might look, and when the sapphires vanished, who would suspect honest Joah Danks? He might well remember seein' Ned Temple in Dalrymple's room.

'What do you want me to do next?'

'Keep your ears open and your eyes peeled — I want to know if Miss Sapphire Hawke turns up. If she does, then we'll have to act —'

'Take 'em, you mean?'

'You know where they are — keys?'

'There's a safe, o' course. Old Dalrymple keeps them on his watch chain.'

'He might lose them, I daresay — have a fall in the street. Terrible number of pick-pockets about.'

Joah Danks looked doubtful suddenly. He thought of Old Dalrymple showing the sapphires to Mr Dickens. 'This Mr Dickens…'

'Another lawyer, is he?'

'No, that's why I'm a bit worried about him.'

'Friend of the parson's?'

'More than that. He's Charles Dickens.' George looked blank. Joah Danks couldn't help smiling — got one over Mr Stoneridge. 'The writer — all them books an' he has a magazine. Big people in this, Mr Stoneridge — very big. That policeman was a Superintendent from Bow Street.'

'Who suspects Mr Temple of some very bad things. It's murder the policeman's after, and your Mr Dickens — well, suppose he does the hard work for us and finds the lady, all the better. Keep your eye on him if he goes back to Clement's Inn — tell him how much you like his books. Big men can take any amount of flattery.'

'Haven't read any of 'em.'

'Skim through one — pick a bit and tell him how good his prose is.'

'I'll need somethin' on account, George — for expenses. Might have to buy a book.'

'So you will, my boy, so you will.' George reached for the sovereigns in his pocket. He looked at Joah, whose thin lips were folded tightly. Two, then, this time, but he'd have to watch Danks. He'd get greedy.

'Meet you at The Ship in Gate Street day after tomorrow. I'll pay the bill.'

Joah Danks pocketed his sovereigns and finished the last of the brandy. A man could enjoy himself with gold in his pocket.

# 28: A LAWYER'S QUILL

Dickens hurried into Bow Street. He had almost run all the way. He knocked on Sam's door, and went straight in.

'In a hurry?' asked Jones.

'I've just found out where Ruby Kiss might be — from Alexander Dalrymple.'

'He didn't say before.'

'He didn't remember until I asked him.'

'Ah, mesmerised him, did you?'

'No — I'm serious, Sam. We should get there as fast as we can.'

'Where?'

'Somewhere off Lantern Yard — that's why —'

Jones saw the memory in Dickens's eyes. He stood up. 'Patience Brooke — where we found — right, let's get up there.' He looked at Rogers, saw that he remembered, and said, 'Alf, you, too — get Feak, or one of the others.'

Lantern Yard was to be found at the end of the crooked lane which twisted out of Whetstone Place. The lane was a jumble of ancient, crumbling houses, the upper storeys looming over, creating a dark tunnel. There was a gaslight at the corner and another about halfway down which flickered on and off, casting a sickly light on the gaunt faces in the crowded street where men lounged against doorways, women sat on steps, and children played in the gutters, heedless of the mud.

They passed through the raucous crowds spilling out of an inn, and turned in to Lantern Yard, which looked very much the same as when they had last seen it. There were several exits from the yard. Dickens remembered only too well the alley into which he had stumbled after Constable Feak, and where he had seen a most terrible thing. He still did not know if the apparition that had leaped at him was ghost or devil, an almost naked thing, crying 'I am Legion' then vanishing. Feak went that way — it had been a dead end, Dickens remembered, like the entrance to a tomb. He didn't fancy venturing down there again. Feak held up his bull's-eye lantern to see if there were a sign for Giff's Court. He came back, shaking his head.

They tried another passage, even narrower. Rogers went first with his lamp, which showed them the greasy walls and running sewer down the middle. Jones came last with his own lamp. Their shadows rose and fell in the flickering light, shrugging their deformed shoulders and dipping their freakish heads. Their tall hats became chimneys, and their coats became rags. At the end of this tunnel, they came to Giff's Court, a ragged huddle of three small houses and broken-down sheds, smelling of sewage and coal, cabbage and stale fish. Rogers went down the court to have a look at the first house. There was a light showing through the ragged sacking which served as curtains. He heard a child cry and went to the second house. The door was open. He stepped in. A woman in a dirty nightgown was putting a frying pan on the bars over a small fire.

He backed out quietly and tip-toed past a tumbledown collection of sheds to the last house, which was in darkness. He went back to Dickens and Jones. 'Kiddie yowling in the first house, woman cooking in the second, third's all quiet.' Whoever Giff was, he wasn't there.

'Charles, you go and ask at that second house. She doesn't need to see the police.'

Dickens went and knocked at the door. He could smell fish.

The woman came and he asked for Ruby Kiss.

'Customer, are yer? Well, she ain't at 'ome, Mister, an' I'm off duty jest now, unless yer wants ter share a nice kipper first.'

'No, thank you.'

'Suit yerself — but I'm tellin' yer, there's no greens next door.'

He heard her laughing as he went away. The door closed. Jones and Rogers came to meet him. 'Bit of a comedian, was she?' asked Jones.

'Let's just say that more than fish was on offer — I meet some very ugly women in your company, Mr Jones. Ruby Kiss lives at the last house, but, according to my new sweetheart, she ain't at 'ome.'

'Let's have a look.'

They tried the front door, but it was locked. There was a very narrow passage between the house and the blind wall that enclosed the court. They went down to see if they could find an entrance at the back. There was a broken-down door into a filthy yard littered with bits of old iron and wooden crates and planks, and against the back wall of the house, a rough sink on a pile of bricks stood under a tap. From under the bricks, a rat scuttled.

'Grim, ain't it?' Rogers said, shining his bull's-eye lamp round the walls.

Jones looked round the yard. 'Maybe Ruby didn't think she'd be here for too long. Perhaps she's gone for good — with her gent. Feak, stay here and keep an eye out.'

The back door to the house was easy to open and led into a tiny scullery where they could see in their lamp lights a little fireplace where an iron pan stood on a grating. There were some pots stacked on a shelf next to a cheap enamel candlestick in which a tallow candle had been stuck. There was an open door through which they went into another little room, sparsely furnished, but clean. Dickens noticed a vase of artificial flowers on a deal table and two old brass candlesticks which somebody had polished; here the candles were wax, not tallow. There was an old sofa, draped with a shawl to cover the holes, and there had been a fire in the grate.

'She probably entertained some of her customers here,' whispered Rogers.

It was pitiable, thought Dickens. Perhaps in the firelight it had looked cosy — Ruby had tried to make some sort of home. A home of sorts, Bella Screech had said. Ruby had her dreams, too. Maybe they had come true.

But there was no one here now. There was not a sound. Jones looked up the rickety staircase, thinking to try upstairs, when they heard voices out in the court. They stood still. Then a door slammed somewhere. They waited until it was quiet again. Rogers moved to the front door which, as in the other house, led straight into the room. Jones and Dickens went upstairs in the flickering light, their shadows going before them.

There was only one room. Jones tapped on the door, but there was no reply. He looked at Dickens, who felt that icy finger on his neck again. The silence seemed to weigh on him. There was a kind of finality about it, as though something had ended here. And, horribly, he thought he could smell the odour of corruption.

'You smell it?' Jones asked.

Dickens nodded. 'Can we get in?'

Jones looked at the gap between the door and its jamb. 'It's on the latch.'

He pressed the metal latch. The noise seemed as loud as a gunshot in the silence. They waited. Jones pushed open the door and raised his lamp. Shadows shifted, as though something was departing. Dickens saw that there was someone on the bed. Jones went in and Dickens followed.

They saw the red curls first — Ruby Kiss, of whom everyone spoke so fondly, even the barman at the Casino de Venise, was absent, vanished with those shadows. She would never laugh at the musical contortionist again. She would never see the lights and the dancers again. Her eyes were dulled now, sightless, all her dreams gone. Then they saw the blood on her chest.

One arm had dropped from the bed, and Dickens saw a knife on the floor as if it had fallen from the dead hand. He looked again at the dead girl and the white breast where the blood congealed like a black flower. 'Suicide?'

'I don't think so. Look how her bodice is unbuttoned and her breasts exposed.' Jones lifted the sheet that was pulled up to Ruby's waist. She was naked. He covered her again quickly, but he had seen the greenish skin on her abdomen, and both he and Dickens smelt the odour of corruption, stronger now. He noted the burnt-out stubs of candles in their sticks on the bedside table. He saw Ruby's skirts tossed to the floor before she had got into bed. 'She was with someone. Someone did this.'

Dickens was bending down. 'Look.' He held out a feather quill, sharpened at the end, which was stained with ink. A quill pen.

'Ned Temple found her?' Jones touched the hand that lay on the sheet — flaccid and cold. Rigor mortis had passed.

The curtains were closed, but Dickens felt a draught. He opened them a crack and saw that the window was open. Peeping out, he saw that below there was a roof of some kind which abutted a wall.

'He could have got out this way, Sam.'

Jones came to look. 'Easy enough to jump.' He leaned out and saw that the roof abutted the wall which separated two yards. 'I'll bet he went into the next yard and away down the alley behind that. Not that it matters much — I think she has been dead for a couple of days. There are the first signs of putrefaction and that smell — and rigor has passed. I'll have to get confirmation from the doctor. I'll need him to come here.'

'Two days since she was at the Casino de Venise.'

'Where Ned Temple was seen by Phoebe Green.'

'The captain was seen with her —' Dickens reminded Jones — 'a chancy sort of character.'

'Yes, that's a consideration, but Temple lied about her, and he might have killed the other two. You painted a most vivid picture: "The cup is bitter to the brim".'

'And he's missing.'

Jones went over to the window and opened the curtains so that he could see into the yard and the one next door. 'I'll get Feak and Rogers to have a look in the alley — see if we can get the mortuary van near. I want to take her out the back way, then Rogers can get Doctor Woodhall or his assistant from the hospital.'

Jones left his lamp and went out. Dickens could hear their voices downstairs. He went to look out of the window. In the fading light, he could see the beam of a bull's-eye lantern travelling across the yard, up and down the walls.

He turned back to the room. Ruby Kiss was hidden by the sheet — he didn't look again, but he contemplated the feather quill in his hand. How had it come to be by the bed? What on earth was Ned Temple doing with a quill pen? There was no ink or paper to be seen — in any case, what could he be writing? Hardly a confession. He could have had a quill pen in his pocket — just as he might have had a knife to cut his quills with. Perhaps, as he had thought before, Temple was the kind of man who absently bundled things into his pockets. He thought of a poet he knew, with a quill pen tucked behind his ear at a fashionable party and a bundle of papers in his pocket.

Perhaps Ned Temple's quill had simply dropped out of his pocket as he had... The horrible scene leapt into Dickens's mind. The half-naked girl, laughing perhaps, a bit inebriated, waiting for her lover to undress. The man taking off his coat, his knife already in his hand, laughing, too, going to the bed, kneeling, stopping her mouth with his other hand, pushing her down. Not laughing now. Ruby's eyes opening, very wide and puzzled, seeing the knife, understanding, and then the terror. The knife plunging in. The blood spurting out.

The murderer leaps back, stands to get his breath, puts the knife in Ruby's hand, picks up his coat. The feather drops, but he doesn't see it, for he hears voices outside or someone knocking at the door, someone shouting for Ruby. Then he's gone, leaping from the window onto that roof and into the yard. He vanishes into the night.

The candles burn down, inch by slow inch, the wax winding its shrouds round the candlesticks. Corpse lights. Then the night gets deeper, darker, and Ruby Kiss sleeps on in her cold sleep.

Dickens saw it all, but he did not see the face of the murderer, for in his reverie, the man was turned to his victim. Even when he was putting on his coat, his back was turned. The coat was — say, on the chair by the door. So why was the feather next to the bed?

Of course, he might not have taken off his coat. Or just put it on the bed. Did it matter? The quill was here, and it implicated Temple.

Jones came back to say that Rogers had gone for Doctor Woodhall. They would have to bring a small cart up the alley to the yard.

Dickens told him his thoughts about what had happened. 'But I wonder why the feather was by the bed.'

'She was in Temple's rooms, according to Joah Danks — and why would he lie? She could have picked it up then, I suppose —'

'Feathers in her hair.'

'So she has.'

They went to look. Dickens saw a peacock feather, what looked like a crow's feather, and that of a seagull, along with some dyed feathers of the kind that Phoebe Green had worn. Perhaps they were her trophies — something she'd laughed about with her lovers. He imagined her laughing as she plucked a quill from Ned Temple's desk and stuck it in her hair. She'd have liked the joke, he thought, and she didn't deserve this end in this shabby house in its dank court, off that crowded lane.

# 29: BODY OF EVIDENCE

Doctor Woodhall, slight and dark, with intense brown eyes and a short beard, black against his white skin, appeared at the doorway, greeted Dickens and Jones, took off his gloves, and went over to look at the body. Rogers came in with a small bowl of water. Jones followed them to the bed with his lamp.

Doctor Woodhall lifted the sheet, looked carefully for a few seconds, sniffed and rolled the sheet back up to Ruby's waist. He examined the back of her head and touched the joints of her fingers. He took out a magnifying glass and scrutinised her left hand, turning it palm up and then looking at the back of her hand again. He dipped a fine piece of cotton in the bowl that Rogers held and examined the place on her chest where the blood had congealed, touching it lightly with the cotton. Dickens saw the blood bloom on the white. The doctor took her right hand to look at that. Finally, he took the knife from Ruby's hand to examine it under his glass.

He looked up. 'I should think she has been dead for two days at least. There are the first signs of putrefaction in the greenish skin discolouration on the lower right abdomen. You saw that, Mr Jones?'

'I did. The smell also.'

'The discolouration of the skin occurs on the second or third day after death. There are signs, too, on the back of the neck. The congealed blood is thick round the heart region — a single stab wound. The blood on the knife is in a partly congealed state, which makes me doubt if it is the murder weapon. You have seen such wounds, Mr Jones, and the knives that make them. A single thrust in and the knife immediately withdrawn would leave only a film of blood which when dry gives to the surface a yellowish-brown colour. When the knife is plunged in so rapidly, the vessels are compressed, so that bleeding takes place only after the knife is withdrawn.'

'It can't be suicide?'

'No, Mr Jones, I do not think so. The congealed blood on the knife in her hand is telling — the murderer may have thought to give the impression of suicide by wiping the knife in her blood.'

'Leaving too much blood on the knife.'

'Exactly. Moreover, you saw me examine her left hand. There is dried blood on the top of the hand and there are marks of fingers having pressed down — finger marks pointing upwards. I do not think she could have done that herself, even immediately after exsanguination. Her right hand would have dropped straight away off the bed as she died. However, I shall have to look closely at the size of the blade and the size and shape of the wound to confirm that this knife did not kill her. I should not like to swear now. There are some healed cut marks on her hands — too old to have any bearing on what happened here.'

'May I ask you to compare the knife wound that killed Felix Gresham with this one? And with the paper knife I sent you.'

'The two cases are connected?'

'I believe so.'

'If you will come tomorrow morning, I will give you more information. Now, as you suggested, we have brought a small cart which is waiting in the alley. Perhaps you might assist.'

Doctor Woodhall wrapped the sheet round Ruby Kiss. Jones laid his greatcoat over her so that she might not be seen. "Deuced dull coat," Dickens had once joked. He hadn't thought it would be a shroud.

Jones lifted her easily. Rogers went to the door with his lamp. Doctor Woodhall followed.

Dickens smelt the bitter taint of putrefaction as Jones passed him. Ruby Kiss was taken away: *having escaped the corruption that is in the world through lust*. Nothing could harm her now.

Dickens closed the door on the dark room.

At Bow Street, Jones provided two glasses of brandy and warm water. *Truly medicinal purposes this time*, Dickens thought, taking a welcome mouthful.

'Is it midnight?' he asked.

'I know what you mean — it seems hours since we walked down that lane.'

'Murder, then.'

'I'm sure, even though Doctor Woodhall needs to do his post-mortem. We have a likely suspect.'

'Alexander Dalrymple went to Bruges — it's easy enough. I wonder —'

'Yes, he could be anywhere. I'm thinking that he went to Screech, killed him because Screech wouldn't budge over money, debts, bills, whatever it was. Having done so, he placed himself under suspicion — he'd be very afraid that Screech kept records.'

'He did. In all Screech's papers, is there something about that five-hundred pounds?'

'Could be — that's fraud on a large scale. We're still looking. There was nothing in that cellar, by the way, except more junk.'

'No corpses?'

'Several wash tubs with what looked like dirty laundry in them and a couple of old mangles.'

'Screech probably tortured his victims down there.'

'He certainly didn't do any washing. But Ruby — did she

become more of a danger to Temple? Did she know something about Felix Gresham's murder? She was very thick with both of them.'

'Ruby left the casino with her gent, though — the captain. Old Sal said he had a temper. Makes you wonder.'

Jones thought about three murders: a stabbing in a stable; a body moved; an old man's head smashed in; and a girl killed in her bed — two stabbings. 'But Screech — I think you're right about a quarrel, about an act committed in rage and desperation. Felix Gresham — another quarrel. But why move the body? Why move it to a public place?'

'They were seen at the stable? It was an inn they knew and were known at — they were drinking there that night — dangerous, that.'

'But why the bookshop?'

'Perhaps he thought to implicate Miss Hamilton — or, more likely, Bella Screech. He knew all about her and Felix Gresham. Perhaps he realised that the boy must be Gresham's.'

'That does make sense — but he's a fool like most of them. Murderers always think they've been clever. Just that one death — it will make all right again. Then some other problem ensues. In the case of Screech, though, he didn't mean to do it.'

'Blind and wild impulse — it's a kind of madness —' Dickens thought about the murderer — 'but it changes him, though he does not know it. Now, he is a wild beast. His own survival is his one idea. He thinks only of what he shall gain by the next murder — not of being caught. He has no balance for the consequences of what he will do.'

'He had no thought of Ruby Kiss. She was just a potential danger. We understand the possible motive, but let's think about the circumstances.'

'She trusted the person. She let him in or came in with him.'

'Ned Temple — he could have followed her from the Casino. Her gent had somewhere to be — his regiment, maybe. As I imagine it, she goes upstairs with Temple — what?'

Dickens was thinking. 'Ned Temple — he wasn't a customer; he was an old friend — yes, she'd had relations with him, but why would she want —'

'And he had no money — what did he offer her for her services?'

'He could have pretended, but somehow, I can't envisage Ruby — but then, we didn't know her.'

'We know she was good-natured, generous, liked a good time. Perhaps they had a few drinks and one thing led to another.'

'That quill — perhaps she took it, then — from his pocket, let's say. They fooled around a bit downstairs. She took the quill, stuck it in her hair as a joke and upstairs they went. I suppose it could have happened that way. And it fell out during Temple's attack on her.'

'I wonder if Joah Danks remembers a quill pen in her hair on the night he helped her up. If he does, then there should have been two if we believe it was Ned Temple who dropped one in her room.'

'There was that crow quill, too. They're used for pens, but I didn't notice if it was sharpened — perhaps she made a habit of picking up quills from all her customers.'

'The quill pen was there on the floor — it might have been dropped by Temple; it might have been in her hair already, but for now, it's all we have. If Doctor Woodhall thinks that the two stab wounds were made by the same knife, that might tell against Temple, too, but until we find him and he confesses, we won't know for sure. And where to find him, I don't know.

He is not at his mother's. Inspector Grove came back with that news. Stemp's keeping watch at Clement's Inn. That's about all I can do tonight.'

'Are you walking home?'

'I am. I've had enough of murder for today. The night inspector knows where to find me.'

'I'll walk with you.'

On the way up to Norfolk Street, Dickens told Jones all about his meetings with Mrs Bradbury and Miss Gauntlett. 'The former a pretty widow; the latter, cold as charity — a disciple of the Temperance Movement. Mrs Bradbury gave me the idea of the Hawke town house and thither I went to find myself touching hands with a glacier.'

'What are you going to do next? Try to find this Josephine Parker you mentioned?'

'I need to speak to Mr Dalrymple again, and I've an idea that I might take the train to Hawke Court.'

'There's something you can do for me before you go.'

'They also serve who only stand and wait, as the poet Milton said — why, I can't recall.'

'You? Standing! Waiting! Steam engine, Rogers says.'

Dickens laughed. 'Never off the rails, that's me. What do you want me to do?'

'Go and get your poetry book.'

'Ah.'

'I shall send Rogers first to tell them about Ruby Kiss. Rogers is to ask if they have any idea of any family we could contact — anyone who might bury her. He is to ask about Mr Temple, who mentioned the bookshop when I first spoke to him, and whom we wish to find. If they have any information about either Ruby or Mr Temple, they must come to see me at Bow Street. The Superintendent is in charge.'

'And very formidable, too. What am I to do — apart from admiring the bookbinding?'

'Inveigle your way into their kitchen for a cup of tea and a hot scone — that's your forte, I believe. I don't know — just get 'em to talk.'

'I could pursue my idea of the piece for *Household Words* — I might get into the binding workshop.'

'You might be able to raise the subject of Temple.'

'Do I mention Ruby?'

'Only if the moment arises. I'll leave that to your discretion.'

'Which is the better part of valour — I am your man for discretion, if not valour.'

# 30: DELIVERED BY HAND

*Iacchimo Guiccolo, who stated himself to be the natural son of Lord Byron, was placed before the Marylebone Police magistrate, very nearly naked, and shivering from head to foot, charged with being drunk…*

Dickens was reading the account of this pitiable matter in the proofs of the *Household Narrative of Current Events*, the news supplement to *Household Words*, giving an account of the doings in Parliament and the Courts, and a narrative of law and crime — very popular, that. Plenty of murders to satisfy readers greedy for sensation. We're all greedy for something, he supposed. Byron was greedy for sensation — what a life he'd lived, and dead at thirty-six. Dickens had wanted to rent Byron's old house near Genoa when he had stayed in Italy. It had turned out to be a third-rate wine shop, fallen to ruin. And a natural son, in the direst poverty. It might be true. Byron had led a very colourful life.

A natural daughter, too, Byron had — Allegra. He thought of Sapphire Hawke and wondered if she was Sir Gerald Hawke's illegitimate child, the so-called ward about whose antecedents nobody seemed to know and who came from somewhere other than Westmorland. Hawke probably had a string of bastards. That was something to ask about when he went to Hawke Court.

Meanwhile, he ought to get on. He had heaps of manuscripts to read, but some could be given to Harry Wills, his sub-editor, for first consideration. The proofs of the next issue of *Household Words* were on his desk to be read and corrected, titles to be altered, additions to be inserted, errors to be expunged. He'd have to work like the steam engine that Rogers had called him if he were to go round to the bookshop by lunchtime — he might catch the ladies then. The shop might not be busy, or it might be closed. Then he would knock until someone came.

He worked on, scarcely looking up. As always, his work possessed him wholly, scoring out, inking in, his pen racing and his mind spinning with ideas to brighten the dullest sentence.

At about half-past eleven, the office boy came in with a letter. Delivered by hand, the boy told him, 'Thought it might be important.'

'Who brought it?'

The boy didn't know. He'd found it in the hall as he was about to go out on an errand for Mr Wills.

*Chancy*, thought Dickens when the boy had gone, and he looked at the envelope. It might not have been found. Somebody who had not wanted to come in — someone, perhaps, who, having, made up his — or her — mind to write, had half-hoped it might be lost. A woman's hand, he guessed, a neat hand. A lady contributor shyly sending him her poem?

No, it was from Bella Screech who had something she wanted to tell him, and would Dickens meet her and Johnny in St. Anne's churchyard at half-past twelve?

*And Johnny* — something Bella wanted the boy to tell, something that would be easier to tell out of doors? Something that Johnny saw? If Johnny had seen the murderer, had the murderer seen him? He would go and tell Sam now. He could call at the bookshop later.

He put his papers in order, making a pile of finished proofs and a pile of those yet to do, wiped his pen, closed the lid of his inkwell, took his hat and coat and sped down the stairs into

Wellington Street. On the corner of Bow Street, there was a woman selling apples from a basket and snowdrops. The woman knew him and found the shiniest red apple she had. He bought a little bunch of snowdrops.

'I'll wrap 'em in a bit o' paper, Mr Dickens, an' they'll be safe in your pocket. Won't spoil 'em fer the lady.' She gave him a wink. 'Enjoy the apple, dearie — can't eat 'em meself —' she showed him her blackened stumps — 'nice Kentish apples, them is.'

Yet another sweetheart. Dickens laughed to himself. *The knave of hearts, I am — turn up the card and find the lady. No time now, though.* He hurried up to the police station.

At Bow Street, Jones had a visitor — two, in fact — Scrap, who served in the stationery shop, ran errands, and did some detecting with Jones and Dickens when they needed a pair of sharp ears, very sharp eyes and a ragged lad who could be invisible as the air when needed. He was looking rather pleased with himself, Dickens noticed. And there was Poll, the little terrier dog with him. Scrap looked after her sometimes for Eleanor and Tom Brim, Sam Jones's adopted children.

'Wotcher, Mr D — ain't seen yer fer a bit. Queer that, I woz thinkin' — two murders, ain't it, so far?'

Jones laughed. 'Detective Scrap has been waiting for the call, but as the call did not come, he is here — with his evidence. He hasn't finished, but he'll start again just to oblige you.'

'Mollie told me about the old man. I asked Mr Rogers when it woz. Day before yesterday, he says. I woz there.'

'At the curiosity shop?' Dickens asked.

'Cuttin' through ter Wardour Street with a parcel. I usually goes down through Dark Entry. Went down Crooked Alley, o' course. Saw a kid.'

193

'A boy?'

'Little 'un. Kickin' all the stuff about outside the shop — load o' rubbish, I'd say. Parrot's cage — no parrot, o' course — stuffed I daresay — screen sort o' thing with a picture on it; some sort o' chair — not meant fer sittin' in — state it woz in, bits o' metal — pans an' that — made a racket.'

Jones interrupted, 'Fire irons?' He wanted to know if the murderer had picked up that poker outside the shop — intent to wound, that might show.

'Didn't see.'

'There was a set of fire irons outside the shop when I was there,' said Dickens. 'I trod on them — there were a couple of shovels, a pair of tongs, and a poker.'

'The murder weapon,' Scrap said, 'bashed on the 'ead, Mollie said.'

'Screech could have taken them in, I suppose — he wanted me to buy them, or pay him for the damage. Not that I could see any.'

'True — what time was this, Scrap?'

'Church clock struck the half hour — 'alf twelve.'

'Was the shop door open?'

'Yes, thought the old fella'd come out and tell the kid ter 'ook it.'

'No one else about?'

'Didn't see anyone. Went on my way. When I came back, the kid was gone. The stuff was still all over the place. The door was closed.'

'Anyone about then?'

Scrap thought. 'Saw a cove in St. Anne's Court jest by that bookshop, an' that Miss Addy was jest goin' in.'

'The man wasn't running?'

'No, jest walkin' along. Saw his back, top hat, dark coat —

nothin' special about 'im.'

'What time were you going back?'

''Eeard the clock strike the hour.'

'Bella Screech said her boy had come running just before one o'clock and she went straight away. She must have arrived after you had passed, Scrap. She said the door was open.'

'So what was the boy doing between half-past twelve and one o'clock?' asked Dickens.

'Did he see? Go in the shop after the murderer came out? Left the door open as he ran for his mother? Was he seen? We'll have to —'

'That's what I came about. I had a note from Bella Screech asking me to meet her and Johnny at half-past twelve in the churchyard. I thought that the boy might have something to tell.'

'Better for you to talk to her for now. I'll be here when you come back.'

Dickens had an idea. 'Scrap could come with me, and Poll.'

'The boy might talk to Scrap — that's what you're thinking.'

'I am. Scrap will know what to ask.'

The apple-seller was still at the corner. Dickens bought more and gave them to Scrap.

'Sweetener?'

St. Anne's churchyard was usually a dank spot, grimly overcrowded and overgrown. It was cold, but there were little sanctuaries of warmth between the buttresses where the sun shone. There were clumps of snowdrops which from a distance looked like patches of snow. At the side of the church, there was sunlight warming a tomb rather like a table. Bella Screech sat there with her face to the sun. Johnny ran along the paths between the crowded graves, heedless of their tenants, sometimes jumping over an unmarked mound. He seemed happy enough. Dickens went to sit beside Bella. Scrap wandered away to meet the boy.

Dickens handed her the snowdrops, which as the apple-seller had promised were not spoilt. 'You could have picked your own.'

Bella took them and looked at the delicate bells which shivered as she held them. 'Not the same, is it? Someone gives you flowers — it's a treat. It's as though you were singled out. Thank you.'

They sat in silence, watching Scrap and Johnny. Dickens marvelled, not for the first time, at Scrap's delicacy. He remembered him with Eleanor and Tom Brim after their father had died of consumption. It was Scrap they had turned to very often. How patient he had been with Tom, playing endlessly with the spinning top and Noah's Ark. Scrap had had a baby sister. Silly, he'd called her, not knowing when he was just a little 'un that she had been Cecilia. She had died, as had Scrap's mother — and no trace could be found of them. Dickens had looked.

Scrap sat on another table tomb in the sunshine, tossing the apples from one hand to the other like a juggler. Johnny caught sight of him, stopped and stared, watching the red apples rise and fall. Scrap didn't speak. Poll sat next to Scrap, perfectly quiet and still. Johnny came forward, still staring. Poll dropped down and went to meet the child and sat in the middle of the path, her head cocked. She didn't bark.

Neither Bella nor Dickens spoke. Johnny by now was crouching down. Poll offered her paw, and they heard his delighted giggle.

'That boy,' Bella said, 'yours?'

'In a way — a piece of me, I think, and the dog.'

'Johnny doesn't know many other children.'

'He'll be all right with Scrap. He's used to children.'

'Why'd you bring him?'

'I thought, perhaps, that Johnny might have something to tell — about what happened.'

'He's had nightmares — about a man who's coming for him — who's under the bed, in the cupboard, looking in at the window, and who shouts at him. It's all a bit muddled, but I think he saw someone, or heard something — voices, perhaps.'

'Scrap told us — Superintendent Jones and me — that he passed by the shop at about half-past twelve. Johnny was kicking the stuff about. The shop door was open. When Scrap came back, the door was closed and no sign of Johnny.'

'But he didn't come for me until near one o'clock — what was —' She looked frightened then.

'Hiding, probably — that's what my boys do — and then he went back in, saw your father, and ran to get you.'

'Suppose he was seen? He might be — the murderer might —'

'Don't worry yet. Scrap will find out, and then we can protect you both. Let them take the dog for a walk. He'll be safe with Scrap. I can swear to that.'

Scrap was coming up the path. Johnny had one of the apples, imitating Scrap polishing it on his thigh. Scrap took a bite of his. Johnny did the same. Scrap bit off a piece and gave it to Poll. Johnny followed suit. Dickens nodded to Scrap, who fastened on Poll's lead.

'Come fer a walk,' he said to Johnny.

Johnny looked at his mother, who told them not to be long. The three went out towards Church Lane.

'He won't take him to the shop?'

'Not unless Johnny wants to. Trust him.'

Bella opened a basket. 'Picnic?' She gave Dickens a stone bottle, unwrapped a pie, and offered him a piece.

They sat in the sunshine and ate. Dickens took off his hat and felt the sun on his face. He drank his beer.

'I'm sorry,' Bella said, 'I shouldn't have accused you of being —'

'A copper's nark.'

She saw that he was laughing, and she laughed, too. She couldn't help liking him, and what he wrote about children — that was true. He'd known about that — about the secret fears and hopes of that boy, David Copperfield. He must have known it himself. And he'd understood about her and Felix and what they'd felt, even though they were just kids.

'Superintendent Jones did want me to find out about your father. But he's a good man. He wouldn't trap you — or Johnny.'

'Does he suspect me? Or Johnny? Johnny was there for nearly half an hour — the Superintendent knows that now, an' I didn't say about Ned Temple and Felix.'

'I told him you'd seen them about the shop.'

'Told him about me an' Felix — an' Johnny?' Her eyes flashed.

'I had to — so he'd understand why you didn't want to say. You weren't concealing evidence — he understood.'

'All right. He'd have found out soon enough, I suppose, an' I might have given him a piece of my mind. I know I'm a bit quick-tempered, but it's Johnny, I have to protect him.'

'Scrap will find out about this man — I am certain he exists, and we'll tell Mr Jones. Anyway, Miss Screech —'

'Bella.'

'Bella, there's someone we know about.'

'A robber — someone who knew what he'd got?'

Dickens told her about Ned Temple, the suspicions about his debts, and the murder of Ruby Kiss.

'Ned Temple did all this?'

'We think he cheated you and your father. Felix's father gave him five hundred pounds as comp—'

'To pay me off, you mean. An' pa got two hundred and fifty an' I got nothin'. I never liked Temple. He thought I would —' her fine eyes had that fierce fire again — 'he thought I was a whore. He had no idea what I'd felt for Felix. Corrupted him, I reckon. This Ruby Kiss, what was she?'

'A good-hearted, generous girl who —'

'A whore, though?' Bella disapproved. She'd kept herself away from all that. She'd skivvied for Widow Jenkins and nursed her when she was dying; she served beer at The Mischief; she'd fought off drunks — an' she'd not asked Screech for anythin'. But some she knew had taken that way. But then, they didn't have Johnny.

Dickens could guess what she was thinking. He admired her steadfastness, but he knew enough about women's lives from his dealings with the girls at Urania Cottage, his home for fallen women — girls like Ruby Kiss. Some of the girls chafed at the routine of the house, the domestic tasks and the lessons. Cribb'd, cabined, and confin'd, they felt, wanting to go back to the pubs, the clubs, the casinos and the penny theatres where the music was loud and the drink was cheap, and there was a good time to be had — until you were half-beaten to death, or threw yourself from Waterloo Bridge, or were pushed, or were murdered in a slum.

'Yes, she was, I'm afraid, but she didn't deserve to be murdered.'

Bella thought about that. 'No,' she said, 'it's men, ain't it, always men. There wouldn't be whores if there weren't any men. Pity there has to be fathers.'

'Plants don't need fathers, I believe. Hermaphrodites, they say.'

'Gracious — I've never heard that word.' Bella picked up her snowdrops. 'Beautiful, they are, white an' pure. Much better than — well, you know.'

'You wouldn't be without Johnny.'

'No, course not, but it ain't been easy. I wear this —' she pointed to a thin gold band on her finger — 'stole it from Pa when I left. People believe it. They think I was his daughter-in-law. Well, they would. You only had to look at him.'

'Do you ever wonder?'

'I do. What I remember of Ma — which ain't much — she was fair and short like him. He never liked me — I never knew why. He used to look at me — as if he didn't know me, and Johnny, it wasn't that he cared about my virtue, he just — I don't know — contempt, I think.'

'Why did Johnny keep going to the shop?'

'I didn't tell him that the old man was his grandfather. Johnny just called him the old man. Pa knew who he was — that made him more bad-tempered. Johnny thought he was — a wicked gnome out of a story book. He was fascinated.'

'Attraction and repulsion — it's terrifying, but, as a child, you can't keep away. My nurse used to tell me the most terrifying stories of a Captain Murderer and a sailor called Chips and his talking rat. I was scared to death, but I wanted more.'

'I suppose — I kept telling him, and now he really is frightened.'

'They are resilient, children — the nightmares will fade.'

'And there's no more Screech. At least Johnny doesn't look a bit like him. P'raps I'm a changeling. Found in a basket on the doorstep. The bastard child of Lady Grace Pierrepont — her monument's inside, all white marble. I used to look at it and wonder what a lady was. Dreams, eh?'

They finished the beer and Bella packed her basket. She swept the crumbs off Sarah-Ann Lesage's table tomb. Mrs Lesage would have been scandalised, perhaps — more so if she could see the state of the churchyard. *Hard luck*, Dickens thought.

Scrap and Johnny came back. Johnny was holding on to Poll's lead. He ran to his mother. Of course, he wanted a dog — now, now. Dickens mouthed the word 'Sorry'. Bella told the boy that one day, when they were settled, a dog exactly like Poll would be his. 'Soon,' she said.

Dickens said he would come to tell her what Scrap had found out.

Scrap and Dickens walked back along through St. Anne's Court, passing Crooked Alley.

'Did he —' Dickens began.

'He saw someone go in the shop — a man — big as a giant, wearing a hat and a long coat, all black. He was just comin' outer Dark Entry. Didn't think anythin' about it. Went ter to do wot 'e allus did — kick the stuff about, though 'is ma'd told' 'im not ter — kids, eh? My pa told me ter do a thing an' I wouldn't — mind, 'e usually wanted me ter go beggin' or stealin'.'

'The man?'

'I don't know, Mr D. Course, 'e saw someone, but I think whoever it was 'as become bigger an' bigger in the tellin' till 'e became a giant. He 'eard 'em shoutin' an' then it all went quiet. He crept under that chair thing I told you about. Saw the man come out, though.'

'Which way did he go?'

201

'Johnny don't know. Kept 'is 'ead down, but the door woz open, so in 'e goes ter see Screech lyin' on the floor an' the blood — runs away ter get 'is ma.'

'Do you think the man saw him?'

'Doubt it. Johnny wasn't at the shop when the man went in, an 'e woz under that chair thing when 'e came out. Reckon 'e's safe enough.'

'Would you run back to tell his mother? It will put her mind at rest. I'll take Poll to Bow Street and see you there in about fifteen minutes.'


'The description's not much help. Scrap, our perceptive reader of human nature, tells me that the man has become bigger. He'd become a giant by the time Johnny told Scrap all about it.'

'Well, I'm glad that the boy wasn't seen. One less worry for us,' Jones said, having listened to Dickens's account. 'There's no news from Clement's Inn. No news from Dacres at Bennett's End — Temple hasn't gone to his mother's. There's only the bookshop.'

'I can still go — I could ask if Miss Finch noticed the man Scrap saw.'

'It's another trouble I'm giving you.'

'The word "trouble" is not in my vocabulary, Samivel. I am in full twig — Miss Bella gave me a very refreshing bottle of beer and a slice of homemade pie.'

'Confidential again, I see.'

'They also serve who only sit and eat.'

'My word, you are in full twig, and so is Scrap.'

Scrap was just coming in to be praised in full measure by his detective colleagues. 'Anythin' else you want me ter do?'

Dickens spoke. 'I might need you to take a little jaunt with me — to the country.'

'Where?'

'To a place not far from Chertsey — a place called Hawke Court.'

'Toff?'

'He was. Dead now, but there's jewels and a missing heiress.'

Jones saw the signs. Scrap's eyes widened. He was already sniffing the air — on the scent. 'You gotter find 'er?'

'For a friend. I might need an assistant if Mollie won't mind.'

'Mollie knows I gotter 'elp Mr Jones when 'e wants me. Same fer you, Mr D. She won't mind. She'll understand.'

*She'll have to*, thought Jones, contemplating his two amateurs. Dickens could be very persuasive — and so could Scrap. 'No murder, I hope. Ought I to warn the local police that you're coming?'

Dickens laughed. 'Just routine enquiries, Superintendent.'

'Make sure they are, the pair of you.'

# 31: SPEAKING VOLUMES

Miss Sarah Hamilton opened the door only partially. Dickens had knocked loudly, guiltily ignoring the sign which read closed. She looked very pale and her face had a pinched look. It seemed to be all nose. Dickens had not thought her pretty or handsome, but that she had an intelligent face, and though she was usually serious, there was a hint of humour in her mouth, which turned up at one side as if she were always about to smile, but never quite managed it — not for Charles Dickens anyway. There was no hint of humour now.

'We are closed, Mr Dickens.'

'I beg your pardon. It is just that I was passing and thought to ask about my book.'

'It is ready.'

She opened the door reluctantly. She knew she could not leave him on the doorstep. Inside, he saw that the door to the binding workshop was open.

'I see that you are working. I wonder, did Miss Addy tell you about my idea for an article for *Household Words* about the process of bookbinding?'

'She did. I suppose it would be all right, but we do not wish to be identified. There are far too many people coming here because of the murders. They do not wish to buy books — they wish only to look at the place where Mr Gresham was killed. And to look at us — as if we might be two murderers. It is — too much, Mr Dickens.' Her voice shook a little.

'Of course, I understand, but I did say that I would place your shop elsewhere — in Chatham — or nowhere. I do not need to mention a place — it is the process I should like to observe.'

'And two lady bookbinders?' Dickens saw the upturn at the corner of her mouth twitch slightly. 'I thought that was your main interest.'

'I have an idea about that. I should explain the process, the tools, the technicalities, and so forth, and end my piece with the surprise that I am referring to two professional ladies.'

'At first they will assume that men are doing the work?'

'Exactly. Do you have time now?'

'I suppose so. You are very persuasive, Mr Dickens. I shall expect more of your custom in return.'

Sarah took him into the workshop where he saw all the tools and leather and paper neatly arranged on the table, the press in the corner, and the shelves stacked with books, more leather and paper. There was the smell of glue and leather, and old books and time.

She took him round the room and showed him the various tools and explained their purpose, telling him of the tools which had been Bartholomew's, and had been his father's, and his father's before that, she believed. 'To think of their hands — that wrought such beauty. Good hands, honest hands, calloused from the work. Yet there are other hands, white and perfumed ... which do no good at all ... do ill... Such simple lives, they led, so tranquil...'

From her wistful tone, Dickens understood why she had felt so violated by the intruders with their raucous laughter and questions, and their leering looks and crude jokes about murder.

'There is great pleasure in working with these — remembering... This is a knife Bartholomew gave me; I think of his hand on this worn wood, which always feels warm to my touch. And this —' her brow furrowed — 'this stitching awl was Thyrza's.'

As Sarah moved on, Dickens saw her face relax and her eyes brighten. She loved her work. She showed him how the press worked, fitting in a book and winding the screw. She showed him the sewing frame and the embossing tools and the gold leaf. There was lovely thick paper: parchment from sheepskin, vellum from calf. She showed him the various leathers for binding. The olive morocco which Bartholomew had sworn was the finest binding material for receiving the impression of a gold stamp. This one, called *Cambridge* with its pattern all over save for the small square in the centre of the boards; the blue goatskin and red morocco with their lozenge-shaped central ornaments and fine gilded border known as the *Harleian*, after Edward Harley, the Earl of Oxford; the now popular coloured calf bindings; the mother-of-pearl used for inlay; the rich velvet and the smooth silks used for the keepsake books. She handled the beautiful things with a kind of reverence and great care.

Then she put on her apron, motioning Dickens to sit near her so that she could demonstrate the paper folding. 'Bartholomew's folding stick,' she said. 'The first thing is the folding, which must be done very carefully — the edges must be perfectly even so that the margins are uniform. You see how the sheets of paper are laid with the signatures — the numbers at the foot of the page — facing downwards.'

She took the stick in her right hand and Dickens watched as she brought the sheet over from right to left, the edges placed carefully together. She used the folding stick to crease the centre. Then she held the sheet down with the folder on the line to be creased and then again, another fold and another…

Dickens observed the way her long capable hands did their work and her complete absorption in her task. He noticed her smooth brown hair, parted in the middle and caught in a net at her neck, her simple grey dress and the ribbon at her neck fastened with a brooch which looked like a miniature portrait. She seemed to be smiling over her work. What was she thinking — of Bartholomew and Thyrza Chantrey? What was her story before that? And what of Miss Addy? Where was she?

Sarah looked up suddenly. He felt caught out somehow. He was about to say something about the work when she said, 'Why are you here, Mr Dickens?'

'The bookbinding.'

'Addy mentioned Constable Rogers, Mollie's husband. You are often in the stationery shop. Addy says that you are all friends.'

'Yes, we are.'

'And you came here after the murder of Felix Gresham. A coincidence?'

'I know Mrs Gresham — I was curious.'

'Like the other sight-seers?'

That stung, but he felt he deserved it. *Copper's nark*, he thought. Sarah Hamilton was remorseless. 'You were there when Mr Screech was murdered. Addy saw you with Superintendent Jones, who came to question us about Mr Gresham.'

'I was.'

'And now you are here again.' She stood up. She was as tall as he and looked him straight in the eye. Her intelligent face was stern. The corner of her mouth was still.

'May we sit down again? I promise I will tell you all.'

'I do not wish to hear. It is enough to know that you have come to spy on us.'

'Ruby Kiss.'

Her face took on that pinched look he had seen first. He had shocked her. He had intended it, but he was sorry to see how her calm had vanished at the mention of Ruby Kiss. But she did not weep. She simply said, 'It is very dreadful.'

'Constable Rogers came from Superintendent Jones to tell you about her death.'

'He did.'

'Tell me what you know, Miss Hamilton — here, in private. It will be easier than going to Bow Street. Superintendent Jones must investigate these murders for the sake of the victims — for justice. You must see that.'

Sarah nodded and sat down, very straight and still in her chair. *Poised for flight*, Dickens thought and sat down again quickly. 'Constable Rogers asked you if you had seen Mr Temple.'

'He did — I wondered if he meant — that Ned was — suspected. I can hardly think — they were friends.'

'Mr Temple had many debts. He owed money to Felix Gresham and to Mr Screech, and Superintendent Jones thinks he may have defrauded Mr Gresham's father.'

'But Ruby —'

'She knew them both — very well, it seems. She probably knew all about the debts. Perhaps she knew something about Mr Gresham's murder. You knew her — is it possible that she knew and did not come forward?'

'She would not have gone to the police. You obviously know the life she had.'

'How did you know her?'

'Addy and I found her one night. Someone had beaten her up. She never said who it was. We brought her here. She would not even see a doctor. We patched her up. Addy thought she had had a miscarriage, but she denied it. She stayed for a month. I tried to persuade her to take up another kind of work,

but she wouldn't, of course. She preferred the life she had —
with all its risks.'

'And Phoebe Green?'

'Same thing. Ruby sent her. She was here the night Felix was
killed. She heard the cab. And she had told us that Ruby had
found herself another lover — a military man. I assume that is
why we did not hear from her — even after Felix died.'

'How did you know Mr Gresham and Mr Temple?'

'Felix used to come when he was a boy — when
Bartholomew and ... well, years ago, and then Ned Temple
came in sometimes. He brought Felix and I recognised him.
They had been at Screech's. Felix was quite frank about
pawning his things — he thought Screech a huge joke. He and
Ned had some secret about Screech's daughter which kept
them amused. There was a touch of cruelty about Ned
sometimes, but I didn't know about his debts.'

'Screech saw Mr Gresham give money to Mr Temple — I
should think it was more than once. Mr Temple, I think, was
so deep in debt that he might have committed some dreadful
act.'

Sarah looked down at her paper and ran her finger up and
down Bartholomew's bone paper folder. Now, she did seem to
be holding something back. *Secrets*, Dickens thought.

'There was a knife missing from here. Thyrza's knife. I don't
know when it was taken.'

'Why didn't you tell the police?'

'I — we — Addy and I — we thought Ruby might have
taken it. She boasted that she could look after herself, that she
carried a knife, but had lost it when she was attacked. I think
she tried to defend herself. She was cut about the hands. She
wanted another knife, but I told her it was too dangerous; she
didn't mention it again. And then when Felix was killed — we

knew, we knew Ruby wouldn't — couldn't have done it. She was fond of Felix; she had a new lover. There was no cause.'

'Could Mr Temple have taken the knife?'

'He came in here — we never thought of Ned. I can hardly believe it now.'

'There was a knife under Ruby's hand. The doctor who examined her does not think it killed her, but he cannot swear to that. However, if it is the murder weapon, Superintendent Jones will have to come back. I will tell him about your knife.'

'I know — I wish we had said something. Ruby might have —'

'I do not think so, Miss Hamilton, but if you think of anything else, you must tell the Superintendent — or tell me.'

'I cannot think of anything.'

'Just one more thing, if I may — did Miss Addy see Ned Temple in the street near the time of Screech's murder? A witness saw a man near your shop.'

Sarah Hamilton paled. 'She did not say so — she — no — she wouldn't — just a man in the street.'

'Then I will leave you, and as far as the piece for my magazine is concerned, let us postpone it until a better time. It will keep.'

'Thank you, Mr Dickens. Addy and I would like to be quiet for a time. We — you cannot know what our lives were like before Bartholomew and Thyrza. When they died — in the cholera — it was the most dreadful thing. We were bereft. It took us a long time to — make our lives — secure again. And now — all this. We might go away — for a time.'

She stood up suddenly, as if afraid she had said too much. It was time for Dickens to go. He could not, in all conscience, ask anything more about the man in the street, but he had seen a man's black coat hanging behind the door, a stain of gold paint on the cuff. Perhaps it was James Semple's — he was a book-edge gilder, a shy, sensitive young man. In debt, yes, but not the killer of Ebenezer Screech. Jones had listened to Constable John Semple's account of his brother and had eliminated James from their enquiries.

Only when he was halfway down St. Anne's Court did he remember his book. That would keep, too. *Dy'd in the blood of recent murder*. Where was Ned Temple?

# 32: A DAGGER OF THE MIND

It seemed that Doctor Woodhall had been busy with his microscope, for Jones was deeply occupied when Dickens went in.

'Any news?' Jones asked, looking up from his papers.

Dickens told him about the stolen knife. 'They did not believe that Ruby could have killed Felix Gresham.'

'They should have mentioned it, though.'

'They found Ruby Kiss after she had been badly hurt — attacked — I suppose they thought they were protecting her.'

'Too late, now, but I don't suppose it would have made any difference. However, that the knife in Ruby's hand came from the bookshop is confirmed by Doctor Woodhall's report. It had traces of leather on it. Minute traces which he saw under the microscope. As for the murder weapon, he believes it is likely that the same blade — not the one from the bookshop — killed Felix Gresham and Ruby Kiss. Likely, mind — he can't swear to it. In court, he can only say that the two wounds are similar in size and that the wounds were made by similar single-bladed knives like the paper knife we found. But, for us, his conclusions point to a single murderer.'

'What now?' Dickens asked as Jones stood up.

'I'm going to ask Joah Danks if he saw that feather in Ruby Kiss's hair. Not that it would necessarily clear Temple. And, even if Danks doesn't remember a feather in her hair, a jury might well discount it as evidence that Temple was there that night.'

'Or a feather to turn the scales against him.'

Jones sat down again. 'To hang him.'

'So light a thing, Sam, to kill a man.'

'I think he was there, but you're right. I shouldn't like to see him hanged on the evidence of a feather. No proof at all that Ned Temple dropped it. We'll have another look at Temple's rooms, too. See if we missed anything. I'll ask Danks about the feather, though — just for my own satisfaction.'

'I wonder if the Dalrymples are missing a knife.'

Joah Danks thought about the Superintendent's question. He closed his eyes as if to remember the scene at the front door of the chambers. He remembered the red feathers. There was a black one, he thought, but he didn't recall a quill feather.

'Did Mr Temple come up here very often?' Jones asked.

'To pay his rent and to borrow a thing or two, sometimes.'

'Such as?'

'Ink, pounce, bit o' parchment — just little things he ran out of.'

'Would he have occasion to come up to see Mr Dalrymple?'

'Not that I know of, sir — more likely to come up to see Mr Alexander in his room. They went about together — casinos, theatres, that kind o' thing. Rich men's doin's.'

Dickens detected a touch of malice in his tone. Spying, he thought. 'You seem to know a lot about them.'

'Just saw them, sir, goin' out together, talkin' about where they were off to.'

'You did not go with them?'

It was there again, that sudden glitter in Danks's eye — a pinpoint of hatred. 'No, sir, I did not. My wages don't allow for gamblin' and such.'

They left him and went in to talk to Mr Dalrymple, who confirmed that he left the matter of Mr Temple's rent to Mr Danks. He rarely saw Mr Temple, except for the occasional legal work he might do. No, he would be extremely unlikely to leave his room unlocked. It was a lawyer's duty to be punctilious about security — documents of great importance were kept, and now, the sapphires. Yes, he supposed that Mr Temple might converse with his son sometimes. Certainly, they could speak with Alexander.

Alexander Dalrymple put down his newspaper rather guiltily. Dickens saw him blush when Jones asked about Ned Temple.

'He'd sometimes come up for a chat — when the governor was in court, but I wouldn't say we were close friends. I told Mr Dickens that Ned tapped me for loans.'

'You know that Ruby Kiss was murdered?'

'Yes, it's in the newspaper. Mr Danks brought it in to show me. It says she was stabbed. He saw her with Ned here.'

'When did you last see Ruby Kiss?'

'I told Mr Dickens about Lantern Court — that was the last time. It was ages ago. I wasn't too keen on the Casino de Venise — too much drink, and I didn't want — those girls… And they were awfully fond of cards. I'm no great hand at cards, Mr Jones.'

'Do you remember a quill feather in her hair?'

Alexander Dalrymple's open face looked puzzled and anxious. 'She usually had feathers in her hair — lots of the girls do, but I don't especially recall a quill. I'm sorry — do you mean to say that Ned had something to do with it?'

'I don't know, Mr Dalrymple, but he is missing, and he knew the young lady. I would be obliged if you would get in touch with me if you hear of him.'

Dickens and Jones went out into the quiet garden and walked to the middle, where the black boy still stood. Mr Justice Silence was nowhere to be seen.

'They knew about Ruby Kiss — they'd have said if a knife was missing.'

'They would,' Jones answered, 'and the feather's no use. Danks didn't remember — why should he? It could have been in her hair, or Temple could have dropped it. The ones in his room are all the same — same as every other lawyer uses. It's just a piece of circumstantial evidence together with the evidence of Temple's debts, his relationship with Felix, and his being here with Ruby Kiss, but, unless we find him, none of it is of any use.'

Joah Danks watched them from his window. He'd heard enough. Temple a murderer? That business of the quill pen must mean something. P'raps they'd found one with the body. An' they'd asked if Temple had been in Dalrymple's room, an' that policeman had been pretty sharp about what things Temple had borrowed. Temple had borrowed things an' he'd taken things. Joah knew that. Couldn't prove it, o' course. But not a quill pen. Temple had plenty o' them. He thought about the newspaper. Ruby Kiss had been stabbed. An' they'd been in Temple's room again. What if they were lookin' for a knife?

*You might remember some other snippets about Mr Temple.* George Stoneridge had said that. Suppose a knife was missin' from Old Dalrymple's chambers. *Honest Joah Danks, ready to do what's right.* It'd be his duty to report it. Too soon, now. Joah Danks wished he'd thought of a missing knife. *Play the long game,* Stoneridge had said. Not too long, though. An' Stoneridge could pay first.

He saw the policeman go out through the archway. Mr Dickens still stood looking at the statue. What was he up to? Joah hadn't liked the way Dickens had said that he knew a lot about Temple and Mr Alexander. Sarcastic. And Joah didn't like the way Dickens looked at him — as if he could see right into him. Now, he was coming back. Joah went up to Mr Alexander's room. He had no wish to see Charles Dickens again.

# 33: A MODEST PROPOSAL

'I wonder, Mr Dalrymple, if you would have any objection to my going down to Hawke Court,' Dickens began cautiously. 'I propose to investigate a little matter.'

Mr Dalrymple's eyebrows rose. 'Investigate?'

Dickens explained what he had discovered from Mrs Pottage, housekeeper at the former Hawke town house. 'And I wonder if Miss Sapphire Hawke might have contacted someone from that house — someone she trusted to help her. After all, she was a girl just come from her convent, and alone in London. Where would she go? This Josephine Parker about whom Mrs Pottage told me possibly went back to Hawke village. Perhaps she is still there.'

Mr Dalrymple looked sceptical. 'After so long? I have already sent Mrs Stoneridge, Sir Gerald's housekeeper, her instructions. The contents of the house are to be auctioned, and Mrs Stoneridge is to give up her keys to the auctioneer. I chose the man myself.'

'When is the auction?'

'At the end of this month. I shall be very glad to have it settled — there are debts to pay.'

'Then I have time to go and make my enquiries.'

'Well, yes, but I really do not see that there is anything to be found out. Mrs Stoneridge could not tell Mr Case anything.'

'I am convinced, sir, that this mystery can be solved. There is someone who knows about Miss Hawke and what happened to her. I should, of course, need your official sanction — in the form of a letter?'

'But what would you wish me to write to Mrs Stoneridge?'

Dickens paused. Now came the difficult part — to put forward his plan without offending Mr Dalrymple's sense of propriety. Mr Dalrymple was already looking at him rather suspiciously. *Well, let us see what he makes of it.* 'The Reverend Octavius Swann —'

'Yes, he conducted the funeral.'

'Mr Case spoke to him. Mr Swann told him that Mrs Stoneridge was employed at Hawke Court as a girl. She left upon her marriage to Joshua Stoneridge. Reverend Swann conducted the marriage.'

'You think that she may have known Sapphire Hawke?'

'I do, but for some reason she denied that knowledge.'

'I cannot think of any reason for her to do so.'

'A mystery, Mr Dalrymple, into which I might delve, if you will permit me. However, I do not think it very sensible for me to go to Hawke Court as Charles Dickens — I would attract too much attention.'

Mr Dalrymple stared at him. His sense of propriety seemed to be too stunned to be offended. 'Pretending — er — to be someone else?'

'Exactly,' Dickens went on briskly. 'What if you required an inventory of the books and valuables? Would you not send a man you trusted to write it all down and assess the value — for the heir?'

Mr Dalrymple did not speak. Dickens watched him. He was astounded to see the side of Mr Dalrymple's mouth turn up. He hoped it wasn't a stroke. But, no, the man was smiling. Lord, he was laughing. Dickens waited until Mr Dalrymple composed himself and wiped his eyes.

'Mr Dickens, you are a most ingenious story-teller, and here I am watching a story come from the very lips of genius. Disguise, Mr Dickens, is that it? Number twenty-eight in a flaxen wig and whiskers?'

It was Dickens's turn to laugh. Mr Dalrymple had certainly read *David Copperfield* — he knew about Mr Littimer's disguise. 'I shall, of course, be more subtle than Mr Littimer. What think you of my scheme?'

Suddenly, Mr Dalrymple looked like a delighted schoolboy offered a dare. His eyes lit up, Alexander Dalrymple peeping from his father's usually grave face.

'Yes, yes — go to Hawke Court and stick a few pins in that sour puss, Mrs Stoneridge — I beg your pardon — but I'll not forget her stringy chops and dusty port. She wouldn't even build up the fire for us. Moreover, Mr Dickens —' there was a definite twinkle in his eye — 'I should very much like your report on the contents of Hawke Court — you never know what you might find.'

A simultaneous thought struck them. Dickens said, 'There is no evidence that Sapphire Hawke did not go back to Hawke Court. All we know is that she was not heard of after she left the steamboat at St. Katherine's Wharf. There might be some evidence that she went to Hawke Court.'

Mr Dalrymple looked grave again. He thought about that empty house and all its damp rooms, its cellars and its attics. He'd never liked the place. 'You almost make me change my mind — what if you were to find...'

'I hadn't thought of that, but I doubt that — er — remains would be easy to discover after so long. I thought only of letters, or someone in the village. Are there other servants besides Mrs Stoneridge?'

'She engages a few female servants, I believe, from time to time, for heavy work. You might be able to find out who they are and whether they remember anything, but, as you say, it is so long ago. I don't know, Mr Dickens —'

'Let me try — for Mr Case's sake.'

'Very well. It can do no harm.'

'I would like to take an assistant — a smart young boy I know who possesses the sharpest of eyes and ears and the swiftest of legs. You will mention him in your letter: Tom Smart and his son, Alick.'

Mr Dalrymple smiled again. He knew the name, Tom Smart from *Pickwick Papers*. A formidable memory, indeed. 'I will, most certainly.' Mr Dalrymple opened his door. 'I will write to Hawke Court about Mr Smart straight away.'

'I am much obliged to you, my dear sir.'

Dickens went out. Joah Danks was there, scraping away with his pen. Dickens bowed to him and went on his way to see Scrap at the stationery shop.

## 34: SHORE OF DARKNESS

Two motionless figures on the foreshore and the grey river licking at the mud, and mist on the water creeping onto the land to shroud a third, prone form, its clothes sodden, its white face staring up at the unforgiving cold dawn light. And a man with a rusty boathook and a boat drawn up on the shore. Not a bargeman or a waterman, or a lighterman, but a fisher of men.

Dickens hurried down Temple Stairs past Constable Feak, who stood at the top and gave him a nod. Jones's face looked raw and grey in the cold. Dickens looked down at the body of Ned Temple.

'Suicide, do you think?'

'Probably — I think so. I've seen enough drownings. See that bit of wood in his hand? That's evidence that he probably went in alive. Doctor Woodhall will be able to confirm it — there'll be water in the stomach, water and froth in the lungs. And he'll look for signs of violence, but I can't see anything. He wasn't knocked on the head or strangled or stabbed.'

'There was a purse in his pocket,' said Rogers, 'some of Screech's sovereigns, I'll bet. And this gold watch an' a gold tooth-pick —'

'Now I remember,' said Jones. 'Temple wasn't wearing a watch chain when I saw him. Perhaps the watch and the toothpick were in hock to Screech. And, this pin, Charles — is this the one that Screech showed you?'

'Yes, it is Felix Gresham's.'

'He had that tin box from Screech's, then — but no sign of Felix Gresham's ring.'

'Sold it, mebbe,' said Rogers, looking at the gold in his hand.

'Worth somethin', this lot. He had enough to get away.'

'He had nowhere to go,' said Dickens.

'Right, sir. Caught on that mooring-chain. Couldn't get out again, even if 'e'd wanted ter,' the matter-of-fact boatman said, 'seen it afore. An' the tide came in. High water at about 'alf past one this mornin'. Couldn't go nowhere.'

Not quite what Dickens had meant, but it made it more awful. Perhaps Ned Temple had stood here, contemplating the black water where the lights reflected like accusing eyes. Perhaps he had stepped forward, his foot in the river, felt its cold fingers at his legs, changed his mind, stepped back, caught himself in the chain, fallen, struggled to free himself, felt the tide rising, covering his face, choking him, freezing him. And at the last, he had given himself up to Death because he had nowhere else to go. And Death had taken him. And there was only a poor clergyman's widow to mourn him.

'I've sent for Doctor Woodhall,' said Jones, looking at the drowned face of Ned Temple and seeing how young it was, all the marks of greed and bitterness erased by death so that he looked just a boy, a boy who had thrown away his own life and three others. 'What a waste,' he said.

'So it is,' said Dickens.

Rogers looked very solemn, too. 'That's it, sir, d'you think? The case is finished?'

'I think so, except for what he's done. That cannot be over — two mothers to grieve for their only sons. I'll send Inspector Grove to Bennett's End and I'll go to see Mr Frank Gresham.'

Doctor Woodhall came to look at the fourth corpse. He agreed with the Superintendent that it looked like suicide, and his mortuary attendants came to take the body to his morgue. Rogers went with them and Feak was sent back to Bow Street to speak to Inspector Grove.

Dickens and Jones went up the stairs into Temple Lane. Dickens wondered what concatenation of ideas had led Ned Temple down Temple Lane, past the Inner Temple and Middle Temple, and down Temple Stairs. His name? His failed hopes? He would never be a member of the Honourable Society of any Temple. The Lord High Chancellor would never call upon Mr Edward Temple, Q.C. to submit his evidence. And the waters of the Temple fountain would continue to plash into their pool as they had done for two hundred years since the first Lord High Chancellor had dipped his fingers in the cool water, and the great river would roll ever onward to the wide sea, its little bit of flotsam forgotten.

The traffic was already slowing in the Strand and in St Clement's Lane. Clement's Inn and its neighbour, New Inn, were already wreathed in fog. Lincoln's Inn and its High Court of Chancery were all but invisible.

Dickens looked at Jones's drawn face. 'Old 'un,' he began — Jones gave him a faint smile. They had not spoken all the way from Temple Stairs. 'Do you want me to come in with you?'

'No, you get home and do your packing — don't stay there too long. Mollie will want Scrap back.' Jones looked through the archway into the foggy garden of Lincoln's Inn. 'Hopeless and hapless, you said.'

'The law?'

'Three murders and the killer got away with it — all for nothing.'

'You don't think — we could be —'

'Wrong? Of course we could. Only Temple's death is a certainty, and the evidence of his debts, but there's no one else.'

'I was just thinking about Ruby Kiss and her toff.'

'I know. Rogers and I will keep making enquiries, but, you know, the Commissioner will be satisfied. Three murders solved and no expensive trial. The Home Secretary will be delighted.'

Jones turned in to Lincoln's Inn to tell Mr Francis Gresham that the probable murderer of Felix Gresham had drowned himself.

Dickens made his way home across Lincoln's Inn to come out at Gate Street, mentally packing his bag with his travelling inkwell, pens and a ledger in which to record the contents of Hawke Court — well, as much as would seem authentic for his fictitious audit for Mr Dalrymple. And he would need his black suit — the lawyer's clerk's suit which he kept for his outings with Jones, his low-crowned hat. A muffler, perhaps, a Bob Cratchit sort of muffler, and some oil to smooth down and darken his hair, and the spectacles. He saw himself fully formed: Tom Smart, lawyer's clerk, near-sighted, stooping, ink on his fingers, a tendency to feel the cold, always humble but cheerful of countenance, and very fond of his lad, Alick Smart. He had suggested Smallweed, but Scrap's face had said enough about that.

Just ahead of him, groping his way through the fog, making his way to The Ship Tavern in Gate Street, Joah Danks was going to meet George Stoneridge. Joah Danks had news — about a knife, and about a visitor to Hawke Court. Mr Dalrymple's door had been firmly closed, and Joah had had to wait until Mr

Alexander went out before he dared put his ear to the keyhole. Someone called Smart was going to do an inventory of the valuables at Hawke Court before the lot went to auction. As that Charles Dickens came out, Joah had heard distinctly that a letter was to be sent to a Mrs Stoneridge — now, George hadn't mentioned her. Wife? Ma? Mr Stoneridge would want to know about that. And a sovereign for each tasty piece of information.

Joah jingled the coins in his pocket. He'd have whistled had he been able to. Joah Danks's lips were not made for whistling.

# 35: SMOKE AND MIRRORS

It was late afternoon when they arrived at Hawke Court. No one had met them at the station, so Dickens had hired a trap and a driver, who had deposited them at the gates of the park. These were padlocked. Clearly Mrs Stoneridge had no intention of welcoming them with open arms.

Scrap, never daunted, dropped his bag and climbed over the gates. Before Dickens knew it, Scrap was looking at him through the rusted scrollwork. 'Nothin' fer it, Mr D., yer'll 'ave ter shin up — ain't that 'ard. Pass me the bags.'

'If you say so.' Dickens threw up the bags, hoping that Scrap would catch his — he had pens and his travelling inkwell in his. He was fond of that bag — his friend, Count D'Orsay, had given it to him. *D'Orsay*, he thought, who had lived with Lady Blessington. He remembered Sir Gerald Hawke's face at that reception so long ago, that smell of corruption, that black obsidian eye. The devil.

He found a foothold to squeeze in his foot, and though he felt the rusty metal give, he heaved himself up. He sat on the top of the gate, from where he could see along an avenue of elms bordered on either side by parkland. He saw the house at a distance, black against the fading light, its tower pointing upwards like a dark finger. It was bitterly cold, and the late sun promised nothing. The dying red looked burnt out, as if it might not bother to rise again.

Dickens dropped down and they began to walk along the avenue towards the house. There had been lawns, but these were neglected now, and clumps of rhododendrons grew wild, spilling onto the path. Eventually, they came upon a broken

226

red-brick wall where a door was propped open, through which Dickens could see more gardens, and the glint of the last light on glass. There had been a moat, but this had been filled in to make a pavement of flagstones, many now cracked. Weeds grew up, the balustrades were broken in parts and ivy crept round them and across the stone flags, winding its way up to darken the mullioned windows. Some of the panes were broken. To their left there was a gravel walk, overgrown with grasses and weeds. It led, Dickens thought, to woods which were encroaching on the house. They were deep in shadow on this raw afternoon.

He looked up at the piles of tall red-brick chimneys and crow-step gables — there was no smoke curling into the grey sky. Some of the chimneys looked as if they might fall were it not for the strangling creeper. A lattice window hung open in an upper room and above that the windows were either shuttered or boarded over. The shutters were closed on most of the lower windows. The door was a great baronial thing studded with big square iron nails. Dead as a doornail — the whole place. Had Mrs Stoneridge fled, leaving Hawke Court to the rooks which perched on some of the brick chimneys? Dickens took up the iron knocker and let it fall. At the sound three black birds rose into the air with a hideous cackle. Dickens and Scrap were not in on the joke.

He knocked again and they waited.

'Creepy, ain't it?' Scrap said, though his eyes were lit up. This was better than servin' in the shop. Place looked as though ten — an 'undred murders 'ad bin done.

'Specs, my lad.'

Scrap took the wire-framed spectacles from his pocket and put them on.

Dickens was about to knock again when he heard the sound

of an iron bar being lifted, then the sliding back of bolts and the turning of a key which he imagined larger than Screech's Newgate key. The door creaked open. There was not, as he was almost ready to believe, a man in sombre black and a white ruff, unsheathing his sword. There was the pinched-faced, unsmiling Esther Stoneridge.

Unlike Meredith Case, Charles Dickens could tell a hawk from a handsaw. He saw the truth of her in a moment — the avidity of the toad-like eyes and the meanness in the compressed lips. He knew in an instant what kind of man he must be.

'Smart, ma'am — Mister. Thomas. Boy — Alick. Smart —' Scrap took off his cap and bowed — 'By direction of Mr Dalrymple — you've had the letter.'

'Yes, sir. Though why Mr Turner, the auctioneer couldn't just — all this inconvenience.'

'Apologies — humble, ma'am. Orders — Mr Dalrymple's. Quick as we can.' All the while smiling.

'Very well. Come in. I've made up a room. A truckle bed for the boy. I suppose that will be satisfactory.'

'Obliged. Small for his age. Smart, o' course. Sleep anywhere.'

Mrs Stoneridge led them into the great hall. Its length stretched away into shadows like a huge cavern and its height into a vast hammer-beam ceiling where shadows and cobwebs hung, too. There was no fire in either of the fireplaces over which hung in military precision a collection of swords and breastplates above a pair of crossed blunderbusses — as if Sir Gerald Hawke had fought for any cause but his own. There was a huge black oak staircase down which the dimmest of red, blue and tarnished yellow light drifted from a large stained-glass window. The light dissolved into dusk, as if afraid to come into the dark below to meet the suit of armour gleaming dully at the foot of the stairs. On either side of the staircase, corridors led into other mysterious regions. All the doors leading off the hall were closed. It was cold and there was a pervasive smell of damp and age — and something else — decay.

'My quarters are down there,' Mrs Stoneridge pointed down one of the corridors. 'There's the kitchen and so forth. I'll thank you not to disturb me.' She looked hard at Scrap. 'No running about my private rooms. Nothing there for your inventory, Mr Smart.'

'Boy — very quiet — ma'am. Not a runner — bookish sort. Like me. Won't disturb a lady. Library, though.' The boy looked suitably timid and lowered his eyes modestly behind the ugly spectacles.

Mrs Stoneridge walked to one of the closed doors to the right of the front door. 'In here.'

Cold as a sarcophagus and as dark. 'Lamps, ma'am. Be obliged. Have to work late — you'll want us to be as quick as we can.'

'I'll bring them and the oil. In the meantime, there are candles on the table.'

Mrs Stoneridge went out and Dickens lit the candles. Scrap looked round in astonishment at the vast bookcases behind whose misty glass were ranks of ghostly books and at the old leather chairs with their horsehair stuffing poking out. Dickens noted the pale squares on the walls where pictures had hung and the dust sheets which shrouded remaining pieces of furniture and what looked like a stack of paintings.

'Blimey, Mr — Pa —' Scrap grinned — 'grim, ain't it?'

'Boy — now — ship-shape, if you please.' Dickens winked and took out of his bag a ledger, several pens and his inkwell and laid them on the table neatly. Scrap's job would be to write down the items Dickens thought were worth noting. He went to look at the books behind the dusty panes.

Mrs Stoneridge came back with two lamps. 'There are two more outside. The boy can fetch them.' She lit the two lamps and the smoke rose to mingle with the shadows and dust. 'Most of the books are gone — burnt for the fires. I should think what's left is only fit for burning.'

'Only need to count 'em — anything of value — when found — make a note. Used to it, ma'am. Quick survey now — rest tomorrow and the other rooms.'

'Most of them are empty — Sir Gerald sold most of the valuables over the years.' Her lips folded in a line. Her eyes were hard.

'What's left — pictures — knick-knacks — china ornaments — silver — know what's what, ma'am.'

'There's bread and cheese in the dining room and some ale. I'll show you your room — it's just upstairs. The other bedrooms are empty.'

'Quick look, ma'am — got to do it all. Orders — Mr Dalrymple's. Whole place, says he. Can't tell a lie.' Scrap came back with his lamps. 'Boy, see. Brought up honest.'

They went upstairs. The bedroom was a gloomy chamber with great black beams in the ceiling and a black bedstead with the truckle bed at its foot. No fire, of course, but there were blankets and a couple of counterpanes. There was a large, black oak coffer with an iron hasp on the bare black oak floorboards which creaked as they went in. *There would no doubt be a bloodstain which could never be got out*, Dickens thought. There was a table upon which to put the lamp and another with a marble top where there were a jug and a bowl for washing — in cold water, he supposed. The shutters were up at the windows and their lamplight did not reach the dark corners, but there was a door by the bedhead which must, of course, lead to a haunted chamber. Scrap's eyes were like moons behind his spectacles.

'Obliged, ma'am. Comfortable enough for us.' Still smiling. Chamber of horrors, more like.

Back in the library, Dickens's fingers itched to remove the dust sheet from that stack of pictures, but he would wait. Mrs Stoneridge might come back. Better to concentrate on the books first. He managed to prise open some of the bookcases. To his relief, most were almost empty. Sir Gerald had wanted to be warm, it seemed. The first case contained a damp set of volumes of *Blackwood's Magazine* — hardly worth noting. He found what looked like hundreds of volumes of Valpy's *Classics* — unopened, of course. *The Sportsman's Library* comprising volumes on hunting, shooting, coursing and fishing — someone had annotated those. In another case there was a set of *The Gentleman's Magazine* and what looked like at least twenty volumes of *The Beauties of England and Wales*. And someone had been on the Grand Tour: there were books on Egypt, Turkey, Florence, Venice — none of any particular value, he thought, with the illustrations all foxed and the bindings damp and decaying. He smiled at the next lot — perhaps Mr Dalrymple would like *Law Forms and Precedents*.

He moved on to another bookcase; the glass was cracked, and the door made a hideous grinding noise as he opened it. Miss Hamilton ought to be here — he noted the red morocco and calf bindings of some more promising volumes. Surely this was what she had called the Harleian binding, the red morocco and the central ornament, a lozenge in finely tooled gold. He looked at the title: *A System of Natural Philosophy*. The date inside was 1748. Valuable, he thought and not in too bad condition. He took out a calf-bound complete works of

231

Shakespeare, and *The Works of Chaucer*, dated, incredibly, 1593, printed by Godfrey, he read. There was a copy of Milton's *Paradise Lost*, dated 1668 and something called *The Muse's Recreation*, 1656. He wondered what other valuable, irreplaceable books Sir Gerald Hawke had thrown on his bonfires. Dickens took them over to the table where Scrap was to enter the titles into the ledger.

'Worth somethin'?'

'I should think so — write 'em in. It'll convince Mrs Stoneridge that we are actually doing the job.'

Scrap removed his spectacles and peered conscientiously at the ledger.

Dickens tried another bookcase. Here were the complete novels of Sir Walter Scott, *Robinson Crusoe* and *Gulliver's Travels* and some volumes of poetry: Alexander Pope, Shelley and Keats. He opened the Keats. It had been read and annotated, and there was a name inside: Millicent Mary Barnard, Hill Abbey, Warwickshire. The first Lady Hawke — he imagined a very young, very pretty Regency lady with her little gold pen sitting by the fire making her notes. And then she'd married Hawke. What a shock that must have been. Dickens took them to the table, which now looked convincingly business-like. He could warn Mr Dalrymple that there were some valuable books. Meredith Case should have something in return for his suffering.

He wasn't sure about the packed shelf of *The Philosophical Transactions of the Royal Society of London*, but they were handsomely bound in blue calf. It looked like one was missing. He put his hand in the space and prised out a little volume which didn't look particularly valuable. It was a volume of the fairy tales of the Brothers Grimm. He looked inside and on the flyleaf; written in a childish hand were the words: *Sydney Trent,*

*Kirkdale, Westmorland, 1827.*

Well, well, Sapphire Hawke surely had been to Westmorland. She must have brought this book here — borrowed it, perhaps. Was Sydney Trent the boy who had survived the fire? Perhaps Sapphire Hawke had been a visitor there for so short a time that no one remembered her — that dreadful fire had erased all memories of what had been before. He slipped the book into his pocket.

*That's enough on the books*, he thought. While Scrap was still writing, he went to look at the pictures under the dust sheet. He found it. It was exactly as Meredith Case had described it: Sir Gerald was holding the reins of a wild-looking horse. Long, cruel hands, one hand tight on the reins, and the other heavy on the shoulder of a young girl with a solemn, unhappy face. Meredith had remembered Sir Gerald's face and eyes with a kind of anguished fear. Dickens saw what he meant. Screech had been a greedy, heartless creature; Ned Temple warped by envy and bitterness; Esther Stoneridge was a miserable, avaricious thing, but this was different. He smelt corruption again as he gazed at the black eyes which looked at the girl, as if the painting gave off its own odour. There was greed, yes, but there was an icy cruelty gleaming there, as if the man calculated what he might do to her, how he might hurt her. And the girl — as Case had said, "too old a sorrow" for one so young. "Poised for flight," he had said. She had escaped, but to where?

Dickens covered it up again. When he stood, he felt a kind of sickness and his legs trembled. Who had painted such a thing? It was not signed. What had the artist felt, having seen what he had seen? Had he simply pocketed his fee and walked away? What had Hawke seen that he should hang it on his wall?

He looked at Scrap. They had come, he thought, in high

good humour. It was an adventure, a lark, and he had thought he might find out something about Sapphire Hawke. He hadn't fully understood Meredith Case's horror, but now he did, and Hawke Court felt suddenly threatening — more than just the pile of old timber and bricks and muddled passages and empty wastes of chambers that you might find in a Gothic novel. They wouldn't stay more than one night — tomorrow afternoon, he would go into the village and make his enquiries about Josephine Parker.

'Let's have our humble supper,' he said. 'We've done enough in here for now. Bring your ledger and we'll write down some stuff from the dining room.'

The bread was not quite stale, the cheese was hard, and the ale had a sour taste. There was nothing else.

'Mean ol' cat,' said Scrap, 'good job I brought this.' He took an apple out of his pocket — with a couple of bites taken out of it.

'Ah,' said Dickens, 'I think that apple is an old acquaintance.' Scrap always cheered him up.

'Beggars can't,' Scrap observed sagely. 'I'll eat the bitten side,' he added generously, 'but that's not all. Mollie gave me this — just in case, she said.' From another pocket he produced a pork pie, which he cut in half. 'Homemade.'

'Bless Mollie Rogers, and may her spoons always shine.' Spoon had been Mollie's maiden name. Scrap smiled — it was an old joke, but Mr D. liked it.

When the pie was finished, Dickens looked in the drawers of a grand sideboard, and Scrap wrote down the items he called out: silver knives and forks in odd numbers, all bearing the Hawke crest; spoons for every conceivable use and some silver napkin rings. In the cupboards below, a set of Sevres porcelain, all sorts of plates, cups, saucers, soup bowls. On top a silver candelabra, two silver salt cellars, wine coolers and silver baskets for fruit and sweets, a silver tray with some dusty decanters and very old glasses, many cracked. That was all. There were still some pictures on the walls, mostly muddy landscapes, an oil painting of Hawke Court in better days, and some pictures of fine-looking horses, one a Stubbs of which he made a special note. He looked in the green fly-spotted glass above the sideboard and saw the haggard likeness of a man he did not know — Tom Smart looked a bit haunted now; even the smile that Dickens tried gave back an impression of hollowness.

'Yer've not lost yer looks, Pa, though there's many as —'

Dickens laughed, and cheery Tom Smart came back. 'Bed, I think.'

Dickens heard Scrap's breathing very soon after they had gone to bed. How pleasant to have a quiet conscience. He hoped he would be able to sleep. Most of the feeling of sickness had passed, but he did like his bed to be in a north-south position. However, he could hardly move this one — it had probably been there for centuries. How many Hawkes had lain here waiting for death, or birth?

That was his last thought. Then Ruby Kiss's face emerged from darkness somewhere, her hair dripping blood. She was wearing the soldier's red jacket from Screech's, and then it was Ned Temple's face, running with water which dissolved into Sarah Hamilton's face. 'Red morocco,' she said, stabbing the leather with a sharp knife. Blood spouted from the cut. 'Exsanguination,' a faceless voice said. But when Sarah looked up, her face was wreathed in smoke and it was Hawke's face which faded into Mrs Stoneridge's eyes and she leant over him. She was offering him a cigar.

The room was pitch dark. Dickens sat up. *That cheese*, he thought, but he didn't move. He strained to hear. The timbers of the old house creaked like a ship at sea. There was a faint scratching. Mice, probably, nibbling at the wood. Soot fell down the chimney and there was a whisper of paper. Scrap breathing. The smell of damp — and something else. The smell of smoke — cigar smoke. Perhaps that had woken him. And then the faintest creak of a floorboard, which seemed to come from behind the door next to his bed. The haunted chamber — he hoped not. He hardly dared breathe. He thought he heard the tiniest click of a door being closed. Someone was creeping about. Surely not Mrs Stoneridge patrolling her domain, a cigar clamped between her teeth.

Or was it the residue of his dream? He had seen smoke and the cigar in Mrs Stoneridge's hand. Yet, he had heard something. He crept from his bed to listen at the door. His hand reached for the door handle, but he drew it back as if scalded. He could hear nothing now. He looked out of the window, but there was only the raven dark — no moon, no stars, no light from any window. Dead darkness lay on all the landscape. He heard the unearthly shriek of a vixen down in those woods somewhere and shuddered. Something white and silent flew past his window. An owl, and then he heard its eerie call and the answering one: 'Who? Who?' Who, indeed? Creatures of the night. What murder was taking place in those hidden places?

The night seemed to hold its breath, listening. He held his, straining to hear, but all was still now. The cold drove him back to bed where he dozed, dreaming of himself in disguise, trying to get home along familiar roads where people turned away, as from a stranger, until the night heaved a long sigh and began its departure, and the dawn light crept into the room.

# 36: PUTREFACTION'S GHOST

Breakfast was bread and cheese — the same bread and cheese, but Mrs Stoneridge had so far extended her meagre hospitality to provide two glasses of milk and an old apple cut in two. Of Mrs Stoneridge there was no sign.

They went back to the library. Dickens opened the curtains out of which clouds of dust flew. In the cold light of a misty grey morning, the library looked more melancholy than before. Dickens looked at the ledger which he had put back the night before with the volume of Keats's poetry on the open pages. The book had been moved — he hoped Mrs Stoneridge had been satisfied by what she had read there.

They peered into various cabinets, but they were empty. Dickens looked at the large, leather-topped desk that stood in front of the window. There were only a bone ruler and a silver-topped blotter there. He thought of his friend Richard Watson at Rockingham Castle and pictured his desk with its silver-handled paper knives, the goose quill pens and silver pencils, the desk portraits of his wife and children — all the paraphernalia that a man of means had on his desk. Nothing of any value was left here. Sold, Mrs Stoneridge had said. He thought of her avid eyes, that flinty countenance and the mean mouth.

And he thought of the little bags they had found at Screech's shop. Portable treasures — never missed. It would be very easy for someone who had access to everything while a sick, half-mad man lay dying. "My private quarters" — he could hardly force his way in.

Time to go upstairs. At the top, they looked along the

rambling corridor which twisted round corners to other wastes of passages and empty rooms. All the doors were closed. There must be twenty rooms along this corridor alone. Looking the other way, the corridor vanished into blackness and before them was another staircase — to the attics and servants' quarters, Dickens assumed. No reason to go there — no reason that he could give to Mrs Stoneridge. He thought about the house in the evening light seen from the top of the gate — that tower, it must be at the end of the right-hand corridor. They went that way, Scrap holding up a lamp, and found a locked door.

Mrs Stoneridge appeared quite suddenly — what a silent creature she was. He had no idea from where she had emerged, but he asked about the door.

'Hasn't been opened for years — never saw a key. In any case, the stairs aren't safe — so I was told.'

'Then Mr Dalrymple must be satisfied, ma'am.' Smiling Mr Smart was not a whit put out. 'Me an' the boy — quick look through the other rooms. Boy has his notebook — mention of any trifle of china, or a picture. Thing worth doing, ma'am, my old ma used to say.'

She nodded and glided away down the stairs he had not seen — back stairs for the servants. She seemed to need no light. Walked in darkness like the night. But he smelt cigar smoke again.

There was nothing to see in most of the rooms. One seemed to have been a salon. The floorboards were rotten. He pulled Scrap back from a treacherous-looking hole in the floor and they tiptoed round it. There were a chipped gilt chair with its legs in the air and a velvet chaise longue with its stuffing poking out, a round table, and an old fire screen, the kind that protected ladies' complexions from the heat. The wallpaper with its faded pattern of birds was peeling off and he noticed damp in the cornices and by one of the windows. Above the mantelpiece there was a portrait of the first Lady Hawke. She looked very pretty and very young — a portrait painted just after her marriage, and on the opposite wall there was a portrait of the same woman with a boy, a pretty, curly-haired boy with large, innocent eyes. Augustus Gerald — the heir who had died raving. The sins of the father.

They walked through a long gallery where long-nosed men and women, all alike in their aristocratic smugness sneered down, the portraits like the line of kings in *Macbeth*, stretching back to the crack of doom. *Another yet*, Dickens thought, pausing at the portrait of a young girl not unlike Sapphire Hawke, similarly delicate, but more composed in her velvet dress and ruff. *Long dead*, he thought, passed to the other side of silence. And the noble house of Hawke was no more — if it had ever been noble. *Bad blood*, he thought, *and black, not blue.*

'Wicked 'un.'

Dickens looked at Scrap in surprise. He had opened a door beyond the gallery and was on the threshold of a bedroom, where Dickens joined him. It had to be the bedroom in which Sir Gerald Hawke had died. He looked at the great black bed with its ragged curtains and the Hawke Crest carved into the black oak above.

'How do you know?' he asked.

'Smell o' somethin' bad, somethin' rotten. Worse than Tom All Alone's — yer knows, down off Chancery Lane. Terrible things down there, but this — it's —'

'I know the place — and this is worse, in a way.' Dickens knew what Scrap meant, but he was curious. How would the boy articulate the mystery?

'My ma — said that there was a thing — evil, she called it.

Niver knowed wot she meant until now.'

Apart from a pair of candlesticks decorated with hideous skulls, there was nothing remarkable about the room — just the bed, stripped of its sheets and counterpane, a few chairs and a huge, empty fireplace. It was cold — *putrefied with cold*, an old woman had said to him once, meaning petrified, but putrefied was the right word here — and, like Scrap, Dickens felt something suffocating in the air as if the corruption were a tangible presence which would infect their very blood. Meredith Case had felt it and it had nearly broken him. The stench of putrefaction was the ghost of Sir Gerald Hawke. He felt a kind of sickness in his bones, as if Hawke's disease infected him. He hurried Scrap out and closed the door.

'We've done enough. Let's be off to get our things and tell Mrs Toad-eye that we have finished.'

The great door closed upon them. Mrs Stoneridge had merely nodded when Dickens told her that he was sure Mr Dalrymple would be satisfied that they had listed all the valuables. No doubt she would hear from the lawyer. He thanked her for her hospitality with all Mr Tom Smart's cheerful ingenuousness. Alick Smart bowed to her. She showed no feeling at all.

Dickens remembered seeing the church beyond the woods. They would go that way, along the path, out into the cold fresh air which would disperse the nausea he had felt in that room. He watched Scrap, who, having dispensed with the spectacles, gazed up at the canopy of tall trees where sunlight now filtered. Then he was running on, picking up sticks, examining his footprint in the mud, climbing a stile, waiting for him, grinning as Dickens hurried to catch up. Scrap would be all right — he had shaken off what he had experienced and was occupied by the wonder of these woods where the thick trees crowded and then separated to show them a clearing and a bright glance of water from which the lingering mist rose.

Over another stile and the path became narrower and the woods darker. They walked in single file, passing a tumble-down cottage or summerhouse, perhaps, squatting toad-like under its ruined green roof. He thought of Mrs Stoneridge — she ought to live there. Scrap still marched ahead. It was very quiet, though there was sometimes a rustle in the undergrowth or the call of a bird. Dickens hoped he had taken the right path, but the trees thinned and there was another stile ahead. Scrap climbed over and dropped lightly on the other side. Dickens stood on the top step to look around. He saw the church spire and made ready to climb down.

The snap of a twig, sharp as a gunshot. A flurry of birds rose into the air with alarmed calls. Someone was there. Dickens knew it and so did Scrap. Dickens pointed ahead. Scrap called out, 'Come on, Pa, yer very slow terday.' They walked on at the same pace, Tom Smart, all good cheer, talking to the boy about the trees, the birds, the possibility that a fox might be hiding in the undergrowth, and Scrap talking to Pa, asking questions and laughing.

And then there was a break in the perimeter wall and they were through, passing by the church, out of reach of Hawke Court. Dickens paused by the rectory, thinking about the Reverend Octavius Swann, but Scrap had other ideas.

'Bet they've got a nice pigeon pie there, hot gravy, mash, peas, p'raps. 'Ot dinner fer two, Pa.' He pointed to the Hawke Arms.

# 37: MISSING PERSONS

The pie was good, the mash was creamy; no peas, but the carrots were fresh and tender; the ale was sweet, and the landlord, a talkative man, curious about the strangers. 'Hawke Court — moulderin' old pile. Bet there's naught left there — sold everythin', folks say.'

'True, Mr Black, there ain't much worth savin', but what there is, the lawyer wants to know about so me an' the lad, we've made our inventory.'

Abe Black watched the boy tucking into his pie. 'Hungry, ain't 'e? Don't suppose Mrs Stoneridge killed the fatted calf.'

'No — she ain't a warm woman, that's certain. Bit of a tartar, I thought. She'll be movin' on, I daresay, now Sir Gerald's dead. Been there a long time — that's the impression I got.'

'Aye — she came back as a widow. Don't think her husband left her anythin'. He was a shambling sort, Joshua Stoneridge, but he came into a legacy and they moved away to start some sort of business — nursery, I think. Didn't come to any good.'

Just as Dickens was thinking about how he could mention any other servants at Hawke Court without arousing suspicion, a woman came out. 'Apple pie, Abe, for the visitors.'

She came out from behind the counter bearing two plates of something hot and sweet, smelling of sugar and cinnamon. Scrap had already finished his pigeon pie. Dickens was just starting.

'Good appetite, your lad,' the woman said.

'He has, ma'am, though he don't seem to grow much.'

'I was sayin', Maggie, that they'd not 'ave got much out o' Mrs Stoneridge.'

'You know her?' Dickens looked at the woman. She was attractive, with dark hair untouched by grey and fine, clear hazel eyes. She would have been a striking young woman, but not, alas, Josephine Parker.

'Knew, more like. She doesn't come to the village — not since she came back.'

'She was here before she was wed?'

'Worked in the kitchen at Hawke Court. You wouldn't believe it, but she was a pretty little girl with fair hair and a neat figure. We was girls together. I went to train as a housemaid. Lots of us village girls went into service up at the court. It was just after Lady Millicent — she was the first Lady Hawke — had died. Mind, I was only thirteen. Sir Gerald didn't come much after that, then he brought his new wife — after his son died. That was in 1819, and Lady Julia came in 1820 — Esther Stoneridge was still there, but in 1820 I married Abe and came to live here with him and his ma and pa —'

Abe Black was called away. 'Cream with that?' Mrs Black asked Scrap as he took his spoon to break into the apple pie. She went to the bar to get the jug and took an order for pigeon pie from another customer.

Dickens was thinking rapidly. The only way was to ask about Sapphire Hawke. Mrs Black seemed a friendly sort — not at all like Mrs Stoneridge. He watched her pour the cream for Scrap and he began, aware of his heart beating that little bit faster, 'Mr Dalrymple —'

'The lawyer?' Dickens nodded. 'I remember him — came to the house sometimes, and he was at the funeral with the doctor and the heir, a parson, folks said. Miserable affair, that was —'

'Mr Dalrymple is anxious to find out what happened to a girl called Sapphire Hawke, who was Sir Gerald's ward —' Dickens plunged into the biggest lie of the lot — 'there's some idea that she might be Sir Gerald's natural daughter —'

Maggie Black laughed — but there was bitterness in it. 'Oh, aye, that I can believe — there was always talk about Sir Gerald and the servant girls and his by-blows. An' his friends — they brought all sorts down here, gamblin', drinkin', parties — couldn't keep their hands off —' her face darkened at some memory — 'I was glad to get out of it, I can tell you. But Sapphire Hawke, I don't know — but I do know — everyone knew — about Esther Stoneridge —'

'What about her?'

'Married off to Joshua Stoneridge —' she lowered her voice — 'an' paid for it. Set 'em up in business, Hawke did. Legacy, my foot — them Stoneridges was poor as charity. We all knew she was expectin' Hawke's bastard.'

'What happened to the child?'

'A son, I heard — be in his thirties now — went in the army, I was told, but he ain't been here for years — they used to come when he was a lad. Esther Stoneridge's mother lived here. She came back; we all thought she might try to get Hawke to acknowledge him — make him the heir — but seems the parson's got it all. That'll have put her nose out of joint.'

'Do you know the name Josephine Parker?'

'Josie — she was Lady Julia Hawke's maid in town.'

'What happened to her? Mr Dalrymple told me the town house was sold.'

'So it was — I thought she'd got married in London. She never came back here. Neither did Lucy Bird's girl.'

'Who?'

'Lucy Bird worked in the laundry. Had a little girl — they lived in a cottage in the woods — ruined now. Supposed to be a widow. Course, everyone wondered about the child. She'd be about the age of Sapphire Hawke, but she ran away — oh, years ago now, back in 1830 somethin'. Never came back. Not surprisin' — the mother was a cruel piece of work, but that girl was an independent little thing. Fought like cat an' dog, or cat an' cat, I should say. She was always runnin' off, roamin' those woods. That cottage, it was a wreck. Lucy Bird lived in squalor after the girl went. Dead now — of drink. Mad as old Hawke at the end.'

'You never met Sapphire Hawke?'

'No — saw her with Miss Henrietta Hawke, Sir Gerald's cousin — they went to church sometimes, an' you'd see her occasionally in the woods with Lucy Bird's girl — lonely, both of 'em, I think. We didn't have much to do with them at the court after Lady Julia's death — it was all mostly closed up.'

The Hawke Arms was filling up. Mrs Black began to clear their table. 'Best eat your pie, sir; it's cold, but it'll still be good. I'd better get on. Sorry I couldn't be more help about Sapphire Hawke. Pity — poor girl. We never even knew where she came from. Makes you think about people's lives, don't it — they come, they go, and you forget them. I hadn't thought of Lucy's girl for years, but they should be important to someone. I've girls of my own — and you've this lovely lad —' she ruffled Scrap's hair — 'he'll be a credit to you, I don't doubt.'

The future credit's smile was almost heart-breaking. Dickens felt the tears sting his eyes. Scrap should have had a mother like this. He fished about for his bag and went to pay the bill, then they went out to hire a trap to take them to the station.

# 38: A MAN WITH A BASKET

There were not many people waiting for the London train, and they did not have to wait long. They settled themselves in a first-class carriage — Tom Smart would have gone second class, but it didn't matter now. Dickens looked idly out of the window. There was no one left on the platform but a tall man in an old hat, wearing the garb of a labourer, a basket beside him, just lounging, smoking his pipe.

Scrap was very quiet. He gazed out of the window at the unrolling landscape. Dickens left him to his thoughts. Scrap would work it all out — his losses and his gains. Sometimes silence was the better wisdom than talk. Dickens was glad to have the time to think.

Josephine Parker — was she a dead end? Was her purpose in this story just to send him to Hawke Court — one of those characters that came in and went out, necessary to the plot, but to be dispensed with when their part was played? Or one of those glimpsed by the protagonist in the street, or in a pub, just part of the landscape, not the face he wanted in his search for a villain? You never knew in writing your story which characters might open out to you — that was the most astonishing thing in invention, how what one did not know sprang up and would be written. He took out his notebook. Perhaps the beneficent power which he believed gave him his stories would show it all to him. *Come on*, he said to himself, whisper to me. He began to write.

*Esther Stoneridge's son — Sir Gerald Hawke's natural son for whom she had hoped a legacy.* He thought of cigar smoke and wondered. Someone in the woods — someone spying on them. Had the son turned up after Sir Gerald had died? Was he after those sapphires? Mrs Stoneridge would know about them. He thought of portable treasures. Perhaps the son had received his legacy by other means.

*Josephine Parker — whereabouts unknown. At the town house sixteen years ago when it was sold to Miss Gauntlett's father. Could have known Sapphire Hawke.*

*Lucy Bird's daughter — whereabouts unknown. Same age as Sapphire Hawke. Played with her in the woods.* Maggie Black hadn't mentioned her name. Still, what good would it have been? She could be anywhere.

*Sapphire Hawke — whereabouts unknown. Last heard of at St. Katherine's Wharf.*

Dickens thought of someone else, a boy whose handwriting he had seen. He took out the little book and looked at the handwriting: *Sydney Trent, Kirkdale, Westmorland* — whereabouts unknown. Could he be traced? He knew Sapphire Hawke. He had given her this book. Adopted by relatives, Meredith Case had written. The Trents had been distantly related to the Hawkes, which explained why Sapphire Hawke had been there. Perhaps Lady Alice Trent whose memorial Mr Case had seen had been a Hawke.

Dickens thought he might give the book to Eleanor and Tom Brim. He thought Scrap — who was now sleeping — might look askance at fairy tales. He looked at the handwriting again and thought about a boy who had lost his parents and who had been sent away to relatives. Another orphan. He hoped the relatives had been kinder than Sir Gerald Hawke had been to Sapphire Hawke. He turned the pages at random.

Here was a story that Sapphire Hawke must have read, for she — or the boy, perhaps — had marked in pencil the opening lines: *There was once a poor shepherd boy whose mother and father were dead, and he was placed by the authorities in the house of a rich man, who was to feed him and bring him up. The man and his wife, however, had bad hearts…*

It must have been Sapphire Hawke — she who had been placed with a rich man with a bad heart. *Poor child*, Dickens thought, imagining her in that cavernous library reading for dear life, finding comfort in stories which told that others had suffered the same hardship. That might give courage. As a child he had read and read, finding solace in *The Arabian Nights*, in all the golden fables of silver palaces and stones of pearl. How did this fairy tale end? Ah, not so well. The boy died and the house of his cruel keepers burnt to ashes in a fire. That part had been underlined, too. Kirkdale Hall had burnt down, but surely Sapphire Hawke had not been there then.

The boy, then, Sydney Trent. Dickens looked back at the beginning of the book. There was more handwriting on the flyleaf: *To Sydney. Take courage. Your friend, Frederick Sutton.* Meredith Case had mentioned a Doctor Sutton who had taken in the boy after the fire. It was a puzzle: someone would have remembered the girl surviving the fire, but no one remembered Sapphire Hawke. She could not have been there, then, in 1827. The boy had survived. The doctor had given him this book — why did he part with it? And if he had been given it after the fire — which the inscription suggested — how had it come to Hawke Court? Could the two orphans, both connected to the Hawke family, have somehow been brought together? Had the boy, Sydney Trent, been at Hawke Court and left his book? He needed to find that boy — though he would be grown-up now, in his thirties. But there must be records of Hawke relatives.

Dickens wrote another note: *Sydney Trent? Burke's Peerage?*

The train was slowing as they approached the terminus at Waterloo. Look for Lady Alice Trent — that would be a start. Dickens got his bag from the rack and he and Scrap got off the train. As they walked along, he saw a tall man with his basket slung over his shoulders, the man who had lounged by a pillar watching the train — a man who walked very tall and erect for a country labourer.

# 39: THE FOLLOWER

It was easy enough to follow them across Waterloo Bridge. It was crowded, but he was tall enough to keep them in sight, and he didn't mind shoving his way through. A lawyer's clerk and his boy travelling in a first-class carriage? George Stoneridge was suspicious. Something didn't smell right. What had they been gossiping about in the Hawke Arms? They'd been in there a long time. His mother had warned him about the inn — Maggie Black, the landlady, had been in service at Hawke Court years ago. She'd remember Sapphire Hawke, if that's who Mr Smart had been lookin' for. It seemed odd to George that Dalrymple had sent someone to count up a load of old books and a few trinkets. Smart and the boy had gone off pretty quickly, too. And they hadn't finished the job. There was all sorts of stuff in rooms that had been shut up for years. Still, all the more pickings for him — he had a good few things in his basket.

Pity old Screech was dead — he'd have to find another fence to take 'em, and he wanted a good price. A man had to live. Screech was a graspin' old cove, but he knew how to keep a secret and he never asked where anything came from, just grinned at the crests on the goods. Well, he'd keep his secrets now. And that was a facer — had the police got their sticky fingers on the Hawke trinkets, or had Screech sold 'em on? George had had his good prices from Screech, but he didn't like to think of what was his by rights in the wrong hands. Good thing he'd kept that diamond ring. Perhaps the police hadn't found the other bits — that shop was packed with cupboards, boxes, bags. Screech would have hidden the good stuff. There was a cellar, he knew — not that he'd been invited down there. Might be worth a look. But for now, Smart was the man to watch.

Ma had thought those two would be there for days and then they were going, but not in so much of a hurry that they couldn't linger at the Hawke Arms. Had Smart found something in those books? You never knew — a letter, a diary — something which pointed the way to that girl. And had he learned something from Maggie Black? It might be time to act — time that Danks learned that you didn't get money for nothing. According to Danks, the coppers had been looking for Ned Temple and a knife. 'You might find that a knife's missing, Joah, my friend,' George had suggested. Ned Temple, the joker in the pack, might well become the ace in his hand.

Smart and his boy were walking up Bow Street. They crossed Long Acre, turned in to Earl Street, and went through Seven Dials, where he nearly lost them. There was an abandoned cart on the pavement outside a pub. He stood on it, sighted them, and caught up with them as they turned in to Crown Street, where about halfway along they slowed and stopped outside a shop window. George stood in a doorway and waited. The boy went in and Smart walked on towards Oxford Street — going to report to Dalrymple, maybe — not at Clement's Inn, but at his house. Now that would be worth knowing. Dalrymple kept his keys on his watch chain. Suppose he was walking home in the dark one night. Ned Temple would know where he lived. Ned Temple who knew Ruby Kiss, Ned Temple who had pinched a knife from Dalrymple's chambers. Danks could remember a missing knife. Royal flush. George hurried on. Smart seemed to have picked up his pace.

Dickens was anxious to get home. He needed to bathe — he felt dusty and grubby and he wanted to wash away the odour of corruption, though the rain was doing that quite well. It was damned cold, too. He walked briskly up Norfolk Street, past Sam's house, but he didn't knock. Carburton Street was quiet, apart from a cab outside a house and the horse steaming in the gas light. He'd be home in a few minutes.

The back of his neck prickled. He knew without turning round that someone was following him, matching him stride for stride. He didn't dare stop, but he wanted to know who it was — garrotter? Footpad? He could knock on someone's door. He knew the family at number thirty-two, but they wouldn't know who he was in his disguise — probably shut the door in his face. He kept his even pace — he'd make a sudden turn in to Norton Street.

Off Norton Street, another narrower street led into Buckingham Place. He paused briefly in the narrow street. The footsteps were heavier, hurrying now. But he'd lose him in this twist of streets. He turned left up Buckingham Place, at the top of which was a little alley leading back to Norton Street. Whoever this was, he might not know the streets as well as Charles Dickens. He hurried down the alley and waited in the shelter of a yard door — he could run if need be. He listened. Sure enough, the footsteps came on. They stopped at the entrance to the alley. To his horror, the door against which he was leaning opened with a creak. He shot into the yard and bolted the door. A dog started to bark — dear God, he thought, garrotted, or savaged. The dog seemed perilously close. He turned to see the animal — rather large and disturbingly frothy about the jaws — but it was chained up. A window opened and a voice cried, 'Shut yer bleedin' racket!' A beer bottle smashed at his feet. The dog looked a bit embarrassed. Night Alley was always a bit on the rough side.

Dickens slid open the bolt and slipped back into the alley, keeping close to the door. The dog gave a farewell growl to preserve his self-respect and all was silent again. He crept back to Buckingham Place and peeped round the corner. A tall shadow was crossing the road, going towards Fitzroy Square — a tall shadow carrying a basket. For a moment, another image of a tall, broad-shouldered man superimposed itself on the shadow. Then he was gone.

# 40: BLADE AND BONE

By means of painstaking cross-referencing, tracing Hawkes and Lambs — which combination rather amused Dickens — Burke's peerage had revealed Lady Alice Trent. Her mother had been Mary Georgiana Elizabeth Hawke, born 1750 at Hawke Court — Sir Gerald Hawke's aunt.

Mary Georgiana had married Richard Lamb, esquire, of Seat Hill, Westmorland in 1775, the year of Sir Gerald's birth. She had borne eight children of whom Alice Lavinia was the youngest, born 1786. Mary Georgiana had died in the same year. Richard Lamb had died in 1805 before his youngest daughter had married Sir Robert Trent of Kirkdale Hall, Westmorland in 1807.

While the Lambs had eight offspring, the Hawkes seemed distinctly unfruitful. Sir Gerald had had one brother who had died in his teenage years and a sister who had died without issue, for which Dickens was truly thankful, for it suggested to him that Sydney Trent had probably been adopted by a Lamb rather than a Hawke.

However, these Lambs — seven of them besides Lady Alice — were, inconveniently, either deceased, leaving issue the length and breadth of England, even unto Cornwall, or, equally inconveniently, were alive — just — and living also in far-flung places, even unto India. A third inconvenience had raised its ugly head in that Lady Alice had three sisters; two of them had married men, naturally with names other than Lamb — not Sheep or Goat, but the perfectly respectable Pengelley of Penzance and the Very Reverend Decimus Morgan of Monmouth. If he were the tenth of ten, Dickens shuddered to think how many children he had sired. One more would hardly make a difference. Suppose Sydney Trent was now Morgan in Monmouth.

It was hopeless; there was nothing more he could do for Sydney Trent who may, or may not, have knowledge of Sapphire Hawke from more than twenty years ago. He had not time to go haring about the country, nor had he time to write dozens of letters. It was a matter for Mr Dalrymple. There were no Lambs now at Seat Hill, Westmorland, but that did not preclude Meredith Case from making enquiries. Dickens had explained it all as succinctly as he could in the letter he had just written to the Reverend Case, who was still nursing his foot at Kirkdale — he could hire a trap, no doubt. The Rector's sister might go with him. Dickens smiled at the thought. Just what Mr Case needed — the company of a charming young woman. He was sure she was charming — and a clergyman's sister. Made in Heaven.

Of more pressing moment this morning — which was why Dickens was putting on his hat and coat — was the matter of the bar sinister on the noble escutcheon of the Hawkes — the bastard Stoneridge who Dickens was sure was the man with the basket who had followed him from Waterloo, and who knew, most probably, where Scrap was to be found. Bow Street first.

Jones was going out, too, with Sergeant Rogers, but he stayed to listen to Dickens's account of Hawke Court, the intelligence concerning the illegitimate son, and the man with the basket.

'You think he's after those sapphires?'

'Well, he didn't get anything else, and the landlady told me that it was thought that Mrs Stoneridge hoped that her son would be acknowledged. Bit of a disappointment, I should think — not that they haven't helped themselves to a good many valuable items. Pair of thieves, I'd say.'

'The important thing is Scrap. Alf —' Jones turned to Rogers — 'get along to the shop, take Scrap to my house in Norfolk Street.'

'Do you want me to meet you at the Blade and Bone afterwards?'

'No, you stay with Mollie — do some shopkeeping just in case. Mr Dickens can come with me. I'll explain to him on the way. Oh, and send Stemp to Clement's Inn again. Tell him to note any strangers about. He's looking for a tall man with a military bearing — as if that helps.'

Eddie Grant, pot boy at the Blade and Bone in Butcher's Row, behind Clare Market, had been told by the landlord about his sister's death. He, Percy Oakes, had read it in the paper and had offered to take the boy to Bow Street, but the boy had been too frightened. The word 'Murder', screaming from the headline of the *Morning Chronicle*, had left him in a state of terror so Percy Oakes, who knew Mollie Spoon's mother and had therefore met Sergeant Rogers, had the idea of going to see him.

Mr Oakes, of some girth and height, was behind his bar when Dickens and Jones came in to introduce themselves.

'Poor lad — he's that shocked. Can't 'ardly take it in — I don't know what to do with 'im. 'E's a good lad, an' Ruby was all 'e 'ad by way of fam'ly. An' she was good to 'im, was Ruby. You know all about 'er, I suppose?' He gave Jones a narrow look.

'We do — it doesn't make any difference to me. Ruby Kiss was murdered, and I want to know who did it, and why.'

Mr Oakes showed them into his parlour where Eddie Grant

sat on a hard chair, staring at nothing in particular. A mug of ale and an uneaten sandwich lay before him on the table. He looked like a badly wrapped parcel waiting to be collected; his large apron from which his arms stuck out at angles was tied with string, his long legs were awkwardly crossed, and his very large feet looked as though they were attached to the wrong legs. His clumsy boots were also tied with string. His hair was tow-coloured and dry as thatch, but he had Ruby's pale blue eyes, which were now red-rimmed. Dickens saw the tearstains on his dirty face. He looked very frightened, very young, and very lost. When he saw them, he wiped his nose on his shirt sleeve.

At a glance from Jones, Dickens went forward to sit on the other upright chair at the table.

'Eddie, take some of this ale and a bite of the sandwich. It will do you good — you'll feel a bit better.'

Used to obedience, the boy did as he was told. Dickens waited for him to eat something and Jones stepped back from the doorway so that the boy should not see him. Dickens would get him to talk.

'We've come about Ruby, Eddie — do you think you could tell me about her?'

Eddie looked at the kindly eyes. 'You her friend?'

'No, Eddie, but I know about her and how people liked her and that she was very good to you.'

'I only 'ad Ruby — she came ter see me. She took me out ter the chop house an' ter the waxworks an' ter the Panorama — seen Egypt once.' The tears spilled over again. 'Wot'll I do now?'

'Mr Oakes will take care of you, Eddie, I'm sure of that. When did Ruby say she would come?'

'Sunday — but she never came. I thort she — she said

things'd be better soon. She was movin' from Giff's an' she'd 'ave some money an' I could maybe live — then she never came, an' Mr Oakes showed me —' Eddie wiped his nose again.

'Was Ruby going to live with someone — a rich man?'

Eddie looked at him. 'I went ter Giff's Court. Saw Ruby, but she was with him an' I came away. See, I 'adn't seen 'er fer a while. Ruby said ter be patient, but I wanted ter see 'er — I wanted ter see Ruby, but I knew she wouldn't want me there when 'e was there. She said she 'ad ter be careful. 'E didn't know I woz Ruby's brother, but she'd tell 'im, she said.'

'When did you go to Giff's Court?'

'Few nights ago — went at night after closin'. Thort she might be there.'

Dickens knew he would have to be patient — to try to tease out some hard facts from Eddie's muddled tale, though Percy Oakes might remember which night it was. 'Did Ruby see you?'

'No, she was a bit drunk an' they woz laughin' an' then they went in. An' I came back. Waited fer Ruby ter come…' The boy's eyes filled.

'Do you know the man's name?'

'Capt'in, she said — Capt'in George — from a rich fam'ly, she said, waitin' fer a lot o' money from a rich man wot 'ad died. But Ruby's dead — wot can I do?'

Eddie put his head down on the table and wept again. There was nothing more to do — the poor boy's grief overpowered him. Just at that moment, a young woman came in.

'Leave him to me, sir. I'm Susan Oakes, Percy's daughter — we'll look after him.'

Dickens went out, but Jones had already gone. He was talking to Percy Oakes in the bar. Dickens stood and listened.

Percy Oakes was explaining, 'Nobody uses it much now, but the captain kept his horse in there. I'll show you — it's out the back. I'll bring a lantern.'

When Percy left them, Dickens asked, 'Did you hear the bit about the boy's going to Giff's Court?'

'I did. I thought it might be more profitable to speak to Oakes. He did remember — Eddie just went, and Percy knew where, but he wasn't long and he was upset when he came back — it was the night Ruby was at the Casino de Venise — the night we think she was killed.'

'The captain was there — at Giff's Court. Eddie called him Captain George — but he was too distressed for me to press him.'

'You won't need to — Percy Oakes knows who he is. Captain George Stone.'

'Stone! Esther Stoneridge's son is or was in the army, so the landlady at the Hawke Arms said. Eddie told me that Ruby's lover had styled himself as a rich man waiting for a wealthy relative to die — Stoneridge was waiting for Hawke to die and Mrs Stoneridge had expectations for her son.'

Jones raised an eyebrow. 'Remarkable coincidence, Mr Dickens.'

'As niver was equalled, Mr Superintendent; there niver was sich a place as London for coincidence — but seriously —'

'I know it, and I'm willing to entertain it. Listen to the rest of Oakes's tale. Captain Stone stayed at the Blade and Bone and that's where he met Ruby — Percy Oakes wasn't too sure about him, but he paid his dues, and seemed fond of her. Of course, he wasn't convinced about the riches nor about any sort of future — George had already told him he was expecting a legacy from his aristocratic family — a family he'd fallen out with, which was why he joined the army. Percy doubted that he'd be returning to his doting mother with Ruby Kiss on his arm, but if he was treating her right and she was enjoying herself, why not?'

'Poor Ruby and her dreams. And that wretched boy.'

'Gambling man, Captain Stone, it seems — very adept with the dice and very skilled with the cards. A number of customers parted with their money and didn't know quite how. The captain left for the country — and this is an important bit — the night Felix Gresham was killed. He took his horse —'

'Which he kept in this stable.'

'He was away for a couple of weeks. Ruby was very anxious, but then the captain came back, and all seemed well. Yes, he told Oakes that he would be moving on — his great expectations had come to fruition. Ah, Ruby, well, he told our Percy, he was fond of her, of course, but — you can guess the rest of that conversation. Percy's a man of the world — he just hoped Ruby had got something out of it. The captain paid his bill and vanished a week ago.'

'And we're looking —'

'For a hayseed.'

'You think —'

'I do — Ruby brought Felix Gresham and Ned Temple to the Blade and Bone —'

'Because they'd all met at the Casino de Venise.'

'So they had — not coincidence at all, then.'

'Fate, more like — and a dark one at work.'

'They went in for card-playing and drinking and general merrymaking — all-night sessions in the stable. Percy Oakes didn't think much about it. They were eating their suppers, ordering bottles of wine — nice profit for him. Of course, they didn't come when the captain was away, but they were back —'

'On the night of Felix Gresham's murder?'

'Percy Oakes can't be sure of that — he thinks it was then or near then, so let's have a look.'

Jones pushed open the double doors — they were not kept locked. "Nothin' to take," Percy Oakes had said.

Could a place retain the imprint of murder? Dickens thought of Hawke Court and the way in which Sir Gerald Hawke had left his impression of corruption in the air as if the atmosphere was his very shape. He sensed it again — something dreadful had happened here. Yet, it seemed very ordinary: a cobbled floor, wispy with straw, three stalls for the horses, a few wooden boxes, some horseshoes fixed to the wall, an old stool kicked over — that might be telling.

In the first two stalls the hay racks were empty, but there was straw piled in the corners. No sign that it had been disturbed. There were signs of occupation in the third one, the hay rack partly full, straw on the cobbles, dried horse droppings and a bucket of water. There was no sign of blood on the cobbles. Jones took the hay fork and began to sift through the pile of straw in the corner. Dickens went out and found a rake. There was no blood.

'There's a set of stairs — a hay loft, I should think.'

Up the stairs, there were hay bales stacked against the walls, but a few had been moved to be set round an old wooden crate. There was another wooden stool, too. Two or three had gathered here, thought Dickens. 'The gambling den?'

'Looks like it.'

'Why in here and not in the pub?'

'High stakes — not much light — two young fools with plenty of drink in them and fancying themselves living dangerously, and the captain a man of the world, I'll bet. In these shadows and all the aces up his sleeve — in more ways than one.'

They went forward and found a playing card — the Queen of Diamonds — and several bottles which had contained wine. They could smell urine, too. Dickens picked up a cigar butt and sniffed it. It was just stale — it did not tell a tale of a man smoking in a secret room. Nevertheless, he showed it to Jones. 'Someone was smoking in the room next to mine at Hawke Court — it must have been George Stoneridge.'

Jones didn't answer; he was shining the lantern down a passage through a stack of hay bales. It was wide enough for a man to get through. As Jones went through, he noted that the smell of urine was stronger here and there was dried vomit on the hay. There was a cleared space between the bales and the wall and here, on the cobbles, he saw the quantity of congealed blood.

'Blood,' he called as he backed out, 'and someone's been sick in there.'

'Felix Gresham?'

'Someone went in there to vomit and to relieve himself. Someone followed and someone was killed — probably Felix Gresham, in whose blood the doctor found hayseeds.'

'And whose body was found on the steps of a bookshop — who took him there?'

'Now that is a question which needs thinking about — Ned Temple? But why would he take dead Felix away unless he killed him and the captain doesn't come into this at all?'

'But he was here, surely — at least Percy Oakes thinks so.'

'"Thinks" ain't enough, Charles — nor is that cigar, before you mention it. In any case, the captain could have left with his winnings and his Ruby, and the other two could have rowed about money. You described it yourself: Felix Gresham laughing it all off, Ned Temple desperate, furious that he's been led into gambling away what he didn't have — that's how he'd see it — all Gresham's fault. And he knows the bookshop — easy enough to pretend his friend is drunk —'

'Ruby Kiss — perhaps she went with them. Maybe she thought that Miss Hamilton and Miss Finch would look after Felix. Perhaps she thought he was too ill to go home. When she finds out Felix is dead, she has her suspicions — Temple realises that and kills Ruby.'

Jones was thinking. After a few moments, he said, 'Ruby Kiss — she very well could have done all that, but with George, not Temple. We could easily suppose that Ned Temple left before the others and George killed Gresham.'

'But why?'

'Same reason — yes, he had his winnings, but what did he owe Felix Gresham? Was he playing with money he'd borrowed anyway?'

'Crooked Alley, off St. Anne's Court, round the corner from the bookshop — I wonder if Captain Stone — or Stoneridge — knew Screech.'

'Wouldn't surprise me. There might be something in those papers of his. A handy address, for example, of a man whose last initial is "S". There was one in Dean Street and one in Noel Street, as I recall. Back to Bow Street.'

'There's something I have to do at the office. I'll come to Bow Street when I've finished.'

# 41: DOUBLE DUCATS

'Not now, not now,' Dickens muttered to himself. 'Look at us,' the piles of papers and letters seemed to say. He only wanted Burke's *Peerage*, which was where he had left it open at the entry of Richard Lamb and his offspring. It was Hawkes he wanted. He scanned the entry, found what he had expected to find, and hurried out again, taking the stairs two at a time, passing Harry Wills on his way up. Wills opened his mouth to speak, but he was too late, the chief was gone — again.

Jones was looking through a heap of dog-eared papers as Dickens went in. 'That was quick.'

'I found what I was looking for in Burke's *Peerage* — it has become my devoted study. Remember those trinkets we found with the monograms? I had a thought when Screech's name occurred to me. Let's have a look at them.'

Jones took the bags from the safe and Dickens separated out several of the monogrammed items. He thought about the portrait he had seen of Hawke's first wife, and of her pedigree. He offered Jones the little gold pencil. 'MMB, I think could well be Lady Millicent Mary, formerly Miss Barnard, Hawke's first wife.'

'And you said that you thought the Stoneridges had helped themselves over the years.'

'Julia Ann Coleman was the second Lady Hawke.' Dickens handed Jones the silver-backed mirror with its entwined initials engraved in the cartouche — a small mirror, a young girl's mirror. Had she seen her future there? A grand staircase where faint coloured light drifted into shadows, its dizzying height a precipice from which she fell, flying to her death, escaping

264

from her bondage.

Jones had picked up a gold snuffbox. 'AAH — another Hawke?'

'Alexander Augustus, father of Sir Gerald Hawke.'

Jones looked at the silver cup. 'What about SMF?'

'The Honourable Susan Mary Flower, third daughter of Maurice Flower, the Viscount Charswell —' seeing Jones's rather twisted grimace, Dickens grinned and finished, 'Sir Gerald Hawke's mother.'

'George Stoneridge, then.'

'Looks very likely.'

'Pawned these things with Screech because selling them might lead to awkward questions, and Screech wasn't a man to ask questions.'

'Screech would have liked having them, miser that he was — he'd enjoy looking at his treasures — kept him warm at night, no doubt. They'd be worth more than he paid Stoneridge.'

'And there's this lot.' Jones poured out a collection of coins which spilled onto the counter in a gold and silver stream.

'Shylock,' said Dickens, picking up a gold coin and examining it. 'Double ducats — by God, it is Venetian. Look, there's the Doge of Venice kneeling to Saint Mark. Not quite three thousand, but worth a mint. Pure gold, this is. Some Hawke brought them back a century ago from his Grand Tour.'

'Now,' said Jones, 'did he kill Screech so he could get them back and keep the money?'

Dickens sat down. 'Little Johnny's giant was no fairy story?'

'So why did Temple kill himself if we think Stoneridge killed Felix Gresham, Ruby Kiss and Screech?'

'He knew he was a suspect?'

'He could have told me about Stoneridge and the card

playing. I asked him if he knew of anyone who owed money to Felix Gresham.'

'Frightened because he owed Stoneridge? Or just frightened of Stoneridge?'

'Let's think this out: Temple had committed fraud on the Gresham family; he owed Felix Gresham; he owed Screech; he owed Alexander Dalrymple; he owed Stoneridge — he was in a mess. He was frightened of Stoneridge because he suspected him of murdering Felix Gresham. He was frightened of me — he thought I suspected him of murdering Felix, and he was also terrified of all his secrets coming out, especially the fraud — which Screech knew about, say, because they'd worked out what to screw out of Felix Gresham's father all those years ago. Ned Temple, of course, didn't understand that he was putting himself in hock to Screech. His instinct is to run, so off he goes to Screech, begs for money for his passage — to anywhere — threatens Screech about the fraud, but Screech doesn't give a damn, turns him down and he grabs the poker in a rage, steals the box where he knows there are valuables and gets away. He doesn't see the child because he's frightened to death. Now, he's a murderer — can't cope with that and ends it all.'

'Past all fear but that of the hell in which he existed — madness, as I said before when we thought he'd murdered Felix then Screech, but the madness of a desperate creature —'

'Not so much past all fear — but in hell, certainly — the hellish thought of the gallows for Screech's murder, though he probably would not have been hanged for that.'

'Perhaps he thought he might be hanged for the murder of Felix Gresham.'

'Even for the murder of Ruby Kiss. He lied to me about her, and he was at the Casino de Venise on the night we think she was killed. He'd know I'd find that out. Perhaps he went to find her just to beg her to keep her mouth shut about the debts and about the night's gambling in the stables — to tell her they were both deep in it. But he didn't find her.'

'And the quill pen was already in her hair — he didn't drop it. Think of it, all these events over which he had no control, winding about him, trapping him in a net from which he could not get free. That's why he killed himself — weak and foolish, and dishonest, but not thoroughly wicked.'

'No — when I looked at his body, I thought how young he looked. What a waste — if he had been more — I don't know — more patient, more diligent, less —'

'Envious — born that way, perhaps, always wanting what he couldn't have. Spoilt by a doting mother — like Felix Gresham, but Gresham had the money to get what he wanted. Gall and wormwood to Temple ... and to Stoneridge.'

'Stoneridge?'

'Same thing — envy, resentment — like Edmund in *King Lear*. "Why bastard? Wherefore base? Now, gods, stand up for bastards!"'

'So, Temple killed Screech and Stoneridge killed Felix and Ruby Kiss. Why Ruby?'

Dickens thought about that. 'She was there in the stable? She knew that he'd killed Felix?'

'But that doesn't sound like the girl we've heard of — the barman at the casino, Sarah Hamilton, Phoebe Green, Old Sal, the brother — all of them gave the impression of a girl with a kind heart. And she was fond of Felix.'

'True — a good sort, Alexander Dalrymple said. Unless — wait a minute — Felix felt ill. He went into the space, vomiting on the way, wanting to relieve himself. Stoneridge follows, does the deed. Tells Ruby that Gresham is really ill. She suggests — don't know why — taking him to the bookshop—'

'Sarah Hamilton looked after her and Phoebe Green.'

'Right. She doesn't know Felix is dead — she's drunk, too. When she finds out, she assumes he was attacked as he lay on those steps, but Stoneridge doesn't trust that, and, Sam, Samivel, my lad — it's all connected —'

'What is?'

'My mystery and yours — they're linked. The sapphires — he knows about the sapphires by now. He went away before Hawke's death. He was there at Hawke Court, waiting to hear what the will said, and he got nothing. He is after those sapphires — he couldn't let Ruby Kiss get in the way — she knew too much.'

'Dalrymple's, then — he needs to be warned about Stoneridge. That's the first thing, and then I'll have to go to Hawke Court. I want Mrs Stoneridge here.'

'Find Sapphire Hawke — what Sir Gerald commanded Mr Case to do. I'll bet Stoneridge is looking for her, too. I wonder if he knows something I don't.'

## 42: A LOAD OF MISCHIEF

Danks was late. George sat in the booth at The Load of Mischief, drinking his brandy, thinking about what that man, Smart, had reported to old Dalrymple. He hoped Danks had his ear to the door. It still worried him that Smart and his boy had left in such a hurry — they hadn't really finished the job. Had Dalrymple sent Smart to find out if there was anything to be known about Sapphire Hawke?

George's mother had said there was nothing to find about Sapphire Hawke — she'd taken down the portrait. She'd not found anything — no letters, no diary — nothing. Dalrymple had sent Smart to see if there was anything of value left. 'We've had the best, George,' she'd said. He didn't trust her overmuch, either. He was sure she had her own stash of Hawke treasures, but she hadn't been in a giving mood. However, he hadn't come away empty-handed after his nocturnal ramblings round the house.

He looked across at the girl behind the bar — lovely-looking piece, but he'd seen her with a little lad. Kids, he didn't want. Somethin' to do with Screech, he'd heard said — daughter-in-law. She couldn't be ugly Screech's daughter, but she'd surely be in for something if that kid was Screech's grandchild. Now, that was useful — she might let him into the shop.

He looked at his dice on the table. Hazard was his game — it all depended on the throw of the dice. Think of a number. His watch told seven o'clock. The dice told six and one. Lucky — he always was.

Danks came creeping in, looking pleased with himself. George thought how much he disliked him. George wouldn't be meeting Danks in Paris, or anywhere else when this was over.

'Drink, Joah.' He poured some brandy. 'Anything on Smart?'

'He ain't been near — only that Mr Dickens came with the Superintendent from Bow Street about an hour ago. Thick as thieves, those two.'

'What did they want?'

Danks looked slyer than ever. George could have taken him by the throat as he watched him drink his brandy. He knew something and he was taking his time about it.

'Well, tell all.' George put his hand in his pocket.

'Couldn't hear much. You know Temple's dead — suicide, they say.'

George looked at his dice — lucky seven, but he kept his poker face, and said indifferently, 'Bad conscience, I should think — murdered a moneylender, it said in the papers. Round here, somewhere. Probably killed that dolly-mop, too, and what's his name —'

'Gresham — I can't say I'm sorry. World's a better place without Temple, I'd say, and his dolly-mop.'

'So would I, Joah, but it's our business that concerns me. Time's going on. What about Smart?' For some reason, Danks was keeping his hand close to his chest — frightened of the policeman, he supposed, but he didn't look frightened; he looked like a man with a secret. George threw his dice again. Six and one. His lucky number. Danks didn't look lucky.

Danks looked at the dice. He fancied himself a gambling man, too. 'Heard your name.'

'Well, you would. Told you, my mother lives at Hawke Court — cousin of Sir Gerald Hawke, deceased. Told you I quarrelled with the lot of them, but I've made it up with her now, and she feels as I do — those sapphires are mine — by right.' George leaned forward — confidential now. 'Joah, my friend, I was a fool — don't you be one. I quarrelled with that old man. Joined the army — thought there'd be time to — well, that milksop parson got in between me and my inheritance. The old man was mad by the end, but if I'd got there in time… Always fond of me, the old man was.'

'They said you're after the sapphires. Warned Dalrymple about you.'

'So I am — you know that, but they don't know where I am, unless —' George leaned back. Danks heard the crack of his fingers as George linked his hands together — big hands, powerful hands.

'I wouldn't tell 'em — you can trust me, George.'

'Surely, I can.' Hazard. He picked up the dice. 'Number nine,' he said. He threw the dice. 'Six and one. You win, Joah; I called nine. I was wrong.' He put a sovereign on the table. 'Yours if I lose again. Think of a number for me.'

'Ten,' Joah said, his eyes on the sovereign.

'Damme, Joah, you're luck's in tonight. Six and one again.' He pushed the sovereign over to Joah, who slipped it hastily into his pocket. George noted the little spark of triumph in his eyes. 'Now, did they mention Sapphire Hawke?'

'Not as I heard — hard to tell — sapphire, sapphires — they ain't shoutin' out, you know.'

'Anything else?'

'There'll be a policeman watching the chambers.'

'But they ain't watching the keys, and they ain't watching you, Joah.'

'But, the keys, George, I can't hardly take 'em. What do you want me to do — hit old Dalrymple over the head? Bit obvious, ain't it?'

George ignored the truculence in Joah's voice — getting

above himself now he'd won his sovereign. 'You ain't wrong there, Joah. Maybe we should think again. What if I were to get those keys — Dalrymple lives up near Regent's Park, don't he?'

'Where did you get that idea? Lives in Caroline Street, up by Bedford Square. Been there with papers — fine-looking house and a garden — pretty daughter, too.' Joah licked his lips — a habit George was beginning to loathe.

George lit a cigar and blew out the smoke. He smiled at Joah. 'Rich man, Dalrymple — money can buy a fine house, a carriage, a pretty wife. Those sapphires —'

'But who else would take the sapphires from the safe? They'll finger me, George.'

'Let me show you something — now watch and learn, Joah.' George took his cards out, shuffled the pack, and asked Joah to choose. Joah didn't know about the long card — it was an old trick — an extra length pasted on one card, placed so that the victim would be bound to choose it. George palmed the card when Joah put it back. Sleight of hand, they called it. George was very good, especially in the gloom of smoky taverns, or an ill-lit hay loft. 'Look at the cards, Joah — an innocent pack of cards. You don't know whether your card's there or not.'

'No, I don't — can't tell from just lookin' at the pack.'

George fanned out the cards. 'Is it there?'

Joah rifled through them. 'It ain't there.'

'The lady vanishes, Joah. Your card was the Queen of Diamonds and it ain't there now.' Joah watched, dazzled again, as George plucked the Queen of Diamonds from behind his ear. 'Mine, Joah, and you didn't see a thing.'

'But what's —?'

'Timing, Joah, it's all in the timing… Suppose you're elsewhere when the sapphires are taken. Suppose you're at home in your innocent bed… Mornin' after Dalrymple's attacked on his way home in the dark, you turn up for work. Mr Dalrymple ain't there and you're sittin' — diligent Mr Danks — on your high stool, scratchin' away with your pen. Mr Alexander comes, tells you about his pa and the stolen keys, but when you both go into Dalrymple's room, all the keys are there and the safe's locked —'

'But there's a policeman watching.'

'No hurry, Joah — few days and no George Stoneridge to be found. Vanished —' George blew out his smoke again — 'in a puff of smoke. The coast's clear. Get a message to me and I'll follow Dalrymple. Bring the keys to you at the office and in we go.'

'Why do you need me there?'

'To let us in.'

'But you'll have the keys — I don't need —'

George leaned forward. 'Partners, Joah — partners in all. That's the way it is, see…'

'But couldn't it be a break-in?'

'No, Joah, it couldn't — no evidence, see. It's a mystery that can't be solved — a card trick. The keys are your Queen of Diamonds. Vanish from the pack only to reappear magically on Dalrymple's desk. Sleight of hand, they call it. But there'll be a break-out because you'll leave a window open.'

'Upstairs?'

'What's downstairs?'

'Temple's old rooms — but that's no good. How'd the robber get in there? There's a little room under the stairs where the laundress keeps her stuff.'

'Likely to leave a window open?'

'Old woman — drunk as like as not.'

'There you are, then. You make sure the window's unlocked

just in case. And we'll close it when we go. Give it two days. On the third day, slip out and meet me at The Ship at noon. I'll wait for Dalrymple to leave the office.'

'What if something happens before that? The woman's found an' the sapphires are hers? How am I to get in touch?'

George hadn't wanted to tell him, but needs must. 'Shooting Gallery, Providence Passage, off Providence Row, by the Artillery ground. But only in dire need — don't want anyone seeing you around there.'

Joah Danks went off. Some of the shine had come off George Stoneridge. Wasn't as clever as he thought — Joah had won that sovereign off him and Stoneridge would do the dirty deed on old Dalrymple. He thought of those powerful hands. What if he killed Dalrymple? Wouldn't matter. Joah's hands'd be clean. They couldn't pin anythin' on him.

George finished his cigar, took a lingering look at Bella Screech, and went out the back to make his way towards Crooked Alley and Screech's shop. He slipped into Dark Entry. Crooked Alley was empty, the shop boarded up. George wondered if he could get round the back and break in that way. He walked to the top of Crooked Alley to see if there were any passageway; at that moment he heard footsteps, a woman's steps, lightly tapping the cobbles. She was in a hurry. He stopped where he was, saw her hesitate, almost turn round. He didn't move, so she had to come on. Her alternative was Dark Entry. As she passed him, she looked up involuntarily and he saw a face he knew. She felt a hand over her mouth and the cold touch of a ring.

# 43: A FACE REMEMBERED

Dickens looked at his watch: ten o'clock. Jones would be there now at Hawke Court with Rogers. They'd have taken an early train. He imagined Jones before that great door, lifting the iron knocker, hearing the rooks fly up and the bolts slide open. Dickens would have liked to have gone — if only to see Esther Stoneridge's face at the sight of two policemen on her threshold, but he'd see her soon enough — in a cell, he rather hoped. She must know where her son was lodging, but would she tell? Dickens could not prove that Stoneridge had been at Hawke Court when he was there — in any case, cheerful Tom Smart had been at Hawke Court, not Charles Dickens. They had the valuables from Hawke Court, but no proof that Stoneridge had taken them, and as for Mrs Stoneridge's pickings, they might be sold already.

Dickens had thought hard about where Stoneridge might be. He thought of the various barracks in Hyde Park, St James's Park; he thought of the Army Pay Office in Horse Guards — surely Sam could trace him there, but that wouldn't necessarily tell them where he was now. And his horse? What had he done with that? A horse was a valuable property. Where would a military man with a horse take lodgings? Another inn with stables? Far too many. A livery stables? But he could have sold his horse.

He thought of the man walking towards Fitzroy Square — did he lodge thereabouts? He saw him in his mind's eye carrying his basket, a tall silhouette in the dark, and then he felt his heart beat faster. A trick of the light — or rather the dark? A real memory? For Dickens remembered that just for a moment, upon the shadow, he had seen another figure, tall, broad-shouldered, upright.

He opened his notebook and looked at the words: Josephine Parker — *whereabouts unknown*. He remembered exactly what he had thought then about Josephine Parker, because he often thought it: *Or one of those glimpsed by the protagonist in the street, or in a pub, just part of the landscape, not the face he wanted in his search for a villain?*

*George Stoneridge*: he had been the man he wanted, and he was the villain. He had seen that tall man with the military bearing before — at the bar of The Load of Mischief. And he had seen his companion with the malevolent eyes: Joah Danks. And he thought of the air astir when he had left Mr Dalrymple's room — the time when Mr Dalrymple had shown him the sapphires.

George Stoneridge wanted those sapphires, so he would still be about, and he had a confederate right inside Clement's Inn.

Dickens was about to grab his coat when he sat down again. His immediate thought had been to go to Clement's Inn — but what to do there? He had no authority to confront Joah Danks. Confront him about a man in a pub? Danks would say he wasn't there, or that he had taken a drink with a stranger — what harm in that? Danks was no fool. And Mr Dalrymple had been warned last night that Stoneridge might make an attempt on the sapphires. Stemp was on watch at Clement's Inn. The sapphires were safe enough for now. It would be better to go to see Bella Screech. He could find out if she had seen Stoneridge and Danks again — she might remember the tall, handsome captain. He remembered Bella smiling at him — perhaps she knew him. He thought about Ruby Kiss and put on his coat.

Someone knocked at the door. Dickens took his hat and stick. Whoever it was could wait — he was in a hurry. He opened the door to see Constable John Semple, his hand raised to knock again.

'Mr Jones,' Semple blurted.

Dickens actually felt the blood drain from his own face. Semple looked pale and most agitated. 'What is it?'

'Mr Jones has gone to Chertsey and I need your help. There's no one else. The lady won't —'

'What lady?' His mind was on Bella Screech.

'Miss Hamilton — she didn't want James to come to me, but he did, then she said you would come.'

'Be calm, Semple, I beg you. Get your breath —' the young man had obviously been running — 'and tell me what has happened. Here, let me give you some water.'

Constable Semple drank and composed himself. 'Miss Finch is missing. She went to James's workshop — my brother — about some gilding, but she never went back to the shop. Miss Hamilton waited and late last night she went to James, but he told her that she had left him at about seven o'clock. Miss Hamilton and James went looking. You know he lives off Wardour Street?' Dickens nodded. 'There's all kinds of courts and alleys about there. They searched all night. They traced the way she'd have come home — past the church — they searched the churchyard, down Dark Entry, Crooked Alley, past Screech's, but not a sign.'

John Semple paused to gulp some more water and Dickens thought of the sinister Dark Entry, Crooked Alley where Screech had been murdered, and St. Anne's Court where Felix Gresham had lain dead. It couldn't be…

John Semple was continuing his tale. 'This morning, James persuaded her to let him come for me. I went o' course and told her I'd get more constables. She asked about Mr Jones, but I told her he'd gone to a place called Hawkstone — she seemed even more distressed — p'raps she thought Mr Jones could find Miss Finch — then she asked for you, Mr Dickens.'

'I'll come, of course.'

'I'll 'ave to see Inspector Grove, sir — get some men on it.'

'Right. I know where the shop is.'

Dickens felt a profound shock, almost as deep a shock as when Constable Semple had blurted out Sam's name and he had thought for a terrible moment that something had happened to him at Hawke Court.

James Semple was sitting on a stool in the shop. He looked shattered and just nodded to where the binding shop door was open. Dickens went in to see Sarah Hamilton standing with Bartholomew's bone paper folder in her hand. Her face, white as paper, was so drawn as to have shrunk to childlike proportions, but it was her eyes — huge and frightened and with such an inexpressible look of sorrow that he knew suddenly who she was.

'Miss Hamilton, what can I do?'

'She would have come home — Addy always came home.' She looked at him with the face he had seen as if all the years had fallen away to reveal the lonely girl in a dusty portrait. 'Come, sit by the fire.' She was trembling. He led her to a chair, for he thought she might collapse.

'Constable Semple is talking to Inspector Grove at Bow Street — they will search everywhere. They will try the hospital — there might have been an accident. Where else other than James Semple's could she have gone?'

'Nowhere — there is no-one.'

'Would she go to someone's assistance — someone who needed help? You found Ruby — perhaps, the same —'

'She would have come back this morning — she would not

leave me. She would know how much — we never —'

*Such anguish*, he thought. Ought he to tell her what he knew and about George Stoneridge? Too great a shock.

'You said that Superintendent Jones believed that Ned Temple killed Felix and Ruby — but Ned Temple is dead, and Screech. What if the same person — has killed Addy — someone we don't know —'

'I don't know, Miss Hamilton. Superintendent Jones will be back soon. He will come.'

She stood up. 'I must go out — I must try to find her.'

'No, please, I beg you, there is nothing you can do but wait — I assure you, the police will search thoroughly. Please, sit down. Tell me about Addy and you and why there is no one else? Talk — it will help. Something might come to you — somewhere she might be — some memory.'

If anything, she looked more anguished than ever. She turned her face away. He watched her long fingers stroke Bartholomew Chantrey's paper folder. She stared into the fire, looking down some long tunnel into the past, he supposed, seeing something at the end which made her tremble and bite her lips, and grip the paper folder. She closed her eyes against the fire and the shadows played across her face like remembered sorrows.

Dickens was conscious of time passing. Sam would come soon and the questions he asked must, given the urgency of the matter, take on a dry official quality, and Sarah Hamilton would retreat into her remoteness, telling Sam that she did not know who would want to harm Addy Finch, and Sam would have to ask about George Stoneridge. But he himself must ask that question, and as carefully as he could.

Sarah opened her eyes and said, looking at the flames, 'I do not want to remember. Some things are best forgotten —

buried deep. You can almost forget, Mr Dickens, if you try hard enough, but a thing may happen that opens the scar, and the pain is as sharp as if one of those knives had cut into it.'

Dickens felt his way as if he wore velvet gloves. 'I know it — we all have secrets, things that cannot be told, even to those we love best because to tell would open the wound to bleed afresh so that the blood might never cease. But you and Addy, yours are shared secrets, I think.'

Sarah dared to look at him now. She almost drew back. Who was he, this man, whose eyes seemed to see into her very soul? But there were some things that she could not bear to bring into the light. He could not know those — not even this man with eyes that held something dark and sorrowful, too, as he looked at her.

She found herself saying, 'Addy and I, we had a life we wanted to forget. Bartholomew and Thyrza took me in off the street —' she looked at Dickens straight now — 'not what you might think — I ran away from my guardian. He was — a vile man, a cruel man. I had been at school, then he summoned me home. I was to marry — a creature of his choosing.'

He was sure. 'Who was your guardian?'

'I cannot say his name — I shall bleed to death. You said so.'

'Miss Hamilton, I must know. Addy's life may depend on it.'

'I do not understand. You know who has taken her? Tell me who it is.'

'Tell me your guardian's name.'

'Sir Gerald Hawke.'

'You are Sapphire Hawke.'

Her eyes, that child's eyes, were wide and terrified again. She half stood. 'No, oh, no — what are you, Mr Dickens? A magician? A spy?'

'No, no, believe me. It is too complicated for me to explain all. Suffice it to say that I am a friend of the Reverend Mr Case—'

'Case? Who is he?'

'Sir Gerald's heir. He was seeking you, but I must ask you something more. Do you know the name George Stoneridge?'

Had she seen a ghost or some monstrous apparition, there could not have been more horror on her face. He almost recoiled. 'Mrs Stoneridge's son? Sir Gerald's natural son?'

'Yes — now, be calm, Miss Hamilton. Let me explain. He has been looking for you, I think. Sir Gerald left the sapphires to you and commanded Mr Case to find you. George Stoneridge wants those sapphires. I went to Hawke Court —'

'You — there — why?'

'Mr Case — I acted for him. Stoneridge was there and he followed me back to London.'

'But how would he find us? I was a child when I saw him last. Addy was a child —'

'Addy — Addy Finch — was her mother Lucy Bird?'

'Yes, yes, oh, God — he would know Addy. She looks exactly like her mother.'

'We will find him. Superintendent Jones has gone down to Hawke Court to bring back Mrs Stoneridge. She will know where he is, I am sure of it.'

'He hated us — George Stoneridge — he would not leave us alone when he saw us in the woods about Hawke Court. He has her, Mr Dickens — and he will kill her. I know it — he has done things which —'

'He must keep her alive until she tells him where you are.'

'She will never do that.'

# 44: A PRISONER

She had known. She had felt the metal ring on her mouth. She had tried to pull his hand away and she had seen it — the black bird on the signet ring — a hawk. Then she was pulled into the darkness. He was too strong for her; one hand clamped like iron on her mouth and the other gripped her arm like a steel band. He had always been too strong for her in those woods, and one day when he had her on the ground and he was inside her, she had been saved by Sarah, Sapphire as she had been then, who had come crashing through the trees, screaming her head off. George had fled, pulling up his trousers.

He'd been about fifteen then. Addy had been thirteen, and he had tried at other times when he had come visiting to his grandmother's — she had been ten years old the first time. She'd never seen him again after the time Sapphire had saved her. But it was too late anyway.

Incest, they called it — a word she'd learned later. Addy knew she was Hawke's daughter — though nothing was ever said. She knew from the way folk had looked at her and whispered. And George Stoneridge was his son. Her child had died. She had been glad of that. Lucy Bird, her mother, had not cared about that child or her own. Addy had endured that cruel, drunken woman for another three years and when the man had come to find her — the man called Bartholomew Chantrey — she had gone with him. He had come with a letter from Sapphire Hawke. Millie Bird was sixteen then, and she had been safe for sixteen years — as Addy Finch.

Now, she wasn't. It was a cellar, she knew that. She was very cold, her clothes were damp, her lip was split and swollen, and she could taste blood. She remembered pain and shock. He must have hit her, knocked her out and carried her to this place. She thought of Sarah, but Sarah could do nothing for her this time. No one knew about George Stoneridge. No one would find her. George Stoneridge wouldn't find Sarah because Addy Finch wouldn't tell him. He could kill her if he wanted, but she would tell him about the child first. Bastard — like George, and she would tell him that she was glad the bastard had died.

She had no idea of the time. She could be anywhere — in any cellar under any old place, workshop, house, shop, or stable. It might be near St. Anne's Court; it might be miles away. She couldn't fight him. She could only hope that he would keep her alive in the belief that she would tell him where Sarah was.

He might not come back. He might have gone after those sapphires which he'd said were meant for Sapphire Hawke. What a fool he was. Sarah didn't want anything from Hawke Court. Jewels meant nothing to her, or to Addy. They had what they wanted — sisters, both with Hawke blood, not that it mattered. They were the daughters of Bartholomew and Thyrza Chantrey; they had each other and the bookshop. It had been hard for Addy to learn to read and write first, but Sarah had been so patient. Addy's little fingers had been deft at the sewing frame and gilding the letters; she had flourished under Thyrza's tutelage, as had Sarah under Bartholomew's.

Sarah had seen that old monster buried — she'd made sure that the tomb was sealed. No one had known her; no one had paid attention to the young man idly watching. Sarah had given a false name at the inn — Frederick Dale — Frederick, the name of the doctor Sarah had told her about. She'd taken one last look at the house and she'd ridden back to London. She would never go there again, she'd said, not even in disguise. It was over. But Hawke had returned in the guise of his son, as bad as his father, and Addy Finch might starve to death in a miserable cellar.

Addy felt the salt tears on her sore lip. Her nose was running, but she couldn't do anything about it, for her hands were bound tight. At least she could crawl to that dirty metal bucket he'd left. There was only the sound of water dripping somewhere, but she had heard faint voices and an odd sound like the distant gun shots she had used to hear in the woods about Hawke Court. She'd shouted and shouted until her throat was sore. But no one came. Perhaps it was night now and the voices had gone home. Maybe they'd come back.

Addy Finch closed her eyes and lay back on the dirty straw.

# 45: FINNY MORTON

It seemed a very long time before Jones came. Dickens sat with Sarah Hamilton. He did not dare leave. He asked her to show him the bookbinding techniques that he had not seen the first time. She didn't want to, but he persuaded her, and they spent a tranquil hour folding paper, cutting up leather, and she showed him how to use the sewing frame, and though her fingers trembled when she impressed a stamp in gold leaf, the work soothed her. Superintendent Jones would come, he kept telling her, and at length, Dickens heard his voice.

Dickens met Jones in the shop and hastily told him the story. 'She is Sapphire Hawke — she and Addy Finch knew Stoneridge when they were children. Miss Hamilton thinks George Stoneridge would know Addy; she is exactly like her mother. I told her that you'd be bringing Esther Stoneridge — that you'd find him.'

Jones looked at him grimly. 'She wasn't there. She'd hired the trap the day before. The driver told me that he'd taken her and her luggage to the London train. Rogers and I went to the house just to be sure. The door was open, the keys on the table — no one was there. We searched, of course, but I could tell. Just an emptiness.'

'Oh, lor, Sam, what do we do now? Miss Hamilton is beside herself.'

'There is one slender thread — Josephine Parker. We were so long because I went to the Hawke Arms and met your Mrs Black. I told her the truth about you and Scrap. She was very taken with Scrap — and you, for that matter. I told her that we were looking for Stoneridge and that it was a criminal matter.

She didn't seem surprised. Bad lot, she called Stoneridge and his mother. I asked her to think very carefully if she could remember anything at all. She said you'd asked about Josephine Parker — she remembered after you'd gone when she was thinking about the old days —'

'Yes, she said how sad it was that you simply forgot people.'

'You did set her thinking. She remembered that Josephine Parker was to marry a soldier — someone from London, she thought. She remembered that there was an aunt who kept a lodging house in Windsor, so Rogers and I went there and found the aunt, Mrs Parker, an old lady now, but she had her wits about her, and she remembered the soldier, Finn — or Finny — Morton, quite vividly — an Irish scallywag she called him, and she didn't like his friend, either.'

'Friend!'

'Exactly — a soldier comrade, a young man, about nineteen years. Morton was in his twenties; his intended bride was over thirty and pregnant. Mrs Parker, who still has very sharp eyes, noted that, and she didn't trust either Morton or his comrade. She thought Morton was after Josephine's money — she'd a bit put by, and she was still a handsome woman. And he made himself very comfortable in the lodging house — dirty boots under the table, Mrs Parker said. Morton and his pal were gambling men, it seems.'

'The friend's name?' Dickens could hardly bear to listen to the details about Morton and Josephine.

'She knew him as George, and that he came from Chertsey.'

'Chertsey — near Hawke Court. But after fifteen or sixteen years, Sam, to find Morton…'

'I know, but the old dame remembered he was an artilleryman, and Finn's not a common name. I'm off to the Army Pay Office and their records. I know his name and I've a good idea of his age. It's the best I can do.'

Distractedly, Dickens ran his hands through his hair. 'What am I to tell her? Honestly, Sam, I never saw such terror. What can I say about Esther Stoneridge?'

'You can only tell her the truth. It's no use giving false hope.'

'I know, I know, hopefulness more painful than sorrow faced. Wait, will you, while I tell her. I don't want to leave her alone —' he lowered his voice — 'James Semple isn't much use. A woman…'

'Elizabeth would come if she's wanted.'

'I'll ask.'

Dickens came back after a few minutes, shaking his head. 'She prefers to be alone, but I've promised to send news as soon as we get any.'

'We'll have to go — it's getting late.'

They left the shop in the hands of Constable Semple and his brother, John. 'No one comes in, Semple. Keep your eyes open.'

Sarah Hamilton sat in the binding shop, holding on to Bartholomew's folding stick. But she wasn't thinking about him. Her eyes were on the fire, and her mind was on those memories which made her heart bleed afresh. But she roused herself. Addy, she thought; there must be something she could do.

# 46: SLEIGHT OF HAND

If there had been a Finn Morton, he could not be found. Jones had sent to every army barracks and Rogers had been to the Army Pay Office. Dickens and Jones had been to the Honourable Artillery Company, but they had no record of a Finn Morton, nor a George Stoneridge.

It was late and beginning to rain when they returned somewhat despondently to Bow Street to find Alexander Dalrymple waiting anxiously for them.

'It's my father. He was attacked near our home in Caroline Street — robbed of his wallet, his watch and his keys.'

'The keys to your chambers?' asked Jones.

'Yes, the safe key, too.'

'Have you been to Clement's Inn?'

'No, I've been tending to my mother and sister. A cabbie found my father and found a policeman who got a doctor in Caroline Street. The doctor knew my father and brought him home. My father was unconscious. The doctor was very good —'

'How is Mr Dalrymple now?' Dickens asked.

'He has come round, but he is very weak — shock, the doctor said. I didn't think what it might mean at first. I thought it was just a street robbery — you know — the watch, the wallet, but my father said "keys" and then I realised someone might have got in — if they were after the keys.'

'We'll go there now. Constable Stemp has been on watch — I shouldn't think anyone would get past him, but I'll bring more men. Have you the key to the outside door?'

'Danks has it — he's usually there first. He has the key to my father's office, but not to the safe. My father had the other set.'

'Where does he live?'

'He has lodgings in Carey Street.'

Jones took an oilskin cape for himself and gave one to Dickens and they went out into the rainy night just as a flash of lightning rent the sky. Dickens glanced up and heard the thunder in the distance. There was something feverish in the air, a sense of something about to happen; he hurried after Jones.

Joah Danks in a greasy nightshirt, his hair sticking up in porcupine quills, and a pair of battered boots on his feet was not a sight Dickens wished to see again. There was a smell of stale lard and old cabbage and worse about him, and he looked very truculent as he answered his landlady's call. She didn't look very pleased, either. They were made for each other. *Made in Hell*, Dickens thought. Danks reserved a particularly malevolent glance for Dickens.

'What's the game? I was in bed — asleep.'

Jones was terse. 'Mr Dalrymple has been attacked and his keys stolen. You have a front door key and I need you to open up — immediately.'

Dickens watched his eyes flick uneasily to Jones and to him; then Danks saw Alexander Dalrymple at the bottom of the steps and changed his tune. 'Oh, I'm sorry to hear that, Mr Alexander — let me get dressed.' He vanished up the narrow staircase and came down wearing a low-crowned hat and a short coat with a moth-eaten fur collar.

'I don't entirely trust him,' Dickens whispered. 'I'm almost certain I saw him in The Mischief when I first saw Bella Screech. He was with a tall, dark man — very like the man who followed me from Hawke Court.'

'Stoneridge.'

'I'll bet.'

'Keep your eyes on him when we get in.'

Stemp was at his post outside the chambers, sheltering in the porch. He had seen no one, only Mr Danks, who had left a few hours ago. Jones left one constable at the archway and directed the other two to look about the grounds. They had their oilskin capes. Stemp remained where he was.

Joah Danks opened the front door. Inside, they saw that Ned Temple's door was firmly closed, as was the door to Mr Dalrymple's chambers, which Danks unlocked. In the outer room, Danks's desk was undisturbed. He unlocked Mr Dalrymple's room. Again, there was no sign of a disturbance.

'The keys,' Alexander exclaimed, 'my father's keys, his watch and chain. That seal with the green stone. My mother gave it to him.' They were there on the desk, as if Mr Dalrymple had simply left them there in a moment of absent-mindedness.

'Could he have simply left them here and forgotten because of the attack? You said he was suffering from shock,' Jones asked him.

'I suppose he could — he sometimes put his watch on his desk, but not the chain. He was so careful.'

'Have a close look, if you will, and see if there is anything missing.'

Alexander took the keys in turn. 'This one opens the drawer.' Jones nodded to indicate that Alexander should open it. 'This second one opens the metal box where the safe key — it's missing —'

'What's the other, small one?' Jones asked.

'It opens a wooden box inside where —'

'The sapphires are kept,' Dickens said, 'inside a velvet box.

Your father showed me.'

'You're sure?' Jones asked Alexander.

'I am — the safe is a Bramah fireproof one and the key is a gold key, stamped with the Bramah name, and the lock is a Bramah lock.'

*Which cannot be opened*, Dickens thought, watching Danks. He looked shocked and there was sweat on his pale forehead. One hand went to his pocket and he wiped it there. Dickens wondered if Danks had the key — was he the attacker, or was he in collusion with someone else?

'Is there a second key at your house?' asked Jones.

'No, the Bramah Company has the master.'

'Then we shall have to get it. Do you know where Mr Bramah lives?'

'I do,' said Dickens, 'Guildford Street, Russell Square. I've met him. I'll go. It's not far.'

Jones would have laughed if the matter had not been so urgent. Not for the first time, he was glad of Charles Dickens's wide circle of acquaintances.

'Rogers will go with you. Make sure Stemp is at the front door when you go out.'

Dickens and Rogers went across the grass to the archway. Stemp remained at the front door. Dickens saw two other constables approach him. They obviously hadn't found anything. Of Mr Justice Silence there was no sign — not that he would have told them. He wasn't Marley's ghost come to tell a tale.

Joah Danks went to work at his books. Alexander Dalrymple went into his own room. For which two mercies Jones was grateful. He had no desire to talk. He had an idea. He took *The Post Office Trades Directory* from Mr Dalrymple's bookshelf.

# 47: THE TURN OF THE KEY

The man whom Jones hoped could unlock the mystery, Mr Edward Bramah, came in. He was a man of about sixty wearing well cut evening clothes and carrying a silk top hat which glistened with rain. He looked prosperous — *well he might*, thought Jones; Bramah Locks was a very flourishing company.

Dickens explained that they had been to 124 Piccadilly, to the Bramah premises where the master keys were kept.

'I have it here,' Edward Bramah said, taking the golden key from his pocket. 'Shall I do the honours?'

Jones nodded and Alexander removed the picture of the long-ago lawyer so that Mr Bramah could get to the safe. 'Let us hope that no one's tampered with it — a safe-breaker might try to use pins or skeleton keys, or even a thin blade. Never works, of course, but such things can do damage. The key has these incised bits at the end — each key is different. The incised bits engage with the spring-loaded steel sliders in the lock mechanism. The sliders are incised at exact points to correspond with the incised depths of the key. When the key is properly pushed in, the slider incisions all align together, allowing the half plates surrounding the central cylinder to be unobstructed.'

A disquisition on Bramah locks was not what they needed, Jones thought, but he could hardly tell the man to hurry up. He glanced at Dickens, whose face had taken on a fixed expression of eager interest, though a slightly raised eyebrow gave him away. Jones knew that Dickens wanted to laugh. Danks and Alexander Dalrymple seemed genuinely fascinated.

Mr Bramah continued. 'Now, let me see…' He took a small magnifying glass from his pocket and examined the lock. 'It seems to be untouched. Now, to operate the lock, one inserts the key and turns it anti-clockwise, rotating the central cylinder — this kind of lock is inset with a rear stud, which engages with the guide plate. The sliding plate is deployed at about the one-hundred-and-eighty-degree mark and moves from right to left — in most cases. With the sliding bolt now —'

Jones couldn't wait any longer. 'And, unlocking, sir, you can demonstrate that?'

'Oh, indeed, of course. I beg your pardon, Superintendent. I am an enthusiast in the matter of locks. Unlocking the Bramah lock is a simple case of reversing the locking procedure; the key is re-inserted, pressed in, and turned clockwise by three hundred and sixty degrees to its initial insertion point. The key will pop out from the front lock aperture.'

They watched Mr Bramah insert the key. There was silence, except that Dickens noted Danks's hoarse breathing. They heard the sliders engage. Then the click. And the key popped out. Mr Bramah opened the heavy door and took out the wooden box and examined the gold lock. 'One of ours — very pretty, indeed. Eighteenth century, I should think. Have you the key?'

Alexander Dalrymple handed him the key. Mr Bramah inserted it and they all craned forward. He took out the velvet case and gave it to Jones, who opened it. The sapphires were gone. For a moment they just stared, and then they all spoke together.

Edward Bramah said, 'Someone had a key to your safe, Mr Dalrymple —'

'My father will be —'

'Stoneridge,' Dickens said.

Jones whipped round. 'Mr —'

They heard the turn of the key in the lock of the door. Jones went to hammer on the door and shout for Stemp. Alexander Dalrymple rushed to unfasten the window shutters. Dickens heard the squeak of the window being raised and dashed to see. There was no sign of Danks, but Stemp would have stopped him. Jones was still hammering and shouting for Stemp when Mr Bramah stepped forward and touched him on the shoulder.

'What?' Jones barked.

'This might do it.' He held out a small pocket pistol. 'One shot, Superintendent Jones.'

Jones pointed it at the door lock and fired. The noise was deafening. Dickens whipped round. What the devil? But Jones was already out, shouting for Stemp, followed by Rogers. Stemp was halfway up the stairs.

'Danks,' shouted Jones, but Joah Danks had not got past Stemp.

'He didn't come out, sir — I swear it. I only left my post cos I 'eard the shot — thought someone —'

'Never mind that — get out and have a look.' Rogers went with Stemp and they all followed to the door, hearing Stemp calling out for the other constable to search.

Dickens remembered a time when he had been forced to hide from a suspect in the room of a laundress at Gray's Inn. He turned back and vanished under the stairs.

'Window,' he shouted. Jones disappeared to go round the back of the building.

He came back in a short time. 'No sign — there's a narrow path down towards a little gate which goes out into Serle Street; the gate's open, but he's gone.'

Rogers appeared to say that Danks couldn't be found.

'No time to waste on him —' Jones knew that Danks would be lost in the nest of narrow, dark alleys off Serle Street — 'he had time to get away. We'll find him. We've somewhere else to go.'

'Chertsey?' said Dickens. 'I remember that Addy Finch was very alarmed when I mentioned — Stoneridge could have —'

'No, no need — oh, I beg your pardon, Mr Bramah, I have not thanked you. I'm much obliged for your help.' Jones handed Mr Bramah his pocket pistol.

'Only as a deterrent,' said Mr Bramah, 'but I'm glad it works. I've never used it, and you'd better keep this —' he handed Jones the safe key — 'for the sapphires when you find them. I've locked the safe again.' He turned to Dickens. 'I am obliged to you, sir. I wouldn't have missed this.' He put on his silk hat and went on his way, his neat little gun in his pocket.

'Charles, will you tell Alexander Dalrymple to go home? I don't want him with us. Tell him that we are following a lead and I'll send to him when we have some news. Stemp, go and collect all the men and bring them here.'

When Dickens came back, he said that Alexander would try to wedge the office door closed, lock up the building and go home to his father. Jones was sending his constables back to Bow Street. They were to change into plain clothes. Rogers was to bring flintlock pistols and they were to meet inside the entrance to Bunhill Fields Burial Ground in no less than half an hour.

Dickens and Jones were to go by cab to the burying ground. 'I'll tell you why on the way.'

'Stoneridge?'

Jones nodded and they walked towards the archway, Jones leading the way. Dickens looked back and he thought he saw the back of a long dark coat vanishing into the trees where the path went through. Mr Justice Silence again? It wasn't Danks — his coat was too short.

# 48: PROVIDENCE

'The burial ground?' Dickens asked, raising his voice as the rain beat down on them while they waited for a cab. Bunhill Fields was another of those densely packed, overcrowded, stinking grounds which ought to be closed — a matter in which he was supporting the Sanitary Commission. On the site of a plague pit, too. People lived cheek by jowl in these infected places. No wonder typhus and cholera were rife. He'd been in the burial ground — the notable residents were Daniel Defoe and William Blake. John Wesley had lived opposite and was reputed to haunt the place — praying for the lost souls, perhaps. The living needed his prayers, too, anyone's prayers.

'The Artillery Ground at Finsbury is where we're actually going. There are all kinds of businesses round there — a couple of gunsmiths, saddlery, harness-makers, coach-makers, a whip-maker — a lady whip-maker, if you please — two farriers, stables, and a shooting gallery. So, while I was waiting for you and the loquacious Mr Bramah, I spent my time reading *The Post Office Trades Directory* — looking at the streets round the Artillery Ground —'

'Lord, Sam, you found Morton.'

'I hope so — the Morton I found runs a shooting gallery in Providence Passage, a narrow twisting alley which runs behind the whip-maker's premises on Providence Row. P. Morton.'

A cab came along, and Jones stood in the road to stop it. 'Providence Row, by the Artillery Ground,' he shouted up to the driver. They got in.

'"P"? Your Mrs Parker said he was Finn or Finny.'

'Phineas Morton, who I am guessing is Finn — I'm thinking

that here's an out of the way place for a man to hole up with an army comrade, a man with a horse to stable.'

'What about Addy Finch?'

'I know, I'm thinking about her, too. Morton wasn't a scrupulous type according to Mrs Parker. Would he object if Stoneridge kept a girl there?'

'She wouldn't stay willingly; that's what worries me.'

'It worries me, but until we get there, we won't know. I've asked the constables to meet at the burial ground because it's at a distance from Providence Passage. There won't be many about there and in this rain, too.' A tremendous clap of thunder punctuated Jones's words. 'The noise of the storm might be good for us, too. I want to have a scout around Providence Passage — get the lie of the land. Rogers knows to wait.'

The cab dropped them in Artillery Place to the east of the Artillery Ground and they walked to Providence Row. The shops were closed now. Only a few people scurried by, anxious to get out of the rain. They passed by a saddlery business, a farrier's, a rag merchant's shop, and glanced down the alley named Providence Passage and walked on, passing The Gunner's Arms just beyond the passage. Fortunately, that seemed quiet, too. They stopped in front of Lamerte's Blacking and Ink Manufactory at number twenty-two.

'Wait here in this doorway while I slip down the passage.'

Dickens looked up at the sign: *Geo. Lamerte*. George Lamerte was a name he knew. Warren's Blacking factory had been at Hungerford Stairs and it was there he had worked as a twelve-year-old boy pasting the labels on the blacking bottles for six shillings a week. James Lamert — without the 'e' — had been the manager, but George, in the same business, had been a connection. Providence, indeed, that all this had brought him to standing in the rain outside a blacking factory — Providence's joke, no doubt. He wasn't amused, only exhausted, wet and cold.

Poor Sarah Hamilton, all alone in her bookbinding room, terrified of what had happened to Addy. He thought of Addy's appealing cat face. They'd had courage, those two girls. Courage, persevere — he said it himself very often, but he felt the rain on his trousers and wished Sam would come back. He heard footsteps and shrank back as far as he could into the doorway, freezing as something rolled at his feet. He looked down. A bottle, a blacking bottle with a label. He put his foot on it to stop it rolling into the street. He was tempted to crush it — for old time's sake — but it would make too much noise. He strained to hear in the rain, but the footsteps seemed to have stopped. Had someone gone down the passage? Someone after Sam?

He went back down Providence Row and listened at the entrance to the passage, but he could hear nothing. To his relief, he saw Jones coming round a corner with his lamp. They huddled in a doorway just as lightning exploded above them, blinding them with livid light. They heard the head-splitting crack of thunder and the rain fell harder like lead shot, beating on a tin roof nearby. They watched the gutter fill, the water carrying the refuse of paper, old bones, old clothes, even a broken chair. Nothing for it but to wait. Jones's face was running with water so that it seemed to be dissolving. Involuntarily, Dickens grasped his arm. They couldn't speak for the noise of the rain and the thunder still rumbling like barrels being rolled through a trapdoor very like the one they were standing next to. Then it was quiet again.

'Umbrella-a-a-as for mendin',' a disembodied voice cried from a distance somewhere in the street.

'Opportunist,' Dickens whispered.

'Optimist,' said Jones and they both felt weak with the desire to laugh.

The rain seemed to ease. 'The shooting gallery is round that corner next to a stable — I thought I heard a horse,' Jones told him. 'The gallery's all locked up.' He wiped the rain from his face, and it was firm and clear again.

'Bramah?'

Jones grinned. 'A simple lock which I can open. There's a light, so someone's there. The passage leads back to Windmill Street — another right-angled turn, so I'll put two men there. Constable Dacres is a good shot. Stemp can stay in this alley — by this trapdoor. We don't know where it leads. Might be the pub, but not necessarily. I'll put Feak at the end of the passage.'

'There'll be guns inside.'

'My thought exactly. Stemp will be armed. Rogers is bringing guns for me and him. I want you to come in because of the girl — but don't get in the way.'

They walked up to Bunhill Fields. The thunder was rolling away now to the west and the rain was not so heavy. The policemen were waiting in their oilskin capes, just shadows in the dark gateway to the burial ground. Their bull's-eye lanterns were shut. Jones gave his instructions, and they went their separate ways at timed intervals. Rogers would see them all in their places before coming to the shooting gallery where Jones and Dickens would be waiting. Before he went off, Rogers took something from his pocket. 'I thought Mr Dickens should have this.' He gave him a small pistol — like Edward Bramah's, thought Dickens.

'Can you use it?' asked Jones.

'I can.' The metal felt cold to his touch. He could shoot, but whether to kill, he didn't know.

'Only if you have to.' Jones looked him in the eye. 'Don't get in the way. Leave the shooting to us. Your job is to get the girl away if you can.'

They waited with the shooting gallery in sight, but no one came or went. Rogers arrived and simply nodded to indicate that the constables were in their places. Under the cover of a distant thunder roll, Jones used a skeleton key to open the door. Then he put his gloves in his pocket and Dickens saw the pistol in his hand. He felt the gun in his own pocket. They waited, but no sound came from the shooting gallery. From the stable they heard the scrape of a horse's hoof on stone and a brief whicker. Perhaps it had heard them, or the thunder had disturbed it. They waited again. Dickens heard the cock of the pistols.

When the thunder rumbled again, Rogers pushed gently at the door and they slipped in through the narrow opening. The place was empty. The walls were bare brick, as was the floor. It smelled of damp, chalk, paint — and cigar smoke. There were two dim gas lights, some whitened targets for rifle-shooting and archery, a rough sort of table with a vice upon it for holding the guns to be repaired and another table pushed in a corner and a couple of chairs. Some pistols lay on the first table and a rifle. Across the expanse of floor, they could see a crude wooden partition which seemed to screen off some other part. There was a door by that which was bolted. Rogers took off his boots and tip-toed across, his pistol in his hand. He went round the partition, looked closely at the door and came tiptoeing back, stopping to look at the guns on the table. He shook his head.

'Those guns won't work,' he whispered. 'There's a rough bed

— someone's slept there — a brandy bottle, a couple of glasses, a pack of cards and some dice. That door must be a back way, but it's locked.'

Jones's eyes travelled to a door on the right side wall. That wasn't bolted. Rogers crept to that and listened. He signalled that he could hear something. Dickens and Jones skirted the walls to get to Rogers, keeping as quiet as they could. Jones gave Rogers his boots back. They slipped off the heavy oilskin capes, which would get in the way. The thunder sounded a drumroll, and Jones opened the door upon a set of steps which they thought must lead to a cellar. Then there was a man's voice and the muffled sound of a woman.

Jones went first, followed by Rogers and then Dickens. Stoneridge was there. He had heard them, and he had Addy Finch in an arm lock with a gun to her head. She looked at them with huge eyes. Dickens thought she looked furious.

'Shoot me and she gets it.' Stoneridge's eyes were black and hard.

'There's no way out,' Jones said quietly. 'Give it up.'

Stoneridge looked up. 'There's a trapdoor,' he said. 'Let me go, and save the girl. Do your duty, Mr Superintendent.'

Jones had no idea where the trap led. He hadn't seen it when he'd looked round. Behind the partition, maybe, or under the table in the corner. He couldn't work out the geography — it might lead to the Gunner's Arms, but Stemp could be standing in the wrong place for all he knew. So could the others. Not that it mattered. Stoneridge, bastard that he was, was right. Jones's duty was to save the girl.

Stoneridge's left arm was pressed hard against Addy's slender throat. She could hardly breathe. Then the gun was pointing at Jones. Jones could take him now.

'I've men surrounding this place — orders to shoot. You

won't get away.'

'Neither will she.' Stoneridge's gun still pointed at Jones. It didn't waver.

Jones's hand was steady. He could shoot him in the face. He made up his mind.

Almost simultaneously, two shots rang out. Dickens saw a flash of gold. Stoneridge's arm fell from Addy's neck, but he didn't fall. He still stared at them, one eye black and hard as a blacking bottle, but Dickens saw how the other eye seemed to bloom like a great black flower and then dissolve into liquid blacking that ran down Stoneridge's face. He tasted sulphur, there was smoke, Jones falling, and Rogers leaping. He spun round to see a young man with his arm raised, holding a gun which was still smoking. There was a stain of gold on the sleeve.

# 49: SAPPHIRES IN THE DIRT

'He missed,' Jones said as Rogers helped him to his feet. Dickens noticed him wince, but there was no blood, only a burn mark and a hole on the shoulder. The bullet must have gone through, just grazed the flesh.

'What happened?' Jones asked. 'I didn't fire.'

'I did,' said the young man with the gold-stained sleeve.

'What are you doing here?'

'I followed you from Bow Street to Clement's Inn. You talked of Stoneridge and I knew. I heard you say that you were coming here. My cab followed yours.'

'And you are?'

'Sarah Hamilton,' said Dickens, *and Sapphire Hawke, and someone else again*, he thought. *I'm sure of it.*

Jones did not say anything — he knew her now and watched as Sarah went over to Addy, who lay sprawled on the straw. Dickens went with her. He knew before he looked because he had seen it happen. Sarah knew, too. She knelt down and lifted up the limp head. Addy's neck was broken. The sapphires lay in the dirt beside her.

'I killed her,' Sarah said. 'I meant to save her, and he broke her neck when I fired — it was my doing.'

'It was his,' said Jones, who had come over. 'He was responsible for Ruby, too, and Felix Gresham. You must not blame yourself. He's dead and it is his own doing.'

'But I should have waited — I was too sure that I could —'

'No,' Dickens interrupted, 'no, Miss Hamilton, she was dead before you fired. I saw. I knew. When we came in, her eyes were furious — she was more angry than frightened.'

'She would be. She hated Stoneridge. She had a child — I told you he would not leave her alone — in those woods after he — it was incest. Addy was Hawke's daughter. The child died.' She cradled the head and her tears dropped on the dead face. 'Oh, Addy, Addy, my brave sister.'

They waited until Sarah Hamilton was ready to speak again. She looked at Dickens. 'But, Mr Dickens, you say —'

'I saw him yank her head back as he turned the gun on Mr Jones. Her eyes were changed. The light went out of them. Then I heard the shots. You were a fraction before Stoneridge. You saved Mr Jones's life because Stoneridge was hit, and his aim wasn't true. But Addy was dead already — dead by his hand.' He pointed to George Stoneridge, who lay with his face in his own blood, one arm stretched out. A ring with the Hawke crest was on the little finger.

'I'm glad he's dead, and I'm glad I did it. I don't care about the consequences.'

'Don't worry about that now,' Jones said. He needed to think fast. 'Stay here while I talk to Sergeant Rogers and Mr Dickens.' They went over to Rogers, who had already been upstairs to stop Stemp from coming down, telling him to send two men to Bow Street for the mortuary van. They were to go by cab. Stemp was to wait for the van at the end of Providence Row. Constables Feak and Dacres were to go off duty. Jones would talk to them in the morning.

Jones beckoned them to go up a few stairs. Dickens and Rogers listened while he explained. They nodded in agreement. Sarah Hamilton did not look to where they were. She sat in her man's coat holding Addy Finch's head in her lap.

Dickens and Jones went back to her. 'You will have to leave her now, Miss Hamilton. I've sent for the mortuary van.'

'She must not go with him — I must go with her.'

'Mr Dickens will go with you. She will be taken to King's College Hospital. Doctor Woodhall will look after her — I know him. He is a good man. Don't think about Stoneridge. I will deal with that.'

'But I killed him.'

'Mr Dickens will explain. You can trust him.'

Sarah Hamilton knelt by her dead friend in the mortuary van. Dickens had to stand. They did not speak. What was there to say? He looked at dead Addy. She looked very young and very innocent and peaceful. Sarah held her hand until Doctor Woodhall came out to receive Addy.

'You must leave her to the doctor now, Miss Hamilton. You can see her tomorrow. I will take you home.'

At the bookshop he made her some tea and gave her some brandy — her face was still drawn into the smallness he had noted before. His heart was wrung with pity for the lonely child she had been and the lonely woman she was now.

At last, she spoke. 'What will happen to me?'

'Nothing will happen. Superintendent Jones has worked it all out. Stoneridge was the kidnapper; he was a thief and a murderer. Superintendent Jones shot him because he feared for the life of Miss Finch. He did not know that Miss Finch was already dead. There was no young man with gold paint on his sleeve. Mr Charles Dickens wasn't there either.'

'So, I won't have to —'

'No, Mr Jones will tell his story at the inquest and Sergeant Rogers will corroborate it. The other constables were outside. They saw nothing, only heard the two shots — George Stoneridge attempted to kill the Superintendent, but the Superintendent's shot killed him. The sapphires that the murderer stole are recovered, and Mr Stoneridge is believed to

306

be guilty of two other murders — those of Ruby Kiss and Felix Gresham. You won't be mentioned at all.'

'He is very good.'

'I said he was — Stoneridge deserved what he got, and you will be spared the telling of any of your and Addy's history. What will you do about the sapphires?'

'Mr Case can have them — for a good cause. He is the heir, after all.'

'Shall I write to him? He is in Westmorland.'

Dickens waited to see if the word had any effect on her, but she turned away and then she said, 'Yes, do that.'

'I will see Mr Dalrymple when he is recovered. What will you do?'

'I shall go away after the funeral. I will close the shop — for a time. I cannot imagine being here without Addy.'

'Perhaps we may talk after the funeral — before you decide.'

'Yes — the funeral will be for Ruby as well as Addy. At St. Anne's. They are closing the burial ground, but I should like Addy to be near the bookshop. I can think of her there with Bartholomew and Thyrza.' He saw the glint of tears in her eyes, but they did not fall again. Frozen in her grief, he thought.

Dickens left her — a solitary and still figure as she stood on the steps where the finding of Felix Gresham's body had made that great rent in their hard-won peace, but he would persuade her to go home. He had worked it out even before he saw her as a young man — by careful computation of the dates. He did not understand it, but he had a book to give her and one to receive.

# 50: NEW COAT FOR OLD

The inquests on George Stoneridge and Addy Finch had gone as planned. The jury had viewed the bodies at King's College Hospital. The magistrate had listened to the evidence of Superintendent Samuel Jones and Sergeant Alfred Rogers of Bow Street. The sergeant testified that Stoneridge had fired, but his shot had passed through the shoulder of Jones's coat, grazing the flesh, but doing no serious damage. Jones had fired at the same time and killed Mr Stoneridge with a shot through the eye. Jones testified that Miss Finch's life had been in danger. When they had entered the cellar, Stoneridge had had his gun to her head. Doctor Woodhall had examined Miss Finch and had found that her neck was broken. It was impossible to say when it had happened, but he was of the opinion that from the policemen's evidence, the sudden yanking of the young woman's neck as he had turned the gun on Jones had caused the second cervical vertebra to snap. Superintendent Jones and Sergeant Rogers testified that Miss Finch was alive when they went into the cellar.

Superintendent Jones and Sergeant Rogers were commended for their courage. On the evidence given, the jury concluded that George Stoneridge was the murderer of Miss Finch. The magistrate expressed satisfaction that the Hawke sapphires had been recovered and that Mr Simeon Dalrymple of St. Clement's Inn, who had been attacked and seriously injured by the guilty man, was recovering. Mr Dalrymple's clerk, Mr Joah Danks, believed to be an accomplice of the murderer, was in police custody.

Jones was glad that neither Dickens nor Sarah Hamilton had

been mentioned. Nevertheless, he felt guilty about poor Miss Addy. Perhaps he should have let Stoneridge go. They'd have found him — they'd found Danks, but he hadn't known that then. Still, in those few seconds when he'd hesitated, Stoneridge had perhaps killed her then. But Dickens had told him she was already dead — dead at the moment when Stoneridge turned the gun on him. It was the sort of thing Dickens would have noticed — he'd have been looking at the girl. Jones had told him that it was what he was there for. 'Leave the shooting to us,' he'd told Dickens. What an irony — that young woman to do it while he, the policeman in charge, had hesitated. He felt a sense of failure and as if he had got away with something at that inquest — the commendation for bravery had made him feel a fraud.

But he was glad to be alive. He thought of Dickens's ashen face, and of Elizabeth who had looked at the hole in his coat and turned pale, too. And Eleanor and Tom Brim — Scrap as well — he was needed. He'd get over his sense of failure — he'd have to. It was all part of the job. And as for those sapphires — he didn't care much about those. Nor did he care about Esther Stoneridge. She hadn't turned up even though the death of her son was all over the papers, but then she had a lot to hide. She was welcome to the goods she'd stolen from Hawke Court. Miss Hamilton didn't care — or rather Sapphire Hawke. What a story that was. And if she'd gained her jewels, she'd lost her best friend.

Jones looked at his black coat on the stand. Dickens would be coming soon. They were going to Miss Addy's and Ruby's funeral.

Dickens came in. 'Skittles,' he said, seeing Jones's sombre face.

Jones gave him a weak smile. 'Just thinking about poor Miss

Hamilton.'

'I know — there's no comfort, I'm afraid — only time, Sam, and a long time at that.' Jones nodded — he knew. 'I have left her alone for a few days, but I'm going to talk with her after the funeral about what she will do now — she said she might go away.'

'Where?'

'I've an idea about that, but I will need to talk to her first. What about Danks?'

'He bumped into Stemp in Providence Passage.'

'I'll bet that gave him a turn.'

'It did. Stemp saw his face all lit up for a moment in a flash of lightning, and as fast as the same, grabbed him, shoved him down some broken archway, and handcuffed him to a handy drainpipe — left him there when he heard the shots. He told Rogers when we got back here. Oddly, they forgot to go back for him until a few hours later. Looked like a drowned rat when they brought him in.'

'Confessed, has he?'

'No, but I've enough evidence to make him. I remembered that you said you thought you'd seen him at The Mischief, so Rogers brought Bella Screech here to have a peek at him in the cell. She remembered him; she could describe Stoneridge, and they were there on the night Addy was taken. She remembered that because Stoneridge was a bit too familiar when he was buying his drinks. She didn't like the look of him.'

'Sensible girl — unlike poor Ruby. Where's Danks now?'

'In the infirmary — caught a severe chill — somehow.'

'My heart bleeds. I thought he was a wrong 'un from the start — something mean about him, and shifty. He thought he'd be in for a sapphire or two, I suppose.'

'There were some sovereigns in his room — fees from

Stoneridge, I don't doubt, and we found a diamond ring on Stoneridge.'

'Felix Gresham's?'

'Not according to Mr Frank Gresham.'

'From Hawke Court, then. I wonder where Esther Stoneridge is — living on her ill-gotten gains.'

'Lord knows, but I don't care much.'

'She was a thoroughly mean sort, too, but another victim of Sir Gerald Hawke, I suppose, and the son — well, what an inheritance he had — bad blood.'

'Thoroughly — though it doesn't always follow that a son inherits the bad blood of his father. Look at Scrap — his father was a wrong 'un, too.' Jones looked at his watch and went to get his coat. 'We'd better get going.'

'New coat?'

'Best coat. The old one has a hole in it.'

'Are you telling me that you could have worn that for our night on the tiles?'

Jones couldn't help grinning. 'Ah — but I was fond of that old coat. I knew you'd dress for two.'

# 51: I AM THE RESURRECTION AND THE LIFE

The snowdrops were almost over, but there were a few spots of pale yellow. *The flower that's like thy face, pale primrose,* Dickens thought, looking at Sarah Hamilton, but she was composed as they went into the church where in the quiet solemnity of the candlelit interior, the priest said the words of farewell to the dead and the words of comfort for the living: *I am the resurrection and the life, saith the Lord; he that believeth in me though he were dead, yet he shall live: and whosoever liveth and believeth in me shall never die…*

Eddie Grant wept for his sister, but he was supported by Susan Oakes and her sturdy father who did not judge the living or the dead, for they knew that the Lord would not judge Ruby Kiss who had been a good sister, and a loyal friend to Phoebe Green who sat with them. She had smiled at Dickens, but lowered her eyes before the policeman who had smiled at her and did not judge. James Semple wept, too, but Constable John Semple was seated by him and touched his shoulder from time to time. Sergeant Rogers was next to his comrade and Mollie Rogers was there for the sake of Addy Finch and Sarah. And next to them were Sam Jones and his wife, Elizabeth. Behind them sat Bella Screech with Scrap, Johnny Screech's hero. Alexander Dalrymple came, for he had liked Ruby Kiss and felt sad for that little red-headed girl with her gurgling laugh. He hadn't mentioned the funeral to his father.

Sarah Hamilton was not alone. Charles Dickens sat next to her with a book of Grimm's fairy tales in his pocket.

They stood by the grave to watch as the coffins were lowered and the handfuls of earth thrown in: *earth to earth, ashes to ashes, dust to dust*. Then they went their several ways. There were to be no funeral baked meats. Sarah could not have borne that. Dickens left her to her thoughts for a while and went to speak to Bella Screech, who waited for him by Mrs Sarah-Anne Lesage's table tomb. She handed him a little bunch of snowdrops.

'The last of them,' she said. 'Put them in with them. I'm sorry for what I thought about Ruby Kiss. She was only a girl.'

'I will.'

'I think you need to come to see me. I've had a letter.'

'I know.'

She smiled at him. 'You would.'


Dickens saw that everything was put away in the bookbinding room — the knives, the awls, the paper folders and the paper was all stacked on shelves. The leather, the velvet and the silks were arranged neatly on other shelves, the glue pots in rows, the brushes in their pots, the gold leaf shut up in its box, all tidied up. He felt sad. Her work was over. He did not think she would come back.

He lit the fire while she took off her black bonnet and black coat and peeled off her black gloves. Her hair was scraped back very severely; her face was pale and drawn into the angular planes of the young man who had shot George Stoneridge.

She made some tea and they sat in silence for a while and drank. He found that he did not know what to say to her. He felt the edge of the book in his pocket, but he dared not bring it out.

'Thank you, Mr Dickens, you have been very kind.'

'You have packed everything away. Where will you go?'

'I don't know.'

'I wondered if you might want to meet Mr Case — in Westmorland.'

He sensed her stiffening, but she forced her question as if she were unmoved. 'What is he doing there?'

'He was looking for you. It was the sapphires; you remember that I said Sir Gerald Hawke commanded him to find you and he left the sapphires to you.'

'A last act of cruelty — he would have enjoyed the joke; to bind me with a jewelled rope even after death. I don't want them.'

'I understand that, but Mr Case, who is a most conscientious man, felt bound to look for you — he saw your portrait at Hawke Court, and Mr Dalrymple told him that he thought you had come from Westmorland. Did you?'

She didn't answer his question. 'What has Mr Case found out in — Westmorland?'

'Something that greatly puzzles him. Sir Robert Trent was the Squire of Kirkdale Hall. He had one son, but no daughter. No one can tell Mr Case anything about Sapphire Hawke, or indeed the son who survived a terrible fire at Kirkdale Hall, Sydney Trent. He spoke to the boy's old nurse, a Miss Robb, but she merely said that the boy had been adopted by relatives, but she didn't know whom or where. She seemed not to care very much, though she had been his nurse.'

The next words tumbled out. 'She did care. She still does.'

Dickens saw the tears in Sarah's eyes. She would tell the truth to defend her old nurse. 'You were there — at Kirkdale Hall? During the fire?'

She nodded and looked at the fire he had lit, remembering, perhaps, that terrible night when she had lost everything, including her name. He still couldn't really understand how

Sydney Trent had become Sapphire Hawke, but that she had been Sydney Trent was the only explanation he could think of.

Dickens took the book from his pocket. 'I found this at Hawke Court. Did Sydney Trent visit you there?' He dared not say what he really thought.

Sarah took the book and read the words on the flyleaf. When she looked up, there was such pain and loss in her eyes that he knew. 'Sydney Trent was sent to Hawke Court and he went away to Bruges as Sapphire Hawke. I will show you something.' There was a kind of weary resignation in her tone.

She rose and went to the desk on which there was a box inlaid with mother-of- pearl. She took a chain from under the collar of her black dress and he saw a key. *The key to this mystery*, he thought. He had guessed from the beginning that she kept secrets and now he would know. She handed him a faded newspaper cutting from *The Westmorland Gazette*. The date was 1817. He read the marked paragraph:

*On the 12th instant at Kirkdale Hall, the Lady of Sir Robert Trent, a son and heir, Sydney Lamb Trent.*

'I am Sydney Trent. My mother's choice in the event that I turned out a girl — which, as you see, I did — a damaged one, it is true.'

*Damaged, indeed*, he thought. Terrible harm had been done, but he said, 'You are complete in yourself, Miss Trent. You have courage, I know, in the face of so much suffering, not the least the loss of your heart's sister, Addy. If it is too — painful, do not tell me.'

She looked straight at him. 'I think you will understand. It sometimes happens — nature plays a trick…'

Dickens understood. He thought of his own little Dora, born

so weak and fragile, and of his sister Fanny's son, born with his deformed legs and dying so soon after his mother. Nature could be cruel like that.

'My father wanted a son, and there had been no children in their ten years of marriage. There might never have been another child. Doctor Sutton could not tell — what I was. My father was dying, so Doctor Sutton told him that he had, at last, a son — and heir. But he lived and my mother kept the secret. Margery Robb told me that she would have told my father, for their second child, born five years after me, was a son. But she had not time. The child died and so did my mother — of childbed fever. My father was distant after that. I was a disappointment to him — I learnt to ride, to shoot, to climb trees, even, but it was as if he knew there was something not quite right about me. It was my fault, too. I knew I was not the son he wanted — I think I knew very early that I was not a son at all. I kept it from him, for I felt the guilt was mine.'

'Could not Miss Robb have told him?'

'She had enough to do to persuade him I was not strong enough to go to school — she dared not do more, and my father was never well after my mother died. What an irony — he survived a serious illness because he thought he had a son… Margery said she would tell him when the time was right — I believed her because I wanted to, but the fire happened. Then, Sir Gerald Hawke wanted an heir — I was to be another heir — another piece on a chessboard. I had no choice, of course, and I was sent to London…'

*The Murdstone tyranny*, Dickens thought; all those parents and guardians who exercised their power over the innocent — and revelled in it, but he said nothing, only waited for her to go on.

'He wanted an heir to marry an heiress and keep the Hawke line going, but he found me out in London through one of the maids. You can guess how —' Dickens saw how her hands clenched. He heard her indrawn breath. He hardly dared breathe when he heard her next words — 'and he looked for himself and he asked me what kind of creature I was. Then there were doctors who — he made me into Sapphire Hawke and sent me to Hawke Court.'

Dickens felt all the sickness and horror he had felt in Hawke's bedroom. He did not want to think about what had been done to the girl in that painting, but he managed to look back at her. 'I met Sir Gerald Hawke — he was a corrupt man. Mr Case saw him on his deathbed — he felt only horror and disgust. He was near to breaking when I met him. Why did he call you Sapphire?'

'He named me Sapphire to tempt — to remind my suitors that there would be a dowry of sapphires, at least — I had nothing else to offer — certainly not beauty. But a suitor might believe there would be a son to inherit the Hawke title. The kind of men for whom I was bait were not interested in my mind. I will not tell you of Hawke's cruelties and depravities, but I will tell you that he wanted to marry me to a man called Arthur Sinclair —'

'The man who committed suicide at Hawke Court.'

'He was as depraved as his mentor. Sir Gerald Hawke knew that I was not able to bear children, but Sinclair would inherit a wealthy estate and wanted an heir — not a wife. He had plenty of women to satisfy his — and the possible title was tempting. Hawke knew Sinclair was not likely to live. Hawke's own son, Augustus, was an example. However, Sinclair did not know that. He thought he was indestructible. Sir Gerald Hawke knew that Sinclair's widow would inherit, but he would be the beneficiary, of course. He needed money, as always. Sinclair came to my room intent on seduction — I shot him. I'm a good shot, Mr Dickens.' He saw the corner of her mouth turn up slightly.

'So I saw.'

'I was sent away to Bruges after the scandal, but Sir Gerald wanted me back. I suppose he had another moneyed, diseased husband in mind. I disappeared from St Katherine's wharf and you know the rest.'

'It is a terrible story.'

'It is. Mother Teresa at the convent knew. I liked the convent. It was so quiet, the silence only interrupted by the summoning bells: matins, prime, vespers. I loved the regularity of everything — the ways the days unfolded like silk from a bale, pure white cloth with no spot or stain. I became used to the simple white dress and blue sash that we wore. The school was spacious and airy, and I found peace in a white room and in the kindly presence of Mother Mary Teresa who was so good to me, and to whom I told my secret, a secret Mother Mary said would never be revealed. "God knows all, and He will reveal His purpose. We must wait, and in patience." That is what she told me.

'I thought I would stay there forever — the life of the nuns appealed to my need for peace. I thought I would become a teacher there, but Sir Gerald wrote to demand my return. Mother Mary told me that all would be well, and that I must trust in God, but I knew it would not be well. I could not tell Mother Mary that the devil awaited me. I knew that my destiny lay in my own hands — and this —' she gestured round the workshop — 'is what I made of my destiny, with Addy, and Bartholomew and Thyrza, of course. They found me on the streets and took me in. I thought the Hawkes were finished. I went to the funeral as Frederick Dale — Doctor Sutton; I took his name.'

'Adeline Hamilton,' Dickens said, remembering Meredith Case's letter about the memorials to the old vicar and his wife in Kirkdale Church. 'Adeline became Addy, and you became Hamilton.'

'They were good people. I wanted to remember goodness after so much. That is why I wrote sometimes to Margery Robb... I wanted to see Hawke sealed in his tomb, but he was not dead. Stoneridge looked just like him. I should have known that that accursed creature would reach beyond the grave. There is nothing now.'

'There is Kirkdale Hall.'

She gave a bitter laugh. 'A ruin.'

'Margery Robb is waiting, and there is your cousin, Mr Case — a good man who has found sanctuary in the open spaces of Kirkdale — in that fresh wind which has scoured him clean of corruption, and there are the Reverend Stephen Hardy and his sister, Jane, who have looked after Mr Case. There is the church which Mr Case writes to me is a place of simple blessed peace —'

'It is, but —'

'And your parents are there, and your brother in that church of white-washed tranquillity where you may find your own... I expect Moses Rigg will meet you at the station in Windermere.'

She smiled shakily at that. 'He is still there?'

'He is — and most unwilling to gossip about the Trent family — the Squire was loved, I think, and his wife. The Trents are missed. That was the impression gained by Mr Case.'

'But who will I be? I am no one now. Sapphire Hawke never existed. Sarah Hamilton was an invention.'

'You will be yourself — you will be Sydney Trent. Your mother chose wisely.'

'But —' She looked down at her black dress.

'I should not think Miss Robb will brook any questions — Mr Case found her somewhat intimidating. Besides, they are your people. They will accept you. And think of the good you may do — with the money from those sapphires. A school, new cottages, a farm, a house rising from the ruins —' he saw the tears well in her eyes — 'Go home, Miss Trent — home.'

He let her weep. It was the best thing — she needed to weep out all her sorrow and her losses until calm came, and though the ache for Addy would never leave her — he knew that ache well — she would lift her head in a moment, and he would see her clearer eyes and know that she was facing a future — her future. All was not lost.

She looked at him at last. 'I think you are a magician, Mr Dickens. I will not ask you how you know all these things — of course, they are in your books, all the sorrows of the bereaved and abandoned, and now you have pierced me to my very soul. All my secrets —'

'Which will never be told.'

'Thank you. I do not know how to thank you.'

'Only by going home and living a life — your life, with a purpose in it. Send to me when you have decided when to go.'

'I will.'

She accompanied him to the shop door and gave him his book. 'I nearly forgot — our last book, mine and Addy's.'

'I shall treasure it, even if it's —'

'Not a very good poem,' she said, her lip turning up slightly. 'I looked.'

Dickens smiled back at her. 'Home — magic word.'

# 52: CINDERELLA

Home — but not for him. He had another call to make at The
Man with a Load of Mischief, but first he had to go to the
stationery shop for Scrap and a parcel he had left there.

'I want you to give Johnny this, and I want you to take the
boy for a walk with Poll while I talk to his mother.'

They walked along Oxford Street to the inn, which was
crowded as usual. They passed by the bar counter where
Dickens had seen George Stoneridge for the first time.
Astonishing, he thought again, the way in which characters
opened up. A stranger in a pub became the chief actor in the
drama — the villain — and his dupe was Danks — who
thought he was in for a fortune. Dickens glanced at the mirror
near the back door in which he had seen that malevolent face.
And Bella Screech? Ah! Cinderella, perhaps.

She looked very smart in a new black silk dress trimmed with
satin which fitted her slender figure very neatly, emphasising
her small waist. He thought how beautiful she was with her
rich hair fashioned into glossy ringlets, and wondered again if
she could possibly be Screech's daughter. Perhaps she was a
changeling — like Sydney Trent, in a way — switched at birth
as in the old fairy tales. Somewhere there might be Screech's
daughter, masquerading as a countess — a very little one, of
course, whose tall, handsome father wondered at her gnomish
ugliness, and looked askance at his once beautiful wife.

Johnny Screech yelped with delight when he opened his
parcel — a dog collar and a lead. For a small dog like Poll,
Dickens told the child. He knew where there lived a small dog
and he had hopes that it might be Johnny's soon enough, but

he did not say so. He thought of the flashing eyes. Bella Screech smiled, however, and told Johnny that they could not buy a dog today — soon, she said. Scrap told Johnny that he could practise on Poll, who submitted to having her collar taken off, and away they went, Johnny holding on to the new lead.

Bella stood by an open trunk with a shawl in her hand. She looked at it critically. 'Bit more wear in this, I suppose.' She folded it and put it in the trunk.

Dickens knew she was waiting for him to begin. Two could play at that game. Bella continued to pack, folding and smoothing, considering a black bonnet, setting it aside, picking up some boots and putting them down again, but she gave in at last. 'The letter.'

'Yes?'

'From the lawyer, Mr Francis Gresham. You wrote to Mrs Gresham — you told her.'

'I did.' He did not apologise for interfering.

'She came and she saw. She said she could see Felix in him.'

'Good.'

'I don't see it myself, but then, I didn't see the old miser in him either, thank the Lord. And I thank Him, too, that Mrs Gresham never saw him. She'd not have —' Bella saw that Dickens was laughing and she couldn't help herself. 'Oh, all right, I am glad, but I've told her we've no need of charity. Old Scrooge left plenty. And I'll not be some sort of half-servant while she —'

'Mrs Gresham won't do that. She needs both of you.'

'I know. I'm not used to being —'

'Cared about.'

'Clever, ain't you? But —' she was smiling — 'I know you are. Good as gold, I know that, too.'

'No secret agony of the soul for Johnny — no lonely roaming.'

'He's to go to school. Mr Francis Gresham has arranged everything, but he needn't think — for all his charm —'

'I'm sure he does not.'

'Oh, not good enough now for Mr Fancy Lawyer.'

'Miss Bella Screech, you are the most perverse young —'

'Woman's privilege, ain't it, or rather, is it not, sir? I'm learning. I'm to be a widow — Felix's secret wife, Mrs Isabella Gresham.'

'Nothing could be more right.'

They heard Poll's bark on the stairs. Scrap and Johnny were coming back.

'I have a gift for you.' Bella took the book he offered and opened it to read the words he had written on the flyleaf of *David Copperfield*: *No more the secret agony of the soul.*

'My favourite child, David Copperfield,' Dickens said.

'Mr Dick — Mr Dick sets us right.' Bella gave him a smile that he hoped she would one day give to a husband. Alas, not for him.

*Mr Dick sets us right* — so Betsey Trotwood always said. Sometimes, in his case — only sometimes.


Dickens and Scrap walked back to the stationery shop. 'That heiress — got her jewels back?' Scrap asked.

'She did, though she lost more than they are worth. She lost her dearest friend.'

'Mr Jones said. That man in the woods followin' us — pity a tree dint fall on 'im. Think she'll be all right — the heiress?'

'I think so. I hope she will go home — to Westmorland, where she came from.'

'Home, eh? That place, that big ol' castle place — yer

couldn't call that home. Yet, they woz rich, I suppose.'

'People are home, Scrap — a house is but four walls and a roof. It's what's in it that counts — the faces that turn in welcome to the solitary traveller who returns after long years to find that though some of the faces are gone, there are still those who remember.'

'Home was where my ma was —'

'And it always will be — you'll not forget, Scrap; those who leave home young always have tender feelings for their first home, but they find others. Here, for instance.'

They had reached the stationery shop where Scrap had found his home with Sergeant Rogers and Mollie, but Dickens knew that Scrap's heart was in Norfolk Street with Mrs Elizabeth Jones, and the adopted children, Eleanor and Tom Brim. And Sam, too — he wouldn't take his eye off Scrap.

'An' Norfolk Street — that's my 'ome, too. Two 'omes — lucky, I suppose. There's folk who have none.'

Dickens went on his way up to Norfolk Street to tell Sam — not all of it, of course. Sydney Trent's secret was hers, and he had promised. Sam would work it out for himself.

# 53: THE SINS OF THE FATHERS

Dickens watched her go — her tallness quite clear and straight in the crowd, her head unbonneted, held erect. He waited until the train vanished, leaving behind its plumes of smoke.

He had written to Meredith Case to tell him that Sapphire Hawke was found. He told him that Sapphire Hawke was really Sydney Trent, but no more than that. Sydney Trent would tell him only those parts of her history that she felt she could. Meredith Case would not ask — he would see her clear, honest eyes and know that she was true, and he would be satisfied.

The sapphires were to be sold, in which matter Dickens had acted for her. He had been to see Mr Dalrymple — still weak from George Stoneridge's attack — and he had told him that Sapphire Hawke had been found and that she had indeed come from Westmorland. Mr Dalrymple knew about Stoneridge's death and the death of Miss Finch, who had been the daughter of a servant at Hawke Court. He had listened gravely as Dickens told his story, but he had not asked questions, even when Dickens had told him that Sapphire Hawke's real name was Sydney Trent, and when Alexander Dalrymple had interjected with a 'Why did she?', he had silenced his son with a look, telling Dickens only that he was satisfied that the matter of the sapphires was closed. Dickens left him to ponder on what he had heard and draw his own conclusions — conclusions which he would never share with his son, or his pretty daughter, Maud.

From the station Dickens walked back to his office in Wellington Street, imagining Sydney Trent travelling up to the north, passing through the stations and seeing the lurid lights of towns and the silent villages, the train steaming through the night to arrive at last in the pure light of that county of mountains and lakes where the taciturn Moses Rigg waited with his cart to take her to Kirkdale where she belonged, and where she would find a home with Margery Robb. Her weary journey's end was her starting place.

His way took him down Norfolk Street, past Sam's house, borne along by the ceaseless tide of the human sea. A man shoved against him, passed without a word, and Dickens found himself up against the window of a familiar grocer's shop on the corner of Norfolk Street and Tottenham Street. He gazed at the apples, thinking of Bella and Johnny Screech in their new home at Richmond by the river. Bella would be all right. She was independent and strong-willed, but tender-hearted, too, as was Mrs Gresham. Johnny would not be forced into the law — nor would he be a little labouring hind in a blacking factory. A poet, perhaps? Whatever came to pass, Bella would keep him on the straight and narrow. He would not go the way of his father.

Dickens looked up at a window above the shop — a window from which he had looked out as a four-year-old child to see the crowded streets in the dusk lamplight, to hear the sound of a barrel-organ, to taste the sulphurous London fog on his lips, and to wonder at the strangeness and mystery of it all. The start of his life in London.

John Dodd — the name flashed into his mind — the grocer who had been the Dickens's landlord, and to whom John Dickens had owed money later when they had lodged here again in 1829. He had looked out of that window as a seventeen-year-old beginning his writing career, learning that fiendish shorthand to become a reporter at Doctor's Commons, that lazy old nook near St. Paul's where ancient lawyers quibbled about wills and marriages and disputes among ships and boats, and lawyerly mice in grey suits nibbled at the heaps of dusty papers.

He thought of the strangeness and mystery of children's lives: Bella Screech looking out into narrow Crooked Alley, nursing a slapped face and wondering at the cruelty of the man who was supposed to be her father; the supposed boy, Sydney Trent, watching his father from a window at Kirkdale Hall and wondering at the distance that separated them; Addy Finch gazing out from a wretched hovel in the woods, seeing a cruel-eyed man pass by whom they said was her father; and George Stoneridge, a bastard son, with contempt in his heart for a man whose business had failed and whose wife despised him, and hatred in his heart for the real father who denied him.

*Home*, Dickens thought, *it's time I went home.* He turned as if to walk back up Norfolk Street to Devonshire Terrace, the house in which he had been happiest, but the lease was up. He must find another house — a new home where he would write his new book about a case in Chancery. The start of another journey which would take him through those tangled regions of bafflement which called themselves the law.

He heard a child's cry and turned round to see a ragged little boy who stared about him, his mouth open in the dreadful grief that only a lost child can show. Dickens was about to step towards him, but a man was before him to kneel to the boy — a labouring man with a hungry, jaundiced face which was transformed when he gently wiped the tears away with his two grimy thumbs. The child buried his head in his father's knees.

Dickens turned back. A sense of dread gripped his heart. Not Norfolk Street. He turned the corner into Tottenham Street — the way that would take him to Keppel Street, where his father lay in his bed and his mother watched. John Dickens was gravely ill. Dickens thought he would not survive this illness. He thought again of Sir Gerald Hawke and the son who had hated him, Ernest Gresham whose son had rebelled against his sternness, and the long-dead Sir Robert Trent whose only son was not a son. He thought of Charley, his own eldest son whose loving, eager face would turn to welcome his father. 'Oh, Pa, what a lark,' Charley would say.

His pace quickened. He must not be too late for this journey's end.

# HISTORICAL NOTES

In doing my research for book six in the series, *The Redemption Murders*, I became fascinated by the work that women did in the mid-Victorian period, especially those who ran businesses or were involved in various trades, including plumbing and ironmongery. There were hundreds of booksellers and bookbinders all over London. I found fifty-two women running bookshops and fifteen women bookbinders. Miss Jane Moore sold medical books at number nine North Gower Street where at number four, years earlier, Mrs Elizabeth Dickens, mother of Charles Dickens, set up her private school. Alas, it was not a success. Perhaps it would have been more successful as a bookshop.

Mrs Mary Ann Bengough ran a bookbinding workshop in Bartholomew Close; there was Mrs Margaret Chip at Amen Corner. Most of her neighbours were booksellers or binders, and there were Miss Foster in Clerkenwell and Miss Jane Wheatley up in Pentonville. The bookselling and binding trade seemed fitting for Sarah Hamilton and Addy Finch, and it was clearly possible. The two Higham sisters, Mary and Sarah, ran a bookshop in Lamb's Passage, off Chiswell Street. I imagined it to be a tranquil occupation for my two young women who had experienced such dreadful pasts — tranquil, of course, until Felix Gresham's body is found on their doorstep.

I didn't actually find a bookshop and bindery in St. Anne's Court, but there were a few around Dean Street, Duke Street and Wardour Street not far away. And there were a couple of businesswomen in St. Anne's Court. Mrs Case was a stay — or corset — maker and gave me the name for Meredith Case, Sir

Gerald Hawke's unhappy heir. Round the corner in Church Court, off Dean street, I found Mrs Sherrin who traded as a plumassier, which I guessed was to do with feathers. It was — usually ostrich for hats. And nearby was Mrs Tisdall, who was a calenderer. I had no idea what this was, but found out that Mrs Tisdall was in the fabric trade. A calenderer or calico-glazer put the finishing waxy substance onto chintz or calico to give it a sheen. Heated rollers — a term I associate with hair — were used to apply the glaze. Apparently, a seven-year apprenticeship was required. Not so for my heated hair rollers.

And of books — it is quite true that Dickens owned a copy of the poem 'The Deluge'. I found the entry in the inventory of Dickens's library. It is listed as anonymous and was published in 1821. I did find it online and stopped short at the line: 'Where are you? Dy'd in the blood of recent murder…' It seemed like fate.

And fate must have pointed me in the direction of Mrs Fraser, who ran a business as a curiosity dealer in St. Anne's Court. There were a number of these curiosity shops around Dean Street and Wardour Street and it is true that in his younger days, Dickens used to visit them, and he did buy a rosewood table. And, of course, he did write *The Old Curiosity Shop* in which he remarks upon Little Nell's grandfather's shop as 'one of those receptacles for old and curious things which seem to crouch in odd corners of this town'. I wonder if Dickens bought his rosewood table from Mrs Fraser, or it might have been from John Schofield in Dean Street. Nell's grandfather's shop is full of suits of mail, rusty swords, strange china and wooden figures and 'furniture that might have been designed in dreams.'

Dickens seems to have been fascinated by the immense variety of shops in the back streets of London, especially those which seemed to sell the most heterogeneous selection of goods. In *Sketches by Boz*, he describes the 'small dirty shop' in 'some by-street' where exposed for sale is 'the most extraordinary and confused jumble of old worn-out, wretched articles.' He gives a list of broken pans, rusty keys, cracked bits of china, pickle jars, an unframed portrait, bottles, cabinets, rags, bones, fire irons and fenders. So that's where Ebenezer Screech's shop came from.

Providence found me a name with which I was familiar, that of George Lamerte who really did have a blacking warehouse in Providence Row, Finsbury. I was actually looking for a shooting gallery in which to put George's army pal, Phineas Morton. Of course, I did wonder whether Mr Lamerte was anything to do with Warren's blacking factory where Dickens worked as a child. James Lamert (without the 'e') managed Warren's Blacking factory and he employed the young Dickens, and he had a cousin George. I couldn't resist putting Dickens in Lamerte's doorway while he waits for Superintendent Jones.

On a topical note: it's extraordinary what you find. My eye fell upon George Lamerte's next door but one neighbour, the Royal Jennerian and London Vaccine Institution, which took its name from Edward Jenner who was the first to experiment with using cowpox to protect against smallpox. In May, 1796, he vaccinated an eight-year old boy, having learned about the virtues of cowpox from dairymaids and farmhands. Publication of Jenner's experiments led eventually to clinical trials in London and wide support for vaccination in the first two decades of the nineteenth century.

In London, the Royal Jennerian Society created vaccination houses across London where children were vaccinated. I'm assuming that the place I found was one of these. The lymph collected from London's children supplied the world with vaccine.

Dickens knew very well the damage smallpox caused. In the novel *Bleak House*, Jo, the boy crossing-sweeper, dies — he has no one to care enough to have him vaccinated; Esther Summerson survives, though disfigured by the disease.

Of course, there were anti-vaccination movements, especially when compulsory vaccine was introduced. However, it is timely to remember that smallpox was the first disease to be totally eradicated — thanks to Edward Jenner, and in part, to that obscure address in Finsbury. Providence at work, no doubt.

# A NOTE TO THE READER

Dear Reader,

A good deal of thought goes into the naming of characters, however minor. As well as the trade directories, graveyards, obituary notices, and notices of births and marriages, the *British Newspaper Archive*, the Bible and the *Oxford Dictionary of English Surnames* are some of the places from where I steal the names of my characters. Graveyards, though somewhat melancholy, are a very useful resource for nineteenth-century names — names you've often not heard before. I came across the Reverend Moister in a churchyard near me. The Resurrection Woman — that's me. He sprang to life as vividly as anything from Charles Dickens. He would be damp about the hands, naturally, moist about the brow, and oystery about the eyes — something of the hypocrite about him, I thought, stuffing the funeral baked meats into his crocodile mouth while wiping away the tears for the murdered man — or woman.

The prostitute Ruby Kiss's name seemed very appropriate, though I admit I stole it from the very respectable businesswoman, Mrs Kiss, a sealing wax maker in Hatton Garden. I'm saving Miss Lorinia Watkins — she's perfect as she is — who was a bookseller in St John's Square. Lorinia, though — someone's sweetheart, surely, in a future life. Perhaps Effingham Wilson's. He was a bookseller at 18, Bishopsgate Within. Made for each other.

Ebenezer was quite a common name in Victorian times. I found quite a few in the *Trade Directory*. The most famous, of course, is Dickens's own Ebenezer Scrooge with its connotations of screw and scrouge, an archaic word for squeeze. I didn't make up the name Screech. I found it in the *Oxford Dictionary of English Surnames.* It dates back to 1279. Robert Screech is found in the historical record, Rotuli Hundredorum. The name derives from Old Norse 'skraekr' meaning to shriek or scream. In the dictionary it comes before 'Scrime' — now that's a name to save for a later date. It's a variant of 'Crime' and derived, so the dictionary tells me, from the name 'Grime', derived from the word 'grim'. Whoever Scrime is, he will be grim. Criminal, certainly. Not Mr Sneezam, though, a carpenter in Wood Street — most law-abiding, I'm sure.

The naming of murderers is a tricky business. Surely Drood with his stony name, Jasper, is the murderer of Edwin. Dickens liked stony names: Bradley Headstone has murder in his heart, and Mr Murdstone is as much a murderer as if he had killed David Copperfield's mother with his bare hands. Cruelty can kill. You can see where Esther and George Stoneridge came from.

But the detective story writer does not want to give away too much too soon. Death — from Middle English 'deeth' — would be tempting were it not one of the aristocratic names of Lord Peter Wimsey, and too obvious, I think. This is why I choose the most glaringly criminal names for minor villains. Blackledge sets your teeth on edge; I've Blackborn and Blackbone in reserve — they sound like pirates.

A last thought: Deadman for the victim? No, I haven't made it up — seventeenth-century tax records for Suffolk!

I hope you enjoyed reading the novel, and I thank you for taking the time to do so. Reviews are really important to authors, and if you enjoyed the novel, it would be great if you could spare a little time to post a review on **Amazon** and **Goodreads.** Readers can connect with me online, on

**Facebook (JCBriggsBooks)** and **Twitter (@JeanCBriggs)**, and you can find out more about the books and Charles Dickens via my website: **jcbriggsbooks.com,** where you will also find Mr Dickens's A-Z of murder — all cases of murder to which I found a Dickens connection.

Thank you!

Jean Briggs

**Sapere Books** is an exciting new publisher of brilliant fiction and popular history.

To find out more about our latest releases and our monthly bargain books visit our website:
**saperebooks.com**